I0731951

Parlatheas Press Titles:

The Cayn Trilogy:

Son of Cayn
City of Cayn
Blood of Cayn

Chronicles of Damage Inc.:

Phantoms of Ruthaer
Mask of the Vampire*

* Forthcoming

Blood of Cayn

The Cayn Trilogy
Book Three

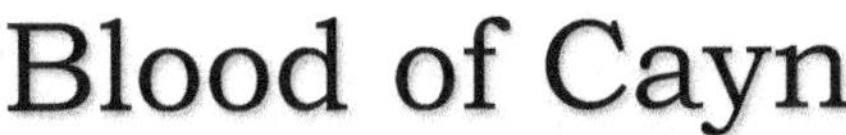

Jason McDonald
Alan Isom
Stormy McDonald

Parlatheas Press, LLC
Hollywood, SC

DEDICATIONS

For Aria and Cerdic, who not only put up with their parents' storytelling obsession, but also participate in our crazy brainstorming sessions. We love you!

Jason & Stormy

For my brothers, Brett and Drew: thanks for always having my back.

Alan

CHAPTER 1
YANA RETURNS

October 28, 4235 K.E.

2:05pm

Squire Patrick Anders burst into Lord Fergusson's command tent. Around the central map table, half-a-dozen knights reached for weapons. Tall, blonde, and blue eyed, Dame Astrid Wolfelschneider, the only female Detchian knight with whom Fergusson had ever served during his years with the Iron Tower, had her blade half-drawn before she recognized the squire.

"Laytenant Marchenkova's back, Sir!" Anders shouted.

Lord Geoffrey Fergusson, sixth baronet of Yorkshire, closed his eyes and counted to five.

"Squire!"

Anders snapped to attention. "Sir!"

"Step back outside and try that again."

"Yes, Sir!" With a nod, the young squire exited. Thirty seconds passed in silence.

"Permission to enter, Milord?" the squire called.

"Granted."

"Laytenant Marchenkova has returned from Chernigov, Sir. They've taken her to the healer's tent."

"Discipline, Squire, discipline. It makes the difference between a live soldier and a dead one," Lord Fergusson admonished.

"Yes, Sir," Anders said with a bowed head. "I'll take you to her when you're ready."

Lord Fergusson signaled for Leftenant Brian Gallagher to carry on with the planning before he followed his squire to the healer's tent.

On the way, they passed the edge of the training field where a small crowd of the curious had gathered to inspect Yana's abandoned glider. The soldiers parted to allow their leader a closer look at the holes riddling the dark silk sail.

After removing three black arrows still caught in the material, Lord Fergusson grabbed a random soldier by the elbow and instructed, "Get those holes patched immediately. Move!"

The man snapped a hasty salute and took off at a run.

Outside the field hospital, a group of camp runners, the young sons of sutlers and camp followers, huddled around one of their number. "...and when the chirurgeon shoved the needle and thread all the way through, blood just *gushed* out..." At sight of Lord Fergusson, the boys scattered, leaving the storyteller behind.

"Zack, I take it Lady Sehraine is inside with Laytenant Marchenkova?"

"Yes, Sir," the boy said.

Inside the tent, a woman screamed in agony. Fergusson saw his squire grow pale. "Anders, wait here with Zack. I'll call you if I need anything."

The wind rider lay face down, her right arm and left side swathed in thick bandages. A streak of bright red blood soaked the white sheets beneath her. Yana maintained a death grip on the edge of the operating table with her eyes shut tight. Sehraine gripped Yana's forearms, tears welling in her eyes.

Yana bit down on a wooden stick and screamed through the block when the healer shoved the barbed arrowhead through her thigh and out the other side. The wind rider dropped her head to the table in exhaustion. A moment later, her torment by the chirurgeon resumed as he stitched and bound the wounds.

Lord Fergusson watched in silence until the bandage was tied, and then said, "I thought I told you to be careful."

"I was," she replied in a raspy voice. "The orcs didn't start shooting and throwing things at me until I blew up the first tower. I have the information you need about their fortifications."

Yana slowly pushed herself up to a sitting position, but it was too much, too fast. Her face drained of color, and she slumped over. Sehraine caught her, holding her tight.

"I'm thirsty," Yana whispered, gesturing toward a cup.

"You need to lie back down," Sehraine said.

"I'm fine."

"Lie down anyway," Sehraine demanded. She eased Yana back onto the table and placed a kiss on her forehead. "Stay still," she commanded before turning to Lord

Fergusson with a narrow-eyed look that reminded the older man of the looks he'd seen some of the sutlers aim at their children. "She needs to rest."

"I can come back later," Lord Fergusson said.

"No, Sir. I'm fine," Yana croaked. "Sehraine, please get me some water."

The elf nodded and crossed the tent to retrieve a pitcher and cup from a trestle table near the washbasins. Beside her, the field chirurgeon scrubbed Yana's blood from his hands. Fergusson saw her lean close to the healer. The two of them whispered back and forth, casting glances at Yana. The man nodded and hurried from the tent, still drying his hands.

The commander waited patiently while Sehraine helped the wind rider sit up. Seeing the two of them sitting side by side, the elf with a slender arm around her friend, it struck him how much the average person could learn about kindness and friendship from these two women.

Yana drank greedily from the cup, draining it twice before she spoke again. "Just so you know, Sir, those dragon pellets are not worth the money you paid for them. They're unpredictable."

He drew in a deep breath and let it out in a short sigh of acceptance. "Some worked, though, correct?" She gave him a single nod in reply. "Considering their age, I suppose we should be glad any worked at all. So what do you have for me?"

"Let's go back to your tent so I can reference your maps." She slid from the table and swayed on her feet for a moment before sitting again.

"Yana..." Sehraine protested.

"Stop mothering me," the wind rider said. "I have a job to finish."

"You need to wait."

"There's no one else who can use that glider, Sehraine, and I'm sure as hell not staying in this tent while Xandor and Jasper are in that cesspool of a city."

"I know," she replied, laying a hand on her arm, "but you need to rest a few more minutes until Bris returns.

"Anders!" Fergusson shouted. The squire stepped inside, eyes carefully trained on the ground. "Take word back to the senior officers: Tell them I'll be there with Laytenant

Marchenkova in ten minutes. Send Zack to ask Knyaz Dorinkov and his senior officers to join us."

Anders bobbed his head and took off at a run. At the tent flap, he barely avoided a collision with the returning healer.

"Normally I recommend bedrest for wounds like yours," the chirurgeon said, "but your friend was very clear that's not going to happen, so drink this." He offered Yana a small glass vial containing a milky, pale blue liquid. When she hesitated, he gave her an exasperated sigh. "It's a healing draught."

"I'm accustomed to blue, but why is it so thick?" Yana asked, tilting the vial side to side. She pulled the cork and took a whiff of the contents. "Ugh! That smells vile!"

"Makes it work better," he replied. "Drink up."

"I think I'll pass."

"You'll drink it if you want to walk out of this tent," Sehraine said. "I'm not above tying you to a cot."

Fergusson bit the inside of his cheek to keep himself from laughing at the wind rider. She'd already lost the argument; it was just taking time for her to realize it.

"Fine," Yana groused and drained the vial in one swallow. Her face twisted in disgust. "That stuff needs to come with a shot of rakiya to get the taste out of your mouth!" Despite her words, her color instantly improved.

"The worse it tastes, the better it works," Bris said, handing her a cup of water.

Sehraine laughed. "In that case, her homemade rakiya should cure everything."

Yana gave her friend a reproachful look. "I'll remember that the next time you beg me to go to the apothecary for a winter ague remedy." The drawn and haggard look she'd worn when Fergusson first entered the tent vanished. Sliding off the table, she tested her leg again and smiled widely.

"Thank you, Bris," she said and patted the healer's shoulder. It was a few minutes' work to get Yana dressed and into her armor.

"I need some silk scraps to patch a few holes on the glider," Yana said.

"Already handled," Fergusson replied. "Let's focus on what you learned." He reached for the door flap, but almost immediately dropped it. He eyed Sehraine. "Milady, you might want to straighten your hat. There is a definite chill in the air these days, and we wouldn't want your ears to get cold."

The elf's eyes grew wide, and she tugged on the hat. "Lord Fergusson, I know it's too much to hope there are any players in the area, but are there any... um... *painted ladies* among the sutlers? I need a better disguise than this hat."

Fergusson shook his head. "If there are, they're among the Rhodinan camp, and not likely to be willing to help. Keep the hat on and stay among friends."

2:30pm

Inside the command tent, a group of men and women milled around, discussing strategies and pointing to the various flags and clay figures on the Knight Commander's map table. A second, older map of Chernigov, the bridge, and the Keep was pinned to another table and propped up where everyone could reference it. Someone had marked the locations of several harpax and small ballistae along the bridge and far shore.

Yana studied the group while Leftenant Gallagher called them to attention, and they shuffled into a semblance of order. Including Brian, there were six Iron Tower knights. An equal sized group of Rhodinans gathered around a middle-aged man with a thick mustache and long, black beard.

"Knyaz Dorinkov, ladies, and gentlemen," Fergusson said, "allow me to introduce Laytenant Yana Marchenkova, in service to the Kral of Trakya, and Lady Sehraine Marchenkova of Pazard'zhik. Laytenant Marchenkova has just completed her reconnaissance of the enemy fortifications." He gestured for Yana to stand beside the map of Chernigov. "Laytenant, you have our attention."

"Yes, Sir," Yana replied. She gave a slight bow to the Rhodinan leader. "Your Highness, thank you for the use of your treasure."

Turning to the others she continued, "Ladies and gentlemen, as the Knight Commander said, I am Laytenant Yana Marchenkova, Black Dragon Squadron, of the Trakyan Wind Riders. We utilize gliders, mostly for reconnaissance and message delivery, but aerial attack is also in our purview.

"Two hours ago, Lord Fergusson asked me to conduct a three-stage reconnaissance. Stage one was the Keep at the eastern foot of the Rainbow Bridge. Stage two was to sweep across Chernigov's port to identify possible transport for Vityaz Dobrynya Sabe's evacuation. Finally, stage three was to overfly the walls of Chernigov and identify the siege engines emplaced there. Afterwards, my mission was to destroy as many of the orcs' war engines along the northern approach as possible."

"Excuse me, Laytenant," interrupted a gangly knight with a purple scar along his cheek.

"Yes, Sir?"

"Stephen Daughtry, Spearhead Patrol." He raised an eyebrow. "Did you say 'fly'?"

"Yes, Sir, I did."

She scanned the small crowd. More than half openly grinned at her. To her chagrin, she realized most, if not all, of them had witnessed her initial antics and minor crashes with the antique flyer. She gave the group a rueful grin and said, "Yes, despite my earlier difficulties, I flew as requested by the Knight Commander, taking advantage of the orcs' perpetual smoke screen."

"Don't let her fool you, folks," Lord Fergusson commented as he passed the three barbed arrows he collected from the glider to Brian for the group to inspect. "The Laytenant and her flyer came back wearing those."

A low whistle cut through the group. "These are nasty business, Sir," a short, broad-shouldered man said. "They're a lot better quality than orcs usually have, too." He gave Yana a sympathetic look. "Franklin Engval, ma'am. Wildcats."

Yana nodded back and resumed her reconnaissance brief. "I'll start with the Keep, since that is our primary target. Your map is accurate, as far as the outer walls and towers are concerned, but they have block and tackle rigs at the towers for hauling up ammunition. They've also widened the battlement walkways on either side of the gatehouse with wooden platforms, giving them enough room for two ranks of archers, possibly three. In addition, there is an onager and two springalds on the gatehouse roof."

Theodore Tolliston, Leftenant Gallagher's squire, marked the platforms and siege engines on the map with a charcoal pencil as Yana described them.

"The eastern face looks pretty solid. Major weak points are the obvious ones: the main gate and the sally port. The eastern towers hold onagers. Based on the debris littering the clearing around the Keep, I'd say their range is the full two-hundred yards to the tree line. These two," she said, indicating the westernmost corner towers, "hold small ballistae on swivels. They also have a handful of scorpions on the western walls."

Gesturing toward the map, she continued, "I counted three buildings inside the Keep, each large enough to house a troop of orcs. I saw no evidence of tunneling, but there's a heavy presence of orcs patrolling the walls."

"I made a final 'just-in-case' pass along the western side. The walls run right up to the bridge abutment and tie into the bridge defenses. The walls themselves looked relatively well maintained, but the steep riverbank is another story. Have your people look at this section along the northwest corner — from the air, it looked like the foundations had partially eroded."

"Mattias and I can check that," one of Knyaz Dorinkov's aides said. "Perhaps an explosion, like the one Lord Fergusson discussed using on the front gate earlier, could drop that corner of the fortification and let us storm the Keep from the waterside."

Knyaz Dorinkov nodded to his senior aid. "Go, Mikhail. Let us know what you find."

Mikhail and Mattias saluted and left the tent without another word.

Yana waited for them to leave and then continued, "The bridge is lined with stone battlements and has small war engines along its length to attack the traffic along the river, but the humanoids could easily rotate them to defend the city from an attack originating on the eastern shore.

"Next, I passed over the docks and identified three possibilities for you. All are single-mast, cog-like boats, but with a little crowding, could hold twenty to thirty men for a river crossing. They are here, here, and about here." She pointed to different piers marked on the map north of the bridge as she spoke, and Tolliston drew a small symbol beside them.

Yana paused and looked at Lord Fergusson.

He raised an eyebrow. "You have a recommendation on which boat?" he asked.

"Yes Sir. At first glance, they are all equal. But this one," she pointed to the southern-most boat, "is crewed by orcs, while dreyri crew the cogs here and here."

"That works well. The tunnel Dobrynya is using will drop them out about here," Fergusson said as he pointed to a blue dot on the map slightly closer to the centermost ship. "This boat is the best option, especially since Dobrynya's men will be on the run. Let's plan on the shortest route. Plus, it's practically within the shadow of the bridge — too close for the engines on the parapet to be of any use."

He pointed at the boat again. "This will be your second mission objective in the morning, Laytenant Marchenkova. We'll need a strike team. Can you handle the planning?"

"Yes, Sir, but I'll have to cancel my next flight to do it," she replied.

"Vassily, don't we have men who know these waters?" Knyaz Dorinkov asked.

"Yes Highness," the Rhodinan knight replied. "I believe the Ivanov twins would be perfect. They were river pirates before they joined our camp."

"Fergusson, Laytenant Marchenkova has a lot on her plate. Let our men take care of Dobrynya's rescue. Besides, pirates are better suited for this type of mission than a wind rider."

The Knight Commander's brow clouded. "You may be right, Highness. Brian, pull a pair of volunteers to assist Knyaz Dorinkov's men."

"You are knights — not thieves," the prince said.

"I may be able to help," Sehraine said. Everyone in the tent turned to her, including Yana, who opened her mouth to protest, but closed it in the face of Sehraine's glare.

Fergusson stared at the elf, hardly believing what he was hearing. "Lady Sehraine, I cannot ask you to put yourself in harm's way. I don't know the circumstances that brought you here, but you yourself admitted to a lack of fighting skills."

"Knyaz Dorinkov is right. You don't need knights," she said. "You need stealth, which means disguises. As a Trakyan Royal Player, I'm an expert."

"Surely you jest! You have no place in this battle," the prince said.

"Your Highness," Yana said, "with all due respect, you're wrong. I personally vouch for her and the value she could add to this mission. We've both been on the Chernigov side of the river and are familiar with the patrols. In fact, she was instrumental in getting our horses and us across the river. However, if she goes, so do I."

"Fergusson, what say you?" Knyaz Dorinkov asked after a moment of contemplation.

The Knight Commander remained quiet as he studied the young-looking elf. Reaching a decision, he said, "Lady Sehraine, it goes against my better judgement but, if you are *absolutely certain*, I accept your help. I believe it will work out better this way, since we need the laytenant to focus on reconnaissance and her part in taking the Keep tomorrow morning. She can join you on the river once we breach the gate."

"Vassily, contact the Ivanovs, and let them know that we have a task for them," Dorinkov ordered.

"Yes, Your Highness," the knight replied with a bow.

"As for you, young lady, this is my second-in-command, Poruchik Vassily Tirinko. Meet him at our camp after this debrief. We'll see just how much you know."

Lady Sehraine bowed.

"Laytenant, please continue with your account of the city," Lord Fergusson directed.

Yana nodded, looked from Knyaz Dorinkov to Sehraine, and then continued, "I overflew the waterfront from north to south, then looped back to check out the eastern wall of the city..." She went on to delineate engines by type and location, beginning with the northeast tower. Tolliston dutifully marked positions on a map as she spoke. That part went quickly. When she got to the southeast tower, she slowed, placing particular emphasis on the eastern wall defenses.

"King Kraagor has emplaced several large siege engines on the walls. He has a mix of catapult-type weapons: scorpions, onagers, and mangonels. Some of the mangonels are unusual. Instead of the torsion system we are used to seeing, they have spring-driven mechanisms; I have no idea how this may affect their range or ammunition capacity."

Lord Fergusson nodded. "I saw them in action earlier this morning. They easily ranged four to five hundred yards with reasonable accuracy." Several of the younger officers exchanged worried glances. "We'll need you to pay special attention to those contraptions on your next flight."

"Additionally, they have trebuchets," Yana continued, pointing to various positions along the walls of the city, with Leftenant Gallagher's squire dutifully marking what engines were placed where.

"The eastern wall is the only portion that I made a second pass. When I got back to the northeastern tower, I climbed for altitude, circled out over the water, and started my attack run.   I hit several of their towers and received heavy resistance."

Yana looked at Brian and said pointedly, "The dragon pellets are not dependable. Most exploded like they were supposed to, but there were a fair number that simply spewed smoke or did nothing at all."

Unconsciously rubbing the fresh wound on her leg, she continued, "We surprised them this time. I don't know if we'll be as lucky the next time.

"I'm confident that I destroyed four or five of their engines. I am certain that I damaged at least one or two more, but not confident on their destruction." She shrugged. "Pending any questions, that concludes my report, Milord."

The Knight Commander responded promptly, "What can you tell us about the numbers of enemy personnel, Laytenant?"

"The Keep looked to be about a hundred. However, after seeing the city, I would double, maybe even triple that count, at the very least. It's hard to tell exactly since they like to stay underground. When I overflew the city, I saw them entering and exiting burrows; however, as I mentioned earlier, there were no visible burrows in the Keep.

"As for actual numbers, there's no way to get even a rough count. I would hazard to guess that fifteen thousand is a gross underestimate."

Lord Fergusson nodded grimly and looked around the tent.   "Ladies, Gentlemen, do any of you have additional questions about Laytenant Marchenkova's reconnaissance or attack?"

When no one responded, he turned to the wind rider. "Laytenant Marchenkova, I suggest you make ready for your next run. The fewer engines they can aim at us in the morning, the better."

With that dismissal, the room came to attention. The officers and squires saluted their commanders, then filed out to prepare their troops.

Knyaz Dorinkov stayed behind, eyeing the map.

"You better be right about this, Fergusson. I'm risking a lot of men on this attack."

"I understand, Your Highness. Our mission is to open the bridge, hold the river, and give our ranger and his team time to cross. Everything else, including extra casualties, is secondary to the information they hope to bring us. I'm not saying that I don't care about casualties, because I do, but if we do not find a cure for the rising plague, many of your countrymen and mine are going to die. In the face of that, we are all expendable."

Knyaz Dorinkov's face soured, "I want that cure as soon as they cross the bridge. I received a message this afternoon from the Korol' — the plague has reached the capital. It started in a fishing village several miles south of here with reports of a ghost ship and spread both north and east. Luckily, we haven't seen any signs of it here in camp. At least not yet."

"Your Highness, we discussed this. I can't guarantee they'll even *have* the cure. My agent has gone dark." Fergusson's eyes flicked to the journal sitting on top of a folding table.

"How do we even know he's alive?" the Rhodinan prince asked.

"We don't, but what choice do we have?" Fergusson replied. "The signal's been given. We attack at dawn."

CHAPTER 2
RITE OF PASSAGE

October 28, 4235 K.E.

3:00pm

Grendel stared into the dark maw of the orc's underground city with a heavy sense of foreboding. He could feel danger emanating from the pit like a cold wind on his skin and wondered if he could have done anything differently. It was too late to change course. To turn back now would not only allow Marko to win, but would, in all likelihood, sentence his friends to a horrible death. He searched the faces of the mass of orcs waiting eagerly for him to pass and saw something he did not expect: acceptance.

He had fought their kind and even hated them on occasion. He never considered that he had anything in common with them, despite his mixed heritage. Now, thanks to Sacha, he had not only walked into their violent society, but in a short span of time had earned a place in their family.

Looking into the dark hole in front of him, he wondered what it would have been like if he grew up in a city similar to this one. Grendel glanced at the óhreint, Skyld, who shared his mixed orc-ogre heritage, and had his answer. These orcs accepted him because he could fight, but he was still an outsider. Like Skyld, he was neither orc nor ogre, cursed never to be truly at home among either race because of his human blood.

Taking a purposeful step forward, he descended into the tunnel.

Xandor was worried. There were so many orcs, and somehow, he and his team had to break out of this place once they found the chuck wagon and its cargo of tainted soap. Sacha's plan ran through his mind again, and doubt gnawed at him. Faith was not one of his strong points and putting that faith in a Zhitomiran was nigh impossible. Nevertheless, he clung to the plan like a drowning man in a sea of storm-tossed flotsam. Could he hold on long enough?

With Grendel at the lead, Xandor set off into the tunnel with Skyld and Sacha just ahead of him. He stopped before entering the cave and looked up at the smoky sky one last time. Taking a deep breath, he held it for a few seconds before exhaling, and plunged into the unknown.

Behind Xandor, Chert studied the entrance and recalled the ancient tale of Deiniol in the Lion's Den. He just hoped they didn't put a stone over the entrance. Looking around, he didn't see anything of a size to use for that purpose, but you never knew. Of course, it would take more than a block of stone to trap him. If only his gran could see him now.

He caught some of the orcs eyeing him suspiciously. Somehow, they sensed he wasn't really one of them. Maybe it was because he hadn't killed anyone yet. They seemed to accept Grendel and Sacha more than one who appeared to be of their own kind. On edge, Chert expected someone to call him out, but no one did. He grabbed Xandor's elbow as the orcs crowded close and pushed him forward.

Inside was a simple, unadorned anteroom. Semi-rotten timbers and planking shored its earth and rubble walls. The orcs had strung crude ropes made of hair between the posts such that when pulled, the whole room would collapse. If someone attacked the city, this is where the defenders would run. Chert's jaw clenched at the grim realization. They had a stone to place over the entrance after all.

The floor of the chamber sloped down to the center, where bare rock lay exposed. Foul vapors emanated from a shaft before them. Chert's eyes narrowed as he spotted rough-hewn steps spiraling down into the stygian abyss. Noises leached from the black stairwell — distant screams of pain and terror, the occasional clang of metal on metal, and the insidious whisper of guttural voices.

Skyld gave Grendel a short bow and asked permission to guide him. Surprised at the amount of ceremony involved, Grendel couldn't help but wonder what Sacha said to make this so formal.

The half-orc accepted Skyld's offer, and everyone started down the stone steps. As they spiraled deeper and deeper, the gloom of the shaft defeated the weak light from above, and the living darkness swallowed them whole. Compared to the wintery cold aboveground, the air washing over him from below seemed warm and fetid.

Sacha gripped his belt. Her feet shuffled from stair tread to stair tread, and she mumbled curses under her breath. The half-orc turned his head so he could see her from the corner of his eye. Silhouetted by the thin trickle of light from above, both Sacha and Xandor lacked their normal confident bearing. Each had one hand on the wall.

It wasn't until he saw the faint golden glow of Chert's eyes in the darkness that Grendel realized Sacha and Xandor were cavern-blind. Behind Chert, a cluster of orcs with red glowing eyes brought up the rear of their entourage.

He turned his attention back to the stairs and the way down. Sacha's plan got them this far, and he was willing to trust it would see them out the other side, but he still worried. No plan, no matter how well thought out, ever worked. Not really. He had a feeling they were going to be relying on improvisation sooner rather than later.

They continued deeper. The limestone wall on their left dropped away, and the carved stairs spiraled down around a massive column into a medium-sized cavern. Lichen growing amid a forest of stalactites glowed faintly with a pale light.

Water dripped all around them, and Grendel was surprised to find a living cavern system. He wondered what Chert thought of it. Then he saw a group of grubby orclings playing amid a cluster of chipped and broken stalagmites, and an orc female chopping meat on a rock formation sheared off to form a table. Grendel knew the dwarf well enough to be certain the orcs' careless treatment of their home would sadden him.

Orc guards armored in shirts of oiled chain stepped aside for Skyld, who directed Grendel and his entourage around the stalagmites and down a muddy path toward the cavern exit.

As enterprising as they were opportunistic, the orcs had added on to the existing cavern system under Chernigov to create their underground city. The group walked through short tunnels dug to connect the various caverns together. Along the way, they passed overcrowded two- and three-story stacked stone huts built against the cavern walls. Their communal nature left no room for privacy.

Even with Skyld guiding them through the network of caverns, Xandor found himself turned around and lost. Fortunately, he had Chert to help him. Not being able to see well in the almost nonexistent lighting, his other senses engaged, and he wished they hadn't. The entire system reeked of unwashed bodies and raw sewage. His nose reacted violently to the stench, and he struggled against the roiling urge to retch.

No signs marked the way, but Skyld moved with a purpose. The winding trail he followed led past several more overcrowded caverns. They finally emerged in an enormous chamber where orc dwellings were stair-stacked atop one another to the ceiling, five stories high. Crude wooden ladders climbed from level to level, and mud-covered orc children constantly scampered up and down them, playing their war games. At the bottom, interlinked pools of mineral water ran sluggishly past broken stalagmites and disappeared into small cracks and crevasses. The raucous laughter of orc women and the cacophony of children playing provided an odd contrast to the occasional screams that echoed. The only thing missing was the smell of cooking fires, and the lack put Xandor's nerves on edge.

Skyld aimed for one of the ladders amid the tallest mud-plastered dwellings. The orc women quieted, and the children stopped playing. They stared intently at the intruders, distrust in their narrowed eyes.

Chert guided Xandor efficiently through the obstacles covering the floor of the cavern to a rickety, wooden ladder.

Skyld climbed to the second level, turned and headed toward the next ladder. The group snaked its way up the cliff dwellings, stopping at the fourth floor. The óhreint turned right, walked down the narrow ledge, and ducked inside the last chamber.

Vile, twisting symbols etched into the clay and limestone surrounding the entrance cast a sickly, pale green phosphorescence over the group. Following Skyld, Grendel stooped and entered the small chamber while everyone else remained on the ledge.

Inside, vivid paintings covered the walls. Some were of a graphic nature while others were abstract and seemed to be vague representations of chaos and the sleeping god, Ka'Sehkuur. Brownish red pools stained the floor.

Faint light from the lichen revealed an orc helrúnan, or shaman, who appraised the newcomer speculatively. Dressed in robes made from human skin, he wore an intricate vest fashioned from rib and finger bones. The shaman carried a black-iron rod topped with a greasy mass of black hair interwoven with tendrils of sinew and moss.

Sacha squeezed into the chamber and bowed politely to the helrúnan. With a gesture, she motioned for Grendel to do the same. Unsure of himself, Grendel bowed his head curtly.

Satisfied, the helrúnan beckoned Grendel to come closer.

With a little encouragement from Sacha, he stepped to the center of the chamber. The helrúnan produced a clay bowl filled with yellow, red, and blue colored pigments. Using a sharp stick, he stirred the contents until they became a brownish-gray slurry. The helrúnan closed his eyes and started to chant. The mixture writhed inside the bowl as the helrúnan's chant reached a fever pitch. With his eyes still closed, the orc swiped his stick across Grendel's massive chest leaving a swath of gray. The slurry moved of its own volition and formed a counterclockwise swirl on the half-orc's skin.

Grendel swayed and staggered back when he felt the cold, slimy mixture slide across his flesh, but Sacha helped steady him. The swirl grew.

Shouting from outside blended with the chanting.

The slurry burned his skin, and Grendel found himself helpless to stop it. He looked down and watched, horrified, as the swirl corkscrewed into his skin. It writhed inside him, and he tried to rip the stuff from his chest. Skyld and the helrúnan shoved Sacha aside and grabbed his arms. Grendel struggled, but the helrúnan's grip was like iron, forcing the half-orc to his knees.

3:23pm

Grendel roared, and the veins in his arms and neck bulged. His dreadlocks whipped back and forth, and his chest heaved.

Sacha held Chert and Xandor back. "It has to be this way," she whispered, her expression more hopeful than confident. "He's strong. He can do this."

Chert shook his head at her and closed his eyes in silent prayer for his friend. After what seemed an eternity, Grendel slumped forward, exhausted, and the helrúnan and Skyld let him fall.

"It is done," the helrúnan said to Sacha in orcnéan.

Still standing in front of Xandor and Chert, she asked, "Will he survive?" Looking at Grendel's limp form, her heart lurched when the helrúnan did not reply.

Skyld directed Sacha, Chert, and Xandor outside and pointed them to the vacant chamber next door. More than thirty feet below, a growing sea of orc men and women stared up at the helrúnan's home with red glowing eyes. Sacha suppressed a shiver.

Chert and Xandor cornered her the moment she stepped into the room.

"What was that?" the two asked, almost in unison.

"The Rite of Passage. All orcs in this region must do it to become one of the tribe."

"Have you ever seen this ceremony performed before?" Xandor asked.

"No," she answered, then quickly added, "but I have heard about it."

"Great. Just great," Chert said in a voice filled with worry, and turned away to look out into the cavern. "This Rite of Passage and becoming a member of the tribe — was it necessary?"

"Yes."

"Couldn't we have just asked the óhreint to take us to Kraagor's throne room or whatever it is he uses to greet visitors?"

"No. Grendel had to become a member of the tribe."

"Even if it kills him?"

Sacha glanced at Chert, and she could see the worry in his eyes. His concern mirrored her own. He took a step forward and said, "I'm sorry."

"I wouldn't have done this if it wasn't absolutely necessary," Sacha said. "All we can do now is wait and hope."

3:33pm

Grendel's heart pounded. Noxious air crawled down his throat to coil inside his lungs. Voices echoed around him, and a looming presence stood over him.

"Arise, Son of Cayn!"

His spent muscles did not respond.

Something struck the stone floor in front of him, and a loud metallic ring resonated in his ears. The harsh sound washed over him and made the chamber vibrate.

"Arise!"

Grendel cracked his eyes open. He was lying face down on the bloodstained floor of the helrúnan's chamber. A shadow crossed in front of him, and the images on the walls came into focus. The vibrant cave paintings swirled and shifted, coming to life. Battles raged across black and red fields: orc versus dwarf, orc versus elf, and orc versus human.

As the images shifted again, Grendel found himself staring at what he first took to be an abstract painting done in shades of grey and black. The image swirled and formed hard edges, reminding Grendel of a rectangular window. Unable to draw his eyes away, he searched the void on the other side of the window and stared intently into the blackness. His mind recoiled when he realized the void stared back at him.

No, not the void. Something from the other side of the window, and its presence filled the chamber with raw, mindless fury.

Chanting called to the slurry inside Grendel, but it was distant and held no meaning. The thing on the other side of the window weighed him, and he struggled to look away. Sweat dripped from his brow, but his muscles remained rigid, his cheek still pressed to the bloodstained floor.

The window and the savage awareness on the other side grew larger and larger. Was he moving, or was it the wall? He couldn't tell, and fear, the likes of which he hadn't felt since before his mother died, gripped his heart. Darkness beyond the window filled his vision, blotting out everything else, and he heard a distant scream.

Grendel inhaled deeply, and the odor of rancid blood from the floor filled his nostrils. Something inside him responded to the smell. It cried out for release, and he felt the urge to rend flesh. The need overwhelmed him, and his hand moved, claw-like, across the floor.

Whispered words slithered through the room, and footsteps soon followed.

Suddenly, Grendel could see through the window. Shock etched his features when he saw his father crouched in a small room, beside an óhreint and an orc guard. But it couldn't be him, could it?

A woman and a man stood behind the orc guard. He ignored the man, but the woman captured his senses. She was beautiful despite her worn and dirty clothing, and he tasted her fear like a draught of cool water. It awakened savage desires deep inside him, but he knew she was too beautiful for the likes of him, no matter how low her fortunes had sunk. His father stared at her, and dread fell like a dead weight in the pit of his stomach. His father would use her to tease him relentlessly, but in the end she would never, *could never*, be his.

'*Vanin, come away from the window,*' his mother's voice whispered from the darkness. '*Close your eyes. Try not to listen.*'

3:33pm

Crouching in the small room, Grendel glared at them with raw hunger. Sacha took a step back, a trembling hand over her mouth, and eyes wide with horror. Grendel's predatory expression made it clear he was lost to them. The creature in that room was no longer her bodyguard.

Xandor turned to Sacha. Shock and alarm vied for dominance in the ranger's expression. "What have you done to him?" he hissed.

She did not respond; she couldn't. She shook her head in denial of what crouched before them, her eyes fixed on those of the half-orc.

Step by cautious step, Chert entered the room. He unbuckled the belt holding his scimitar, and it clattered to the floor.

Grendel snorted at the noise. His eyes shone violet and bored into his onetime friend with no hint of recognition. Now, they held the savage glint of a predator that kills for the simple joy of spilled blood and has found its next prey.

Chert removed Sacha's necklace. The orc form melted away, revealing his true self. He dropped the chain on the ground at Sacha's feet.

Grendel stared at the dwarf. His brow furrowed, and his head tilted as though he was trying to understand what he was seeing.

With a prayer on his lips, Chert took another step forward. "Grendel, I am your friend," he said, raising his arms in a gesture of peace.

Rage flooded Grendel as countless years of racial hatred surged forth. He lashed out at the stocky dwarf with the fury of a savage beast. His battle-axe forgotten, Grendel's clawed hand slashed toward Chert's cheek. Instead of hitting flesh as expected, Grendel's hand hit a solid surface of light.

Surprised, Grendel took a closer look at his prey. The dwarf held a small, round shield of pure energy. On its surface, the dwarven symbol of creation — a cross-shaped hammer suspended over an anvil — shimmered brightly in the dim chamber. In his other hand, he held a glowing war hammer. Together, the two gave off enough light to cause the helrúnan to cover his eyes with his arm and remain hemmed in at the back of the chamber.

Grendel dove at Chert with both clawed hands extended. Rather than strike with his hammer, the dwarf brought up his shield and let Grendel ride over it. At the last second, Chert shoved up at an angle, sending Grendel flying into the wall with a solid thud.

Chert counted himself fortunate. The half-orc's attack lacked his normal finesse; otherwise, there would've been no way out of this chamber alive. At least this way he had a fighting chance. Acutely aware of the helrúnan skulking along the edge of the room, Chert circled, keeping one eye on the orc. The helrúnan, for his part, seemed content to hiss and spit curses at the shield of light.

Grendel climbed to his feet, slow and wary. The two eyed one another. The half-orc clasped both his hands together in a hammer-fist and brought them down on Chert's shield with a crushing blow. The dwarf staggered, holding his shield tightly, unable to do anything but stay on the defensive. Grendel struck repeatedly, driving the dwarf toward the helrúnan.

CHAPTER 3
BREGU KRAAGOR

October 28, 4235 K.E.

3:38pm

Orcs in chain and plate armor burst into the cavern below amid the raucous echo of orders shouted in their guttural language. Xandor and Sacha watched Bregu Kraagor stride into the cavern accompanied by Marko, Kourash, and Gregori. Around them, a dozen of the bregu's personal guard held flaming torches.

Soldiers scaled the ladders, blocking off any chance of escape. Xandor whispered the command word and the cord around his wrists loosened. He slipped it into his pocket while picking up Chert's scimitar. He let the weapon's scabbard drop over the ledge and waited.

"Give up, ranger!" Marko shouted from below.

"Come up here and get me!" Xandor replied with a rakish grin.

"Surely, you realize you can't win. Make it easier on yourself."

Swiping the sword in front of him, Xandor replied, "Maybe not, but I will take as many of you with me as I can."

"Lady Aleksandra," Bregu Kraagor bellowed, "I'm surprised to find you here. Your brother said you were dead."

"You should never believe anything my brother tells you," she replied coldly.

"And what about you, my dear? What brings you here?"

"I came to steal your throne, Bregu Kraagor."

"You've got mighty big balls, for a woman," Kraagor said with a laugh. "How did you plan to do that?"

"The Rite of Passage."

"The Rite of Passage? You are not one of us."

"Not me. My bodyguard."

Marko leaned close to the orc king and whispered a few words in his ear. Surprise flooded the orc's face. "Does he live?" Kraagor asked.

"Why don't you come up here and find out?"

"Don't toy with me, Lady Aleksandra. You are meddling with powers of which you have no understanding."

At a snap of Kraagor's fingers, a line of orcs produced their short bows and aimed them at the people on the ledge.

"He lives. If your archers shoot up here now, before the challenge, it may be misconstrued as an act of cowardice."

The orcs hesitated and their bows dipped slightly.

Kraagor made a show of looking around and asked, "Why do I not see him?"

3:38pm

Grendel pinned the dwarf to the floor. He pushed against the shield, slowly crushing his smaller opponent. Chert gritted his teeth and pushed back, but it was no use. Grendel was by far the stronger of the two. The helrúnan approached with his iron rod in one hand and Grendel's battle-axe in the other.

Grendel pushed harder, trying to kill the dwarf. His hands sank lower until the shield disappeared, and the half-orc found himself pressing his hands against the bloodstained floor of the chamber.

The helrúnan yelled and cursed the half-breed for letting the dwarf get away. Grendel turned on the orc, a deep rumbling growl echoing from his throat. The shaman's eyes grew wide, and the scent of fear filled the room. Grendel's hulking form slowly rose from the floor, blocking the helrúnan's path to the doorway.

Chert popped through the stone and fell to the floor of the chamber directly below. He landed with a hard thump, followed by a few choice words in dwarven. Dusting himself off, the dwarf took stock of the earthen room. Several orclings had him surrounded. Waving his hands in the air crazily, he yelled, "Boo!"

The orclings ran screaming, and the cavern erupted with shouts and vile curses. Bregu Kraagor's roaring voice cut through the din of the crowd. A dwarf had violated their city!

Chert didn't need to understand orcnéan. He turned and fled into the wall of the cavern.

3:45pm

Sacha turned to Skyld, noted the uncertain look in his eyes, and asked, "Do you want to survive this?"

The óhreint's brow furrowed. A crunch of bone echoed out of the helrúnan's chamber, pulling his attention from the bregu's entourage below to the beast at their back. He nodded.

"Do exactly as I say."

Again, he nodded.

Weapons drawn, orc soldiers lined the narrow ledge and cautiously approached the cloaked ranger with savage snarls on their faces. They were almost within reach. Sacha turned to Xandor and whispered, "Are you ready?"

He looked over his shoulder at Sacha. In her hand, she held her dagger. "After you, Milady," he replied sarcastically.

Making sure everyone below could see her, Sacha pressed the tip of her knife against the back of Xandor's neck, paralyzing him. Skyld slipped past Sacha and hefted Xandor's now-frozen body.

"Bregu Kraagor! I seek an audience with you!" she shouted.

"Where's your bodyguard?"

A loud, ripping sound answered from the shaman's chamber.

Throwing a quick glance behind her, she said, "He's still inside with your helrúnan!"

"Ask him to come out!"

"I don't think he'll listen. He's rather busy."

Behind the orc king, Marko and Kourash had their heads together, gesturing up at her. Marko nodded to his bodyguard, then murmured something to Kraagor. The king nodded and gestured for the knight to speak.

"You seem to be having trouble holding on to your servants, sister," Marko called. "Where is the cook, and how did you come to ally yourself with this ranger?"

"The cook is buried under the monastery. You're welcome to search the wreckage for his body," she replied. "As for the ranger, we share a common enemy, little brother." Dismissing him, Sacha turned her attention back to the king. "I have a proposition for you Bregu Kraagor. Will you meet with me?"

A smile spread across the wretched king's face, and he said graciously, "Of course, Lady Aleksandra. I would be happy to meet with you. Please, bring your friends."

Bregu Kraagor clapped his hands, and his orcs stopped their advance.

Sacha bowed toward the king and aimed for the nearest ladder, followed closely by Skyld, who carried Xandor's stiffened body. The orcs in front of her fanned out of the way and gave her room. They eyed her warily as she strode toward them like a queen. Once they reached the cavern floor, Sacha walked directly to the king.

At a signal from Bregu Kraagor, several orcs cautiously entered the helrúnan's chamber with scimitars drawn. Moments later, a shout erupted from the fourth floor and an orc soldier sailed through the air across the cavern. Another cry echoed from above, cut short in a sickening, wet gurgle.

Kraagor turned to Sacha. "What have you done?"

She didn't answer. She simply stared up at the helrúnan's dwelling in fear. Black blood dripped from the ledge and glinted in the torchlight.

With a sigh, the orc king said, "I have heard it said that the ritual will awaken the primal spirit inside half-breeds who suppress their true nature. Your bodyguard is lost and must be put down." His words sounded as if he were declaring judgment.

The king gestured again and a dozen more guards entered the room. They wore blood-red mail shirts, marking them as his elite guard. Each carried a long, iron pole with a spiked iron tether attached to one end. At their hips, they wore long, saw-toothed scimitars.

The leader of the Red Guard stopped and bowed to his king.

"I want him alive," Kraagor said.

The orc bowed again and marched to the ladders, followed by his team.

"I should kill you for what you have done, but your brother says it would be far worse for you to be taken home in disgrace."

Sacha cast a withering glance in Marko's direction but otherwise remained silent.

With an expansive smile, the king continued, "As a parting gift before you go, I would like to present you with some entertainment."

Sensing a trap, she asked cautiously, "What kind of entertainment?"

Watching the Red Guard climb the ladders, he responded, "I'm going to pit your bodyguard against your ranger."

She glanced at Xandor and felt a sinking feeling in her stomach. Her plan was falling apart.

3:50pm

The harsh sounds of bones splintering and flesh shredding echoed within the dark chamber. Covered in black gore, Grendel crouched with his back to the door, pulling apart the body of an orc. Behind him, a boot scraped on stone. Dropping the arm in his hand, he turned and rose. He focused on the red-clad orcs rather than the poles they carried until the iron tethers snapped open, revealing tiny spikes.

Grendel grabbed at the first pole as its tether snapped closed around his left calf like a bear trap. Pain lanced through his muscles, causing his back to arch. Another tether snapped around the thigh of his right leg, and the pain instantly doubled. Taking a quick step backward, he jerked the pole out of the orc's hands. That orc backed away, and another took his place.

Focusing on his legs, he didn't notice when the orcs on the ledge snuck two more long poles into the room. They hovered around his arms, waiting for the opportunity to strike. Grendel grabbed one and jabbed the orc on the other end, hurling him off the ledge. He screamed all the way to the bottom.

A spiked tether bit into Grendel's left arm, and the half-orc bellowed. Spasms of pain filled his entire world and red rivulets of blood trailed from the edges of the tethers. He tried to move and fight the effects of the Red Guard's weapons, but cramps seized his muscles where the iron bands gripped him.

Another tether latched onto his right arm. The coup de grâce was the band that snapped around his neck, its vicious metal teeth delivering pain directly into his spine.

With five poles attached to the half-orc, the Red Guard dragged him from the helrúnan's dwelling. Grendel was like a wild, rabid animal, his face, neck, and body covered in red and black blood. His manic eyes glared at the orcs with such raw hatred that they flinched as if struck, but the Red Guard knew what they were doing. They stood on both sides of the half-orc, careful to avoid the occasional flailing arm.

The three orcs holding the poles attached to Grendel's arms and neck heaved while the two holding the poles attached to his legs twisted the shafts to release their tethers.

Using their poles, the three orcs shoved Grendel over the ledge, letting him dangle for a moment or two. With a final twist of the shafts, the orcs released their tethers, dropping the prisoner to the guards poised on the ledge below. The pattern repeated and, in a matter of minutes, Grendel landed heavily on the cavern floor beside a broken stalagmite.

The fourth group of Red Guard attached their poles to the iron tethers with quick snaps of the wrist and dragged the still-writhing half-orc to Bregu Kraagor.

The orc king studied him briefly and said, "Take him to the throne room."

4:00pm

Vanin spat blood and dirt from his mouth as he pushed himself up from the arena floor.

"Od's blood, boy! You're half óhreint! Start acting like it!" the trainer shouted.

The lanky boy stared daggers at the broadly built minotaur. "I may look like Grendel, but I will never be like him," he muttered.

"You have something to say, boy?" the swarthy-skinned J'Belan asked, taking a threatening step forward and raising the whip in his hand. When Vanin shook his head, the trainer sneered. "Good. Then get back to your mark and go again."

With swift efficiency, the Red Guard raced down the ladders and formed up on the cavern floor to await further orders. Their leader stepped out in front and pointed toward Grendel. Immediately, three orcs peeled away to help guard the prisoner.

"Herewísa, there's a dwarf in the walls!" Kraagor shouted. "Flush him out."

The Red Guard leader bowed and shouted additional instructions to his warriors.

Before she followed King Kraagor and his entourage, Sacha noticed the female orcs and their children gathering across the cavern from their dwellings and wondered what could instill such fear in them in the heart of their city. A new sound came from a tunnel on the far side of the cavern, reminiscent of a landslide. It started with a shushing, slithering sound like sliding sand and pebbles, followed by the clack and grumble of falling stones. The orcs grew silent and still.

The creature that emerged from the tunnel was a heavily muscled, ovoid-shaped beast, bound with multiple leashes. Three savage looking orcs in rust-colored studded leather clung to the ends of the leashes, each leaning all their weight against the creature's pull to slow its progress. Its four long-toed feet gripped the cavern floor and made tiny furrows with its claws as the creature stretched the leashes to their fullest.

Sacha had never seen its like before. It stood thirteen hands high at the withers and measured ten feet from the end of its pointed nose to the tip of its stubby tail. Sharp plate-like scales protected its slate blue body, and beady eyes set into each side of its pointy-head peered about warily. As it moved, the scales scissored back and forth, producing a unique hissing sound.

Something attracted the creature's attention. It sniffed the ground, similar to a bloodhound, and pulled one of its handlers off his feet. Sacha turned, holding up the procession of orcs, and watched the handlers remove the leashes.

It leapt forward and climbed the side of the cliff dwellings, its scales still emitting their uncanny sound. Sacha heard it sniff once and then disappear inside the chamber directly below the former helrúnan's home.

CHAPTER 4
SEHRAINE

October 28, 4235 K.E.

3:00pm

Sehraine made her way through the heavily wooded Rhodinan camp in the long shadows cast by the late afternoon sun. Hidden amongst the trees, a small city of pale grey tents spread like a blanket of low-lying fog. The effect was strange yet beautiful with their spider webbing of guy ropes. It fascinated her that the soldiers and sutlers dared to be so close to the humanoids, with a few scant miles of new-growth forest between them.

Zack walked ahead of her with another boy about his age, somewhere in the neighborhood of ten summers. The two whispered earnestly, and the new boy, Afon, kept glancing over his shoulder at her. She smiled and shook her head. No need to wonder what — or who — they discussed.

Still wearing a hat to hide her ears, she wished, once again, that she had access to theater makeup to create a better disguise. When Xandor explained the local prejudices against the elves, she hadn't worried. She expected to be among the Glaxons, not the Rhodinans. Now, she was walking into their armed camp, with only a knit hat and a few judicious smears of mud for protection. Although Lord Fergusson offered her an escort, she feared it would arouse unwanted attention and refused.

She glanced at the men and women she passed and couldn't help but think that, in her case, their resentment was justified. Jasper's account of the vision from the black book they stole from Asenov's office haunted her. Even without seeing it for herself, she felt certain it was her father's wagon in Jasper's vision, sitting in the center of a village with the Blood of Cayn pooled around it.

If only she hadn't been so stupid that day, had not run away. If she had stayed to watch the wagon as her father asked, there might never have been a plague or a war.

She swallowed her rising emotions as she passed a section of tents and almost ran into the back of a leather-clad warrior who stepped between her and the boys, seemingly unaware she was with them. Only when he drew close enough to hear the boys' conversation did she begin to take note.

The man was shorter than average, only half-a-head taller than her, with the heavy build of a laborer... or a thug. She had seen men like him in Pazard'zhik more than a few times. Although they lacked muscle definition, they did not lack for strength, and most had an even bigger attitude.

The boys turned down a lane between the tents while the man kept going straight, but when Sehraine followed the boys, she caught a glimpse of another man, identical to the first, following her.

Pretending he wasn't there, she kept going, searching for a place to step out of sight. She saw an opening ahead that greatly resembled a farmer's market with its makeshift stands to hold fruits and vegetables. The drone of conversation fought with the sounds of pigs, chickens, and other livestock as people sold their wares.

Just before she reached the clearing, the man behind her vanished inside a tent. '*What was that about?*' she wondered, unconsciously checking the brace of small knives sheathed in the worn leather adorning her forearms.

The boys stopped at the market to let her catch up.

"Did you see the two men following us?" Afon asked. Sehraine nodded, and he continued, "Good. They are the Ivanov brothers. Not armiya and not militsiya. Poruchik Tirinko only lets them stay here because they're useful against the vragi on the river."

"How so?" Sehraine asked, curious what the Rhodinan runner knew.

"Miyka saw them go out on the river early one morning, just before the sun rose. Soon after they returned, several of the vragi boats caught fire and sank."

"Hmm... that's interesting. I look forward to meeting them." At the boy's sharp intake of breath, she looked at him askance. "What is it?"

"They are dangerous, Dama."

"Yes, I could tell. However, dangerous men are exactly what I need for my mission. Come, your poruchik is waiting."

The two-story stone tavern Knyaz Dorinkov had commandeered for his headquarters looked ancient, with its thick tufts of moss outlining weathered black and grey stone blocks. Sometime in the past year, someone repointed the blocks near the foundation and corners with fresh mortar. They gleamed in the afternoon sun, making the repairs stand out even to the untrained eye. Pale wooden shakes covered the roof, and the dark-stained door looked new. A clearing surrounded the building, dotted with stumps intermingled with several pavilions.

A single, ancient oak cast a long shadow across them all. The half-green, half-red, autumn leaves looked as if they were dipped in blood. Touching her forehead, Sehraine made a quick sign to ward off evil.

She and Zack followed Afon as he mounted the short flight of steps and knocked on the door. The specific cadence of the knock was not lost on the elven actress, and she wondered what someone giving the wrong code would find waiting within.

Hearing a man call out permission to enter, Afon opened the door and stepped into the dimly lit room. He advanced far enough for his charges to enter and closed the door behind them. Sehraine moved to the center of the common room. A narrow table with a lit candelabra and a pair of closed doors took up the right-hand wall. Straight ahead, a pale swath of flooring marked where the bar once stood between the room and an arched corridor that passed under the stairs to a back room. A single door near the foot of the stairs occupied the left wall.

"Sir! Dama Sehraine as requested!" the boy declared to the leather-clad guard standing in front of the arched corridor.

"Eto ne mesto dlya malen'kikh devochek," a deep voice whispered in Sehraine's ear, sending an icy shiver down her spine even as she dropped into a crouch and spun to press the tips of her daggers against sensitive and vital areas of the man's anatomy.

The man yelped and leapt back. He took a swipe at her, knocking her knit hat to the floor. Looking up, Sehraine wasn't surprised to see one of the Ivanov brothers scowling at her.

A deep-throated laugh came from behind the guard. Someone gave the man a slight push from behind, and the second brother stepped into the room.

"What did I tell you, Lev!" he said, "This kotenka has claws, da?"

"*Da*," the scowling brother replied. He glared harder as she rose from her crouch and turned to keep both men in sight.

Zack and Afon peered out from under the table, their eyes wide with fright. Afon inhaled sharply. "*Ona fyeï!*" he exclaimed. Sehraine snatched her hat from the floor and pulled it down on her head, but the damage was done.

The cold hiss of the guard's weapon leaving its leather scabbard filled the room. His face was a hard mask of hate, and he started across the room. "*Grebanya fyeï!*" he spat.

Sehraine darted away from Lev and the guard, trying to escape before either laid a hand on her. An arm snaked around her waist, lifting her from the floor, and a hand gripped her wrist.

"Don't move, kotenka," Lev murmured in her ear. "Don't make a sound."

"What is going on out here?" demanded Poruchik Vassily Tirinko. He stood in front of the door at the foot of the stairs with his arms crossed.

Lev dropped Sehraine on her feet and stepped away.

Sehraine straightened and turned to the Rhodinan second-in-command. "The Ivanov brothers and I were getting acquainted, Sir, and I'm afraid your guard mistook me for an enemy."

"Is that so?" Vassily asked, taking in the dark look exchanged between the brothers and the expression on the guard's face.

"She's a filthy elf, Sir," the guard declared.

"Soldier, hold your venom for the orcs and the battle tomorrow. This young lady stands with us against the vragi."

The guard glared openly at Sehraine and said nothing.

"Do I make myself clear, soldier?"

"Yes, Sir," the guard grated, barely within the limits of civility.

Poruchik Tirinko turned his attention to the Ivanov brothers. "You two!" he barked. "The prince lets you stay in this camp because you are very good at what you do. Do not give him a reason to change his mind. Into my office. NOW."

Turning to the young boys, he commanded, "Afon, take Dama Marchenkova's guide outside until we are done, and stay out of trouble."

Sehraine followed Vassily and the Ivanov twins into a former dining room with shuttered windows. Maps covered the walls like tapestries and another map lay across the central table. Cyrillic markers identified various fortified positions.

The brothers continued giving her appraising looks as they arranged themselves opposite her.

"Dama Sehraine, these are Yevgeny and Lev," the deputy commander stated. "Please do not ask me which is which. I cannot tell them apart."

She studied the two brothers. While they did look remarkably alike, she noted subtle differences, particularly around the eyes. They were mirror images rather than exact copies.

"Can't you, Sir?" she asked. Pointing to the one on her left, she said, "This is Yevgeny, and that is Lev," she added pointing to the other. At their looks of surprise, she gave them her most mysterious smile.

"How can you tell us apart?" Lev demanded.

"No one, except our parents, can tell us apart," Yevgeny said.

"I think that shall remain my secret, if you don't mind. Once a secret is spoken, it loses its power."

The brothers eyed her speculatively but nodded their agreement.

"What's the plan, Vassily?" Lev asked.

"This isn't my operation. The lady is in charge," he answered. "Can the two of you live with that, or do I need to find someone else?"

"Tell us the job first, then we'll decide," Yevgeny stated.

"As we speak, there are a number of your countrymen stranded in Chernigov," Sehraine explained. "Some of them are wounded and unable to attempt the swim, even if the weather were warmer. My plan is to cross the White River tonight, steal a boat, and bring those men home."

"You've taken a ship before?" Yevgeny asked, his eyebrows raised in surprise.

"Of course," she said mockingly. "The laytenant and I took one just this morning after killing a dreyri patrol."

"Your boyfriend must be one hell of a fighter," Lev said, his voice tinged with doubt, "to kill a dreyri patrol singlehanded. Is he coming on this rescue, too?"

"My boyfriend?"

"Your laytenant."

"Oh. She's not my boyfriend, but yes, she is rather good with her blades. She plans to join us on the river tomorrow."

The brothers looked from Sehraine to Vassily, waiting for one of them to give away the joke.

"It's true," Vassily stated. "One of Mikhail's scouts confirmed the story earlier today."

The brothers looked at Sehraine with newfound respect.

"I heard a rumor that the two of you are good at burning vragi boats."

"Ships," Yevgeny corrected.

"Ships," Sehraine replied with a nod. "Of course. The laytenant has already scouted the available craft and found three that suit our needs. Our job will be to set up a diversion and liberate a ship, allowing your countrymen to escape."

"That is not a plan," Lev growled. "That's suicide."

"How so?"

"To start, we will need more than three and a half people to take a ship and pilot it across the river," he said with a sniff and a slight raise of his chin.

"We'll have more than four people," she countered. "Vityaz Dobrynya Sabe and his men will be waiting for us when we get there."

Yevgeny studied her carefully and asked, "How will they know where to meet us?"

"We have a prearranged signal. More importantly, how do you normally sneak up on the boats, I mean ships, without raising an alarm?" she asked.

The brothers shared a look. "We swim," Yevgeny finally answered.

Sehraine raised one elegant eyebrow. "Swim?" she queried. "In that river, in this cold? That will never do."

4:15pm

Sehraine exited the old Rhodinan tavern late in the afternoon. The sun had already sunk below the smoke pall above Chernigov to the west, turning the forest gloamy. The shadows of the day grew deeper with each passing minute, and the play of light and shadow wreaked havoc on her vision.

To all outward appearances, she was the epitome of calm, but inside, an amalgamation of fear and excitement roiled in her belly, similar to what she experienced during the opening night of a new performance. Of course, the consequences of a poor performance tonight were bound to be more dire than anything she might have faced from even the most unruly Trakyan audience.

She sighed. The danger was unavoidable.

Pulling her hat more firmly down on her head, Sehraine stepped away from the short stoop and began her journey back to the Iron Tower camp. She wished she hadn't sent Zack away earlier with messages, and then admonished herself for being a coward. She had years of experience passing herself off as human, and she was a Royal Player, after all.

Her mind wandered, and she contemplated the late arrival to their meeting. Sergei Nikoloff was a fit man, handsome for a human, with inquisitive eyes. He introduced himself as a rasskazchik, and the others in the room laughed, asking him to play them a tune. He smiled at the invitation but declined, saying he left his gitara in his tent. The man had made many useful suggestions and provided Sehraine with an interesting source for supplies. After the Ivanov twins left, she remained with Sergei, working out a list of items they would need for the disguise she planned. By the time she emerged from the map room, a new guard stood at the entrance. A shiver danced along Sehraine's spine as she thought about the heated glare of the guard who recognized her as an elf.

Despite Vassily's warning to the guard, she knew word would spread through the camp as fast as the most sordid court gossip. She was glad Sergei took the news well. Not being able to avail herself of his help would have made her mission a lot more difficult.

Letting caution get the better of her she turned east, intending to circle around the edge of the Rhodinan camp. A flicker of movement caught her attention. Pausing for a moment, she scanned the shadows but saw nothing. "Privyet! Who is there?"

No answer came beyond the soft rustle of a tree limb overhead. Eyes closed, she shook her head. '*Just a squirrel,*' she thought.

Walking on, she skirted the lines of tents and the few buildings, opting to stay closer to the forest and pass behind the corrals. Campfires flickered amid clusters of tents, and she caught the smells of supper cooking here and there.

The hairs on the back of her neck stood up, and she swore she felt eyes watching her. Sehraine whipped around but only saw the normal comings and goings of the camp through the trees. She berated herself for being paranoid, thinking about what Yana would say.

A horse approached the corral fence and watched her draw closer. With a soft smile, she stopped and rubbed the animal's nose. The mare contented herself with the attention for a minute, and then pushed her head out to sniff at Sehraine's clothing.

"Fyrirgefðu, engin epli," Sehraine said softly. *Sorry, no apples.*

In response, the horse snorted, shook out her mane, and backed away to join the rest of the herd. Sehraine sighed. Apparently, even Rhodinan horses disliked elves.

The shadows grew. It was time for Yana to leave for another flight over Chernigov, and she wasn't there. There wasn't a strict timetable, but Yana, being Yana, was impatient, not to mention prone to worry. Sehraine hurried on, paying little heed to the noise she made in her haste. Yana would not approve, but Sehraine had no time for stealth.

Following what she thought was the trail back to the Iron Tower camp, Sehraine's heart jumped into her throat when a Rhodinan soldier appeared around a clump of underbrush and aimed a crossbow in her direction.

"Ostanovke! Kto idet?"

A guard! Thank the gods. "Dama Sehraine Marchenkova of Trakya," she announced. "Can you tell me if this is the path back to the Iron Tower encampment?"

"You're Iron Tower?" the man asked suspiciously.

"No, not really, but I'm helping them," Sehraine answered, not sure how much she should say.

"Come. It's that way," he said indicating the direction with his head. "I'll make sure you don't get lost."

He walked beside her, but she noticed that he kept the crossbow trained on her more times than not. Sehraine swallowed hard, uncertain what to do. To run would look guilty of a crime, and she didn't want to be shot over a misunderstanding. She hoped Yana would wait for her.

The guard beside her seemed to know where he was going, but she had to admit it — she was lost. Angling in what she believed to be the right direction, Sehraine prayed for a sign that they were nearing the Glaxon camp. An elf lost in the woods. She would never live this down, even if she lived to be a thousand years old. Her human family would pass the story down like a damnable heirloom.

The trail entered a clearing and she found four soldiers waiting for her, including the one who saw her ears earlier. She slammed to a halt, only to have the guard, who was now behind her, shove her forward.

"Walk, fyeì."

"Why are you doing this?" Sehraine asked.

"Shut up and move," the guard answered, using the tip of the bolt to push her.

She stumbled forward, barely catching herself.

"It was your kind who caused the last plague," one of the other soldiers said. "The Glaxons let you run free, and now there's another plague. We will not let you infect our people again."

"No!" Sehraine cried. "I swear upon my father's soul, I came from Trakya seeking a cure!"

"Where you came from doesn't matter," the guard from Dorinkov's headquarters said. "It's where you are going that is important to us."

"Please, I mean no harm! You have countrymen trapped in Chernigov! I'm here to help rescue them. Why don't you believe me?"

"You have brought the plague among us!"

Sehraine looked at the men who moved to surround her. Her options were vanishing faster than the light. In desperation, she slammed an elbow into the gut of the man behind her and sprinted away from the others.

A crossbow bolt slammed into the tree beside her. She darted away, sliding in the pine straw and leaves until she gained traction and took off again, flying between the trees like a deer pursued by hounds.

It frightened her that she couldn't hear them over the sound of her own footfalls and racing heart. Not daring to look back, she frantically searched for the way back to the horse corral and the main camp.

Sehraine leapt over a fallen tree and felt something snap underfoot as she landed. Her feet jerked out from under her, and she screamed as she went down hard, a tangle of roots and vines wrapped around one leg. She pulled furiously against the snare, but it only grew tighter. Gulping in deep breaths, Sehraine drew a dagger and worked furiously to free herself.

As the last vine parted, a calloused hand clamped over her mouth from behind, and a blade pressed against her throat.

"Drop the weapon," a man growled. When her dagger hit the bracken, he pulled her to her feet. "You're going to be sorry you elbowed Anton," he said. Footsteps crunched in the underbrush, and he shouted, "Yuri, I found it!"

His unwashed stench overwhelmed her. Sehraine struggled against his tight grip as the man forced her to walk. The other three joined them. They gagged her, bound her hands and feet, and took away her other dagger. Her captor carried her away from camp.

Her mind reeled. Were the men right? Rather than its victims, were the elves responsible for the plague thirty-some-odd years before? She thought back to Jasper's vision and the derelict wagon. She didn't know the meaning of it, but she was certain her father had not been a willing participant.

Sehraine let out a muffled grunt when the man carrying her bumped her against the low-hanging branch of a tree.

"Careful! If you spill her blood, we all get sick!" someone hissed.

Somehow, they knew she was infected. How did they know? She had been so careful. Tears welled in her eyes. In the gloom, no one noticed the grey tinge.

CHAPTER 5
DANGER AT EVERY TURN

October 28, 4235 K.E.

4:30pm

*Y*ana paced away from the glider and back. Everything was ready, but Sehraine had yet to arrive. The runner said to wait for her, but what if he got the message wrong? He was just a little boy, even if his job was carrying messages for Lord Fergusson and Leftenant Gallagher.

She considered going to look for Zack and send him to verify the message but decided against it. What if Sehraine arrived while she was gone? With a huff, Yana dropped to the ground next to the flyer.

"We make a pretty good team, old girl," Yana said, "even if you did try to dump me in the trees at the beginning."

The glider remained silent.

"I wish Sehraine would hurry."

Yana wondered, for the dozenth time, what was keeping Sehraine. Hope rose when she caught a glimpse of movement on the far side of the field, but it quickly vanished when two stocky-built Rhodinans emerged from the trees and headed her way.

Rising to meet them, she studied the two men. They moved with a quiet grace that belied their unfit appearances, like otters on a riverbank. Their hair shone the golden brown of dried river reeds, furthering the image.

"Are you Dama Sehraine's laytenant?" one asked.

She nodded and replied, "You the Ivanovs?"

They nodded in return. "I'm Yevgeny," the twin on her left said. He hitched a thumb at his brother. "That is Lev. Sehraine asked us here to meet you, so we are all familiar with one another. We left her with Dorinkov's rasskazchik, talking about disguises."

"She sent a message to wait for her, but that was close to an hour ago," Yana replied. "She knows I want to leave before dark, so she'd better be along soon." She appraised the two men and asked, "You'll help us take and hold a ship?"

"Da," Yevgeny replied. "Your fyei has a good plan to get us close without notice."

Yana looked at them sharply. *"My elf?"* her voice held a sharp edge. Xandor's warning about the Rhodinan attitude toward elves flashed in her mind. She scowled and searched the trees again. Under normal circumstances, Sehraine hid her identity under an excellent disguise. Years of working in the theater with make-up and costumes made her an expert, but on the backside of nowhere with few resources, her options were limited to Xandor's knit hat, dried mud, and the bracken along the riverbank.

The brothers had the good manners to look embarrassed. "It is my fault," Lev stated flatly. "I startled her, she drew a blade, and I took a swipe at her head. We all saw her ears."

"All?" Yana snapped. "How many was that? Is she in danger?"

Yevgeny put up a placating hand. "The two of us, Poruchik Tirinko, the runners, and one of Dorinkov's guards saw her."

Lev added, "Vassily ordered the guard to stand down and leave her alone. He will not go against orders."

Yana glared at the two men. "You hope."

"If she is not here before you go, we will find her, Laytenant."

The wind rider's expression hardened as she stared at the two men. Could she trust them? Had they done something to Sehraine on the way here?

Seeing the look on her face, the brothers glanced at each other and nodded. Yevgeny stepped forward and gestured for Yana to do the same. When she was near enough, he leaned down and pushed back the hair covering his ear. Where a human's ear would have a smooth curve, his was scalloped, as if something had taken a bite out of it. Behind and below it, three vertical slits marked his skin — gills.

With a gasp, Yana breathed, "You're river elves."

Yevgeny straightened and gave her a single nod. "Now you know our most guarded secret. If we betray you, that is your weapon against us. To reveal it would be our deaths."

Yana stared at the two, weighing the pros and cons of trusting them. The brothers neither fidgeted nor looked away. She finally nodded. "You can call me Yana. Sehraine told you about the three ships?"

"Da. You and she are crazy, expecting to take that ship with three and a half people, but we have ways to distract the vragi when the time comes."

"You think we can't do this? Men are depending on us."

"We did not say we couldn't," Lev answered. "Doesn't change the fact that you're crazy, though."

Yana glanced at the darkening sky and heaved a frustrated sigh. "I can't wait any longer if I want the orc's lookouts to see me north of the city."

"Do not worry," Yevgeny stated. "We will find Dama Sehraine. She will be here when you return."

4:45pm

Sehraine did not know how long they had walked. They entered another clearing, and the man dropped her on the ground, bruising her arms, legs, and back in the process. She could see the one she elbowed earlier sitting several yards away, still holding the crossbow. His smile held no warmth.

On the far edge of the clearing, an open crate sat beside a mound of fresh earth. Two men stripped to the waist stood beside it leaning against their shovels. When she saw the box and the pit beside it, Sehraine renewed her desperate struggle against her bonds and tried to cry out despite the gag.

"My father was a little boy when the plague came," one of the soldiers said, gripping her tighter. "It took his parents from him — my grandparents. All of us here lost family to the plague."

One of the men spit on her face, but she was too stunned to feel it. She met each of their gazes one by one. She saw anger and hate, but she also saw fear. Guilt gnawed at her. These men wanted to save the camp. She could see the conviction in their eyes.

"I hope you enjoyed your little display back there," Anton said. He flinched a little as he rose from his seat and walked forward. She didn't think she had elbowed him that hard or that her blow was that well placed. Surely, she hadn't broken a rib. The man drew closer, and her mind focused on the hard edges of his leather boots, caked with dirt.

Her vision went black when one of the boots drew back and kicked her in the side. The breath whooshed out of her lungs, and pain exploded through her gut and chest. She sucked in, and the gag went deeper into her mouth, choking her. Sehraine struggled to rise, but her pain and bonds kept her on the ground, writhing in agony.

Then she felt it. Something stirred and twisted in her blood. Jasper's tale of the dwolma and the dying elf flashed in her mind.

"No!" she thought, fearing the sickness she felt signaled the beginnings of her own transformation. She squeezed her eyes shut and forced back the darkness in her veins.

The heavy weight of despair flooded her thoughts. She didn't want to die, but perhaps these men were right. Her presence endangered everyone. How could she help these people when deep inside, she carried their death?

One of the men grabbed Anton and stopped him from kicking her again. When she heard the scuffle of feet, she glanced up, praying that whatever they did wouldn't wake what was inside her.

The men did not speak again. They grabbed her by the arms and legs and dumped her in the box. Sehraine closed her eyes and waited for a crossbow bolt that didn't come. Darkness consumed her. She heard pounding, and then the box dropped.

Sehraine pounded on the lid with her bound fists. The gag hung loose around her neck.

"Please! Please don't leave me here!" she cried.

She heard the men talking, but the thud of dirt on the lid drowned out what they said. Panic set in as the whirl of thoughts pulled her over the edge. Buried alive, the dwolma would still take her. Then, it would escape from the crate and earth, and attack the camp. The Rhodinan guards had unwittingly sowed a seed of the plague — not expunged it.

Jasper's signet ring shifted under her shirt. She tugged at the leather cord tied around her neck, pulling the ring free. Her fingers traced the dagger-pierced globe on its surface, and her mind focused on the symbol, wondering at its meaning. One thought crystalized: Jasper would find the cure, and he would use his ring to find her.

Panic overcame her despair. Sehraine did not want to die. She had to escape.

She kicked at the lid and shouted at the men. She screamed until her throat grew raw and her voice became a raspy croak. Fear wormed its way back into her mind, and her efforts grew frantic. She kicked and beat at the box until her feet and fists were bruised. When that didn't work, she dug into the wood with her fingernails, not caring if they broke and bled. Her breath came in labored gasps, and her limbs grew heavy until, finally, her mind could take no more, and wrapped itself in darkness deeper than her prison.

CHAPTER 6:
THE THRONE ROOM

October 28, 4235 K.E.

4:30pm

*P*ain became Vanin's entire world as he stumbled and fell to one knee under a hail of blows rained down on him from all sides. Running the gauntlet of experienced fighters at the end of a day's training was the closest the young trainees came to the merciful escape of death. But it was just a tease — like everything else.

They started at one end of the arena and had to survive long enough to reach the other side. It hadn't taken him long to realize the older gladiators enjoyed the chance to dish out a bit of pain, and their skills were honed sharper than a razor's edge. He'd seen the bruised and battered evidence written on the faces and bodies of the slaves held by the arena owner for the pleasure of the fighters who won their bouts and drew crowds.

Someone kicked him in the ribs, and he struggled to regain his feet. He hurt all over. In most ways, he was lucky his dark skin did not show bruising easily, although he sometimes wished for the pale skin of an elf that showed the slightest mark. There were those, like his father, who took it as a personal challenge to leave a mark on his hide, especially if it meant breaking bones and drawing blood.

With his jaw clenched in determination, Vanin pushed on. He would get through this; he had to, or there would be no one to avenge his mother and those like her who suffered and died in this hellhole.

5:00pm

The journey to the throne room seemed to last forever. Sacha fought to maintain her cold façade as the Red Guard pushed and shoved Grendel along the trail. He often fell, and the orcs hauled him up roughly. It did not take long for her to figure out the constant, petty torture by the Red Guard was both sport and meant to keep the wild half-orc off balance. They walked through several more tunnels, each lined with spectators as news of the king's arrival preceded him.

A rough-hewn, arched entrance gaped at the end of the passage, swallowing the procession by twos and threes. Beyond stretched a vast, rectangular cavern with a smooth floor. Veins of semiprecious gems decorated the walls. The crystals captured and magnified the dim lichen-light, sparkling like stars. At the far left end of the cavern, cold water arced out of the wall and splashed against a pile of glossy rocks, causing it to spray out in all directions. To their right, sitting atop a raised dais with a half-dozen steps, was a glassy throne carved from a single block of obsidian. There was no telling where Bregu Kraagor acquired such a piece of furniture, and Sacha could think of several lesser monarchs who would sell their soul to possess such an item. It would have been beautiful had it not been for the company.

Bregu Kraagor walked straight toward the raised dais. His personal retinue of guards fanned out behind him and took their positions. Marko, Kourash, and Gregori followed him to the foot of the dais, where they stopped and took positions at the king's right hand.

Skyld and three orc guards escorted Sacha and Xandor down the long center of the rectangle to stand at the foot of the dais. Xandor looked around, finally free of Sacha's spell. They had not spoken after the incident, but she had a feeling that they would have words if they survived this. Skyld remained by Sacha's side, but whether he was her bodyguard or one of her wardens, she couldn't tell.

News of the goings-on spread, and orcs flooded into the throne room. They jostled for position, each wanting to be the first to see these outsiders. The cavern quickly filled with their shouts and the occasional quarrel.

Bregu Kraagor turned with a flourish and sat on the throne. He snapped his fingers, and a human female slave with downcast eyes appeared from behind the throne and offered her master a heavy, jewel-encrusted goblet. He took a sip and watched the Red Guard drag their prisoner across the cavern to piles of chain affixed to the stone floor with thick iron rings. There, they made Grendel wait on his hands and knees while male slaves fastened the iron shackles on the other ends of the chains to his wrists. Grendel snarled and growled at them, but the orcs used their long poles and pain-filled tethers to keep him subdued.

As the slaves scurried away, the Red Guard unlocked their mancatchers and retreated. Grendel climbed to his feet. With a loud scrape, the metal links became taut, but they were too short and forced him to remain stooped. He yanked on them, testing them, but the chains and iron rings were secure. Unable to break free, he glared at everyone and settled into a crouch, a predator waiting on his prey to draw near.

Bregu Kraagor handed his goblet back to his slave. The woman sank to her knees beside the throne, her expression hollow and empty. He turned to his right and nodded to a burly orc sporting many scars along his arms and cheeks and wearing a heavy black breastplate.

The captain of the guard raised his hands and shouted, "Hwæt! Cayn cynne hlystest þin brytencyning!" *Hear me! Clan of Cayn, listen to your powerful king!*

The noise from the crowd slowly subsided, and all eyes turned to their king.

Looking down on the assembly, Kraagor said loudly, "Lady Aleksandra, it was so good of you to join us."

The audience chamber erupted in uncouth laughter.

"Don't mince words with me, Bregu Kraagor," Sacha said when the noise died. "Get this charade over with. I had hoped we might reach an accord, but I can see now you are nothing more than Marko's puppet."

Her words slapped the king in the face, and he leapt to his feet, intending to proclaim punishment. Resisting the impulse, he took a deep breath, resumed his seat, and said, "Lady Aleksandra, I forget that you are a Madasgorski, and thus a master manipulator. I will not let it happen again."

He clapped his hands, and a male slave approached the throne. After a few whispered words, the slave left and shortly reappeared carrying a length of dirty cloth knotted in the middle in one hand and a thin, braided leather cord in the other.

"You wouldn't dare!" she hissed when she realized the slave's intentions.

"Mind your tongue, Lady Aleksandra," Kraagor sneered. "Either you submit to binding, or I'll have it cut from your mouth. It matters not to me."

With his eyes down, the slave approached Sacha and waited. Staring daggers at the vile king sitting on his throne, Sacha closed the distance to the slave and opened her mouth. He placed the knot inside and tied the cloth tightly around the back of her head, then waited for her to hold out her hands. When he was done, she knew she would find neither sympathy nor help among the dispirited shells of humans in Kraagor's demesne.

Kourash hissed at Xandor and stepped forward, his red eyes narrowed to slits. "Bregu Kraagor, I claim vendetta against this man," he announced in a sibilant voice.

Marko's brow furrowed.

Kraagor's face split into a broad smile. "Explain yourself, servant."

"Your Majesty, this man raided my home and, with his companions, murdered my brother. He owes me a blood debt."

Xandor eyed the Seldaehne suspiciously. Kourash stared back, open hatred writ across his face.

The ranger stepped forward and said scathingly, "You betray your heritage. You are half-dragon and yet you work as a hired blade. My, how the mighty have fallen."

"All because of you and your comrades."

The Seldaehne unsheathed his massive sword. The crowd of orcs distanced themselves from the two warriors and formed a wide circle around the perimeter of the room.

Holding his weapon in both hands, Kourash walked into the clearing and said, "Are you afraid? You're alone, mage, with no one to hide behind."

A dim nimbus of light appeared around the ranger. Xandor's form melted away, leaving Jasper in his place. The pudgy mage held out his hand, and his wooden staff appeared. Murmurs echoed in the cavern, and Kraagor moved to the edge of his seat. His personal guards shifted and drew weapons, waiting for a signal from their king.

"I never needed to hide from you," Jasper replied confidently.

Marko and Gregori stared, open-mouthed, at the mage.

Kraagor saw the looks on the two humans' faces and laughed. "Clan of Cayn, change of plans!" Gesturing toward the mage, he said, "Kourash, you have my leave to seek resolution of your vendetta. Fill my goblet with his blood."

The orc king motioned to Skyld, who took Aleksandra by the elbow and half-guided, half-pushed her through the crowd toward Kraagor. Rough hands pawed at her along the way, their owners watching her with lust burning openly in their eyes.

Grendel stared at the two combatants. Pain made it hard to focus, but somewhere deep, deep inside him, the vague beginnings of a memory stirred. It seemed to be something important. Nevertheless, it ducked and skittered through the shadows of his mind, avoiding his attempts to grasp it and pull it into the light.

Marko tugged on Gregori's sleeve and nodded toward the mage, who was slowly making his way to the middle of the cavern. A loud clap sounded behind them, and several orc guards moved closer to the two men.

"You will not interfere with this fight," Kraagor said from his throne.

The two humans faced the king and bowed their heads in acceptance before turning back to the coming spectacle. The knight glared at Jasper, watching the mage prepare to die. "Cook, where is the Kral's ranger?" he demanded.

The pudgy man grinned. "I really don't know. Last time I saw him, he was helping Dobrynya and his men escape the city."

Shock and rage burned through Marko. He turned to the leering orc king. "Bregu, I'm going to check on my crates."

"Of course, but hurry back or you'll miss the fight."

"I assure you, this will not be a fight. It will be a slaughter."

"We'll see."

Marko bowed curtly. He strode toward the exit, Gregori on his heels. Before he reached the line of guards, the knight stopped and leaned close to the young-looking mage. "Remain here," he said softly. "Make certain things remain on track for us to leave this city with my sister in tow. A Madasgorski will never be a slave. I intend to offer her heart to Sutekh personally."

Gregori gave the knight a short bow and returned to the dais.

From her position by Kraagor's throne, Aleksandra watched her brother disappear into the crowd, all too aware of his intent. She hoped the ranger would reach the wagon in time. While she wanted to be the one to drive a blade through her little brother's heart, she knew the ranger was the key to ruining Marko's enterprise and placing her on even footing with him in their family.

Wracking her brain for a plan to escape Kraagor's court, she found herself torn between searching for a way out and watching Jasper face Kourash.

CHAPTER 7:
LOST AND FOUND

October 28, 4235 K.E.

5:00pm

Yevgeny and Lev were on their way back to Dorinkov's command post when a runner came around a curve in the path and collided with them, knocking the boy to the ground. The child paled when he saw them.

Lev glared down at the boy, who was already climbing to his feet. "Watch where you're going, boy!"

"Yes, Sir. Sorry, Sir," the boy babbled. "I have to find Zack."

Yevgeny grabbed the boy by the scruff of the neck and lifted him off the ground. His eyes burned into the boy's as he asked, "The Glaxon runner? Why do you need to find him?"

"Afon sent me to check on Dama Sehraine," the boy stammered, his eyes growing wide.

"Why?" Lev growled. "What do you know about her?"

"Nothing! I swear! I was at the corrals with Afon, feeding the horses. We saw Yuri Stefanov and Anton Guryev with some others a few minutes ago. They were smiling and laughing. Anton and Yuri are never happy unless someone else is miserable," the boy said. "Afon said something about Yuri knowing the Trakyan lady's secret, and sent me to find out if Dama Sehraine returned to her camp. That's all!"

"She has not returned," Yevgeny said dangerously. "Where is Afon?"

The boy swallowed hard. The look on Yevgeny and Lev's faces scared him even more than Yuri's smile. "I... I don't know. He left the horses when I did."

"What is your name, boy?" Yevgeny demanded.

"M... M... Miyka, Sir!"

"Miyka, go to Poruchik Tirinko. See if Afon has been there. If not, tell him what you told us. Then tell him we will bring Yuri and Anton to the corral even if we must drag them."

Miyka shivered at the tone in Ivanov's voices, but he grinned as he turned and bolted back toward Poruchik Tirinko's office.

Yuri dropped his empty bowl and spoon in the pile of dishes waiting for the scullery boys. The pile toppled over and spread across the ground. He laughed at the dark looks cast in his direction.

The Ivanovs watched him swagger toward his tent. All around him, groups of soldiers gathered around the campfires, checking their armor and weapons. Yuri had few friends among them, and no one called out for him to join them.

The soldier was halfway into his tent when Yevgeny grabbed him by the ankle and yanked him back out. He scrabbled and clawed at the ground, but Yevgeny's grip tightened. The river pirate twisted Yuri's foot to a painful angle but stopped short of breaking bones.

Lev knelt beside the struggling man and pressed the point of his knife to the soft skin beneath the soldier's eye.

"What do you want?" Yuri snapped. He tried to pull away from the blade, but Lev hoisted the soldier to his feet and shoved him at his brother, who wrapped an arm around the man's neck.

"Where is the Trakyan girl?" Lev demanded.

"Trakyan? You mean that damned fyeì?" Turning beet red, he slapped at Yevgeny's tightening arm until Lev gave his brother a miniscule nod.

Yevgeny grabbed a handful of Yuri's hair and pulled the soldier's head to one side until the man could see him from the corner of his eye. "You should have listened to Tirinko, Yuri," he growled. "What did you do to her?"

Yuri bucked in Yevgeny's grip, but the stocky man's hold remained firm.

Lev nicked the tip of Yuri's nose with his dagger. "Tell us where she is," he said, "or my brother and I will take you out on the river and leave you."

"Kill me, and you will never find the bitch's body," Yuri spat. "Kill me, and the entire camp will know you for fyeì loving scum." Yuri smiled. "There are many who feel as I do. You might find yourself on the wrong end of a rope."

Lev's eyes narrowed. "Is that a threat, Yuri?"

Yevgeny pressed harder on his prisoner's throat. He could feel the man's pulse throbbing against the pressure. "No one cares what we do to you, Yuri," he said. "We know you and Anton were together earlier."

"Who..." Yuri's voice cut off abruptly as Yevgeny tightened his grip. His eyes bulged from his head, and a trail of spittle ran down his chin.

Yevgeny shook him. "Where. Is. The. Girl?"

"Go... to... hell."

"You first," Lev replied and nodded to his brother. The struggling soldier slumped like a broken toy when he fell unconscious. "Take him to the corral. I'll fetch Anton."

He found Anton lying in his tent, curled in a ball on his side. The man's pallid skin reflected the dim light from the tent flap, and beads of cold sweat dotted his forehead. A faint moan escaped him, as he lay deep within a dream.

Lev kicked the man's booted foot. "Wake up!"

"Leave me," came the muttered reply. "Can't you see I'm sick?"

"Come out!"

Lev dragged Anton from the tent by his feet, despite the weak cry that escaped him. The soldier squinted up at his attacker. "Ivanov? What do you want?"

"What's wrong, Anton? Guilt eating you? I know a cure for that. Tell me where the Trakyan is."

"The thrice damned suka gave me the plague. She can rot in Hell for all I care," he cursed. "Who gives a damn about the fyei anyway? They're animals. Across the border in Vologda, you can buy them in the slave market — cheap."

"You don't have the plague, moron," Lev growled. He bent down, grabbed a handful of Anton's shirt, and jerked the man up from the ground. "You shouldn't listen to rumors. Now show me what the two of you did to that girl or, so help me, I'll cut you up and feed you to the fishes, piece by piece."

5:32pm

Poruchik Tirinko, Leftenant Gallagher, and six Iron Tower soldiers stood ringed around the two men digging in the clearing. Several held torches that lifted the gloom from around them to the branches above and cast the hard looks on everyone's faces into stark relief.

Overseeing the digging, the Ivanov brothers stood on either side of the deepening hole, their expressions growing darker with each shovelful. It was taking too long to get to Sehraine, especially if Yuri and Anton were telling the truth about how long she had been underground.

"Dig faster," Vassily ordered.

Grumbling escaped from the two diggers, but they continued their work. Finally, when the hole was waist deep, one of the shovels struck wood with a hollow thud. They reached to climb out of the hole, but Lev and Yevgeny barred their path.

"Clear it off," they said in unison.

Again, the culprits dug, lifting less dirt with each scoop until the Ivanovs gave Sir Brian nods of approval.

Yuri and Anton crawled out of the hole, and Yevgeny took their place. He knelt and called out to Sehraine, but received no reply. He pulled a small pry bar from his belt and inserted it between the lid and the side. Working the bar back and forth, he listened to the wood and nails protest.

Worry crowded his features, mirrored on his brother's face. With a resounding crack, part of the board broke free and Yevgeny tossed it to his brother, who threw it at Yuri. The board hit the soldier across the back, and he cast a murderous look in return.

Another board, longer this time, came up from the ground, followed quickly by a third. Even in the torchlight, it was easy to see the blood-soaked marks on the boards from Sehraine's fingernails. Yevgeny passed his brother a fourth board, and the sounds from the pit stopped.

Lev watched his brother push the tangle of hair away from Sehraine's face, revealing tear-stained cheeks. She remained limp and unresponsive to his brother's touch, and he couldn't tell if she breathed. He looked to Yuri, and his own guilt for revealing her race mixed with his rage at the ignorant men.

Lifting gently, Yevgeny pulled Sehraine into a sitting position so he could get an arm around her torso. With one hand behind her head, he pushed himself to his feet, drawing her legs from under the remains of the lid. When she was free, he carefully adjusted his hold and lifted her up to Lev.

Together, the brothers approached Poruchik Tirinko and Leftenant Gallagher. Neither brother looked at Yuri or Anton as they passed. Yevgeny leaned forward and said something only the two officers could hear.

The two knights shared a look, then Vassily said, "Leftenant Gallagher, in light of their crime, these two men, and the others who helped them, are hereby surrendered to you for justice. As I did not insist on her accepting an escort back to your camp, I will make any reparations to her family that you or they see fit."

Leftenant Gallagher frowned as he took in the two Rhodinan soldiers. "Poruchik Tirinko, we appreciate your offer. I will discuss it with Lord Fergusson."

At a gesture from Sir Brian, two of his men grabbed Yuri and Anton and bound their hands behind their backs. The other Iron Tower soldiers formed up around their prisoners, ready to escort them to camp.

Sir Brian came forward to take Sehraine from Lev. The Rhodinan stepped back. "We promised Laytenant Marchenkova we would personally see Sehraine back to camp," Yevgeny said to the knight. "We will keep our word."

6:00pm

The chirurgeon looked up at Sir Brian and the two grim-looking Rhodinans standing on the opposite side of the cot. "Other than bandaging her fingers, I'm afraid there isn't anything I can do for her."

"What's wrong with her, Bris?" the knight asked.

"Je ne sais pas," the field surgeon replied. Seeing the puzzled looks on the Ivanovs' faces, he remembered the language barrier, sighed, and repeated himself. "I don't know."

"You are a healer, da?" Yevgeny asked.

"I'm a surgeon!" came the snapped reply. "I remove arrows and stitch wounds, set broken bones, and patch people up the best I can. There is nothing physically wrong with this woman other than a few bumps and bruises, and the damage she did to her hands clawing at that box."

"Are there any other fyeì in your camp?" one of the brothers asked.

"One or two half-bloods, but no full-blooded elves," Brian replied. "What do you think an elven soldier could do for her?"

The brothers shrugged. "Perhaps one of the fyeì would recognize this and know how to wake her."

"She just had an incredibly traumatic experience. Perhaps letting her sleep it off would be best," the chirurgeon said.

The knight nodded in response. "Maybe. Thank you, Bris. I'm sure you have preparations to make. Laytenant Marchenkova should be returning soon."

"Sir Brian, I strongly recommend the Knight Commander ground the laytenant."

"I'll pass along your concerns, but I don't think she will listen to us or him at this point."

The chirurgeon shrugged and said, "You're probably right."

CHAPTER 8:
BATTLEGROUND

October 28, 4235 K.E.

5:12pm

When Jasper reached the middle of the cavern, he faced Kourash, raised his staff, and struck the butt on the stone floor. Bright light exploded from the staff head, illuminating the circle Kraagor's subjects left for the battle. The crowd of orcs cursed and squealed, hiding their eyes.

Kourash cautiously stepped into the light.

"I have waited three long years for this moment," the burly half-dragon growled. "When I'm done, you will beg for death."

"I guess it was too much to ask for, hoping you didn't recognize me that night in the kruchma. Why didn't you come after me sooner?" Jasper asked in a conversational tone.

Kourash advanced, scenting the air as he stalked the mage. "I was curious," he said. Kourash took several more steps, putting the mage within range of his long blade.

Jasper did not move. He waited and watched the other approach. "You know what they say about curiosity?" he asked.

With a quick snap, Kourash lunged, thrusting with his blade. The sword easily cut through Jasper, and the half-dragon stumbled forward. There was none of the expected resistance of flesh and bone. Kourash looked up and found himself surrounded by duplicate images of the mage. Seven in all, they danced and swirled about him. The eyes of the half-dragon narrowed, and he assumed a defensive stance.

Vanin squinted in the bright flare of light that burned through the slowly opening arena door. The sun was directly overhead, beating down relentlessly on the pristine white sand and reflecting up into the crowded stands where the unkempt masses took the brunt of the heat. Above the commoners, the wealthy sat in well-shaded box seats.

Behind the half-orc, nine other fighters of mixed races waited in nervous anticipation. They all wore masks of one sort or another as part of the day's spectacle: a battle scene from the historical drama Unda Sanguinis. Vanin and those with him would play the part of invaders from Tirnna Flain and face the champions of the first-circuit.

He didn't like it. The younger fighters lacked the skills required to pull off this kind of show without being injured or killed. To make matters worse, Vanin was familiar with this particular story, and it did not end well for the invaders. If he knew Novius, a turma of upper-circuit fighters would descend on their battle, ending it in a blood bath.

The crowd was already loud and boisterous. He knew they were making wagers and drinking liquor like water.

On the far side of the sand stood the special box seats reserved for Novius and his guests, usually minor bureaucrats or, occasionally, a nobleman from one of the larger cities. Today, he could make out the figure of the arena master with a single guest and various servants. The man appeared to have brought a gift for his host — a woman stood nearby, her stance regal despite the gag and her bound wrists.

For a fleeting moment, recognition teased him, her name on the tip of his tongue, but the vague memory slipped away, swallowed in the darkness of his thoughts.

Aleksandra studied the throne room, trying to pierce the darkness along the far walls and behind the waterfall. There had to be a way out that didn't involve wading through a sea of slavering scum.

She wondered how she ever thought Grendel had anything in common with these creatures. Her eyes sought his and, for a moment, she thought she saw a flicker of recognition. The moment passed, and she could again see the violet glow under his hooded lids. His expression was even more horrible than before, and she shuddered involuntarily.

The crowd roared, drawing her attention back to the fight.

"Your petty tricks won't work on me," Kourash growled.

Timing his strike, Kourash swung at the image to his left. His blade easily sliced through the neck of the illusion. Pressing forward, the half-dragon took a short step with his left foot and suddenly reversed his swing, hitting another image with all his strength. This time, the sword hit something solid and drew sparks.

The sound of metal hitting stone resonated throughout the chamber, accompanied by a raucous cheer from the orcs. Jasper sailed through the air, landed hard, and slid several feet. The duplicate images evaporated into mist.

Kourash leapt after the mage with his sword held high.

Pointing his staff, Jasper yelled, "Vrontí kai Astrapí." Thunder rumbled as bluish-white lightning arced from the staff, striking Kourash in the center of his chest. With a grunt, the half-dragon flew backward, a cloud of ozone trailing after him.

Battered and bruised, the two climbed to their feet and appraised each other anew. Kourash brushed away singed bits of his leather tunic, grimacing at his blistered chest. His blood-colored eyes glittered with malice when he raised his sword and charged toward the mage.

"Remember, we were like those kids out there not too long ago," Vanin growled to the others on his team before he led them onto the sand.

"It is kill or be killed out there," someone muttered. "There will be no mercy today."

The so-called free men and women of the empire packed the arena. The closest spectators cast jeers and catcalls in their direction, along with bits of rotten fruit. He hated every one of them. They were nothing more than rabid beasts despite the thin veneer of civility they wore outside the stands. Civilization was a mask just as real as the shaped leather covering his own face.

Kourash swung again. He cut at Jasper's head, but the mage dropped low and jabbed the half-dragon with the end of his staff. Instantly, the air surrounding Kourash shimmered and congealed. The warrior struggled against it, like a swimmer fighting a rip current.

Jasper's lips twitched. "You know, old age slows your reflexes," he taunted as he staggered back, barely dodging another life-ending swipe of Kourash's blade. "It inhibits certain bodily functions."

"I'll rip off your head when this is over, mage!" Kourash bellowed but, like everything else about him, the words seemed slowed. Fury burned in his eyes as he fought against the mage's spell.

Jasper sucked air in and pondered the half-dragon as he lurched away from another swipe of the long blade. He could not avoid that sword forever. He had to come up with a real way to damage the Seldaehne before he ran out of magic.

Sacha tore her gaze away from Jasper. She had to find a way out. Whether or not Xandor killed her brother, there was very little chance he or Chert would come for her. She was an outsider, and they would have a hard enough time escaping, themselves. Even entering Kraagor's audience chamber, she never expected that they would have to fight their way out of the heart of the orc hive.

Her gaze fell on Grendel, still crouched in his chains, and crushing pain constricted her heart. Although he appeared to sleep, his breathing was still the rapid pant of one under strain. Stifling a sob, she wrestled with unfamiliar guilt.

She found herself hoping... praying to whatever god her bodyguard followed... that he would fight off the thing that possessed him and return to her. A deep sense of shock coursed through her. He was the closest thing to a friend she had ever had, and she desperately wanted him back. She needed to apologize, to make it up to him. Not just for this mess she'd pushed him into, but for everything she did to manipulate him from the moment they met.

Vanin and his teammates faced the last of the first-circuit fighters in the center of the arena floor. With a sudden boom, the arena gate flung open, and the roar of the crowd renewed as the team of fifth-circuit fighters charged over the bloodstained sand. He turned to face them. The knowledge that this might be his only opportunity to avenge his mother lay hard and cold in the pit of his belly.

He kept a tight grip on his anger as he scanned the running warriors for Grendel. He might die, but he intended to take recompense from the old óhreint's hide before he did. The trick would be separating himself from the rest of the fight long enough to reach the sorry bastard.

The older fighters spread out as they crossed the sand, and Vanin saw him.

"Grendel!" he bellowed. "I challenge you!"

For one crystalline moment, in the space between one heartbeat and the next, Vanin saw everyone and everything in the arena cease to move. His eyelids descended slowly in a blink that may have lasted hours.

When he opened them again, he stood alone before Grendel and wondered when he'd become as tall as his father. Novius had been careful to keep them apart the past two years, and Vanin could hardly believe the creature standing before him was the same towering beast who haunted his darkest nightmares. Even so, he did not make the mistake of thinking Grendel had grown soft or weak since their last encounter. He knew the creature before him, half-orc and half-ogre, had only grown tougher and more wily.

Vanin's focus was so intense upon his opposite that he hardly noticed the barren emptiness of the arena around them. He reached over his shoulder for his weapon and saw Grendel reach back as well. With the precision of mirror images, they simultaneously drew huge, double-bitted battle-axes.

The óhreint flashed a wicked grin full of sharp, pointed teeth the color of egg yolk. "You ready to die, boy? The sleeping god requires a blood offering, and you're it."

Vanin refused to answer. He knew Grendel was only trying to bait him, make him nervous enough to make a mistake. Instead, he stepped to the side in a circling maneuver, beginning the intricate dance he knew could have only one conclusion. In the end, only one of them would walk away.

Kourash and Jasper circled each other.

The orcs, finally accustomed to the brightness, crowded around the dome of light. They jeered and yelled, but they seemed to have split into two groups. Odds were calculated and wagers placed. Even Bregu Kraagor edged closer to the fight. He stood on the top step of his dais, sipping from his goblet, with a human female slave kneeling forlornly at his feet.

Holding his massive sword with both hands, the half-dragon sliced angrily at the air in front of him. The movement was slow, as if he was fighting underwater. He strained against the current, putting all his anger, all his rage, behind each swing.

"Did you lose your hair all at once, or did it fall out gradually? Must of come from your father's side of the family," Jasper said in a tone that seemed more at home in a laboratory than a fight. "Was he human?"

Kourash shifted his grip and raised his sword, inch by inch, to his left shoulder. A vein throbbed at his temple. His steps were painfully slow, like a cat stalking a mouse.

Raising his left hand, Jasper yelled, "Sfaíra!"

In response, a ring on that hand glowed and five streaks of light streamed and spiraled toward the half-dragon. Kourash tried to block them with his sword, but the magical spears deftly avoided the slow advance of the weapon and struck him in the chest.

At first, it seemed the attack had little effect, similar to the lightning. Kourash took another step forward before he felt the burning sensation from two small pinholes dotting his chest. Everyone in the throne room saw the reaction, and a groan went up from half of the orcs while the other half cheered madly.

"Huzzah!" Jasper smiled in triumph. It wasn't much, but it was something.

Furious, Kourash plowed toward the mage with an insane look in his eyes, and Jasper's look of triumph disappeared.

Sacha snuck a quick glance at Skyld and breathed a silent thanks to the powers-that-be that the big oaf was more interested in the fight than guarding her. He'd turned his back to her and taken several steps forward in Kraagor's wake, as if certain she would remain where he left her. The haughty smirk that crept onto her face spoke volumes of what she thought about Kraagor and his minions.

She glanced at Grendel, and the look on her face melted away. She was a fool to think he was anything like these beasts. Reprimanding herself, she cast around for a way to free herself while everyone was distracted.

Keeping low, she surreptitiously approached the obsidian throne, hoping to find a hard edge to cut her bonds, but once she got there, she realized that it would offer up no help. The throne gleamed like polished glass, every surface and corner carefully smoothed and rounded. Sacha tried to reach her dagger, only to find she was unable to get her fingers on the hilt to draw it free. In desperation, she pulled and twisted her hands and arms, but the braided leather cord only dug deeper into her skin.

Grendel sneered at the masked youth before him. He knew it was a boy because he lacked the scars a seasoned fighter would sport. The boy was probably trying to make a name for himself, challenging the longest-reigning champion the arena ever had. Fool. The only thing he'd get would be a slow, bloody, and painful death.

He pushed his lower hand out as though drawing back for a swing, just to see what the boy would do. The kid tensed but recognized the feint before committing himself to a block that would have left his flank exposed. The older warrior pivoted and swung his axe low, aiming at the boy's legs even as he shifted his massive body to avoid the inevitable counter swing.

Both blades missed their targets.

Grendel drove his axe-head through the crystalline sand and flung it toward his opponent's face. A cloud of dust enveloped the young fighter.

Vanin leapt aside, barely avoiding the blinding spray, and closed before Grendel could bring his axe back into position. He slammed his axe haft into his enemy's mouth, sending teeth and blood flying.

"First blood, old man."

Grendel spat in the sand and glared at the upstart boy. Kid was getting cocky. He'd show him a thing or two. With a roar that had unnerved many an enemy, the óhreint charged forward. Vanin brought his axe down in an overhead swing intended to cleave the old óhreint's head in twain, but Grendel caught it on the wrapped haft of his own, stopping it cold. Before the boy could pull free, Grendel released his axe with his left hand and jerked the weapon down to the right, locking the weapons' blades together. He continued his downward swing with enough force to pull the younger fighter off balance. He swung his left fist with all his might, catching the boy just below the ribs on his right side.

Vanin let out a grunt of pain but did not retreat. Instead, he smashed his boot-shod foot against Grendel's leg, just below the knee. The óhreint staggered back from the blow, but their weapons remained tangled. A strange tug of war began as both fighters struggled to retain their own weapon and take that of their opponent.

Without warning, Grendel leapt toward Vanin and dug the claws of his free hand into the boy's upper arm, eliciting a roar of pain. Grendel bared his teeth and dragged his claws down, leaving deep gashes in their wake.

"You cannot beat me, boy," he growled. "You do not have the savage heart of an orc."

Vanin flinched involuntarily, but he felt the slow spark of anger hidden deep in his soul glow brighter at the reminder of all he had suffered from that savage heart.

"Do not think I don't know who you are behind that mask," Grendel said. "Hiding your face will not change what you are or what you could have been."

"What would that be?"

"You could have been the greatest warrior the world has ever known. You could have been a king. Instead, you chose to be ashamed. Weak. Human." Grendel spat out the last word as if it tasted vile.

The words pounded against Vanin, driving him back as surely as a hail of physical blows.

"You should have grown tough instead of hiding behind your mother like a whipped cur."

"No..." Vanin whispered, shaking his head.

"Melika made you soft."

"No..." he moaned.

"Her death was the best thing that ever happened to us. I know it, and you know it. I have come to life, more and more, since that day, despite what you did to hold me back."

"No!"

"But no more. I will be the one to walk out of here today and take my rightful place on that throne. And when I do, I will give our wench what she has been begging for, but you have been too scared to give her."

Grendel's spite-filled words were the fuel that sent Vanin's hidden anger into a towering blaze of rage. Images of the friends he had made and the woman he wanted to save from herself swept through his mind, clearing the haze in his thoughts. He saw them all clearly — recognized who they were, but one kept coming to the forefront, one he had not thought about in a long time: a grizzled old man who taught him about the balance of nature.

With an inarticulate cry, Vanin leapt forward, swinging his axe in a rain of ferocious blows that drove the hated figure before him across the sand.

No more words were wasted. The two struggled for dominance in a landscape that began to flow and change around them as first one, then the other, held the upper hand.

Vanin's mask ripped free, revealing a face that was an idealized version of Grendel. The two fought each other, not as father and son, but as mirror images of the same person.

Blood and sweat flowed over their skin, and still they struggled. Somewhere in the fray, their weapons were lost, and they went at each other with tooth and claw. They paid and repaid insult and injury until each gripped the other by the throat, inexorably choking the life from one another.

As one, they collapsed, first to their knees, then prone on the sand, their hands still locked around one another's throats.

Sensing blood, the volume of noise from the orc crowd reached a fevered pitch as they watched the half-dragon charge the portly mage.

Fueled by his fury, Kourash fought against the thick air that surrounded him. He held his two-handed sword high over his head. There would be no escaping the killing blow.

With each step, the air surrounding the half-dragon seemed to increase in thickness, and it took more and more effort to swim through it. The frustration increased his fury.

From the other side of the circle, Jasper watched Kourash's progress with a calculating eye. His free hand dipped into one of his pockets and he waited.

An emotional maelstrom charged toward the waiting mage. '*How dare the mage just stand there?!*' Reaching deep, the half-dragon drew upon his reptilian heritage to combat the air surrounding him. He poured all his rage, all his hate, into each step, but the more he fought the mage's spell, the more it resisted him. Each step became a bigger struggle, and Kourash's muscles bulged from their effort.

Still, Jasper watched and waited.

The half-dragon's fury and hatred boiled inside his veins. He would rip out the arrogant mage's beating heart and eat it while the light died in the human's eyes.

By the time Kourash was within striking distance, he was almost stationary. The air was so thick around him that he felt like he was drowning in it. Forging ahead, he moved inches instead of feet, and even that seemed to be slowing. Panic added to the mix of emotions, feeding the spell surrounding the half-dragon.

Jasper regarded Kourash curiously. The raucous sounds of the orcs faded away. Kourash's nostrils flared, and his breathing came in gasps, but the intensity in his reptilian eyes held the mage.

Letting his staff rest against his shoulder, Jasper drew his hand from his pocket. In it, he held a small wooden box with a hinged latch. A leather cord hung through the latch's eye, the knot already worked loose. Jasper removed the cord and opened the box, his movements as slow as the half-dragon's. He cast a furtive glance at the surrounding orcs. They gave him their undivided attention.

Jasper reached into the container with his thumb and forefinger and pinched out a portion of orange powder with red flakes. He snapped the lid closed and retied the knot one-handed, without spilling a single grain of powder.

Kourash's eyes grew wide when his super-sensitive sense of smell registered the potency of the seemingly harmless mix. Muscles strained near-to-bursting, and the half-dragon pushed forward another inch.

With a precise flick of his fingers, Jasper launched the powder toward the still-flared nostrils. The orange and red flakes flew across the gap between them and slowed as they entered the air surrounding the half-dragon.

Kourash's red eyes slowly widened, tracking the various flakes' paths. He tried to turn his head. As a last resort, the half-dragon tried to reverse course, but it was no use. His face entered the drifting spice cloud. Multiple red flakes and countless dots of orange adhered themselves to his lips, cheeks, and the insides of his moist nostrils.

For a brief moment, Jasper stood transfixed, watching the powder sit there. Then, within the blink of an eye, the flakes disappeared, inhaled by the half-dragon.

The effect was instantaneous. Tears developed along the rims of the half-dragon's eyes even as his eyelids slowly descended to clench shut. A flush of red started at his nose and crept across his normally pallid skin. Kourash tried to keep his eyes open and found them fighting against him.

The powder overwhelmed the half-dragon's senses, causing an agony unlike anything he had felt before. A burning sensation ignited within Kourash's sinus cavities and ran down his throat. His head felt like it was on fire from within. He tried to turn his head and shake the stuff out, but the spell seemed to feed off the increased emotions and grew more powerful. The air surrounding him solidified.

Still holding the small box, Jasper trudged over to Kourash. The half-dragon's vision blurred as water streamed from his eyes, and his pulse pounded in his ears. Kourash saw the movement, but he could not focus on what Jasper was doing. He was helpless, and he knew it.

Holding up the box, Jasper said, "Chili powder. My grandmother's secret blend."

Kourash tried unsuccessfully to blink the water from his eyes. Long strings of mucus ran freely from his nose.

"I probably should give it a name. Maybe I'll call it *dragon slayer.*"

The orcs who'd bet on Jasper whooped and laughed as money changed hands.

"You really are a mess. I normally cut that powder with water and other ingredients, so I don't know how long the effect will last. Could be minutes... or hours. Maybe even days," Jasper said as he contemplated the helpless Seldaehne. "Just remember, I could have killed you."

He had bested the half-dragon, and everyone there knew it — but he also knew that if he let the Seldaehne live, he would never give up. Ever. Especially after this humiliation.

Jasper dropped the box into its pocket, turned his back on the half-dragon, and staggered across the circle of light to face the orc king.

"That spell was a nice piece of work."

Jasper's head jerked toward the speaker. For a moment, the sight of a leather-clad man sporting an eye-patch among the orcs confused him. Then, he remembered Gregori. The dark mage performed an intricate weave with his hands. The motion stopped abruptly, and bright orange and yellow globs of viscous flame spat forth, filling Jasper's vision. At the last second, the portly mage raised his left hand and called up a shimmering field of magic.

The sticky mass coated Jasper's shield, and dark circles appeared as the liquid fire slowly burned holes through it. The dome of light from Jasper's earlier spell winked out, throwing the cavern into darkness except for the gout of hot flame that splashed the floor.

Confusion reigned in the throne room, and Kraagor shouted at the dark mage. Orc guards drew their weapons and closed in on Gregori.

The dark mage, still spouting liquid fire from the palm of one hand, raised the other. Touching his thumb and middle finger together, he turned his hand palm up, and a small ball of lightning appeared, casting off a pale, bluish-white light.

The orcs hesitated, most still more than two sword-lengths away.

With a flick of his middle finger, he shot the ball at the nearest orc. It flew toward its target, growing to two feet in diameter. Multiple forks of electricity licked the ground as it sailed along, and a strong smell of ozone followed in its wake.

A gurgling scream escaped the hapless orc's throat as the floating ball hit him in the chest. Finished, it passed over the burnt shell of the orc and floated toward the next one, who backed away, his eyes widening in fear.

The other guards hesitated. More crackling orbs orbited Gregori. They hovered briefly before they streaked toward the surrounding orcs.

Screams and shouts rang out. The globules of lightning flashed and burned their way across the chamber as they chased the orcs toward the exit.

Near the middle of the cavern, a small moat of molten stone surrounded Jasper and steamed with noxious fumes. He knelt on one knee with only his failing magic to protect him. A thin line of blood ran from his nose as he poured more and more energy into his shield, shoring it up and repairing the holes.

He cursed his own lack of foresight.

'I can help you,' a voice whispered.

Jasper raised his eyes, searching for the speaker.

'I can give you the power you need,' the voice hissed. *'All you need do is ask.'*

"Who... who are you?" Jasper panted.

'*Knowledge at your fingertips,*' the voice whispered.

He should have known. His hand fumbled to open his sporran.

Fire dripped onto his back through his collapsing shield, and he screamed in agony. His hand spasmed around the book, and cold energy slid over his skin, quelling the burn.

Back against the obsidian throne, Sacha hid, trusting the bulk of rock to shield her from both Gregori and Kraagor. She reached up and wrestled the sour-tasting rag from her mouth, then flashed a satisfied grin as she listened to the orcs fleeing the throne room. In the confusion, she had lost sight of Kraagor and his guards and could only hope that they had fled with the rest of the mob.

Sacha carefully peeked around the throne. Across the cavern, blue and white balls of lightning devoured orc after orc. In the eye of the chaos, Gregori continued his attack on Jasper, his face lit by the glow from the stream of flame. It was the face of a lunatic.

Movement at the corner of her vision drew her gaze to Grendel. She watched in terrified fascination as he wrapped the chains around his wrists, before clasping them in his huge fists. With excruciating slowness, he rose and leaned forward. Clanking, the chains binding Grendel became taut.

Mad laughter echoed in the cavern.

The half-orc's head snapped up and his chest heaved as if he had just come through a fierce battle.

Sacha let out a startled scream when Kraagor grabbed a fistful of her hair. He dragged her toward a small exit hidden behind the dais.

"Let me go, you filthy goblin!"

"Pretty girl, I am going to cut out your tongue so the only sound I have to listen to will be your grunts while I beget myself an heir to the Zhitomiran throne."

She struggled violently against the orc king, but his grip wouldn't loosen. Holding the door open to a hidden exit behind the throne, Skyld towered over the squad of Kraagor's personal guard. He watched the fight between the two mages and urged the warriors through the exit.

Desperate, Sacha kicked and bucked. Other hands grasped her body and legs. As she passed through the hidden exit into the darkness of the king's private chambers, she screamed, "Grendel!"

CHAPTER 9:
FIGHT OR FLIGHT

October 28, 4235 K.E.

5:32pm

Chert leaned over with his hands on his knees, trying to calm the beating of his heart. Wet mud coated his beard and mustache, and the orc shirt he wore hung in shreds. A newly stolen shield guarded his back. Red, swollen teeth marks dotted his abdomen where the vile beast bit him and throbbed painfully with each step. Blasted overgrown pangolin!

He could not believe his luck. Chert had given the creature the slip for the time being, but it wouldn't be long before it was back on his trail. To top matters off, he was lost. A dwarf lost underground! Shaking his head, he heard his cousins laughing at him. He stopped. The laughter echoing in the cavern wasn't his imagination.

Hugging the wall, he searched the darkness and listened. Excited breathing reached him from a cluster of stalagmites up ahead. Chert retreated into the wall of the cavern.

Without a sound, he reappeared on the far side of the stalagmite cluster. Chert crept up behind an orc crouched beside a puddle and caught him in a headlock. The orc exploded into a frenzied panic. He stomped on the dwarf's foot as hard as he could and elbowed him in the gut, but Chert squeezed tighter. Wiggling like a worm, the orc splashed in the mud and sprayed water everywhere.

With rocks in their hands, four other orcs burst from behind their cover to defend their companion.

Chert saw them and realized he was facing mere children, two girls and three boys. They stood about his height or shorter, all except for one boy, who had a few inches on him.

A rock sailed through the air and smacked the dwarf on the cheek. He let the young orc go and stepped backward, using the back of his hand to wipe his face.

Instead of running away as he hoped, the orclings closed on him. The dwarf yelled and growled, trying to scare them.

Another rock came at him, and Chert dodged left, letting it strike the wall behind him. He needed them to show him the way back to the orc city, but he couldn't speak their language. Maybe he could follow them through the walls.

The tallest orc glared at him. A fresh scar showed on his chest, and he had the look of someone wanting to prove himself. Drawing back, he held a rock tight in his fist and took aim.

Chert raised his hands in a gesture of peace and took another step back toward the wall. He was about to duck inside when he heard the shushing hiss of sliding sand drift down the tunnel.

The pangolin was coming.

The children heard it, too. They cast fearful glances down the tunnel, the dwarf forgotten for the moment.

Again, Chert made to step inside the wall but stopped. He looked at the orclings, at the wall, and then back at the children. The vision of the orcs killing Sky came unbidden, and he shook his head to dismiss it. These were children, even if they were orcs. Could he leave them to the pangolin? He needed them as guides, but they could also buy him some time to escape. Conflicted, he hesitated, and a feeling of deep shame crept around the edges of his thoughts.

Before he could decide, the older of the two girls raised her hand, pointed to his bite marks, and asked, "Do they hurt?" She spoke in halting Rhodinan, and the words came out mispronounced but recognizable.

"Aye," Chert replied, staring into her eyes. He realized with a start that they were pale blue.

The sound drew closer, and the children searched the darkness for its source. Chert shrugged and sighed deeply.

"You're the dwarf who escaped the helrúnan," the girl said, wide-eyed.

Surprised, Chert nodded and cast a quick glance down the tunnel.

"Did you hurt the beast?" she asked.

"Only a love-tap on the nose."

The girl gave the dwarf a confused look, clearly not understanding his odd turn of phrase. He lifted a spiked orc hammer from his belt, and her face lit with understanding. She translated for the others, and Chert read the fear in their eyes. Even though they were orcs, he couldn't let the pangolin slaughter children.

"You should run away," he whispered to the girl.

She said something to the tall boy, who shook his head and answered her. Chert didn't need the girl to translate.

"We stay," she said. "We fight."

"You don't have any weapons," Chert said gruffly.

"Doesn't matter. It knows we are here. It will catch us before we reach home if we run."

The matter-of-fact way the little girl said it touched Chert deeply. "I am honored to fight by your side."

The boy stood straighter when the girl relayed what the dwarf said. Adulthood came early to orcs, it seemed.

In the stygian recesses of the tunnel, the pangolin sniffed at the base of a stalagmite and caught the dwarf's scent. A low, grinding noise escaped its throat. The sleek, armor-plated head swiveled back and forth as its beady, black eyes scanned the cavern for signs of movement. Not sensing any, it followed the dwarf's path. It splashed eagerly through water and mud, excited that it was closing on its prey.

The pangolin came to an abrupt stop when it saw a glimmer of light ahead. Its claws scored the stone floor and saliva dripped from the corner of its mouth.

Chert held his new shield before him in his left hand and the spiked hammer in his right. Both gave off a dim glow. The pangolin broached the edge of the light, revealing a pale spider web of scars running down its blue-grey face.

Behind the dwarf, the five orclings stared at the creature. Their eyes were wide but, to their credit, they held their ground. One of the orc children gasped. The dim light reflected off a dimpled portion of the pangolin's nose where Chert's hammer had recently crushed it.

"This chase is over!" Chert yelled, brandishing his glowing hammer.

In response, the beast snorted and flexed its claws, drawing deep furrows in the stone floor. Chert expected the beast to charge at any moment. Instead, it clawed another furrow. He could see it sniffing the air and imagined the blended scents of dwarf and orc confused it.

Waves of fear rolled off the orclings arrayed behind him. He raised his shield, angling the light to hit the pangolin's eyes and drive it back toward the shadows. The creature gave an eerie creaking trill and lowered its head to the broken ground at its feet. Sharp scales flexed in a scissoring motion, breaking the hard ground into passable sand. In a matter of moments, only the creature's scale covered spine remained visible. Another moment passed, and nothing remained but soft earth.

Panicked whimpers escaped from the youngest orc. Chert murmured a prayer, asking the Eternal Father for guidance and courage. He turned and handed the tallest orc his shield and hammer.

"Take these."

The glow from the items lit the boy's face as he gripped the hammer and shield.

"Lóclóca!" The smallest child in the group pointed with a trembling hand. The pangolin's back broke the surface of the tunnel floor like a shark's dorsal fin and headed directly for them, its scales flexing and cutting the ground around it, leaving a swath of sand and gravel in its wake.

Facing the pangolin, Chert knelt and pressed his fingertips to the floor. His shoulders tensed as he sank his hands into the stone, followed by his wrists. Pushing harder, he reached down into the rock, all the way to his elbows, before he found the calcite filled fractures in the limestone beneath them. He moved his hands back and forth, sending out rich, harmonic waves.

A loud, guttural roar erupted from within the earth.

"Run!" Chert gasped between clenched teeth. "It can't sense you. Go! Now!"

Not needing to be told twice, the children turned and fled down the tunnel. Chert listened to the receding patter of their feet to make certain they were gone. However, the glow from his hammer and shield never wavered. He stole a glance over his shoulder and spied the tallest orc and the older girl who spoke Rhodinan standing behind him.

"We will stay by your side, dwarf."

"Fine," Chert replied. "Get ready."

"Ready for what?"

No sooner than she spoke, the ground before Chert split open and the pangolin lunged at the kneeling dwarf. Its mouth opened wide, emitting a deep, rumbling growl that sounded more like a cave-in than something produced by a living throat. Chert threw himself to one side, barely avoiding the pangolin's dagger-like teeth, and locked his hands around one of its forelimbs. Clenching his jaw, the dwarf tucked his head and prepared for the worst.

Pressed against the side of the tunnel, the two orclings watched in horror as the momentum of the pangolin carried it and the dwarf into the air and then back down onto the cavern floor. Its claws and scales burrowed into the rock, taking the dwarf with it, leaving only a patch of loose sand. The pangolin's growls became distant whispers.

Staring at each other wide-eyed, the girl and boy were too afraid to move. The boy's clenched fists gripped the glowing shield and hammer. However, compared to the pangolin, they seemed grossly inadequate.

A sudden yell attracted their attention, splitting the brief silence asunder, and Chert appeared, skimming along the floor of the tunnel. Dirt plastered every visible inch of his skin. Clinging to the underside of the pangolin, one hand still held onto the creature's leg while the other dug at the creature's hollowed-out eye socket. Red-grey blood oozed from the wound.

Twisting its head, the pangolin snapped its teeth and tried to catch Chert's arm, but the dwarf kept just out of reach. With a burst of speed, the beast burrowed into the tunnel wall.

Its passage broke loose small stones and left a mound of coarse shifting sand and gravel in its wake. Vibrations rattled the tunnel ceiling. With a boom, a stalactite split at its root and crashed to the floor. Shards of rock exploded outward, pelting the glowing shield. Behind it, the two orclings held each other, too afraid to look.

In a deluge of dirt and rock, Chert crashed to the tunnel floor with a loud crunch. He groaned in pain as he stood. Long scratches ran down his arm, and thick blood coated his hand. The orclings started toward him, but he raised his good hand to stop them.

Stomping loudly, the dwarf moved farther down the tunnel, away from the children.

The pangolin's back briefly broke the surface of the floor before it dipped back down and disappeared again.

Peeking around the shield, the orclings stared at the floor, expecting the pangolin to return at any moment.

Chert waited in the middle of the tunnel. His eyes scanned the ground for signs of the pangolin. This one seemed gifted with a cunning intelligence, and Chert didn't expect the monster to give itself away easily. That didn't mean he couldn't hope — especially while life still coursed through his veins.

He turned when the pangolin burst from the tunnel wall and struck the glowing shield a violent blow with its nose. The boy grimaced and snarled at the creature but did not cry out. Turning its head and opening its mouth wide, the beast gripped the shield between its teeth and ripped it away. The glowing shield sailed down the cavern.

With a savage cry, the boy smashed Chert's hammer down frantically on the pangolin's armor plating. The creature turned its good eye toward the boy and growled.

Chert slammed into the creature with all his strength and knocked it on its side. Its sharp scales dug into the rock as it slid.

"Hammer!" Chert yelled and extended one hand.

Understanding the gesture, the boy tossed the hammer to Chert. The dwarf caught it and brought it down on the pangolin's exposed, light-grey underbelly. The blow snapped a thick rib with an audible crack, accompanied by a squeal of pain from the pangolin.

Raising the hammer, Chert smashed it down again, breaking another rib.

The pangolin writhed and flipped over, catching Chert underneath it. It reared up and plowed its pointed nose into the surprised dwarf's stomach. Meaty thuds echoed throughout the tunnel as Chert struck the creature's armor plating repeatedly with his hammer, cracking it.

The pangolin burrowed into the ground, taking Chert with it.

The children quivered with fear. The boy's arm hung limp by his side, and the girl clung to him with her face pressed against his chest.

Darkness returned, but it no longer comforted the orclings. They knew what lurked under their feet, and if it killed the dwarf, they had no doubt they would be next.

The tunnel shook, causing the two orclings to lose their balance and fall to their hands and knees. The boy clenched his teeth around a grunt of pain, refusing to show weakness by crying out when his arm collapsed under him.

A rough four-foot wide by eight-foot-long chasm opened as a section of the floor dropped out of sight. Cracks and fissures spread up the tunnel walls, almost to the ceiling. Dark liquid sprayed rhythmically out of the crack in the floor, hit the tunnel roof and fell as rain. Each following gout came weaker than the one before.

The orclings cautiously crawled to the lip of the crevasse and peered down. Ten feet below, blood oozed out from under a pile of rubble. Lit by the glowing head of his hammer, Chert crawled out of the stone face of the chasm.

Another feeble spray drew their gazes to the source of the dark liquid. Halfway up the wall of the chasm, a quivering mass of red flesh embedded in the rock oozed bodily fluids, sheared off as if someone had cut it with a massive blade.

Chert met the wide-eyed gazes of the two orclings before he knelt and prayed. Blue light seeped into his injuries and healed them. Once finished, he snatched up his hammer.

Covered in mud and blood, Chert looked a sight when he crawled out of the hole in the floor and approached the two orclings. They stared at him with a mixture of amazement and fear. The dwarf tried to give them a reassuring smile, but it was hard to see behind all the muddy gore caked in his beard.

"Boy, what's your name?" Chert asked.

The girl translated, and the boy hesitated before answering, "Daegal."

"Well, Daegal, do you mind if I look at your arm?"

The girl translated again, and the boy turned his body to hide it.

"I promise that I can fix it," Chert said softly, urging the boy to show him his arm. When he touched it, the boy winced and barred his tusks.

Tugging, Chert brought the arm out farther and looked at it under the light of his hammer. The shield had done its job, but when the pangolin wrenched it away, the shield took some flesh with it. A long, bloody scrape ran down the boy's forearm and his swollen wrist appeared broken.

"This is going to feel strange," Chert warned.

Closing his eyes, the dwarf prayed. Blue light seeped into the boy's arm, and the child's eyes went wide with wonder.

Daegal's skin stitched together, and his bones mended. He grimaced and tried to pull away, but Chert held him tight, letting the arm heal.

When he was done, Chert asked, "How does it feel?"

The boy made a fist and worked his arm back and forth. He smiled at the dwarf for the first time, revealing a mouth full of pointed teeth. After making certain neither child had other injuries, Chert dug in his pouch.

The two watched him curiously.

Chert asked the girl, "What's your name?"

She replied, "Yfellice."

"Name doesn't really fit. Did your momma give you that name?" he asked, still rummaging. He pulled out a small piece of purplish-burgundy stone pockmarked with ugly grey flaws.

"My name is Chert," he said. "Am I the first dwarf you've met?"

The two nodded.

The children remained silent as they watched Chert rub the stone. He worked it with both hands, flaking off rough spots and polishing out the flaws. Gem and mineral dust drifted to the ground. After a while, the milkiness went away, replaced by a heart of dark purple. Chert worked it some more, and the rough edges became smooth planes. He did not stop until it shone.

"Remember, we are all ugly little stones. But, with the Eternal Father's help and a little pressure, we can be shaped into something wondrous."

As he said it, he held the gem up to the glowing lichen. The orclings' mouths dropped open.

"Watch this," Chert said with a glint in his eyes that matched the gem's sparkle. White light appeared in the palm of his left hand, and the gem turned forest green. At its heart lay the shape of a deep purple rose in full bloom. He closed his hand around the light, and the stone turned back to burgundy.

The orclings' eyes grew wider.

"This is one of the reasons I travel both above and below ground," Chert said. "If we stay in the dark, we miss the beauty that's only visible in the light."

He handed the gem to Yfellice, whose face lit up when she took it. The two stared at the piece of rock in her hand.

"Can you do the light trick again?" she asked in a whisper.

With a smile, Chert opened his hand and the light fell on the stone, turning it green again. Deep inside, the purple rose sparkled.

"Now," Chert said, "I have a favor to ask. Can you help me find my friends?"

CHAPTER 10:
THE CRATES

October 28, 4235 K.E.

5:32pm

Marko rushed down the dark tunnel. His metal-shod feet pounded on the stone floor and echoed off the earthen walls. Orcs glanced up from their chores and watched from a safe distance. Intent on his mission, the knight passed them without a second glance. He traveled through multiple passages, both natural and orc-made, turning this way and that. Occasionally, he stopped to listen for someone following him, but each time, all he heard was the sound of the orcs working.

Two orcs guarded the narrow, dark tunnel of packed earth leading to Marko's crates. The knight neither stopped nor spoke. He had no faith in the creatures' ability to stop the ranger and saw no need to waste his time talking.

Marko passed under a half-dozen rough-sawn posts and lintels before he finally reached the mouth of the small orc-made chamber where the crates were stored. The knight paused, unslung the shield from his back, and drew his sword. He scanned for signs that someone else was there, but nothing looked out of place. Step by cautious step, he eased into the room.

The lighting from the few torches was dismal at best, but it was enough for him to survey the chamber. In the middle, four heavy timber posts set in a rough square surrounded the remaining four crates from the chuck wagon. Above them, a grid of wooden girders held tongue-and-groove planking against the earthen ceiling.

D'yakon Krovos' enchanted silver nails still held the crate lids firmly in place, and the destination mark on each was unmarred. He eyed the cargo, suspicion still gnawing at him. Aleksandra entered Chernigov with the mage and a dwarf, which meant the Kral's ranger was still unaccounted for.

A grunt from one of the orcs guarding the entrance preceded the fleshy thud of bodies falling to the floor. Marko shifted into a fighting stance, his shield to the fore, and peered over its edge. He could not see the two orcs at the far end of the tunnel, but he had no doubt they were already dead.

"Took you long enough," Marko said confidently.

"Sorry, I needed a guide," Xandor's voice answered from the tunnel.

The knight cursed his own stupidity as he tightened his grip on the hilt of his weapon.

"Catch!" the ranger called from the shadows.

Something small and silver glinted in the torchlight as it flipped through the air. Marko responded instinctively and batted it aside with his shield.

With a metallic ping, the coin bounced off the cave wall and rolled to the pile of crates. Marko stared, brow furrowed in confusion, unable to understand why the ranger had tossed a silver lev at him.

Laying on the floor, the coin shimmered with an eerie inner light. Intricate runes etched onto its face glowed dull red and silhouetted a thin thread that bound a single black bead to the coin.

The thread sparked. Marko's eyes went wide in surprise, and he dove for the exit.

The coin exploded and darkness swallowed the wooden crates along with their contents. Waves of heat billowed out of the chamber, followed by a jet of black flame. The concussive force hurled Marko against the tunnel wall and into one of its support posts. He crashed to the ground, uncertain if the ringing sound he heard was his armor or his ears.

"Mighty Sutekh, make me your hand this night that I might vanquish your enemies," Marko prayed to his dark god.

The black blaze retreated, replaced by tongues of bright flame that licked their way up the wood shoring, growing larger and hotter as it continued its ravenous search for food. Blue and white flames rolled along the room's ceiling like ocean waves. They sprouted out of the surrounding wood, crawled over its surface, and danced along the beams' edges.

Dirt and rock rained down on the knight through gaps in the charred planking. Rolling onto his knees, he climbed to his feet.

Marko swore he would make that ranger pay in pain and blood before offering up the man's heart and soul to Sutekh.

Xandor leaned against the wall of the tunnel and waited inside a shadow created by the raging fire in the crate room. For once, he was happy Jasper had a habit of overdoing things. From the far mouth of the tunnel, he heard orders shouted by orcs coming to investigate the explosion.

Ominous grumbling erupted, punctuated by the sharp staccato of splintering wood. Tendrils of fire streaked along the ceiling and each of the timber girders, probing for more food. Thick smoke roiled, and Xandor settled into a combat crouch.

Another deep grumble followed the first, closer this time. A cloud of dust billowed toward him, making it difficult for the ranger to see if the knight survived.

'*That wasn't supposed to happen,*' Xandor thought to himself. A knot formed deep in the pit of his stomach. He felt trapped. He glanced up the tunnel toward the exit but didn't see any orcs yet.

Iron footsteps rang on the stone floor, and Xandor spun to face them. He brought up both of his blades in a cross-block, catching Marko's crushing blow at its apex. The whites of Marko's eyes shone brightly and contrasted with the black soot staining the edges of his shield and armor. With a grim smile, the knight smashed his steaming shield into the ranger's chest and shoved him backwards. Steel hissed on steel as their blades slid apart.

Behind the knight, a sudden gout of red and orange flames broke through the thinning dust cloud. It licked the mouth of the crate room, silhouetting the two combatants. One of the charred timber girders inside the tunnel buckled, and the ceiling framing groaned under the weight it supported.

With a grunt, Xandor stopped his backwards motion and slashed at the knight's exposed face with his dexter blade.

The knight swayed back, letting the flaming tip slip past. As it did, he lunged with his sword extended.

Steel struck steel as Xandor dropped the tip of the blade in his left hand. He rode the parry all the way to the cross guard of his hilt.

"You can't win this fight, ranger."

"I already have," Xandor replied, nodding toward the flames devouring the crates and the evil they contained. Only two of the wooden posts remained standing in the room. Both were pillars of light. One bowed crazily and could snap at any moment while the other stood straight but had assumed the shape of a blackened hourglass, thick at the ends and narrow in the center.

Xandor saw a hint of doubt in Marko's eyes, but the knight's ego quickly squelched it.

Orcs gathered at the tunnel entrance, drawn by the explosion and sounds of battle. Limned in firelight, the ranger and the knight went at each other with a ferocity to rival even the most savage humanoid. Their blades flashed back and forth in a blur of motion. Smoke billowed along the ceiling between flaring sparks and tongues of flame. At the far end of the tunnel, the timber posts groaned like ancient men.

Raining blow after blow on Xandor's defenses, Marko's lip drew up in a snarl as he shoved the ranger back against the wall with his shield. To those watching, the knight's steel armor seemed to shimmer in the heat. Eyes filled with triumph, he swung his sword in a descending arc aimed at the ranger's head.

The ranger raised his right-hand blade and caught the knight's sword on the quillions. A flash of steel glinted in the firelight as he thrust with the blade in his left hand.

Marko leaned hard to the left, avoiding the attack.

With the knight off balance, it gave Xandor the opening he needed. He side-stepped away from the wall and cut toward the knight's exposed flank. His left-hand sword crashed against the metal breastplate, drawing sparks.

Passing back with his right foot, Marko swiped at the sword, knocking it aside, and pushed the ranger with his shield.

Xandor tucked his head and attacked the knight with a series of short vicious slashes.

Retreating, the knight was hard pressed to keep his shield up. Like a hammer on an anvil, each strike reverberated down his arm, causing it to grow numb. Out of desperation, Marko swept his sword counterclockwise.

Knees bent, Xandor ducked and stretched his right arm forward. He snagged the quillion of his sword on the sharpened edge of the knight's shield and yanked.

Already numb from wrist to shoulder, Marko couldn't stop his shield from banging into his sword arm.

Twisting at the hip, Xandor thrust with his left-hand blade and drove the upper rim of the shield into the knight's nose.

Marko backed off, spitting blood.

With the smoke growing thicker, Marko's breath came in ragged gasps. He could see the ranger's chest heaving with the effort to extract oxygen from the poisoned air.

The ranger's step faltered, and Marko lunged, shield first. The heat shimmer threw off his aim, and his shield glanced off the ranger's shoulder. The ranger spun, striking with his right-hand blade, but lost his balance and disappeared as a cloud of smoke engulfed him.

Marko drove his sword through the cloud, hitting empty air. Blinking away the stinging tears from his eyes, he crouched in preparation for the ranger's next attack. When none came, Marko retreated toward the exit and the crowd of watching orcs.

Deep vibrations shook the ground, sending Marko staggering to the wall to brace himself. He squinted, trying to pierce the acrid smoke and find the ranger. Dirt and small rocks rained down faster, extinguishing flames and breaking up the smoke. The very air around him seemed to vibrate. With an explosive crack, the last column in the burning chamber snapped, and the earthen ceiling collapsed, burying the ashes of the Blood of Cayn.

The earth groaned, and the blackened lintel at the mouth to the crate room snapped.

His head down, the ranger charged past Marko toward the tunnel entrance, but he wasn't fast enough to escape. A cloud of dust erupted from the debris and hit the two warriors, coating them. The blinded ranger stumbled over loose rocks and careened into the wall.

Like a house of cards, the next pair of columns splintered and fell. The third pair leaned drunkenly but held their load.

Marko shoved away from the wall and slashed at the ranger, knocking one of Xandor's blades to the ground with a loud, metallic clatter.

Grinning over his shield, Marko turned and pressed his attack, driving his opponent back toward the cave-in.

Xandor switched to a defensive stance and parried Marko's thrust. He backpedaled and narrowly avoided a smashing blow from the shield.

Again, Marko thrust forward.

Closing, the ranger caught Marko's blade on his quillions, twisted, and jammed it into the rim of the shield, trying to bind the two.

Marko push-kicked the ranger, sending him staggering back. "Orcs! Bring your archers!"

"Coward," Xandor taunted. His voice came out raspy and hoarse.

"We don't have much longer, ranger. The roof over our heads is about to collapse. Surrender to me now and I'll see to it that you die nobly, not buried alive."

The ranger stared at the knight from behind his sword. "If I go, you go with me."

Marko smiled grimly and saluted the ranger. "I expected nothing less from you. But know this: I am the only one stopping the orcs from killing you outright. I die, and they will shower your body with arrows."

"Stop wasting my time, Marko."

With a quick step forward, Xandor came at Marko's exposed flank with the tip of his blade.

The strike was faster than Marko expected, and he missed the parry. The ranger's sword slid under his right arm, piercing the chain protecting his armpit. Sword arm hanging limp, Marko grunted and slammed his shield into the ranger. A loud crack rewarded his effort.

Xandor wrenched his blade free. Bright red blood dripped from the edge.

"Got you, you bloody bastard."

Marko's eyes went wide, but he wasn't looking at the ranger.

Above them, one of the remaining timbers split down the middle. Orange and yellow flames filled the inside of the hollow beam. The two warriors could only watch in horrified fascination as the timber broke in two pieces and the ceiling crashed down on top of them.

The last thing Xandor saw was the chunk of granite that knocked him to the floor.

CHAPTER 11:
FIRE

October 28, 4235 K.E.

5:32pm

The air reeked of burnt flesh and ozone. Flashes of light from the ball lightning subsided as their energies fizzled. Charred orc bodies lay strewn about the floor. The last of the spectators were long gone. Aside from Jasper and Gregori, only Kourash and Grendel remained. A few of the deadly orbs hovered near the cavern's entrance, silent guards against any interruption.

Gregori allowed the stream of liquid fire to dissipate. The dark mage stood for a second or two and listened to the sound of Jasper's labored breathing over the spitting and bubbling of the molten stone. With his hand still held palm out, he walked toward him, watchful for an attack.

Hunched over with his head down, Jasper was on his knees. He leaned against his staff, his heavy-lidded eyes surrounded by dark circles. Sweat drenched his clothes. Smoking holes in his sleeves and along his back revealed raw flesh and gave evidence to his shield's failure. He slid his hand out of his sporran and refastened its buckle.

"You did well against the Seldaehne. Too bad you used up all your magic," Gregori taunted. He stopped at the edge of the molten stone moat and studied his portly opponent. He clenched his fist and a ball of shimmering red energy surrounded Jasper.

"Are you... going... to kill me... now?" Jasper panted. The ball of red energy contracted to within inches of his skin. "If you are... get it over with... I'm too tired... to listen to a diatribe."

"Not just yet," Gregori replied, smiling. "First you're going to tell me everything you know, even if I have to go inside your head and get the information myself."

"We could be here... for a while."

"I have all day," Gregori replied, ignoring Jasper's attempt to provoke him. "Talk to me. Tell me everything."

Jasper mumbled a reply.

"What was that? I didn't hear you."

"I said sauces... must be simmered slowly... if you heat them too fast... they burn," Jasper panted.

Frustration slowly crept into Gregori's eye, and he hissed, "No, you idiot. Why are you here?"

"...working as a cook. Here by accident..."

"Do not lie to me!" Gregori screamed, spittle foaming on his lips.

Jasper held the small reservoir of strength from the *Veritas autem Sutekh* deep within. While part of his mind searched for a way to defeat Gregori, he stared at the dark mage and said evenly, "I didn't lie."

Gregori appraised him anew and said menacingly, "I know that you and that ranger work for the Kral. And I know it was you who broke into the guild."

The dark mage watched Jasper for a reaction but didn't get one.

"So, was it you pulling Asenov's strings?" Jasper asked.

"I'm the one asking the questions!" Gregori yelled. "How did the Kral discover Asenov's betrayal?"

"How should I..." his words died in a scream of pain as the sphere around him contracted, lashing him with its searing energy.

Gregori shouted over Jasper's screams, "You and that ranger have nearly ruined everything! What did you do to Asenov? Where is the book?"

White knuckling his staff with both hands, Jasper shook convulsively, and his eyes rolled back into his head.

The other mage smiled cruelly as he watched. After a few long seconds, he allowed the sphere to expand away from his prisoner.

Jasper collapsed to the floor, coughing blood.

Gregori knelt and said, "That was just a taste. Lie to me again, and I'll give you a bigger dose. Now, tell me. What... happened... to Asenov?"

"Swear... I don't know!" Jasper panted.

Gregori gestured, and the shimmering sphere shrank.

Jasper saw it closing in and said between gasps, "Saw him at the guild... He tried to kill me... I escaped and went for help... He was alive when I jumped out the window."

Gregori's scowl deepened, and he asked, "Where is his book?"

"What... book?"

"I told you that I'm asking the questions, not you!" Gregori shrieked, battering Jasper again with pain.

Under the barrage, Jasper curled into a ball. The sounds of his pain soaked into the stone.

With a low growl, Grendel heaved on the chains. It was not the frenetic jerking from earlier. This was a consistent, concentrated upheaval.

Yelling defiantly, Grendel gripped the chains and heaved. The massive muscles in his legs and arms bulged under the tension.

A narrow crack snaked out from under one of the mooring plates anchoring the rings to the floor. It wasn't much, but it was enough. Gritting his teeth, the half-orc pulled harder.

The sound of grating stone filled the air, as the mooring plate broke loose from its foundation. The chain, ring, and plate arced up and hit the floor with a loud clang. A pyramidal-shaped chunk of stone fell apart, exposing the mooring pins. Taking the other chain in both hands, he struggled against his bonds. Both the plate and the stone beneath refused to give way.

Changing tactics, he grabbed the loose mooring plate with both hands and chipped away a small portion of stone near the other anchor. Standing, he again took the chain in both hands and pulled. Sweat streamed down his body and his muscles quivered from the exertion, but a small crack finally appeared in the cavern floor. Seconds ticked by. Cracks shot out in all directions, and a section of stone broke free, releasing the second mooring plate.

Chains dangling from his wrists, Grendel stalked across the throne room.

5:33pm

Rough orc hands had stuffed the vile gag back into Sacha's mouth, but it didn't fit as tight. Her brow creased in concentration, she slowly pushed it back out of her mouth with her tongue. All she needed was a little more... just enough to get the knot past her teeth.

Kraagor's guards carried Sacha down a long hallway that exited into the king's main living room. Ornate pieces of mismatched furniture lined the walls, many of them covered with a thin layer of white mold. They seemed out of place in the underground chamber. She counted at least half-a-dozen similar hallways arrayed about the room.

Several of Kraagor's females and a small horde of orclings occupied the chamber. They fell quiet when the orc guards entered bearing their prisoner. The older orcs barely gave Sacha a passing glance, but the children stared at her, wide-eyed, and soon the room filled with questions — the type only the very young would ask.

"Who is she?" Sacha heard repeated, but the one that truly worried her was the child who licked his lips and asked, "Are we going to eat her?"

Despite being the focus of their attention, Sacha ignored the little stares as best she could and tried to mark the passage leading back to the throne room mentally.

"Where do you want her?" one of the king's personal guards asked.

Kraagor didn't answer. Instead, he stood near an exit at the opposite end of the chamber, listening. Orc voices echoed from the tunnel, probably the tribal leaders — his tohan. From the sound of it, they were arguing. Kraagor glanced toward Sacha and then back toward the voices. She heard his name mentioned frequently, often preceded by a curse. They blamed him for the sudden chaos: a powerful mage loose in the throne room; a pangolin chasing a dwarf; rumors of Rhodinans loose in the city; and, not the least of which, a Trakyan Wind Rider raining fire and death from the skies.

The king shook his head and glanced at Sacha again. She could see the calculating look in his eye.

"Sire, where do you want her?" the guard repeated.

Kraagor jerked and spun to face his guards. Sacha thought he looked startled, as if he'd forgotten their presence. He growled and bared his yellowed canines. "You, Skyld," he said, pointing. "Have one of my girls show you where I keep my new slaves. Take Lady Aleksandra, strip her down, and lock her up. I'll deal with her later. Guard her door after you are done — and Skyld: do *not* damage her."

Sacha's eyes narrowed in fury as Skyld wrapped a heavy hand around her arm.

The orc king laughed at her. "I've heard that you Madasgorski women have quite the appetite when it comes to your bedchamber. When I get back, pretty girl, I want you ready, not all banged up."

He turned to his guards. "As for the rest of you, split up. I want those two mages and Lady Aleksandra's pet óhreint dead. Do not engage them. Seal off the throne room and flood it."

The captain bowed and struck a fist to his chest before he hurried down another exit with two of the guardsmen.

Kraagor turned to one of the few members of the Red Guard who had managed to escape the throne room. "Go find out where, by the eye of Ka'Sehkuur, young master Madasgorski has gotten, and find out if that dwarf is dead yet!

"Everyone else, with me."

Skyld gripped Sacha's upper arm tighter and said to the gathered women, "Take us to the slave chambers."

An old female orc dressed in dark robes came over and appraised the white woman. The look in her eye was disapproving. She reached up and pinched Sacha on the arm, leaving a red mark.

"She's all bones. Hardly worth the effort of a king. She should be given to a guard."

Moving her jaw, Sacha finally slipped the gag past her teeth, so it rested on her chin. She drew up and spit at the old woman.

The orc woman slapped her hard across the face. Sacha fell back, then lunged and tugged against Skyld, trying to claw the old crone.

Skyld enveloped Sacha in a bear hug and turned, interposing himself between the two women. "Móðor Kraagor," he said, "your son gave specific orders that she is not to be harmed."

"Very well," the crone said in a disappointed voice, heading toward one of the exits. "This way, Lady Aleksandra."

Sacha slowly calmed down. The óhreint's arms were steel bands wrapped around her torso. Her thoughts of escape subsided, though not forgotten.

The trio traveled down the dark passage for some ways before turning left and entering another smooth-walled cavern. This one was small and appeared to have a single purpose. Old blood stained the floor, and the room stank of fear. A long wooden table dominated the room, and, on the opposite side, two rows of shackles lined the wall: one row high, and the other low.

Móðor Kraagor ushered them in with a gesture. Amused, she stood there for a moment and watched Skyld drag Sacha into the room. "She's all yours," she cackled as she left.

Skyld pushed Sacha against the wall with his body and bound her wrists with the shackles. After verifying they were secure, he reached down, removed her boots, and bound her legs. He tossed the boots into the corner of the room and produced a small knife. Placing a hand around her neck, the óhreint ordered, "Don't move."

He carefully sliced open the front of her leather tunic and bodice.

Despite the danger she was in, Sacha stood unflinching, her eyes staring into the middle distance, unseeing. The image of Grendel, chained like a beast in Kraagor's throne room filled her inner eye. What had she done?

No matter what Bregu Kraagor did, she had survived worse. Only now, she felt she was losing something much more precious than the petty finery she surrounded herself with in Pazard'zhik. She looked around to find something to distract her, but the room was painfully devoid of anything interesting. Her eyes settled on Skyld and watched as he cut off her clothes. At first, his actions were very precise and careful, but after her shirt came off, a change came over him. Sacha felt him groping her breasts and sliding his hands down the small of her back. She struggled and tried to bring up a knee, but the chained shackles prevented it.

Skyld knelt and started to work on her pants. He looked up at her hungrily. Light flickered in his eyes, a reflection, really. In it, she was not alone. Instead, she saw herself and her demon the night they formalized their pact. He reached and sliced the leather along the inside of her thigh, causing her to flinch.

"Demon! What are you doing here? Are you here to free me or just grope me?"

Razrushitel grinned using Skyld's mouth and continued to remove her pants, piece by piece.

"I thought I would drop by and see how things were going. Fortunately for me, this óhreint has a weak spirit."

"If you are not here to help me, then go. I preferred the company of the óhreint."

With a sly grin, the demon said, "I heard that your taste in men has, shall we say, gone wild. Had I but known sooner."

He pulled away one whole pant leg and started on the other. A chill caressed her skin, and Sacha suddenly felt very exposed.

While working, the demon said conversationally, "Poor half-orc. He never had the chance to tell you he loved you. What a loss."

She pretended to ignore the demon, but his words struck a nerve. She bit her lip and tried not to cry.

"Too bad, really," he continued. "Now that his savage half has consumed him, you're just supper to him."

Sacha glared down at the demon as he cut away her other pant leg.

"He will seek you out if he survives and kill you for what you have done. I have foreseen it."

"I am tired of your prognostications, demon. They have only led me deeper into misery."

"My desire is to protect you... and him," the demon said meekly. Stepping away, he dropped the torn garments in the corner near her boots.

"What do you mean — *him*?"

Razrushitel turned and walked back to her, Skyld's face full of concern.

"I have my orders: the half-orc's soul is to be delivered to my lord and master." He leaned closer and said in a conspiratorial voice, "However, I can only do that if I am the one to kill him, and I can only kill him to protect you from death. That is our deal — that is our pact."

Anguish and grief filled the words of her next question, "Are you saying that if Grendel tries to kill me, you will kill him and take his soul?"

"Yes, but if you were to kill him before I could save you, then his soul would be free to go where it chooses."

Sacha looked up to the ceiling with tears streaming from her eyes. "Oh, wretched beast, why do you torment me? I cannot kill him."

"Then he will kill you. The madness you set upon him has consumed him. Remember, you did this, not I. I only offer you a way for him to be free in the afterlife."

Sobs wracked her body, and she desperately searched the demon's face, looking for the truth in his words. "Why?"

Whispering, Razrushitel said, "I suspect that if my master had to choose between his soul and yours, he would want yours."

"But he already has mine."

"Not yet he doesn't. At least not all of it."

She glanced about, seeking different answers, a different path than the one presented by the demon.

"Take this." Grabbing her hand in his, Razrushitel slapped something into it. As soon as she touched it, she knew what it was, even though it was invisible to the naked eye — a dagger forged deep in the pits of the abyss. She stared at her hand as if it belonged to someone else.

Demonic weapons served only one perverse purpose: to kill. Uniquely crafted for a specific target, rumor claimed they killed with a single scratch. Razrushitel must have had the forges of Hell blazing to complete this one: a weapon designed to kill a half-human who was also a quarter orc and a quarter ogre.

"I can't kill him," Sacha said, still staring at her hand.

"You must, because if you don't, I will."

5:38pm

A thunderous boom shook the walls of Bregu Kraagor's throne room. Gregori continued his barrage of pain, oblivious to the sounds around him. His manic laughter mingled with Jasper's screams.

Out of the shadows, Grendel's huge form loomed behind Gregori. With a clink of metal, heavy chains looped around the madman's neck and clinched tight, cutting off the nerve-wracking laughter at the source. The instant the iron chains touched the mage's skin, his spells dissipated, plunging the chamber into darkness, leaving only the bright red glow from the ring of molten stone surrounding Jasper.

Gregori raised his hands and struggled against the chain at his neck. He pulled, but it was pointless — the chain wasn't going anywhere. The dark mage grew still, as if accepting his fate, then slashed at Grendel with a short, thin blade.

Growling, Grendel let go of the chain, grabbed the mage's wrist with one massive hand, and squeezed. The small bones resisted the pressure at first, but then slowly ground together.

Gregori turned and, ignoring the pain in his arm, swung a fist at the half-orc's jaw. The hit connected poorly, delivered by one unaccustomed to brawls, but one of Gregori's rings scratched the half-orc across the cheek. Grendel's eyes glowed with violet fire.

Belatedly remembering the fate of the guards sent to collect the huge beast before him, Gregori tried to pull away, but could not escape the iron grip on his wrist.

Water sluiced across the floor. It hit the molten ring of stone, and steam geysered into the air, turning Jasper's island into a sauna. The spray of hot water jarred the portly mage, spurring him to action. Muscles protested and cramped, but with the aid of his staff, he managed to stand upright.

Through the vapors, he watched Grendel snatch away Gregori's small blade and wrap his hand around the mage's throat. He had to stop Grendel from killing Gregori... if he could get to him. He looked down at his feet and watched as more and more water flowed across the molten floor. The rapidly cooling stone took on a glassy smoothness, and through the ring of heat, he felt the occasional waft of bone-numbing cold. He sought the source but couldn't see it. Then he remembered the waterfall at the far end of the hall.

Jasper edged his way around the perimeter of his island and prodded at the rehardened surface with his staff until he found a solid-seeming spot. Backing up a few steps, the mage pole-vaulted through the steam. The glassy surface crunched under his weight, and the staff sank several inches into the stone. Fortunately, Jasper's momentum carried him over the moat. When he landed in the water, his feet slipped out from under him, and he fell with a splash.

The near-freezing temperature was like an electric shock. Jasper climbed to his feet and turned to Grendel and his prisoner. He needed to neutralize Gregori. Inspiration struck, and he searched the floor for the body of a Red Guard.

The huge half-orc continued to grip Gregori by the throat. He growled into the evil mage's face, a sound that was both warning and threat. The dark mage turned purple as his fist slowly closed.

"Don't kill him," Jasper gasped as he drew near. "If you do, he'll just move into another body, probably yours, and then he'll kill us both."

Grendel tore his gaze away from his prisoner, and Jasper staggered back a step. The look on the big man's face was truly terrifying. It was more animal than human.

Jasper mustered his courage. "Grendel, think about what you're doing."

A smile crept onto Gregori's face when Grendel's hand relaxed, allowing the mage room to breathe.

"Here," Jasper said, holding up a guard's mancatcher, with its iron-spiked tether open wide. "This will work better. Move your hand."

Grendel stared at it, and the mages saw the muscles in his jaw twitch with remembered pain.

"Do it, man! We have to get out of here. The water's rising."

Grendel blinked and looked down at his feet, as if noticing the cold water for the first time. He nodded to Jasper and let his hand drop to the chain draped at Gregori's shoulders.

Jasper slipped the tether around Gregori's neck and muttered, "Let's see how this works." He twisted the shaft the way the Red Guard had, and the iron tether snapped closed. He twisted it again, and Gregori screamed and clawed at the iron collar. Blood welled up along the lower rim and trickled from underneath. Jasper handed the pole to the half-orc while he sought for the release to Grendel's shackles.

Free of his chains, Grendel held the long mancatcher pole tight, his face a mask of fury.

Jasper laid a hand on his arm and said, "That's enough. We need him alive to talk."

The water had filled the throne room up to their ankles, and the cold seeped into the marrow of their bones. Grendel stared at Jasper and then back at Gregori. Hatred and rage filled the half-orc's face as he wrestled for control. He forced the dark mage to his knees.

"Grendel, we haven't much time," Jasper urged.

The portly mage pointed emphatically toward the end of the cavern. "Kraagor must have plugged the waterfall pool and sealed this chamber. Right now, it's pouring tons of water onto the floor, and Kraagor intends for us to drown. As cold as it is, we'll probably die from exposure long before that happens. Do you understand?"

Grendel struggled with the urge to rend the man at his feet limb from limb. Jasper raised his staff, and the head began to glow. The feral part of the half-orc's brain construed it as a threat. He snarled at the fat man but then stopped short. *'What was he doing?'*

With a twist, Grendel released the pole from the tether, dropped it into the water in disgust, and turned away. A spasm wrenched through his gut, and the half-orc doubled over. The spasm coursed through him again, along with a wave of nausea. He dry-heaved, but nothing came out. Pain ripped through him, and he roared.

Nausea hit him again, and his stomach heaved, knocking him to his knees. Grendel coughed up the grey slurry, purging his system. It slid out almost of its own volition and slithered into the water. Groaning, he fell to his hands, his limbs trembling.

Gregori laughed. The half-orc's head jerked up and he twisted around to face the two mages. It seemed they moved in slow motion. Jasper extended a hand toward the one-eyed mage, the words of a spell forming on his lips. Gregori crushed something in his fist, releasing a cloud of pearlescent silver dust. The cloud swirled and grew, hiding him from view.

"Next time, mage!"

The dust swirled faster and faster, preventing Jasper or Grendel from reaching Gregori. It pushed back the water at the dark mage's feet, then suddenly shrank in upon itself.

Gregori vanished with only the echoes of his manic laughter left behind.

"Damn it! I knew I should have checked his pockets," Jasper said, his teeth chattering.

"Where is Sacha?" asked Grendel, slowly coming to his feet.

Jasper worried his lower lip between his teeth. Finally, the mage said, "I don't know. Last I saw, Kraagor had her behind that obsidian throne."

Grendel leapt up the dais steps. Leaning on his staff, Jasper followed at a slower pace. The water hadn't reached the top, but it wouldn't be long.

"There must be a secret door," said Grendel as he faced the blank wall. "Can you find it?"

Closing his eyes, Jasper pressed one hand to the stone. After a few minutes, he shook his head. "No. Not using magic. This seems solid. Maybe there's a mechanism."

While Jasper used the light from his staff to search for the door, Grendel cast about for weapons. His battle-axe was gone, but he found the floor littered with scimitars, spears, and iron poles. Giving Kourash a quick glance, he picked up a few swords and walked back to Jasper.

"Why is the Seldaehne still here?"

Still searching, Jasper replied, "He's trapped, and with the spell I used, he's the only one who can release himself."

"Release himself?"

"The spell feeds off his emotions. He has to relax."

"How long will he be that way?"

"Depends on him, but with all that's going on, it will probably take a while." Jasper shrugged and stepped away from the wall. "I'm not finding this door."

Hefting one of his newfound weapons, Grendel asked, "Want me to chisel a way through?"

Jasper looked at the cavern and calculated in his head. "The blocks of stone sealing the exits have to be heavy and set in grooves to hold back the water once it reaches the top. We aren't getting out that way."

"What can we do?"

"We're trapped unless we can find another way out."

Jasper thought some more until an idea lit his face. With a gesture, he said, "Bring something sharp."

Grendel looked at the mage, perplexed, and wondered if the scimitar in his hand was sharp enough.

Using his staff for support, Jasper staggered down the steps of the dais into the water. It had risen to mid-calf, and the temperature in the hall dropped noticeably.

"We won't last much longer in this," Jasper said absently as he trudged through the icy water.

The mage walked to the glowing ring of glassy stone. The water was warmer here, but the red hue had turned several shades darker as the stone cooled. Jasper turned to Grendel and pointed toward the ring. "Try here."

Grendel gave him an incredulous look.

Jasper pointed at the floor. "*Look*," he demanded.

"All I see is water."

"What else?"

Grendel was about to reply, "Nothing," but then he noticed eddies in the water hovering over small fissures in the floor.

"It cracked when I jumped across," Jasper said.

Again, Grendel gave him a look that plainly questioned the mage's sanity.

Jasper sighed and said, "Just strike here."

Shrugging, Grendel took the scimitar in both hands and stabbed down into the glassy stone. The sword sank almost halfway up the blade, and the surface fractured into myriad large and small cracks.

"Where does this go?" Grendel asked, surprised.

"How should I know? But the water has to drain out somewhere."

Grendel struck again and again. The glassy stone cracked and split with each blow. When Grendel pulled out his scimitar after the last strike, water poured into the fissure and fresh steam hissed from the opening.

"Don't stop. Make it bigger," Jasper encouraged.

With each blow, the glassy stone fell away and disappeared into whatever void lay beneath them. It wasn't large enough for a person, especially one as large as Grendel or Jasper, but the water swirled away like the drain of a bathtub.

"It's not big enough. The water's still rising."

Grendel cast away his battered scimitar and took up a fresh one. He jabbed it into the stone repeatedly, producing a trench conforming to the shape of the ring of black glass.

Between jabs, a crack spread its way beneath their feet. The floor around them split into several sections and shifted. The piece under Jasper tilted, sending him stumbling for balance. He held up his hands for Grendel to stop, but the half-orc raised his scimitar and aimed for the new crack.

"What are you doing?" Jasper asked. "The floor will collapse!"

"I know."

"You don't know how far we'll fall, or if we can survive the landing."

Grendel stared hard at the mage and asked, "Is there another way out of here?"

Jasper didn't need to look. He heaved a sigh. "No."

"I am going after Sacha. Are you with me or not?"

"I'm with you, but..."

Before Jasper could say anything else, Grendel struck the fissure's end. He hit it with such force that the blade of the scimitar snapped at the hilt and lodged in the stone.

At first, nothing happened. Jasper stared at Grendel, his eyes wide. Water continued to rush around their calves and flow into the various cracks and crevices. Without warning, Grendel leapt into the air and smashed down onto the end of the crack with both feet.

A fountain of steam spewed from the floor, and sections of stone canted farther. With a loud groan, the floor lurched and opened up. Both Grendel and Jasper slipped in the water and slid toward the yawning, jagged hole.

"I hope you know what you're doing!" Jasper yelled at Grendel. The half-orc threw him a fierce grin as they both plummeted into the dark void, surrounded by sheets of water.

Growling all the way down, Grendel landed on his stomach with a wet splat. Mud spattered the sides of natural columns and stalagmites, and the falling water from above quickly washed it away. Jasper, on the other hand, floated down and gently landed in the mud. He held up his staff and lit the various cave formations around them.

Grendel picked himself up, and they both looked at the cavern ceiling roughly fifteen feet above them. Cracks and fractures scored the stone in multiple places where Gregori's fire had weakened it. Frigid water poured from the rents and glistened like multicolored gemstones in Jasper's light. It formed a frothy stream and wound its way around the undulating floor of the cavern.

Jasper peered in one direction and then another. The cavern was ancient, evidenced by the massive natural column formations that abounded in the area. Stalagmites climbed toward the ceiling, reflected by a matching stalactite above. Water coursed down the formations, and streams of white-grey sludge merged with the deluge from the throne room.

"Any idea where we are?" Grendel shouted over the roar of the water, wiping his hands on his pants.

"No idea. You?" Jasper asked. He sank to the floor and leaned back against the wall. "Give me... a moment... to rest."

"Let us go downstream. That is the same direction they took Sacha." Grendel looked around when the portly mage didn't respond, and found him fast asleep.

CHAPTER 12:
RETRIBUTION

October 28, 4235 K.E.

6:19pm

Leftenant Brian Gallagher had just completed his report to Lord Fergusson when Anders appeared at the tent flap.

"Sir, Yana's returned."

"Milord?" Brian said.

"Go. I'll have Anders alert the staff."

By the time Brian reached the training field she was already gone, but the collection of arrows in the glider's sail confirmed where to find her. He ordered repairs to the craft and headed to the healer's tent.

There, he found the Ivanov brothers sitting on either side of Sehraine's cot. Across the tent, Yana glared at the brothers while the chirurgeon stitched a deep cut in her leg.

"That looks like it hurt."

"It did, but not as bad as last time. Mostly bruises."

Sir Brian winced in sympathy. "Have you talked to the Ivanovs?"

"One of them met me at the field." She inhaled sharply as the chirurgeon tied the last knot. "Do they have to be so tight?"

"Do you have to let the orcs shoot you?" the harried man snapped in reply.

"They were instrumental in Sehraine's rescue," Sir Brian said, ignoring the byplay between Yana and Bris. "Without them, I don't know if we would have found her in time. As it is..."

A muscle jumped in the diminutive Trakyan's jaw, and she interrupted the officer. "I want the men who did this to her."

"The Rhodinans turned them over to me for justice. Poruchik Tirinko offered to make restitutions. He feels responsible because he didn't insist on an escort for her." Sir Brian shook his head. "She refused an Iron Tower escort as well. We should have sent someone with her anyway. Can you help us contact her family?"

"Sehraine is an orphan. I'm the closest thing she has to family," Yana replied.

Sir Brian eyed her curiously and waited for her to continue.

Yana stared across the tent at Sehraine's unconscious body. "My aunt is a patron of the Trakyan Royal Players. She discovered Sehraine begging in the street outside the Naroden Teatar and took her in when I was a little girl. It came as a bit of a shock, discovering she was an elf pretending to be human, but I think it made my aunt love her even more. She and my uncle adopted Sehraine. Aunt Nevena arranged for Sehraine to study at the Naroden Teatar with the great actress and singer Tatyana Nozharova.

"Not too long afterward, my brother and I went to live with Aunt Nevena and Uncle Bate. Our parents... died. Sehraine and I became friends, and she helped me find the light in those dark days." She scowled at Brian. "I'll take my reparations from the men who hurt her. If Sehraine wants something from Poruchik Tirinko, she can ask him herself."

"You know what's wrong with her, then? Why she won't wake up, I mean?"

Yana shook her head. "They must have done something to her." The expression on the wind rider's face grew harder as she spoke, and there was a savage anger in her eyes that caused the knight to step back without thought. "When I'm done with them, they'll wish they buried themselves instead of Sehraine."

"They aren't going anywhere. The troops I have watching them may even offer to hold the culprits down while you hit them," Brian said, his normally crisp voice softened. "However, Lord Fergusson is waiting for your report. Will you do all of us a favor and see him first?"

At her nod, he offered her an arm to lean on and they made their way to the Knight Commander's briefing tent.

6:30pm

Lord Fergusson leaned over a model of the Keep, studying it. He turned and spent a silent moment taking in the look on Laytenant Marchenkova's face. "I'm sorry about Sehraine."

The laytenant glared at the Knight Commander. "I want those men, Lord Fergusson," Yana growled. Her hands hovered near her weapons, ready to draw and lash out at any moment.

"Laytenant!" Lord Fergusson barked as he straightened, and she instinctively snapped to attention. As he stepped in front of her, it occurred to him that, for such a petite woman, she was terribly intimidating.

"We have done everything we can for Lady Sehraine, and the men responsible for this are in our custody," Lord Fergusson said with a hint of finality.

"But, Sir..."

"Forget those men, Laytenant. I cannot have you distracted right now; too many lives are at stake." Lord Fergusson held Yana's gaze. "We cannot afford to lose you now. You are too critical to this mission." He saw her resolve waver, but he could still see her anger simmering just below the surface.

Anders appeared at the door and waited for Lord Fergusson's permission to enter. The Knight Commander made eye contact, and the squire said, "Your officers are assembled, Milord, and Knyaz Dorinkov is waiting."

Lord Fergusson turned back to Yana and placed a hand on her shoulder. "Are you ready, soldier?"

"Yes, Milord."

"Good," Lord Fergusson said and turned to Anders with a nod.

The squire stepped aside to let the Rhodinan prince and their officers enter. They gave the barest attention to formalities as everyone took their places. When they were ready, Lord Fergusson said, "Tell us what you saw. How did the orcs respond to your initial attack? Did they replace their engines like we thought?"

"During my flirting with them, I noted that the towers here and here," she pointed at the north wall, "were partially repaired. From what I could tell, they moved engines from the western gatehouse here and here. Additionally..."

The conversation delved into particular engine types and orc deployment. As information came out, Anders dutifully recorded it in his notes and on the map as appropriate.

"Regarding numbers of enemy personnel, we need to up the estimate. The city looked like an anthill that had been kicked over."

By the time she answered their final questions, another twenty minutes passed. Lord Fergusson stood and addressed Yana directly. "Laytenant, you have given us more assistance than I expected and far more than I asked; thank you," he said earnestly.

"You're welcome, Sir," she said. "I wish I could do more, but unless we can come up with additional ammunition, I think we will have to cancel the next two flights. There was not much ammunition to begin with, and I know you thought it would stretch a little farther — perhaps I should say hoped it would. We have plenty left for the attack on the Keep tomorrow morning, but not enough for anything else." When Leftenant Gallagher shook his head, she continued, "In light of Sehraine's injury, I'd like to coordinate final details for Vityaz Dobrynya's extraction with the Ivanovs."

"All right," Fergusson agreed.

The discussion moved on to the specifics of what Lord Fergusson expected of each commander, where each needed to be at dawn, and which signals to expect. In less than an hour, they rehashed the plan, with the respective commanders verbally rehearsing their actions. Fergusson and Dorinkov made minor adjustments to their earlier plan, incorporating their new information.

"Fergusson, don't forget that the orcs have engines on the bridge itself," Knyaz Dorinkov said. His tone was that of a man on the downside of a familiar argument.

"Highness, I have not forgotten. They will be taken care of."

Knyaz Dorinkov nodded his acceptance, but his expression shouted that he was unconvinced.

Lord Fergusson swept the group with his gaze. "Questions? No? Then..."

"Milord," Anders interjected, "Mikhail and Mattias are back."

The two woodsmen entered the tent behind him.

"Well?"

"As the wind rider said," Mikhail nodded at Yana. "The river has eaten under the northwestern wall and tower. It is a deep cut, but short. Too wet for fire," he shrugged.

"Thank you, Mikhail," Fergusson said. "We were afraid of that, but we can still use it. It might work with our explosives." He shrugged as well. "We will just have to try and see."

"Mikhail, can you and Mattias get back to the cut without being seen?" Knyaz Dorinkov asked.

At Mikhail's hurt look, he laughed and continued, "Sorry, old friend; that was a silly question. I never doubted your ability."

He turned back to the Knight Commander. "Fergusson, how many of these explosives are available, and how do we employ them?"

"Anders, take the woodsmen to our quartermaster and have him instruct them on using our fire-sticks."

Patrick left with the two men in tow.

"Ladies and gentlemen, get back to your people. Let them know what we know. Get them prepared for tomorrow."

He dismissed them, and the knights filed out of the tent in quiet conversation with Yana trailing behind them.

"Excuse me, Lord Fergusson?"

"Yes?" he responded. He turned to find a middle-aged man, bone thin, with his dirty blonde hair pulled back and plaited in the twin braids of a Rhodinan court style two decades past. Sir Brian and Yana hovered in the doorway behind the man.

Fergusson turned to Dorinkov with a questioning look.

Dorinkov responded by saying, "I asked the Korol' to send us a battle mage. I got a bard instead. Lord Fergusson, may I introduce Sergei Nikoloff."

Sergei bowed low.

"What can we do for you, Mister Nikoloff?"

"You said you lack enough ammunition for Laytenant Marchenkova to make any more air attacks against the enemy. Have you considered any alternatives?"

The Knight Commander gave the man a sharp look.

"What do you have in mind, Mister Nikoloff?"

The man gave a gentle chuckle. "Just Sergei, Milord; a rasskazchik ever in search of a new tale to tell or epic to recount. I'm certain you've already searched high and low for something at least marginally destructive that is light enough for a glider to carry and, obviously, haven't found anything. I'm guessing, however, that you have only gone through your own stores, and possibly those of Knyaz Dorinkov. Have you taken stock of the sutlers and other camp followers? I think I might be able to pull enough ingredients together to make something formidable. It's one of my specialties."

Lord Fergusson eyed him warily. He was not certain exactly what the man had in mind. He glanced at his second, who had remained behind. No doubt, his natural curiosity held him back. "What do you think, Brian?" he asked.

"We should at least hear the man out, Sir," Brian replied with a shrug.

Lord Fergusson studied Sergei for a second more.

"Quite right. Tell us what you have in mind."

7:15pm

Yevgeny sat beside Sehraine, cradling her bandaged hand. Her skin was cool to the touch, and he had to resist the urge to rub her hand between his. He cast a worried glance at his brother.

Lev walked to the doorway of the overlarge tent. He made a show of stretching before exiting the field hospital to take stock of who was nearby. In theory, they were safe in the Glaxon camp, but one could never be too careful.

Yevgeny waited patiently for his brother's return, listening to the muffled chatter of a group of camp runners. Finally, Lev stepped inside the hospital tent and gave his brother a short series of signals. Yevgeny nodded, and Lev retreated, and closed the heavy canvas tent flap behind himself.

Yevgeny eased his short stool closer to Sehraine's head and leaned close to her ear. "Sehraine," he whispered. "Sehraine, fyrirgefðu." *Sehraine, I'm sorry.* The elven words tasted unfamiliar after so many years unable to speak his native tongue freely. "Fyrirgefðu að þessi skrímsli meiða þig, en þú verður að vakna núna. Vinsamlegast. Sehraine, ekki fara. Vertu hjá okkur... með fjölskyldu þinni. Systir þín þarf þig núna. Við höfum verk að vinna."

"Isä?" came a hoarse reply.

Yevgeny's eyes snapped to Sehraine's face, but her eyes remained closed.

"Komdu, Sehraine. Það er kominn tími til að vakna."

"Mig dreymdi hræðilega draum," she whimpered. *I dreamed a terrible dream.*

"Sehraine." He spoke her name, a little louder this time, and he felt her hand tense in his.

Her eyes flew wide, and her face filled with panic. Kicking at the blanket covering her, she struggled to sit up and her eyes darted wildly around the dim tent.

Yevgeny grasped her shoulders and gave her a gentle shake. "Sehraine. Shhh. You're safe now. Well... at least as safe as anyone can be right now."

She cringed and scooted away. "Don't," she rasped. "You mustn't touch me. I was exposed to the plague."

Yevgeny offered her his hand. "I don't care," he said. "Besides, it's too late. Lev and I brought you out of that hole."

Tears welled in her sapphire eyes.

The stocky riverman pulled her into a gentle embrace and let her cry on his shoulder. No words could ease the horror of her experience, so he simply held her.

"How did you find me?" Sehraine finally asked.

Yevgeny shrugged. "We asked around."

Startled by his comment, the elven actress drew back. Her eyebrows arched high, and she gave an incredulous laugh tinged with a bit of hysteria. "You asked around?"

"Well... You really have the runners to thank. Afon and Miyka saw the pack of curs returning from their sport and realized something was amiss. Miyka ran into us on his way here, told us he had to check on you, and what they saw. Lev and I simply persuaded their leaders to tell us what they did."

"Where are they now?"

"The Glaxons have Yuri and his comrades. Gallagher was waiting to speak to you and Laytenant Marchenkova before he punished them. However, I think Yana wishes to deal with them herself."

Sehraine nodded. "That sounds like Yana: protective to a fault and just a bit overzealous in her methods. If there's one thing she excels at, it's taking things to an extreme." She sighed. "Do they know I'm alive?"

Yevgeny shook his head. "No, but I can't say the same for the rest of either camp. Not with that pack of runners outside."

She shivered. "At least we won't be here much longer. I can't be lucky all the time."

"If you would learn to fight with a real weapon, you wouldn't have to rely on luck," Yana said from the doorway. The wind rider tried to maintain a serious expression, but her relief to see the elven woman awake won.

7:30pm

Yevgeny leapt to his feet, surprise written across his face. Sehraine realized he hadn't heard Yana and Lev enter the tent either.

"So you've said before," Sehraine replied. "If I hadn't gotten tangled in a snare, they never would have caught me."

"But they did catch you."

"Yes, they did."

Yana crossed the tent and crouched by the cot. "Are you alright? I heard that old saw-bones gave you a once over and was disappointed there was nothing to stitch or cut off."

"Yana!" Sehraine exclaimed, feigning a shocked expression. "You'd better be glad he knows how to sew, or you'd have to get one of the sutlers to patch you! Besides, I'm sure he found my minor injuries a refreshing change of pace."

The wind rider motioned to Yevgeny, who excused himself and went to join his brother guarding the door.

"How late is it?" Sehraine asked.

"Not very. A little over two hours since sunset is all. Are you thirsty?"

Sehraine nodded. While Yana retrieved a cup and the water pitcher, Sehraine studied her bandaged fingertips and thought about what would happen if they failed to help Xandor and Jasper. If they failed to find the Tear of Havel. Fear slithered up her spine. "Yevgeny told me the Rhodinans turned over the soldiers who did this to Sir Brian for justice."

Yana nodded. "Did he tell you everyone is preparing for an execution?"

Sehraine accepted the cup Yana offered. "Not everyone... only you."

"What is that supposed to mean? Sehraine, the bastards buried you alive! I'm not about to let them get away with it."

The elf drew her knees up to her chest and gave her friend a sad-eyed look. "Yana, think about what you're saying."

"I am thinking. They're worse than midden sludge and will only try to hurt you or someone else if given half a chance."

Sehraine sighed. "Let me rephrase. Think about this logically rather than emotionally. Lord Fergusson and Knyaz Dorinkov need every fighter they can get tomorrow. Even men consumed by hate and fear. We can't risk Jasper and the others' lives by diminishing the forces here by even one soldier."

Yana scowled. "Fine. *But*, if I see any of them after our friends are safe, they're dead men."

CHAPTER 13:
AFTERMATH

October 28, 4235 K.E.

6:19pm

Xandor startled awake with the coppery taste of blood in his mouth. At first, he couldn't remember where he was or what happened, then the fight and the fire came rushing back. *'Don't blow up your friends,'* he mused. Eyes still closed, he took stock of himself, flexing and relaxing muscles from his feet up, assessing his various aches and pains. He let out a sigh of relief when everything responded as expected and turned his attention to his surroundings.

Rough stone and debris pressed against his back and right side. He cracked open his eyes to semi-darkness, and discovered he was wedged between the passage wall and a broken timber. An errant trickle of air touched his cheek, and warm, orange light blossomed, revealing a smoldering hollow no more than twelve inches from his face.

Turning his head up and to the left, Xandor could see a small, black, triangular hole that was the source of the air current. *'It must lead to the tunnel exit,'* he thought. He raised his head enough to stare down the length of his body. Less than a yard beyond his boots, the narrow hollow he lay in ended in a mass of crushed wood and rocks. *'At least I'm facing the right direction.'*

Exhaling all his air, Xandor pushed with his feet and tried to slide free, but the ruined timber held him fast. He raised his arms and gently pushed. The rocks and boulders shifted ominously. Dirt cascaded on his face, and he jerked his head aside to avoid getting it in his eyes.

"That was a mistake," he muttered.

Xandor inspected the timber that trapped him. The surfaces not glowing were charred black, and grey with ash. The wood would not last much longer. It was a miracle it lasted as long as it had. He groped blindly and found one of his swords partially buried under the debris. Several long minutes passed before he was willing to admit the second blade was lost.

It was awkward working on his back in the confined space, but eventually, he freed his sword and maneuvered it across his body. Gripping the blade in one hand and the hilt in the other, Xandor tried to chip at the hard packed earth and gravel wall next to him, but he didn't have enough leverage to make any real progress.

The ranger glared at the boulder above him and tried to think of a way out. His mind raced through options, but his inability to move fed his fears. Panic hovered at the edge of his thoughts, and try as he might, he could not banish it. He closed his eyes and breathed through his nose, taking as deep a breath as possible. When he did, he realized the air was smoky but still relatively fresh — all things considered. It dawned on him that the small fires were still burning. He glanced toward the exit again, encouraged by the thought that it might lead all the way out. If he could just move the timber.

An ember flared in the distance, revealing another fallen ceiling timber. That one rested with one end propped on what remained of its support post.

He looked again at the timber directly above him — the support post was gone. Probing the surface of the floor around him with just his fingers, he found part of it beneath him. Dirt and small rocks covered the wood post, but Xandor was sure he could move it. A surge of hope filled him, and the crippling sense of claustrophobia receded.

The ranger dug his into the loose dirt and rocks until he found the end of the post. The timber above him groaned as he moved, and a fresh stream of dirt fell onto his face. Ignoring the distractions, Xandor braced his hand against the end of the fallen post and pushed it with a slow, consistent effort toward his feet.

Sweat beaded on Xandor's forehead, mixing with the dirt. With an abrupt lurch, the post broke through some unseen obstacle. Xandor raised his head and looked down the length of his body. Everything seemed stable, at least for the moment.

He continued to push the post and slide it farther toward his feet, opening a small gap. It wasn't much, but it was enough for him to squeeze past the beam above him. Rolling onto his stomach, he brought in his elbows and positioned one arm so that it lay inside the newly made hole. The pressure of the beam resting against his body disappeared.

Keeping his elbows tucked underneath him, Xandor inched forward and eased out from under the timber and into the triangular-shaped hole. He grabbed his sword and cautiously worked his way down the narrow shaft using only his feet and forearms.

The ranger hugged the wall as best he could, but the sides were rough and irregular. He often found himself forcing his way through the tight spaces by using his body to push small boulders aside and make narrow openings wider.

By the time he reached the next post, Xandor was exhausted. His body took up the entirety of the hole, so it was impossible to look behind him. This was a one-way trip with no going back. He stopped, dropping his forehead to the dirt floor. '*Just a few minutes rest*,' he thought, and closed his eyes.

6:43pm

Yfellice and Daegal struck off down another tunnel. They splashed through puddles, dodged past large boulders, and jumped over obstacles with carefree ease, the horrors of the pangolin left behind. Chert found himself liking the pair of orclings.

He followed them through narrow passages, around limestone spires, and behind fragile stone curtains. Strange patterns created by the different geological strata decorated every surface. White calcite stripes meandered over onyx columns, crystals sprouted from pockets and fissures, and pools of still water mirrored the glow of lichen.

As they neared the borders of the city, Chert began to see damage to the living stone, places where careless hands brushed stalagmites and stopped their growth or something chipped a formation. The smells of rotting meat and unwashed bodies drifted through the tunnel, causing Chert to slow.

The orclings continued. He followed them, wary of the increasing signs of the orc civilization that thrived beneath Chernigov.

The two suddenly stopped in front of an orc-made shaft and listened. Above them came frequent growls and screams, marking one of the entrances into the city.

"Stay here," Yfellice said. "We will find you a disguise."

"Hurry back."

The two disappeared up a set of steps carved into the side tunnel. Chert sat down with his back to the wall, ready to dive in and hide at a moment's notice.

After what seemed like an eternity, Yfellice and Daegal returned. Daegal carried the pelt of an adolescent winter wolf with its head and snout still attached. Chert stared at it, amazed. Under all the dirt and grime, the wolf's coat still glistened silver and white. It would have fetched a handsome price in Pazard'zhik.

"It was the only thing we could find," Yfellice said apologetically.

Neither offered any information about the source of the pelt, and Chert didn't ask. He draped it over his shoulders, pleased to see it was large enough to wrap around him completely, leaving only his mud-caked boots exposed. He raised the wolf's head over his and peered out through its silver-white teeth.

Yfellice scrutinized his disguise. She scooped a handful of mud and smeared his beard and cheeks, then tugged around the cloak. After a few moments, she stepped away and said, "Now you look like one of us."

Chert wasn't sure how to take that, so he simply nodded and kept his mouth shut.

When they emerged from the shaft, Yfellice and Daegal walked on either side of him and guided him into the outskirts of the orc city. Like everywhere else, this part of the city was a mixture of natural caverns and orc-made tunnels.

Mud-covered children ran and played on the floor and narrow ledges leading to the orc dwellings. Chert realized that the true danger of orcs didn't lie in their strength or ferocity in battle. It was their numbers. A place like Chernigov, with its walls and caverns, provided the orc population a safe haven in which to expand. With each generation of orcs growing exponentially, it was little wonder no one had been able to remove their foothold.

But there was something else. Along the fringes of the city, groups of ogres, dreyri, Repha'im and other beasts he did not recognize congregated in various caverns. It struck Chert as odd. He saw few, if any females among the other races, and no children. It occurred to him that, if the Plague Wars returned, Kraagor would be ready.

The three didn't linger. As they traveled deeper into the city, the orc population swelled, and Chert counted himself lucky that he was the same height as the orclings. They walked in plain sight without receiving a second glance. The adult orcs paid little attention to the children, provided they stayed out of their way. If the path became too crowded, the threesome took advantage of the multitude of smaller, secondary routes. Chert kept his eye out for anything familiar, and even though he was loath to admit it, he was still lost.

Occasionally, their path took them near human slaves. Chert studiously avoided eye contact, painfully aware of the hopeless way they carried themselves. He hated how it made him feel and knowing that the humans would eventually end up as food only made him feel worse.

Chert studied the orc children who guided him. They ignored the humans. They were property, like beasts of burden, nothing more. He shook his head and walked past the slaves too.

Yfellice and Daegal were careful to avoid the routes used by the Red Guard and those who worked directly for Bregu Kraagor, but guards were not the only danger.

In a large cavern filled with three levels of dwellings stacked along two of its walls, Chert's wolf pelt caught the eye of the younger orcs, and they pulled at their mother's skirts and pointed. Chert kept his head down, but behind them, he heard harsh whispers and the patter of feet.

A rock struck the dwarf's back.

The three turned around and faced a gang of juvenile orcs. The tallest stepped forward. He bore three scars on his chest and wielded a flint dagger. He carried himself like an adult, and it was obvious from his swagger that he spent most of his time bullying the others.

"Give me the wolf fur, and I'll let you go."

Daegal stepped in front of Chert and Yfellice. He carried no weapons, but that didn't seem to matter. He growled and gave the older orc a harsh glare.

"You only carry one mark. I have three," the older orc bragged, pointing to his chest with his thumb.

Daegal didn't back down. Instead, he took another step forward and clinched both his fists.

The gang of juveniles formed a semicircle behind their leader.

Chert watched Daegal and, although the youth wasn't scared, it was going to be a one-sided fight. The juvenile orc had him by at least a foot and easily outweighed him by twenty or thirty pounds.

The dwarf closed his eyes and prayed.

Daegal kicked loose dirt in the taller orc's face and plowed into him, shoulder first. The boy doubled over, the wind knocked out of him.

The gang yelled taunts and jeers at Daegal. One of them picked up a rock and threw it, striking him in the leg. Others followed suit and picked up rocks of their own. As they were preparing to throw, a soft, azure-colored flame ignited around their feet and crawled its way up their legs to their bodies. When it reached their heads, it danced along their scalps and in their sparse black hair.

The rocks fell from their hands.

Panic set in among the gang members. Some dropped and rolled in the dirt, while others slapped at their skin, trying to put out the flames. Terrified screams rang out; however, they weren't shrieks of pain. Chert grinned. The boys were too frightened to realize their skin wasn't actually burning. The light from the dancing flames simply limned their bodies and played havoc on their low-light vision.

Chert grabbed Daegal and Yfellice, and the three ran as fast as they could. The shouts of superstitious orcs echoed in their wake.

After a long stretch of hard running and randomly ducking down this tunnel and that, they finally slowed. Daegal backtracked to check for anyone following. Once satisfied, he resumed a more casual pace, leading them away from the fringes of the orc city.

The clangor of steel on steel and the hissing of steam preceded the next cavern. Curiosity got the better of him and Chert motioned for the other two to follow.

Yfellice tugged at the pelt and said, "We're not allowed in there," but the dwarf had already moved on.

Harsh fire light from the many forges set against the walls illuminated the cavern. Smoke filled the upper third of the space, collecting around narrow cracks in the ceiling on its slow journey to the world above. Filthy male humans formed two long lines beside a muddy stream meandering through the cavern's center. One line exiting into a dim tunnel, while the other line returned carrying bundles of cordwood on their backs. Orcs wielding rawhide whips walked up and down the lines, making sure the humans kept moving at a brisk pace.

On the opposite side of the stream, barrels waited for leather apron clad orcs working at black anvils to fill them. Orcs worked in teams to beat and fold glowing metal, while others poured molten steel into molds. One of the smiths raised his work from the anvil face to appraise it before plunging it into a barrel of water.

"They're creating weapons," Chert said. "How many of these caverns are there?"

"I don't know," she said, "at least six, maybe more."

Chert looked up and tried to guess how deep they were. He glanced back toward the line of humans and watched them go by. The dwarf rubbed his nose thoughtfully.

"That's a lot of wood," he mused.

Yfellice shrugged, "I guess..."

"What are you doing here?" a guard shouted.

Heart in his throat, Chert dashed past an orc with a whip and tugged hard on a bundle of cordwood as he went by, knocking it off the back of the slave carrying it. He plowed through the next line, hurtled the stream, and headed toward the nearest exit as fast as his short legs would carry him.

Daegal and Yfellice struggled to keep up. They ran into the orc with the whip together, bowling him over into the line of slaves, and kept moving. Chaos ensued as humans and cordwood went flying.

Orc guards alternated between yelling at the orclings to stop and yelling for the humans to get back in line. The air came alive with the crack of whips.

Daegal and Yfellice raced after the dwarf, just ahead of the guards, and followed him down the tunnel. A crowd of humans carrying buckets of iron ore suddenly appeared in front of them. Without stopping, the dwarf and two orclings lowered their heads and wove their way through them.

The pursuing guards rushed blindly into the tunnel, and the two groups collided.

"This way," Yfellice said, grabbing Daegal's wrist, her face flush with exertion. She and Daegal slipped through the humans and ran inside a narrow crack in the wall, where they hid behind a slimy limestone column as the guards ran past, their iron-shod feet drawing sparks on the stone.

The noise and excitement gradually died. Chert crouched beside a puddle with his hands on his knees. Feeling eyes boring into him, he looked up and met the angry gazes of the orclings.

"That was stupid, dwarf. You almost got us caught," Yfellice hissed. She threw an apprehensive glance back toward the main passage. "We must leave before the guards return."

"Alright, let's go."

The three filed out of the narrow crack and traveled cautiously down the main passage. They took the first side passage they found, moving fast and close together, and soon found themselves back amongst the populace. Chert's saturated pelt earned the occasional odd look, but no one stopped them.

Still not finding anything familiar, Chert pulled Yfellice aside and said, "We need to find my friends."

Yfellice said something to Daegal, and he ran off into the crowd to gather what information he could.

They didn't have to wait long. Daegal came back, excitement filling his face. He relayed what he learned to Yfellice who quickly translated. "Kraagor has sealed his hall and flooded it. They say he trapped two galdreas inside."

"Galdreas?" Chert asked.

"Magic men," the girl whispered in a fear filled voice.

Daegal spoke again, and her fear turned to shock.

Yfellice turned to Chert. "He also says that when the ground shook, it collapsed two tunnels and part of a cavern near here. Many of his kinfolk were injured. They're still digging people out."

Chert's brow furrowed in thought. Had he caused this in his struggles with the pangolin? He felt certain that he had kept the collapsing of the small section of tunnel isolated.   He didn't have it in him to cause the mass destruction she described, at least not on purpose.   Chert thought about the sound waves he used to distract the pangolin away from the children.   As his gran said, everything is connected.   Guilt and doubt gnawed at him. They were orcs, why should he care if they died?

"Will you help them?" Yfellice pleaded.

Chert was torn.   He met the orclings' expectant gazes, and suddenly found himself preferring to face a dozen hungry pangolins rather than say no to these two children. He let out a sigh and said, "If you can take me to the tunnel without getting caught, I will see what I can do."

The trio walked through several more side passages linking larger caverns.   Traffic increased with every step they took toward the collapsed tunnels, but the adults paid them scant attention in their haste.   Daegal guided them down another passage, which opened into yet another vast cavern of orc dwellings.   A section of homes lay in a heap of rubble. Shocked women and wailing children huddled together.

Across the chamber, frantic shouts preceded a team of dusty orcs carrying chunks of boulder out of a makeshift tunnel.   Behind them came a wave of injured orcs.   They flooded into the cavern, some carried on litters, and others sporting dirty bandages.   As soon as the path cleared, more orcs joined the search.

Chert and the two children mingled with other orclings and adults resting from their endeavors.   They entered a tunnel that seemed to snake around the collapse and passed an injured orc warrior sitting on the ground with his head in his hands.   Sweat-streaked dust covered his dark skin, and one of his legs lay mangled where something heavy had crushed it.   Chert hurried the orclings past the orc before he noticed anything suspicious.

A warrior?   The dwarf glanced back.   Maybe this wasn't just a mercy errand after all.

More orcs rushed past them.   Shouting followed, coming from the junction of several tunnels where orcs loaded rocks and broken timbers into handcarts.   The trio made their way into the dust-clouded chamber and past the workers, climbing over the rocks strewn across their path.

An orc near the end of the line shouted at them, and Daegal raced into another tunnel. They stopped in a lichen-lit cavern half covered by a shallow pool that reflected a variety of glistening rock formations. Numerous ledges and narrow drifts dotted the far wall.

"That's it," Yfellice whispered in Chert's ear, pointing to one of the lower tunnels. "That leads back to the cave-in."

Handing her the wolf pelt, he said, "Stay here."

10:30pm

Xandor woke and pushed onward, uncertain how long he'd slept. He lost count of the number of times he had to exhale completely to squeeze through a gap between rocks. Raw scrapes covered his arms, and his muscles ached with every move. Visibility dwindled the farther he traveled from the burning timbers, and he was reduced to crawling and scraping his way along blindly.

Behind him came a loud rumble and his small tunnel belched dirt and dust. The ranger closed his eyes tight and prepared for the worst. The ground trembled over his head as the area he had just passed collapsed.

Total darkness consumed his path and with it came despair, but the slabs of stone above him remained in place. When the noise subsided, Xandor tried to look around again, but everything was black as pitch. He closed his eyes and reopened them, but it made no difference. He inhaled through his nose and held his breath. A gentle shift of air tickled the stubble on his cheek. He sighed in relief.

The ranger wiggled his hand into his pouch and slipped out his journal. A few sharp shakes activated the stylus, and he shined the light around. It revealed more rocks and more dirt. The triangular-shaped gap continued parallel to the wall. Another cracked timber beam lay at the edge of his light. At least this one wasn't smoldering.

Putting away the stylus and journal, he tucked his elbows beneath him and wormed his way forward.

CHAPTER 14:
CLANDESTINE JOURNEY

October 28, 4235 K.E.

11:40pm

It was a little before midnight when Yana returned from her third flight over Chernigov. Sehraine and her Iron Tower escort waited outside what was left of an old barn. She arrived just in time to help the man hoist a bulky satchel onto the back of one of Jasper's wormy horses.

"What on earth is in this bag?" Yana demanded as she tied it down. "You do realize you are getting into a boat, don't you?" Already saddled and ready, Xerxes and another horse watched them from a safe distance.

"Just some things we need tonight. Sergei got them for me," Sehraine answered, sidestepping the question.

"Sergei Nikoloff?"

"You've met him, then. Isn't he a treasure?" Sehraine grinned at Yana. "As far as finding just the right supplies, I mean. I wasn't suggesting we invite him to dinner."

"Yes, he's very good at finding supplies," Yana conceded. "He came up with a potion of liquid fire for my latest flight. Of course, he wants an account of how I used it as payment. I'm not sure when he thinks I'm going to have time for tales."

She pulled Sehraine up onto Xerxes' saddle behind her and caught sight of the bandages on the tips of the elf's fingers. "Sehraine, are you *sure* you want to do this? I don't want you getting hurt, or worse..."

"Yana, we've been over this. I want to help Yevgeny and Lev take that boat. Rescuing Dobrynya and his men is important to Xandor and Jasper."

The wind rider nodded to their Iron Tower escort. He turned and guided them down the trail to the White River. After nudging Xerxes to follow, Yana glanced over her shoulder at Sehraine. "I still think the Ivanovs can handle this without you."

"I can't sit in camp alone, waiting for the rest of you to return. I have to do something. For all we know, one of them has the cure I need."

"I beg your pardon?" Yana half turned in the saddle. "The cure *you* need?"

"If what Jasper learned is true, it's my fault. The plague, the war, all of it, because I abandoned my family. I have to prevent it from happening again."

"I thought you meant you're sick," Yana said with a relieved sigh. "What happened thirty some-odd years ago isn't your fault. If I had to guess, I'd lay the blame at the Madasgorski family's doorstep." She patted Sehraine's knee. "Now tell me what's in that heavy bag of yours."

"Not yet, but I will tell you that I had to recruit Sergei to help me find what we needed, and he knew exactly which one of Knyaz Dorinkov's quartermasters to see. He called him a Plyushkin." A bubble of laughter escaped her at the reference to the old Trakyan theater character known for his greedy, packrat ways. "Based on the supplies he brought, I believe the description truly fit!"

They both laughed.

"So what's in the bag?"

"A surprise."

Yana shook her head and let the matter lie. It was no use arguing with Sehraine.

Sergei waited at the shore with a smile and a boat. A very small, *old* boat, whose age was exceeded only by its odor.

"Hello, ladies!" He greeted them with a courtly bow and a flourish. "I think this craft meets your needs. Just don't ask its provenance." He grinned at their dubious expressions.

The Trakyans looked over the boat. It seemed dry enough inside, and Sehraine announced that it would do nicely. Sergei and Sehraine talked a bit more as she walked with him up the path a short distance and then sent him on his way.

A few minutes later, the twins joined them at the edge of the river, carrying a crate between them. Yevgeny and Lev looked over the fishing boat while making disapproving sounds.

"Did you dredge this off the river floor?" Lev inquired.

"No, I did not," Sehraine replied primly. "However, appearance is everything tonight. If we don't look exactly right, it won't matter whether we speak orcnéan or not."

"Will that thing stay afloat with all three of you in it?" Yana inquired.

"Of course it will." Sehraine threw her a mock glare. "I think."

Yana looked at the massive bag the Ivanovs unloaded from the horse. "So, what's in the bag?"

"Stuff we need," Sehraine said absently.

"Uh huh. Right." Yana turned to the twins. "What did you two bring to the party?"

With mischievous grins, they unpacked their crate and showed her several dozen ceramic balls, a handful of rags, and a pair of jars whose viscous contents glittered in the moonlight. She picked up one of the ceramic balls and heard something inside rattle. "What's this?"

"Eitureldi," one of the brothers replied, and the two men laughed.

The darkness of the sound sent a shiver up Yana's spine. The Ivanovs were like two violent boys showing off their favorite toys. She took Sehraine by the arm. "Last chance. Are you *sure* you want to do this?"

Sehraine hugged the wind rider and replied, "Stop worrying. I'll be fine. Besides, I have you as my guardian angel."

"Good luck." Taking the horses' leads, Yana mounted and headed up the trail to the waiting soldier. Xerxes looked back at the boat. Yana patted the horse on the neck and said, "I worry about her, too."

At the top of the bluff trail, she found a strange little man with a dark stained crock whose lid was fastened with leather straps. He nodded to her and scurried toward the river's edge, leaving the stench of sour fish guts in his wake. Yana muttered, "I really don't want to know," and hurried on her way, her fourth and final flight of the night a few short hours away.

Sehraine gave Lord Fergusson's short, stocky assistant cook a bright smile. "Egan, thank you so much for bringing it. This will add just the right touch." He blushed bright red, ducked his head, and hurried off without a word.

Lev wrinkled his nose at the stench rising from the pot. "Ugh!"

Sehraine shot him a sly grin. "We have to sell the idea that we are a fishing boat, so we have to look and smell like a fishing boat."

"That will certainly cover the smell part!"

"And this," she said, opening her big bag to reveal an assortment of old, ragged clothing and a large net, "will make us look like orc fishermen!" She grinned triumphantly at their shocked expressions. "Did you think we could just row into their midst looking like ourselves? I told you: appearance is everything."

They grinned sheepishly at her and reached for the clothing. As they dressed, Yevgeny asked from beneath a garishly colored tunic, "Can we wait until the last minute to open the pot?"

CHAPTER 15:
LOST?

October 29, 4235 K.E.

12:03am

Voices. Orc voices.

Xandor rested his forehead on his hands and listened. He didn't see any light, but he hadn't expected to. The orcs practically lived in darkness. Voices meant he was close to the end of the cave-in.

A groan to his right drew his attention.

Sliding out his sword, the ranger tried to locate the injured orc by his breathing. He reached out with his hand, feeling along the surface of the rocks and found a wet spot. Inching toward it, Xandor reached farther and followed the trail of blood. His hand became slick as he continued his search. The orc's ragged breathing became louder, and the stench of unwashed flesh grew. Xandor extended his sword toward the noise. The weapon's tip found an obstacle that gave under pressure.

The obstacle groaned in response.

Silent as a snake, Xandor reached back, prepared to plunge his weapon into the dying orc. Before he could strike, the overpowering scent of wet dog rolled over him, and something grabbed his hand. If not for his training, he would have screamed.

The newcomer held Xandor's arm in a vice-like grip and prevented him from moving.

A bearded face brushed against Xandor's arm and whispered, "I wouldn't kill that orc unless I was absolutely certain he would go quietly. There's a whole horde of them out there searching for survivors."

"Chert?"

"Aye."

"How did you find me?"

"Accident," the dwarf replied. "Are you hurt?"

"Just a nasty headache," the ranger whispered. "What are you doing here?"

"Believe it or not, rescuing orcs. Sort of."

"What?"

"Long story. Suffice it to say, I made a deal. What are you doing here?"

"Trying to get out."

Chert ran a hand over the ranger's head and found a lump the size of a duck egg on his forehead.

"Where are Marko and the crates?" the dwarf asked.

Xandor motioned back down the tunnel with his head and replied, "Marko's in there somewhere, buried. The crates burned."

Chert peered into the small hole leading deeper into the debris. "You crawled through that?"

"Yes," Xandor replied. "Feels like forever." Dust tickled his dry throat, and he struggled against the urge to cough. "Water?" he croaked.

Chert handed Xandor a water skin. He took a sip, swished it around, and spit the grit from his mouth before taking a real swallow. "Thanks. Please tell me you know the way out."

"This way." Chert pressed his hands into the tunnel wall and pushed aside the rock. He kept the opening small, and slowly worked his way through the earth.

Xandor entered the new hole on his hands and knees, following the scent of wet dog. They crept along, with Chert's impromptu passage resealing itself inches behind Xandor's boots. He lost all sense of time worming through the cave-in. In an effort to reset his internal clock, he counted the seconds as he followed the dwarf.

Using the walls of Chert's tunnel to guide him, he was surprised when he felt the occasional void open up to one side or the other. Orc voices carried through these shafts, and at times, he felt they were right on top of them. Chert kept moving, their path as sure as the North Star.

A breath of moist air wafted over the ranger's skin a moment before his forehead collided with Chert's outstretched palm.

"Why are we stopping?" he whispered.

"Just checking. Thought I saw movement." Chert stepped away. After a minute, he returned. "Must have been my imagination," he said. "This way."

He led Xandor into a natural, low-ceilinged drift. The earthen passage became rough and gradually sloped downward. They traveled a little farther, and the walls became wet to the touch. Beyond Chert, Xandor caught a glimpse of glowing lichen. It was the most beautiful sight he'd seen since passing the Stena. He lowered his head and thanked his Maker.

Xandor emerged from the tunnel and stood stiffly. He stretched his arms out wide, rolling his shoulders and neck to relieve the aching stiffness, and drew in a deep breath. The ranger's skin prickled under the weight of someone watching him, and his eyes snapped open to find a pair of smaller than average orcs almost upon him. He sprang away and yanked out his sword in a single motion.

The orcs darted out of the weapon's reach.

"They're friends!" Chert exclaimed, interposing himself between man and orclings.

A pain-filled groan came out of the darkness. The ranger stalked around a pile of rubble and found wounded orcs lying on the floor. They drifted in and out of consciousness. Some had limbs wrapped in blood-soaked bandages, and others had makeshift splints.

"You've been busy," Xandor said, his tone rife with disbelief.

"I told you I made a deal," Chert explained.

Xandor studied the two orclings. The boy came up to his chest. He stood proudly and eyed the ranger warily. The girl was a little shorter. She blushed under his scrutiny and turned her head away. The ranger grabbed her chin and stared into her eyes.

Daegal clenched his fist, preparing to defend the girl, but Chert intervened. "Xandor, remember they are our *friends*. They helped me find you, even if it was mostly happenstance."

Letting the girl go, he said, "You're half-orc."

Yfellice took a step back behind Daegal.

Emphasizing their names, Chert said, "Her name is Yfellice, and his name is Daegal. What difference does it make?"

"A lot. She has free run of the city and a young protector. Who is your father?"

Chert studied her a little more. It was difficult for him to see the human blood, except for her eyes.

"Answer me. Who is your father?"

Daegal faced the ranger and growled. Xandor gripped his sword tighter, expecting the young orc to charge at any second.

Yfellice placed a hand on Daegal's shoulder and answered timidly, "Bregu Kraagor."

Chert and Xandor stared at her ragged clothes and unkempt appearance in amazement. She was a far cry from any princess either man or dwarf had ever seen.

"What were you doing in the tunnels?" Chert asked.

Yfellice answered meekly, "Playing."

"Why in the tunnels?"

"My older brothers and sisters don't like me," Yfellice said with a fleeting smile. "My father doesn't like it when I sneak out. He'll beat me when I get home, like always, but it's worth it." Her matter-of-fact tone was a testament to the type of life she led, and it made the two pause.

Daegal turned to her and said something. She frowned and shook her head.

"What did he say?" Xandor asked.

"He wants me to run away, but I can't."

"Why not?"

"Daegal is the son of Toha Ruugar. He only has one scar and won't be of age until he gets five. No tribe would accept us if we ran away now."

"So you sneak out often?"

"As often as I can."

"Can you take us to your father?"

Her face clouded with worry.

Chert stepped closer. "We are looking for our friends, and your father will know where they are." He stretched to his full height as a sudden thought struck him. "*Jasper...* Oh, no."

"What about Jasper?" Xandor asked.

"Yfellice, when did Kraagor trap the mages — the galdreas — in the throne room? Were they alone?"

"I don't know," she shrugged. She spoke with Daegal in rapid-fire orcnéan. The boy shrugged as well, gestured to one of the orcs, and walked away. He crouched beside the injured warrior, asking him questions.

Xandor clenched his fist around his sword hilt, ready to call its flames to life.

The boy returned. Yfellice listened to what he said and translated for Chert. "Oergnath said Bregu Kraagor trapped the two galdreas, the dragon-man, and a wild óhreint. Unless the ground shook and broke there, too, they all drowned.

Chert dropped to his knees. "Eternal Father, please let us find our friends alive," he prayed.

"We need to have words with your father," Xandor said.

Chert reached a hand to Yfellice. "Please take us to him," he pleaded. "The óhreint is my friend. I must find him."

Daegal pulled Yfellice back from the dwarf and the ranger. The children conversed in whispered orcnéan.

It occurred to the ranger that he could probably force the female to guide them. Looking at the two orclings, he could see why Chert had befriended them, but deep inside, there was a bitter hardness to the ranger. He needed to reach Kraagor, find the others, and escape. One way or another, the girl would cooperate.

Chert nudged Xandor, jarring him from his thoughts. "You need to let the Iron Tower know Kraagor's massing an army. Not just of orcs, but ogres, dreyri, and others — even giants."

"The few we saw outside the monastery hardly make an army," Xandor argued quietly.

"What we saw outside is nothing compared to what I've seen in the past few hours, Xandor. There are caverns full of them, *and* they're forging weapons. Kraagor knows about the plague. He must think the humanoids are immune to it, and if he's right, your people's history will repeat itself. He'll cross the White River with this army and there will be no one to stop him."

"Do you think Kraagor is the answer to the riddle of who wants the plague to run rampant?" the ranger asked. "I don't see him masterminding infectious soap."

"What about the Madasgorskis? Gregori?" Chert replied.

"Maybe. I still think there's a puppet master out there who's pulling our strings. Someone we haven't seen yet."

"Who else could possibly want this war?"

Xandor shrugged. "That's the question, isn't it?"

Chert thought for a moment, and his brow creased in concentration before he said, "Marko's dead. Gregori? He's the only one left. You think he's working for someone?"

"Zhitomir and the Grand Sha'iry," the ranger suggested. "They were responsible for the original Plague War, and they're responsible for this one."

"That's too easy. It explains Marko's connection, but they're just as susceptible to this plague as anyone else is. From what I can tell, not even Gregori is immune to it. Why don't you send a note to your friends aboveground and see what they think?"

"I'll do that," he said, reaching for his journal.

"There's something else. I recognized the symbols in the helrúnan's cave. They were symbols of chaos. These orcs worship something other than the Dark One. What happened to Grendel was primal — savage," Chert said.

A cold wind cut through the cavern, and Chert stepped closer to the ranger and asked quietly, "Do you have my armor and other gear? I need to get out of these wet clothes."

As his answer, Xandor produced Jasper's box. He unfolded it until Chert's hammer and helmet became visible.

While the dwarf made himself ready, Xandor penned an update to the Iron Tower.

Daegal and Yfellice turned back to Chert and Xandor. The ranger stuffed his journal into his pouch, and Chert slipped into his chain shirt.

"I will take you, but you cannot kill my father. Promise?"

The dwarf struggled before answering, "We can't make that promise."

The ranger cast a hard glare at the dwarf.

Ignoring Xandor, Chert said, "I will not lie to you. All I can say is that we will do everything we can not to kill him."

Yfellice turned away and relayed what Chert said to Daegal. After a brief discussion, she turned back to Chert. "Follow me," she said. "After we leave, Daegal will bring someone down here to help these orcs."

Chert placed his great helm over his head and dropped his trusty hammer into its belt loop.

12:09am

"Face it, we are lost," Grendel growled.

"No, we're not. I know exactly where we are," Jasper replied.

"We have passed that same rock three times."

With a forced laugh, Jasper said, "Three times. How did you get that number?" Jasper took a few more steps before he realized that Grendel had stopped. When he did, he turned around and shined his light where Grendel pointed. Three rough lines scored its surface.

"That is how."

The two stared at each other. Jasper's head dropped. "I should have thought of that."

Grendel searched the cavern for another way out.

The rush of water from the throne room no longer guided them. It disappeared down a narrow fissure some way back, and the two pressed on, trusting to fate and the mage's rough sense of direction.

"What now?" Grendel asked.   "Can you magic us somewhere?"

A look of exasperation overcame the mage. He leaned against the rock and said, "No, it isn't that simple. Some of my magic has returned, but only enough to get one of us out, maybe."

Grendel thought some more and said, "Then why stay? Save yourself. Maybe you could bring someone back."

Jasper looked around at the cave formations. He listened to the constant dripping of water and felt cool air caress his cheek.

He shook his head. "If I leave now, I could never get back. There's not enough here for me to remember this exact spot. Besides, I'd miss all the fun."

Grendel silently let out the breath he'd been holding. "Thanks."

The mage simply smiled and nodded.

"So, what now?" Grendel asked.

"You're the half-orc. Aren't you supposed to be an expert underground?"

"I was raised in an arena," Grendel answered. "If you want, I could fight my way out, I guess. How about you?"

"Born and raised in the city," Jasper said.

"So what made us think we could find Sacha and the others in this big maze?"

"Well, I would say it was our big, brass balls," Jasper grinned. "When you have those, there's no need to think."

"Uh-huh," Grendel replied. "I thought mages had crystal balls."

"Nah, they'd clink when I walk," Jasper laughed. "In all seriousness, though, do you remember how to get back to the water?"

"I think so."

"Let's backtrack. At least that way, we'll be in familiar territory."

1:04am

Xandor and Chert followed Yfellice through chamber after chamber. Occasionally, the sounds of the city drifted down to them, but for the most part, it was just the three of them.

"Where are we?" Chert asked.

"We're under the city. A lot of our trash gets thrown down here, so be careful where you step."

Both Xandor and Chert slowed and looked down at the floor.

Smiling, Yfellice said, "Trust me, you will smell it first."

"Don't the orcs come down here?"

"Sure they do, but something has everyone busy. Kraagor has many of the adults aboveground tonight."

Chert stopped. "You mean there's more?"

Yfellice replied, "Yes, a lot more."

The orcling set a fierce pace. They pushed to keep up, and Xandor fought the feeling that she was leading them into a trap. He tried to map the twists and turns in his head, but there were too many. From the look on Chert's face, he suspected the dwarf was just as lost. Xandor had no choice but to put his faith in the girl.

In the darkness, there was no way to track time. They stopped when Yfellice stopped and moved when she moved. Xandor's mind began to wander, and, when his stomach grumbled, it dawned on him that he hadn't eaten all day.

After a long walk through a narrow cavern, the orcling finally stopped. At her feet, a stream of water rushed by. She frowned, and the two stared at her, concerned.

"Are you lost?" Xandor asked.

"Huh? No. No, I just haven't seen this stream before."

Xandor reached down, dipped some up in the palm of his hand, and took a tentative sip.

"This is fresh — and cold."

He dipped some more and slurped it down. Chert did the same. They splashed the cold water on themselves, cleaning off some of the mud and grime.

Yfellice stared at them. She canted her head to one side, and a smile tugged at her lips.

"What? Do you not bathe?" Chert asked.

Surprised by the question, she answered, "Of course not! Orcs get sick if they take a bath. Didn't you know?"

"Are you sure?" Chert prodded.

"Yes. Orcs do not take baths," she said, crossing her arms.

"Well, I know a half-orc who bathes and doesn't get sick."

Her eyes grew wide, and she asked, "You know a half-orc. Like me?"

Chert stared at her before answering, "A little. He's the óhreint you said Kraagor trapped in the throne room. Hopefully, you'll get to meet him for yourself."

The three continued farther, walking beside the stream.

Xandor raised a fist, and everyone stopped.

Something splashed in the water behind them.

The ranger put Yfellice behind an earthen column while Chert took up a position close to the wall. Moving slowly down the cavern, Xandor positioned himself behind another column. It was far enough away not to reveal the orcling's position if someone attacked, but close enough to defend if necessary. Another splash echoed down the cavern. Chert stepped inside the wall and disappeared. Xandor gripped his sword, reflecting the glow of lichen on the edge of its blade.

A faint echo of voices reached the ranger. Ears straining, he couldn't make out individual words, but it sounded like an argument. Two, maybe three, individuals.

Xandor checked Yfellice's position. A hint of red eye-shine near the bottom of a column revealed the girl peering into the darkness.

Using the voices for cover, the ranger ran to the next column and waited. Bringing up his blade, he tried to catch a glimpse of who was approaching. A beam of light struck his blade, blinding him. He raised his hand to his eyes, trying to rub away the spots.

More splashes echoed, and Xandor cursed his blindness. He put his back to the earthen column and hoped that whoever it was hadn't spotted him yet.

"Why are we backtracking all the way to the throne room?" Grendel asked.

"Because we know that the entrance to Kraagor's chambers was behind the throne. Based on that logic, if there is another entrance, it shouldn't be too far from where we started."

"Is that not the same logic that got us lost in the first place?"

"For the record, you found the water; thus, we are no longer lost."

"I do not see how..."

Jasper stopped and held up his hand in warning. He flashed his light near a column but didn't see anything.

Grendel looked around. He splashed through the water, trying to draw out whatever was there. When nothing happened, he turned back toward the mage with a shrug. Jasper cast his light about, trying to illuminate a row of columns, but it only seemed to generate more shadows.

"Maybe it was just my imagination," Jasper ventured.

"Jasper?"

Grendel spun around while Jasper aimed his light in the direction of the voice.

"Who's out there?"

"It's Xandor! Stop blinding me with that bloody light!"

Chert emerged from the wall and raced to Grendel. The half-orc knelt and wrapped the dwarf in a bear hug.

"I am truly sorry, Chert. I never meant to hurt you."

Gasping for air, the dwarf said, "Next time, let's skip seeing the witch doctor."

The two backed away from each other awkwardly, acutely aware of Xandor and Jasper watching.

"I agree," Grendel said. Sniffing, he asked, "Why do you smell like a wet dog?"

"Long story," Chert said.

Xandor stepped forward and asked, "What did you do to my cloak?"

When the ranger moved to retrieve it from Jasper, the dwarf spotted Yfellice standing behind Xandor, shielding her eyes from Jasper's light. Chert motioned to Jasper, who immediately dimmed the glow to that of candlelight.

"Grendel, Jasper, this is Yfellice, daughter of Bregu Kraagor."

Grendel swung around, expecting to see a hideous monster. Instead, he found a blue-eyed girl.

He stopped.

She walked up to the giant and said in wonder, "You're a half-breed like me."

Grendel glanced at Chert and then back at the little girl. A battle of emotions waged across his face. Was this some kind of trick?

Chert nodded some encouragement to the half-orc.

"Yes," Grendel answered.

"Are you here to kill my father?" she asked.

"Yes."

"Why?"

"He took my woman."

Jasper and Xandor watched the exchange in silence.

"Is she pretty?"

Grendel nodded.

"I hope you find her, but please don't kill him."

Grendel took a step back, unsure how to respond.

Chert glanced between the two of them and said, "We have one more friend to rescue. As I said earlier, we cannot promise that your father will not be killed."

Yfellice stared down at her feet.

Touching her softly on the chin, Chert gently raised her face and said, "But we will try to find another way."

CHAPTER 16:
AGONY AND REGRET

October 29, 4235 K.E.

2:45am

Sometimes, Kraagor wondered why he had bothered to become king of Chernigov. Between the general rabble expecting him to solve a thousand problems at once and the tohan council, who acted as though they couldn't organize patrols or move a single war engine without consulting him, it seemed that there was always something demanding his attention. Other times, he knew exactly why he wanted to be king.

This was one of those times.

The orc king stepped past Skyld and walked into the torcher chamber, closing the door behind him. His eyes roamed over the scene before him, took in the pile of ripped clothing in the corner, and settled on the naked woman chained to the wall.

He took his time, drinking in the view of every inch of her soft pale skin, the curves of her hips and breasts, and the thick white scars on her thighs. The exquisite expression on her face managed to blend both her rage and her revulsion.

In all, the perfect end to a not-so-perfect day.

A toothy smile formed on his face. It was by no means a pleasant expression. He enjoyed nothing more than breaking a new slave, especially one as spirited as Lady Aleksandra Madasgorski. Kraagor mulled her over in his mind, thinking that one like her would take time — possibly weeks, if he played it just right — and he planned to make every minute count.

He swaggered to the table, unmindful of the dried blood, and laid down an oilskin-wrapped bundle. Watching out of the corner of his eye to make sure Aleksandra noticed, he carefully untied the bindings and rolled out the cloth to reveal his toys. The scents of leather and steel mixed with that of the room, and Kraagor inhaled deeply, exhilarated by the fresh scent of her fear.

The orc king ran a hand lovingly over the tool kit, trying to decide which to use first. He had made most of them himself as new ideas struck him. However, the more interesting pieces were for later, when he was tired of playing with her and ready to break her entirely. For now, he would start with something light. He untied another cord and produced a short-handled scourge, its three thin leather cords evenly knotted and seasoned with blood.

Kraagor let the ends hang by his side and approached Aleksandra. He rubbed one coarse, calloused hand over her scars, liking the feel. He dug his thumb and clawed fingertips into her leg, and the chain clinked as she tried to squirm away from his touch.

"Where's your razor tongue now, wench?" he asked, letting her go.

"Get your hands off me, gryaznaya svin'ya," Sacha said and spat in his direction. Kraagor took a quick step back and laughed as the spittle fell short.

"Filthy dog, am I? I'm going to enjoy breaking you, woman."

He raised the lash to the height of his waist and backhanded Sacha's thigh and hip with it, drawing angry red lines and small, blood-filled blisters.

Sacha hissed and flinched at the stinging pain but did not scream. She ground her teeth.

The orc king swung again, harder this time, at the other hip and leg. The knots bit deeper. Blood welled and trickled down her leg in slow-moving trails.

A vicious light grew in the orc king's eyes, and he rained blows on her legs and arms in earnest. She managed to hold back the scream, which surprised him, but she could not staunch the tears that streamed down her face.

The tears pleased him.

Sacha didn't want to cry. During childhood, her parents had schooled it into her that tears were for the weak. Tears were for victims.

On the opposite side of the table from the orc king, she could make out the shadowy form of Razrushitel leering at her, thoroughly enjoying her torment. She had always loathed the demon. Now, she planned a thousand-and-one ways to slay it.

She flinched as the lash struck again and a tiny whimper of pain escaped her. The demon's grin grew wider, and he ran his own hand and eyes over Kraagor's torture kit, fingering some of the more frightening pieces with interest.

Sacha thought about the invisible blade still clutched in her fist and the demon's words. There was no doubt in her mind that the demon intended to kill Grendel at the first opportunity, but as for the rest of his words... She kept repeating to herself that they were meant to cause her pain and couldn't be relied on for even a modicum of truth. She wanted to drop the dagger to the floor but knew the demon would simply retrieve it and use it himself if she wouldn't.

One thing she did believe — not because the demon said it, but because not believing would mean losing all hope that she could survive this — Grendel would come. He might or might not want to kill her, but he would come.

Bregu Kraagor didn't stop using the lash until his pretty new pet sagged limply in her chains, unable to stand. Sweat trickled down the king's crooked nose, and he found himself breathing heavily from the effort.

She had lasted longer than any woman before her. Stripes of red crisscrossed her body and her head hung down, perhaps unconscious, but she still clenched her fists.

Taking his time, he placed the scourge on the table and walked back to the woman. He wrapped one hand around her pale throat to hold her head against the wall and licked the blood from her arm. He closed his eyes as a shiver ran down his spine. It was even better than he imagined, full of hate and fear, with just a hint of sadness. Disappointed that she didn't react to his touch, he fought the urge to take a bite out of her. It was too soon for that pleasure.

He stared down at her body, so close to his, and felt the heat rising from his loins. It did not matter if she was unconscious, he had waited long enough to make this vixen his. Adrenaline coursed through his veins and rippled through him. With his free hand, he worked the laces of his pants.

He had barely loosened the knot at his waist when the door crashed open, and a rumbling growl echoed through the chamber.

"Get your hands off my woman!"

Kraagor spun around to face the intruder. Anger burned away the pleasure of the moment before.

In front of him stood Grendel.

The king's eyes went wide. The óhreint should have been dead. Kraagor drew himself up to his full height — he almost made six feet.

"*Your woman?*" he demanded. "I think not. I am king here, and she forfeited her freedom and her life when she attempted to depose me."

Kraagor studied the óhreint, admiring his physique. He had a lifetime of experience dealing with orcs. He knew what they wanted most, and he was in a position to give it to them.

"I can see that you've got potential, now that you're not acting like a rabid dog, so I'm going to make you an offer. You become my toha, and I'll give you your freedom and the leadership of the tribe you won this morning." As an afterthought, he added, "I'll even give the girl to you as a slave after I'm done with her."

Grendel barely kept control of his rage.

"If you refuse my generous offer," the king continued, his voice dropping into a warning growl of his own as he moved close to the table opposite Grendel, "I will have you flayed alive, and your flesh used to fill the troops' stew pot."

"How about you give her to me now," Grendel countered, the tension in the room rising to deadly levels, "and I let you keep your throne and your pathetic life? I take her, gather those we came here with, and we leave, never to return."

Kraagor looked surprised and began to laugh.

The sound grated on Grendel's nerves.

"I'll give you points for your brashness, but you must not have much in that thick head of yours," the king said, pointing a finger at Grendel. "None of you are leaving Chernigov alive. Not you. Not your friends. Not Marko Madasgorski. And certainly not this luscious tidbit."

Grendel stalked toward the king, his expression cold and hard. "I will kill you before I let you touch her again," he growled.

The orc king held his ground. The table between them was easily nine feet long by four feet wide, more than big enough to keep a lesser opponent at bay. Grendel, however, had other ideas. The table looked heavy. Six stout legs topped with thick planks so deeply stained with blood and body fluids that it was impossible to tell what type of wood they were. He gripped the edge of the table and pushed it forward, lifting as he went.

Kraagor's eyes grew wide as he realized the table was actually moving. Neither his slaves nor his strongest guards had ever managed to move it more than a few inches. Now, the rumbling protest of wood on stone filled the chamber with reverberations that made his teeth ache.

"Guards!" the king yelled.

Anger fought against the rising panic, and the king pushed back against the table, but it was no use. The table kept coming.

It was all too obvious that the óhreint meant to crush him between the table and the wall. His eyes darted to either side and he realized he could not get around the table before it trapped him.

"Guards!" the king yelled again. Where were they? Kraagor dropped to the floor and rolled under the table.

Pain exploded through the king as something slammed into his head, knocking him back against the wall. Dazed, he tried to roll out of the way of the table and found himself staring up at the portly mage Kourash fought in his throne room, that damnable staff in his hands. Kraagor had the briefest moment to wonder how the human could still be alive before he felt the table edge crash down across his legs, shattering both. Darkness swept over the king like the comfort of a lightless cave, and he knew no more.

Grendel rushed to Sacha. Her body hung limp on the chains, but life still beat within her. He reached down and quickly opened the shackles around her ankles. She dangled by her arms, so Grendel reached around her waist with one arm to relieve the pressure on her joints. When he did, a groan escaped her lips as she slowly floated back toward consciousness. With his free hand, he unscrewed the clevis pin in the shackle at her left wrist and moved to the next one.

Sacha's head flopped forward onto Grendel's chest. He placed a kiss on top of her head and inhaled. His fingers worked faster to undo the shackle.

As the shackle-pin holding her clenched right fist came free, Sacha's head lolled to one side. Her hand jerked down, and she struck Grendel full in the chest. A grunt escaped the half-orc. Her fist snatched back, holding a blood-coated blade.

The half-orc collapsed to the floor with Sacha on top of him, plunging her dagger repeatedly into his chest.

Jasper swung his staff as Sacha raised her arm for another blow, knocking the now-visible dagger from her hand with a clatter.

A sepulchral chill slid through the room, carrying the scent of brimstone. Sacha's glazed eyes snapped into focus, and she saw Grendel lying beneath her.

Sacha opened her mouth, but nothing came out. Horror contorted her features and tears rained onto Grendel's face as she collapsed forward over him.

Jasper wrapped his arms around Sacha from behind, pinning her limbs against her body. He tried to pull her away, but she fought the mage, not wanting to leave Grendel's side. Then, she began to scream.

Xandor and Chert rushed into the room, weapons drawn.

Sacha's scream became a constant wail as she struggled against Jasper. In one fluid motion, the ranger sheathed his sword and helped the mage wrestle her to the floor.

Chert threw down his hammer and helmet and knelt beside his friend.

As soon as Sacha was clear, the dwarf placed both hands on the half-orc's chest and closed his eyes in prayer. Blue light coursed down his arms into the half-orc, closing the wounds, but Grendel didn't respond.

The dagger had done its job.

CHAPTER 17:
KRAAGOR'S EXIT

October 29, 4235 K.E.

3:25am

"Move, Jasper," Xandor said through clenched teeth. "She killed Grendel."

Xandor knelt on the floor with Sacha's legs trapped beneath him. As he spoke, he drew a dagger from his belt and pressed the tip against her bare ribs, poised over her heart.

Jasper still had her arms pinned but let go when he felt her stop resisting. The mage stared at the fallen dagger.

"Look!"

Xandor followed Jasper's pointing finger in time to see the last of a shadowy blade melt into the stone floor, leaving only a blackened stain. "What was that?"

Jasper reached around Sacha and laid a hand on Xandor's, cautiously moving the blade away from her heart. "If I had to guess — an abyssal weapon," the mage replied in a whisper.

"So, her demon gave it to her."

"Yes, but I doubt she meant to use it on Grendel."

"Why?" Xandor glanced at Sacha and back toward the stain. "You think he tricked her?"

Harsh laughter erupted from the overturned table. Even through his pain, Bregu Kraagor reveled in the irony.

Jasper ignored the orc king and watched Sacha. She sat motionless on the floor, staring at Grendel's still form. Taking Xandor's cloak, he draped it over her shoulders. "I do," he said, answering Xandor's question.

Skyld stepped into the room. He cast a quick glance at Grendel lying on the floor and warned, "Hýðweard Bregu Kraagor néawung."

Xandor didn't understand the óhreint's words, but he heard the thudding of iron-shod feet heading down the hallway. He surged to his feet and said, "Chert, whatever you're going to do, be fast."

As Xandor and Skyld rushed to intercept the orc guards, Chert bent over Grendel and rhythmically compressed his giant rib cage. Bolts of bright blue light shot into Grendel's body, causing it to spasm.

The dwarf muttered, "Please, Eternal Father, do not take my friend. Please, Eternal Father, do not take my friend..."

He repeated the supplication each time he pushed on Grendel's chest, and each time, Grendel's body shook as the pulse of blue light traveled through it.

Metal on metal clashed outside.

The pool of healing light grew under the surface of Grendel's skin, spreading farther with each repetition of Chert's prayer to the Eternal Father. The light grew brighter and brighter until it became too painful to look upon. Dark shadows fled the room, and the noise of the fighting outside became distant. At its center, Chert hunched over Grendel, continuing his prayer.

Suddenly, the light flared and winked out. Chert felt the beating of Grendel's heart. He sat back on his heels, a prayer of thanksgiving on his lips.

Grendel's eyes flew open. He took in a ragged breath and let it out slowly. He sat up gingerly and glanced around, trying to recall how he ended up on the floor.

Beside him, Jasper stared at Chert.

The half-orc saw the dwarf resting with a tired smile on his face, but Chert looked different, older. Lines radiated from the corners of his eyes where none existed before, and a streak of grey ran through his beard.

Then he noticed Sacha, and it all came rushing back. He remembered sharp jabs of pain in his chest, but when he looked down there were no wounds. He ran a hand over his heart and felt shallow dimples marking two new scars.

Sacha huddled under a cloak, her eyes unfocused.

Harsh shouting erupted in the hallway, and everyone in the room looked at each other as if waking. The dwarf stood and offered the half-orc a hand. It was symbolic and Grendel knew it, but he nodded and took it anyway.

At first, Grendel felt fine, but once he was on his feet, the room spun. Chert grabbed him around the waist and kept him from falling down.

"I do not know if I can walk," Grendel said. His brow pinched with worry.

"You have to," the dwarf replied. "We're getting out of here."

Jasper recovered his senses when he heard shouting in orcnéan. He knelt beside Sacha and spoke her name, but received no response. He grabbed her by the shoulders and shook her gently. "Sacha. Sacha," he repeated, calling her back to the present.

She turned her head, and her eyes focused on the mage's face.

"We need you. Snap out of it."

Her lips moved, but nothing came out.

"Sacha," Jasper repeated more urgently.

Tear-filled eyes pleaded with Jasper. "I killed Grendel," she whispered.

"I know, but it wasn't your fault."

"I killed Grendel," she repeated, her voice tinged with rising hysteria.

Jasper gripped her shoulders tighter. He felt her shudder under his touch, and her eyes grew distant. Giving up on being nice, he slapped her cheek. "Sacha! We need you, now!"

Her cheek turned pink where Jasper struck her, and he felt guilty; however, the shock jarred her from her thoughts. She glared at the mage, and he watched some of her haughtiness return.

"Hearde hildefrecan! Ætstandaþ!"

Everyone turned to look at the door, even Kraagor.

A shriveled female orc dressed in dark purple and red robes entered the room, flanked by Xandor and Skyld. Behind them, a horde of orcs armored in red chain stood shoulder to shoulder in the narrow hallway, iron mancatchers gripped tight in their hands.

The orc matron glanced at the small group and then down at her son. A frown spread across her face when she saw his condition. There was none of the motherly concern Jasper would expect from a human, elf, or dwarf — only cold calculation.

She turned around and barked at the Red Guard, "Sweðraaþ!"

The orcs snarled and growled their displeasure but did as she said and backed away.

Xandor asked, "What's going on?"

Jasper turned to Sacha, who stood next to him, studying the old crone.

"Hwæt syndon gé?" she asked. *Who are you?*

The old orc pointed to Kraagor, lying on the floor, and answered, "Bregu Kraagor's móðor."

As soon as she said it, Sacha remembered their previous encounter. Trying to control the maelstrom of emotions inside her, she glanced from one to the other and said, "Hwanan éowre cyme syndon?"

The crone was quiet for a moment, her eyes drawn to the red lines that scored Sacha's body. The orc licked her lips, and the light of hunger burned in her eyes.

Seeing where the old orc was staring, Sacha drew Xandor's cloak closed and said, "Mínne gehýrað ánfealdne geþóht: ofost is sélest tó gecýðanne." The threatening tone in Sacha's voice was unmistakable, and everyone in the room gripped their weapons tighter.

Switching to Trakyan, the old lady turned to Grendel with a toothy smile and said, "Your kuchka needs some lessons in manners."

Sacha glared at the old orc and made to step forward, but Jasper held her back. However, Xandor didn't hesitate. He stepped closer, making sure the old orc knew that he was right behind her with the point of his sword.

"Why are you here, crone?" Grendel asked, still supported by Chert.

Móðor Kraagor stared intently into Grendel's eyes. To Jasper, it seemed she measured the tall half-orc, and he came up wanting. "You have not killed Kraagor. You could have been Bregu," she said with a certain amount of amazement.

"I do not want it," Grendel stated simply.

Her face fell, and everyone saw her thinking about her next question. "How do you plan to leave this city alive?"

Xandor said from behind her, "We'll take Kraagor hostage and use him to get out."

The old orc laughed and turned to face the ranger. "You don't know very much about us, do you?"

Unsure what she meant, he remained quiet, some of his previous confidence gone.

Sacha gestured to Jasper. He let her go and followed her to Kraagor. The bregu's eyes were those of a wounded animal. Together, he and Sacha stared at the king's crushed legs.

"Wounds like that, he'll be permanently crippled," Jasper murmured.

"Xandor, if they see him like this, they'll kill him," Sacha said finally. "He's of no use to us as a hostage."

Móðor Kraagor cackled.

Jasper searched the faces of the Red Guard waiting in the hallway. They didn't know. They hadn't seen their king — not yet.

Looking to both Sacha and Móðor Kraagor, Xandor asked, "If he dies, what happens to his family?"

Chert's eyes snapped up.

Jasper could see the worry in the dwarf's expression and recalled their bargain with Yfellice. He began to understand their perilous situation, and he answered the ranger's question. "They die, too."

"Doesn't Kraagor have a son or brother who would step forward?" Sacha asked, standing back up.

Móðor Kraagor answered, "He does, but he will be challenged by each of the toha before they accept him as the new bregu."

Jasper asked the crone, "If we make Kraagor look healthy, could we use him to get out of these chambers without having to fight every guard?"

"Maybe," she hedged.

Jasper turned to Xandor and said, "I have a plan."

The groans were audible, but no one stopped him.

"It won't get us out of the city, but it might give us some breathing room."

Everyone glanced at the guards. They were getting restless and looked ready to charge at any moment.

With a curt nod, he said, "Do it."

Gripping his staff, Jasper concentrated on the table. The magic was slow to respond. Sweat beaded his brow and his vision swam. Forcing himself to focus, the table rose slowly and righted itself.

Once the table was out of the way, he knelt beside Kraagor and noticed the odd positioning of his legs and the stain of blood on his robes — a compound fracture.

"Chert, I need your help."

The dwarf walked Grendel to the table's end before he assisted the mage. The two bent over the orc king.

"What do you think? Can you mend them?" Jasper asked.

The dwarf looked like he had a bitter taste in his mouth when he pulled up the hem of the orc's robe and examined his legs.

"Not all the way, but enough to get him on his feet if we splint them."

Kraagor smiled back at both of them.

"We do this, and you get us out of here. Agreed?" demanded Jasper.

The orc king quickly nodded his head and gasped, "Of course."

Jasper worked beside Chert, cleaning the wounds, and exposing fractured shards of bone that poked through the green-brown skin. Finding a leather strap, Jasper offered it to Kraagor. The orc king glared at the mage as if insulted. Instead, he nodded toward the dwarf.

Under Kraagor's steady gaze, Chert cut the swollen flesh with his knife, releasing a stream of cloudy grey humors. Beads of sweat dotted the orc king's forehead and his jaw muscles bulged under the pressure, but he remained silent.

When both ends of the bone were exposed, Chert gestured for Jasper to hold Kraagor's leg just below his knee. The dwarf shifted around, gripped the orc's ankle, and pulled with slow, steady pressure until the bone ends aligned.

Jasper reached for his magic. It slipped through his mental fingers like sand. He cast a furtive look at his companions and slipped a hand into his sporran. His fingertips brushed the black book. An icy chill slithered over his skin, spiking adrenaline into his blood. He reached for his magic again and wove shadowy strands around the bones to hold them in place as a splint.

At the same time, Chert pinched the orc king's flesh closed and prayed for healing. When he finished, angry-looking scabs covered the wounds. He frowned. "That's the best I can do for him," he said. "We'll have to bind the bandages tight and hope he can walk."

"We'll make it work," Xandor said. "One way or another, we're getting out of Chernigov."

Chert sighed and reached for the other leg.

While Jasper and Chert worked, Sacha stared down at her shredded clothes. The tattered remnants were a fitting metaphor for her life. It took all she had not to break down. Instead, she focused on getting out alive. She pulled on her boots, then knelt and rifled through the rags. She tucked her dagger inside her boot and fastened her necklace around her throat.

Sacha watched the others through the veil of her hair, all too aware of her precarious position.

Skyld resumed his position as Grendel's protector and said, "Nú ic, Grendel, þec, secg betosta, mé for lindgestealla wylle heald forð tela níwe sibbe."

Grendel didn't understand what Skyld said, but that didn't seem to matter. The óhreint turned his back and stooped to retrieve the dwarf's hammer, shield, and helmet. Skyld handed them to Grendel and turned to watch the door.

After Chert finished binding the wounds, he and Jasper helped Bregu Kraagor stand. He took a tentative step forward and breathed a sigh when his legs held his weight. A cunning look crossed the orc king's face.

"Kraagor, we own you," Jasper warned, his voice laced with a cruelty that seemed out of place for the portly mage. "You do as we say, and you might walk out of this alive. You lead us into a trap, and I'm taking you down with me. All I have to do is reverse the magic, and your legs will snap."

The orc king grinned. "All I have to do is yell for my guards, mage. Do not pretend to threaten me." He gripped Jasper's upper arm as though the mage were his prisoner. "Let's go. I want the lot of you out of my city."

Jasper escorted Bregu Kraagor to the door and down the hallway toward the Red Guard. Behind them, Xandor and Skyld walked with Móðor Kraagor.

Grendel, with Chert's assistance, met Sacha at the door. She glanced up at Grendel and placed her hand on his chest. The half-orc flinched at her touch. Hurt and shame warred in her heart, and she stepped back, eyes downcast.

"You need to go first," Chert said. "Stick close to Kraagor and that old crone so they don't double-cross us."

With a quick nod, she pulled Xandor's cloak tighter and slipped out past them, sparing a glance at Grendel. The look of hurt and confusion in his eyes sent another lance of pain through her.

In the hallway, Kraagor barked orders at his guards, demanding updates from the surface and sending others scurrying away to confirm Marko and Gregori's deaths. He gave Sacha a smug grin. The orc king's message was clear: *he* was in control here.

The group passed down a dark tunnel and emerged in the main room where Kraagor's children lived and played.

Chert spotted Yfellice sitting by herself. Winking at her as they passed, he caught the barest glimpse of burgundy when she stuffed her hands in her pockets. One of the female slaves stared at the little girl: her mother. She was a shapely woman with a haunted look in her eyes and a history of old bruises and scars writ across the exposed portions of her skin. She watched Bregu Kraagor with a mixture of despondency and fear. All the human women in the room had the same look.

Helplessness seeped into his marrow as he observed the different women and children. Looking at his companions, he saw it in their eyes, too, but didn't know what he could do. How could they save all these people? What about the slaves in the forge? And once they got to the surface, what then? The orcs would slaughter these people. Would they prefer that to the horrors of their everyday life? What if saving them jeopardized finding the cure to the plague ravaging Pazard'zhik?

He looked at Yfellice again. Somehow, she had found a life in this dismal place — found someone to share it. Would she even want to go?

Kraagor led them through the chamber and down a side passage. After a few turns, it emptied into a narrow tunnel with an arched ceiling. At the end was an ironbound door with rusted rivets. Taking a key from his pocket, he inserted it into the padlock and twisted. The gears and tumblers shrieked from lack of use, but eventually, they fell into place and the lock clicked. He pulled open the door, revealing inky blackness.

"This leads to the surface near the center of town, but it isn't guarded. As you can see, I haven't used it in a long time."

"This better not be a trap," Xandor said.

"Ranger, this is the quickest route to the surface. Trust me, I want you gone as much as you do."

"Is there a path that can get us outside the walls of the city?" Xandor asked.

"No. I'm afraid all paths up lead into the city. I didn't want someone accidently stumbling across an unguarded back door."

Xandor peered into the stygian depths, thinking about what Kraagor said. It made sense, but he couldn't shake the feeling the king was holding something back. Finally, he nodded. "All right. Let's go."

CHAPTER 18:
A MOTHER'S CHOICE

October 29, 4235 K.E.

5:36am

Stepping past the threshold, Jasper held up his lit staff to get a better view. Gossamer webs filled the narrow passage, clinging to the stone walls like glistening curtains. Multi-faceted eyes winked back at him before scurrying into the shadows. At the front of the line, Skyld sliced through the layers of webbing, creating a path for the group. Behind him, he heard the distinct click of the lock after Kraagor shut the door.

"Jasper, you still have a connection to that magic in his legs, right?" Xandor asked uncertainly.

"Yes. If this is a trap..." Jasper trailed off.

"There's a set of stairs," Chert announced. The light revealed rough-hewn steps that began a slow spiral to the surface. Shrouded with even more cobwebs, jagged walls loomed to either side.

One behind the other, they traveled clockwise up the stairs. It seemed backward for normal construction until Jasper realized it was built to defend the caverns. Then again, the walls were so close, it didn't matter which way the attack was coming.

Cobwebs coated his clothes and hair, and he felt weighted down by the sticky strands. He had lost track of time and distance, and instead, focused on placing one foot in front of the other.

A zephyr of fresh air tickled his nose and with it came a sense of relief. They were finally getting out of the city.

"I can't do this," said Chert.

The group stopped.

"Do what?"

"Leave without rescuing those women and children."

Xandor stared up the stairs and back down at Chert, who was still assisting Grendel. "How do you propose we do that? Reaching the surface is just the beginning. We'll have to fight our way out and, with every orc in the city standing against us, there's no guarantee we'll survive, let alone anyone who comes with us."

"I don't know, but I can't just leave them."

"I agree with Chert," Grendel said, his deep voice resonating off the walls.

"Can you even fight?" Xandor asked candidly.

"I will sure as hell try."

Jasper could see the ranger felt the same, but he didn't know how they could manage it. Wiping his face with his hand, he closed his eyes. A short nap and a meal would do him a world of good right about now.

"You know most of them will die if we do this," Xandor said.

"They'll die anyway, the difference here being a slow death or a quick one," Chert replied.

"Let's at least give them the choice," Sacha said. Everyone stared at her, surprised.

Grimacing, Xandor took out his journal and scribbled something on the blank page. He wished he could be there when Lord Fergusson read *that* message. "Fine. Let's go back down."

Jasper wove his magic into the old padlock, letting it work the tumblers. After a few seconds, the padlock snapped open and fell to the floor with a metallic jangle.

Blade drawn, Xandor pushed the door open with the toe of his boot and entered the hallway. The group formed up behind him and listened.

"We'll be on the run so, Grendel and Skyld, stay here and hold the hallway," Xandor said. "The rest of you, with me."

Grendel rested with his back to the door while Sacha translated. After she finished, Skyld nodded and unsheathed his massive two-handed sword.

Chert and Grendel clasped wrists. "Good luck. Bring back Yfellice. I like her," the half-orc said.

"Will do."

Xandor led the small group down the narrow tunnel and into the hallway. Deserted chambers and side passages went by in a blur as the ranger backtracked.

Outside the entrance to the main room, Xandor stopped and motioned for Chert and Jasper. After a few words, the two disappeared, Jasper using his magic, and Chert slipping into the floor.

Children played in the large room while their mothers watched. There was no sign of any guards, so Xandor stepped into the room, followed closely by Sacha, and found the nearest human. It was difficult to tell through all the dirt and grime, but the red-haired girl appeared to be young, in her late teens at most. Holding the hem of her ragged skirt was a little boy with a pudgy face who had the wide, unsteady stance of one who recently learned to stand.

When she saw the ranger, her eyes flew wide, and she froze in place like frightened deer.

Móðor Kraagor hissed when she spotted Xandor and Sacha. She lifted her robes above her ankles and ran toward the nearest exit, but before she had made it halfway, a dwarven hand reached up from the floor and tripped her. She screamed as she fell and struggled to regain her footing.

Wrapping both his hands around her, Chert dragged her below the surface of the stone, her wails for mercy cut short.

Jasper gestured with his staff, and a mass of air congealed around several orc matrons, muffling their shouts as sure as the tightest gag.

"We don't have much time," Xandor announced. "If you want to leave with us, decide now. I can't guarantee that we'll make it out alive, but I promise you we'll give it our best."

The women stared at each other. Suspicion clouded their eyes, but there was also a hint of desperate yearning.

An orc barked an order from one of the passages, and guards in red chain appeared at all but one of the exits, their eyes shining in the dim light. Kraagor must have expected they would return.

Xandor shouted, "Let's go!"

Many of the women and some of the older children snatched up the younger ones and rushed toward the one exit absent of guards. Others simply ran. It was impossible to tell how many there were. They disappeared into the passageway, leaving behind those who chose to stay or who became separated by the advancing orcs.

Chert found Yfellice and knelt beside her.

"Come. We can get you and your mom out of here."

Yfellice's mother watched, but didn't interfere.

With huge tears forming in her eyes, the young girl shook her head.

"I can't. Not without Daegal," Yfellice said.

Chert looked from daughter to mother. They had the same intent look in their eyes.

"As you wish," Chert said sadly. Before he stood, he placed a hand on her head and said a silent prayer.

"Come on!" Xandor shouted. He had taken a scimitar from an opponent and had his longsword coursing with bright flames.

Jasper guided the children down the passage using small glowing balls colored red, blue, yellow, and green.

Guards erupted from the tunnels.

Chert stood and held out his hand to Yfellice's mother.

The woman stared at her daughter and said, "I stay where she stays."

Chert gripped her arm tightly. Letting it go, he ran after the trail of women and children.

Lights flared down the tunnel from Jasper's magic, and Chert hurried forward, worried the mage might try something more extreme. Sounds of fighting echoed in the hall, and the screams of women and children followed.

Using a side passage, orc guards had outflanked the line of people and hewed mercilessly into the crowd.

Chert couldn't throw his hammer, so he pushed inside the cavern wall. He came out behind the orcs and grabbed one by the jerkin. Swinging his hammer underhanded, he crushed the orc's knee, causing him to fall into one of his companions.

More blood splattered when an orc ripped into one of the fleeing children.

"Heofonléoht!" Chert yelled and pointed. Light poured from every orifice in the orc's head. Screaming, the guard dropped his weapon and clawed at his eyes. One of the fleeing women scooped up the fallen sword and ran him through.

The line continued to move forward, and Chert lost track of how many orcs he killed and how many slaves died. More orcs streamed out of side passages, and Chert found himself surrounded.

Scimitars clashed against Chert's shield as he spun around, forcing the orcs to focus on him rather than the line of retreating people.

A dark shape loomed next to him, appearing as if from nowhere, and tore the ring of orcs asunder. At first, Chert thought it was Grendel, then he realized it was Skyld. The óhreint cut a swath through the orcs with his two-handed sword.

The two stood back to back in the dark hallway as they fought against the ever-increasing tide of orcs, shifting and turning in a slow retreat. The line of women and children was gone. All they had to do was keep backing slowly and give everyone time to get into the stairwell. Orcs fell before them, but more took their place, stepping over the bodies.

Chert slammed his shield against his opponent and heard a loud crack from the orc's wrist. Skyld swung over the dwarf's head, taking advantage of their different heights and his longer weapon to wreak havoc. The two fought well together and continued their steady progression toward the shaft leading to the surface.

A flash of red chain appeared in front of them, and an iron tether shot out from behind the wall of orcs. The collar clanged against Chert's shield and disappeared into the crowd.

Chert yelled a warning to Skyld, but he couldn't tell if the óhreint heard or even understood.

Another iron tether shot out. It was another blind attack that crashed against Chert's shield. The dwarf deflected it and slammed his hammer into the body of an orc. The iron rod bounced off the shield and jerked to the side, catching Skyld on the leg. The tether closed around the plate armor. Lacking contact with the óhreint's skin, it could not cause pain, but it hampered his movements.

Skyld kicked, driving the pole attached to his leg into the crowd. The next moment, an orc tripped over the pole, fell, and brought his neighbor down with him. The added weight on the pole pinned the óhreint in place. Several orcs launched themselves at Skyld, and their blades clanged against his cuirass. Using only one hand, Skyld slashed with his sword and cut down one of his opponents.

Chert shoved with his shield, forcing the orcs back. Beyond the crowd, he heard deeper voices yelling. The orc guards had reinforcements.

More iron tethers launched from the crowd toward the óhreint. He swung his sword and deflected two of them, but a third clasped around the vambrace protecting his wrist. His sword stroke went wide and struck Chert's helmet a glancing blow.

With two of the collars attached to him, the Red Guard slowly dragged Skyld into the writhing mass. Chert beat at the iron rods, but all it did was jerk Skyld around.

A nervous chattering sound grew from the orcs. They glanced at each other fitfully, and then a loud booming sound echoed down the hall. Chert risked a quick glance behind him and thought he saw the exit. However, he also saw another crowd of attackers rushing toward him. Among their number came several ogres carrying iron spears with wicked hooks at their tips.

They were surrounded.

Skyld twisted his arm around, grabbed the rod attached to his vambrace, and jerked it from the orc on the other end. He gave the rod a sharp twist to release it, and swung the pole in a whistling arc, opening a small gap in the attackers. Through it, Chert saw more ogres surging toward the front. They crushed the orcs in their way. One picked up an orc body and threw it toward the two warriors. Skyld ducked to the side to avoid it, and the body landed beside him in a heap of torn flesh and gore.

Another body sailed through the air, bounced off the ceiling, and slammed into Chert's shield. Off balance, the dwarf took several steps back, and a pair of orcs took his place. They struck at Skyld from the side while others attacked him from the front.

Chert crashed into them with his shield, but the damage was done. He and Skyld were separated.

With a bellow, Skyld launched himself at the orcs, yelling and slashing with his weapon. He threw a quick glance at Chert and shouted something in orcnéan.

The surrounding orcs threw Chert back against the wall. He pushed and shoved to get free, but the press of bodies kept him pinned.

An ogre got a hold on the iron rod at Skyld's leg. He jerked the óhreint's leg out from under him. Skyld crashed to the floor, and another ogre plowed through the line of orcs to grab Skyld's other leg.

Yelling, the dwarf struggled to reach the óhreint, but with each orc that went down, another immediately took his place. It was a battle of attrition, and Chert grew more exhausted by the minute.

Skyld growled furiously and sank his teeth into the ogre's leg. Black blood gushed, but the ogre ignored the wound, snatched a scimitar from a nearby orc, and plunged it deep into the óhreint's armor. Skyld snarled and slashed at the ogre. In the brief moment of respite, the óhreint found the dwarf and shoved his weapon toward him. "Grendel!"

Chert clenched his jaw and tried to shut out the orcs' victory cries. With a prayer on his lips, he retreated into the wall.

CHAPTER 19:
CROSSING THE KILLING FIELD

October 29 , 4235 K.E.

5:56am

Predawn light cast the foggy world in a surreal glow. Hidden by the low hanging streamers, Sehraine and the Ivanov brothers glided across the water toward the orcnéan port. Moving north against the sluggish shoreline current, they crept past small, dilapidated vessels moored to listing docks.

Sixty feet above the river surface, the orange glow of fire marked the top of Chernigov's shrouded walls. Disembodied voices drifted down to them as the orcs and their allies vainly searched the smoke and fog for the next attack or worked on repairing the damage caused by the wind rider.

One by one, the stone piers and arches supporting the Rainbow Bridge appeared from the fog. The stygian shadows made each one seem like a portal to the underworld. From their position, Sehraine could only make out five of the fifteen arches that carried the bridge deck over the White River. The openings were wide enough for two ships to pass without fear of collision. Sergei Nikoloff told her the centermost spans had room for two huge ships and a full-grown dragon overhead, but she felt certain the bard was joking. Then again, humans seemed to love grand architectural statements.

Sehraine whispered, "There's the first cog," and pointed to a dark, blurry shape. The deck looked deserted.

They slowly worked their way north among the other boats and ships dotting the water, all in varying states of disrepair. Lev looked around one last time, took his sack, and slid into the frigid water, trying not to rock the boat as he went. A plume of rainbow colors marred the surface where he disappeared.

A cargo boat bearing down on them shattered their calm.

"Hwæt!" exclaimed Yevgeny. He pulled hard on the oars, frantically moving them out of the other boat's path.

Sehraine's sharp elven sight picked out the dark-furred form of a dreyri hovering over the bow, vulture-like. Beneath a shock of white hair, his cruel short-muzzled face reflected his disappointment at not having run them over. Her first emotion was a tingle of anger, quickly replaced by the thrilling knowledge that their costumes had passed their first test. She grinned beneath her hood and tossed out her fishing line. Then she bolted upright.

Yevgeny looked up at her in concern. "What?"

"Which cog was that?" she whispered urgently. It was a silly question, and she knew it, but could not stop herself asking, "Was that our boat?"

"How the hell should I know?" Yevgeny whispered, and then ducked his head. "Beg pardon," he murmured.

They continued on their way, searching for the ship they planned to use to rescue Dobrynya and his men. When they passed under the bridge, Sehraine peered up into the gloom, trying to estimate its height.

"Yevgeny, how tall is this bridge?" she whispered.

The river pirate shrugged. "I haven't measured it myself, but I was told the two arches under the bridge apex clear over a hundred and fifty feet, depending on water level and the season."

Sehraine shook her head in wonder.

A handful of boats similar to their own headed back toward the shore. Their crews wore hoods pulled low to protect sensitive eyes from the burning rays of the rising sun. The soothing darkness of night was almost over.

She supposed fishing was a necessary evil for those in the city. The orcs, of course, preferred the taste of warm-blooded creatures, but it was unlikely there were enough humans or herd animals to support a population as large as theirs, leaving them a choice between fish and cannibalism.

Sehraine turned her attention back to the docks. They were about fifty feet away from an empty stretch of pier, one she recognized from the maps of Chernigov they'd studied. "Our boat is gone!"

"What now?" Yevgeny asked urgently. "Abort?"

"No. Dobrynya and his people are counting on us. Continue as before. Go for the third boat."

"Will the wind rider know?"

"Yes." Her voice sounded much more certain than she felt.

Yevgeny nodded and pulled on the oars again, moving them around the pier and farther northward.

6:18am

Sitting atop his warhorse, Knyaz Dorinkov turned to Poruchik Tirinko. "Are our men in position?"

Vassily smiled behind his beard. The prince's anxiety was showing. He had asked the same question three times in the last quarter hour. Not once in that time had they received a messenger from the last unit, stating readiness. "Not yet, Highness. Soon."

"That's what you said five minutes ago," replied Dorinkov.

The western sky was still dark, even without the ever-present smoke above Chernigov. The sun wouldn't rise for at least another half hour. There was barely enough light to illuminate the tops of the city walls roughly a mile away. The knyaz took a sip of tepid kofe from his tin.

The light grew with each passing minute. Separating them from the bridge were the fifteen-foot-high walls and towers of the Keep. The Rhodinan prince had a clear view of the bodies hanging from its battlements, some of whom he recognized. A layer of decades-old grime covered the black and grey streaked walls. Above it all, a moon-and-skull flag flew from the ramparts of the gatehouse, mocking them — but it also told him they had a favorable wind.

Staring through the trees, Knyaz Dorinkov studied the two hundred yards of killing field in front of the Keep. He grimaced.   Old foundations stuck up like tombstones. Reports suggested the ground was firm, but the orcs might have dug pits. There was no way to know for sure until they crossed it.

Sunrise crept closer.

Mikhail and his shadow, Mattias, ran up, their breath fogging in the frigid air. "Knyaz, Vityaz Valenki and his men are ready."

"Are the charges set?"

Mikhail nodded.

"Excellent," Dorinkov said. "Return immediately and tell him to start the attack."

Mikhail and Mattias saluted smartly and raced away.

Knyaz Dorinkov looked down at his kofe. It had grown cold. He tossed it out and grumbled, "I hate waiting."

Several minutes later, a cloud of smoke plumed from the far side of the Keep, followed closely by the distant, rumbling boom of an explosion. Trumpets blew, signaling the first wave of Dorinkov's men north of the Keep to charge the walls.

Grey smoke obscured the killing field, and battle cries split the air when four ranks of soldiers armored in chain and hard leather raced from the line of trees and across the open field. It was a mixed crew, with the first and third ranks bearing tall pavise shields, the second armed with longbows, and the fourth carrying scaling ladders in addition to their normal weapons. A standard-bearer with a cotton broadcloth gonfalon, checkered purpure and argent, kept pace beside the men.

The men of the front rank stopped midway on the field and set their shields by shoving the foot spikes into the ground. The second rank took aim and fired at their foes on the ramparts.

The screams of wounded orcs filled the air in response to the whistling hail of Rhodinan arrows. Whips cracked and guttural voices barked orders inside the Keep. The orcs behind the battlements returned fire. Sporadic at first, the orcs' black arrows buried themselves harmlessly in the ground or the large shields, but as the orcs recovered, their return fire rapidly increased in volume. The soldiers' shields gave them decent cover, but several arrows snuck through the makeshift wall, claiming the first Rhodinan casualties.

6:50am

Leftenant Gallagher watched the sky from his vantage point in a glen east of the Keep, waiting for the signal to attack. A dull boom echoed through the trees, and smoke streamed into view. Brian waited a few short minutes before giving Yana a curt nod. She nodded in response, secured her barbute, and kicked off with her flyer, rising out of the small clearing. Once over the trees, she headed southwest. He watched until she disappeared, then turned to his runners. "Tell the troops it's time. When the gate blows, follow me."

They nodded and ran to their units.

CHAPTER 20:
ESCAPE

October 29, 4235 K.E.

7:00am

Inside the narrow tunnel, Xandor stood behind a wall of air. On the other side, orcs and ogres struck the barrier with anything they could lay their hands on, including feces and body parts. Beside him, Jasper continued concentrating on his spell. Xandor tried not to notice the growing pallor or the fever blotches blooming on the mage's sweat streaked face. They needed him to hold the wall.

At least the women and children were all inside the stairwell, climbing to the surface with Sacha leading the way.

"Where are Chert and Skyld?" Xandor asked.

Grendel stood beside them, his face lined with worry.

Chert suddenly emerged from the tunnel wall. Propped against his shoulder, he held a long two-handed sword that still dripped with black blood. The scrapes, dents, and gore covering his armor spoke more than any words.

The furrows in Grendel's brow deepened as he searched the horde beyond Jasper's barrier for signs of Skyld. There was a flicker of sadness in the big man's expression when he took the sword Chert offered him, but the look was gone in an instant, replaced by grim determination.

"Let's move," Xandor said.

Chert eyed the door, noticing they could neither lock nor brace it from the stair side. "The three of you go. I'll lock up out here and join you." When the dwarf appeared inside the stairwell a moment later, he grinned. "That should hold them."

Jasper almost collapsed when he released the wall of air. Exhausted, yet determined to see freedom, he leaned heavily on his staff and started up the slow spiral.

Heavy pounding from the ironbound door echoed. Pulling up the rear, Chert helped Grendel navigate the steps, and the two struggled to match the ranger's pace.

"Hurry up! Sacha's almost at the top!" Xandor yelled down to them.

The two scowled but didn't say anything. They pushed harder and continued climbing.

With a loud metallic bang, the door below burst open, and the clank of iron-shod feet followed.

Grendel and Chert stared at each other briefly — *not again.* While Grendel continued the arduous climb, Chert knelt, dipping his hands into the stone tread, and fashioned sharp spikes of rock. After repeating the process with several more steps, he turned and took off after Grendel.

Xandor worked his way through the knot of refugees. They cringed away from him and huddled together for comfort. Despite their fear, the desperate need for a miracle shone in each of the women's faces. He just hoped he could give it to them.

The ranger found Sacha waiting at the foot of a wooden ladder. She pointed up with the stylus from his journal, illuminating a trapdoor made of oaken planks. She placed a hand on his arm and whispered, "Good luck."

"Thanks," Xandor replied as he climbed the ladder. At the top, he tested the trap door and found it secured in place. Why was nothing ever easy?

He climbed two rungs higher, folding himself into a crouch, braced his feet, and shoved a shoulder into the door. It creaked and groaned, revealing a few inches of the black void beyond. Xandor motioned to Sacha for the light.

Orc growls echoed up the stairwell. The women and children cast fearful glances behind them and jostled closer to the ladder.

Bracing himself again, Xandor shoved the wooden door the rest of the way open, letting it slam against the floor above with a sharp crack. His light spilled into the bare cavern. On the far side, another ladder led up to a trapdoor secured by a heavy timber set into a series of rusted brackets: two riveted to the wood door and two set into the adjacent stone.

A loud thunderclap, followed by the clash of weapons, started several of the smaller children crying. He clenched his jaw and resisted the urge to reprimand them for the noise, knowing it would only make matters worse. Instead, he slid down the ladder and passed the light to Sacha.

"Get them up there. We'll be right behind you." He didn't wait for her to reply, or to see if she followed orders. Taking the steps two at a time, he charged back down to find his friends.

The sounds of fighting grew louder. Flashes of white light illuminated the dark stairs followed by guttural screams and shouts.

Jasper, one hand on his staff and the other buried in his sporran, stood several steps above Chert and Grendel. The three faced off against the orc horde. Dead bodies lay on the steps in front of them.

Pointing his staff over Chert's head, Jasper yelled, "Astrapí!" Lightning arced, striking the front line of orcs, blasting them backwards.

Orcs pooled into the gap and piled the bodies of their comrades, creating a makeshift barrier. Archers moved into position and fired at the trio. Their arrows hit a shield of air and snapped with a clatter.

"What's going on?" Xandor asked when he reached them.

Jasper replied, "We've got them stopped, but the more we kill, the more there are."

Patting the mage on the shoulder, Xandor said, "Let me pass." As the mage shifted back, the ranger dug through Jasper's box, turning and folding the various compartments until he found what he was looking for, a compartment filled with various flasks and jars. '*Two will have to do,*' he thought to himself, pulling out two glass bottles filled with a clear liquid. "Get ready to drop your shield"

"You sure?"

"Yes." With the refolded box back in his pouch, the blonde ranger twisted the wax-coated corks free. He stepped beside Grendel and said, "Now!"

The air shimmered as the spell collapsed.

Squeezing in front of Chert, Xandor zinged the stoppers at the archers and doused the wall of bodies in front of them.

"Everyone run!"

Jasper turned and staggered up the stairs, heavy gasps following each step. In his wake, hastily shot black arrows struck the walls and ceiling.

"Chert!"

"Got it," the dwarf grunted, hoisting up his shield. Behind him, Grendel's swept Skyld's large sword back and forth over Chert's head, using his long reach to keep the orcs at bay.

"Grendel, get going," said Xandor. "I'll help Chert."

Chert kept his shield raised, giving Grendel time to disengage and retreat. As Grendel stepped back, Xandor jumped into his place, shouting, "Aduro!" Flames coursed up his longsword, filling the stairwell with dancing shadows.

"Ready?" the ranger asked.

"For what?" Chert said, maneuvering his shield to cover them both.

"Something nasty."

Xandor plunged his burning blade into a body at their feet. The lamp oil burst into flames, engulfing the fallen orcs and dangling webs. Smoke filled the shaft, hiding them from the archers.

Crouching low, Xandor said, "Let's go. Maybe that will buy us enough time to get out of here."

Chert looked at the burning orc bodies and wrinkled his nose at the smell, then raced after the ranger.

CHAPTER 21:
ONCE MORE UNTO THE BREACH

October 29, 4235 K.E.

7:00am

From their position across the river, Sehraine and Yevgeny watched smoke billow up from the riverside wall of the Keep, following the boom of an explosion. Muddy water lapped against the newly exposed foundations. The outer wythe of blocks between the bridge and the northwest tower teetered a moment before collapsing and spilling out into the river. She willed the inner wythe to fall as well, but it held, evoking a sigh of disappointment.

Sehraine's keen hearing detected a series of explosions, tiny by comparison and almost inaudible against the cacophony of frantic orc voices along the waterfront, as fire and smoke marched across the Keep's eastern battlements. The shadow of a single smudged shape flitted through the smoky air, and Sehraine could imagine orcs, rubble, and pieces of war engines raining down both inside and outside the compound.

"There go the engines on the eastern wall," she muttered so low that Yevgeny, sitting next to her, didn't seem to hear what she said. She cocked her head, straining for the next sounds.

7:01am

Screams erupted on the killing field when the few engines on the north wall fired into the first wave of soldiers. Head-sized stones whistled through the air, propelled faster than a herd of warhorses, and plowed through the line of pavise shields, some bouncing as far as the tree line.

The remaining Rhodinans raised their shields in a turtle formation and raced to the foot of the wall. Ladders sprang into the air, followed by grappling hooks attached to thickly braided ropes.

A single horn rang out, and the second wave issued forth from the wood line. Like the first wave, shield-bearers lead the way for archers and skirmishers.

A screech of metallic protest caused everyone to pause. Orcs yanked on ropes attached to gears and pulleys, and the catapult on the northeast tower rotated into position. It fired, and a volley of stones cut a twenty-foot swath through the second wave of soldiers, leaving the shattered remains of broken bodies in the bloodied mud. As more volleys fired, the Rhodinan casualties mounted horrifically.

Knyaz Dorinkov's jaw clenched, and his fists tightened as he watched the carnage through his spyglass. He forced himself to stand still and watch. The main attack had yet to start. '*Where the hell are those Glaxons*?' he thought. He expected to see them at the eastern treeline by now, but the forest was dark and still.

He scanned the Keep and saw a few of his people fighting along the top of the wall.

The wind rider streaked out of the smoke, targeting the catapult. The top of the northeast tower exploded, raining down chunks of stone. She swept over the courtyard and released the last of her arsenal. Orc archers turned away from the army on the field and fired into the air after her.

In her wake, the engine lay in ruins and burned furiously, its smoke rising to join the hanging clouds.

Taking advantage of the sudden reprieve, the survivors of the second wave raised their shields and raced forward, dodging around the bodies and furrows left by the boulders. They added their numbers to the soldiers in the first wave and grabbed up the ladders and hooks that lay scattered on the ground.

Knyaz Dorinkov panned over and saw Vityaz Valenki send the third wave of soldiers charging across the killing field. Linking shields, the group kept a tight formation. At the last moment, a large, brown, dome-shaped object protecting two men broke away and ran toward the Keep. The few remaining archers on the wall sighted on the leather-wrapped siege bell and fired. Some arrows stuck, but most bounced harmlessly off the scale-like layers.

The siege bell continued its run. It reached the east wall and raced along its base as hand-held boulders rained down, trying to stop the odd contraption. Dorinkov watched the wood frame shudder under the onslaught, stones rolling down the sides and bouncing across the ground, but the men inside kept moving. Ahead of them loomed the gatehouse.

The siege bell paused, first on one side of the gate, then the other, before racing away toward the southern tree line. It was halfway across the killing field when an explosion rocked the countryside, and a fountain of rocks and wooden debris flew into the air. Smoke shrouded the main gate. Knyaz Dorinkov smiled grimly as he listened to the distant clamor of voices raised in a war cry.

7:15am

Through the slits of his visor, Lord Fergusson watched the Rhodinan attack on the Keep. He raised his sword on high. As the doors blasted apart, he shouted, "For the Eternal Father, the Highlord, and the Tower!"

He swept his sword down and forward while spurring his charger. The Knight Commander's bugler sounded his clarion call, and dozens of throats roared their battle cries.

Leading both Iron Tower and Rhodinan knights, Lord Fergusson galloped across the killing field, jumping boulders, and dodging old foundations. A war engine on the Keep wall trained on the knights, and he vaguely heard the whistling of missiles over the thunder of their hooves. A horse screamed as it tripped over a shallow stone wall and crashed to the ground, throwing its rider.

Lord Fergusson didn't slow until he reached the smoke cloud clinging to the wall. Visibility dropped to practically nothing. He proceeded cautiously, letting the smoke thin. The explosion had torn the right half of the gate completely off its hinges and tossed it into the courtyard beyond. The left half dangled precariously by one hinge. He kicked it as he went by, nudging it open farther, and heard the knights behind him do likewise.

With silent murder holes above them dripping black orc blood, they clattered over the fallen gate. Still shrouded in the grey-and-white cloud, they entered the courtyard. The Knight Commander waited a few heartbeats at the threshold for his troops to regroup.

Two stone and brick buildings spewed a stream of screaming orcs to reinforce the north wall. On the far side, the Rainbow Bridge with its massive, fifty-foot-wide deck stood empty, framed by the Keep wall.

Lord Fergusson spurred his horse into a charge toward the orcs guarding the main thoroughfare. His horsemen followed behind him and crashed into the roiling mass of bodies like a hammer hitting a rotten melon. They burst through the outer fringe with little resistance, leaving broken bodies behind, but the resistance increased the farther they went until, finally, they slowed to a sticky crawl. Red and black blood mixed freely over the flagstones, making them slick.

The orcs quickly recovered from the shock of the explosion and the surprise of finding knights of the Iron Tower in their midst. Hulking shapes appeared behind the orc ranks as ogres waded forward, carrying long, barbed spears. They thrust them into the cavalry, felling horses and horsemen alike. One ogre punched his spear completely through a knight's shield and vambrace. He yanked it back, and the barbs dragged the knight off his horse into the mass of orcs.

"Push through!" Lord Fergusson shouted. "Forward!"

The mounted warriors swung their swords and axes in vicious arcs, hacking at the orcs around them. Their horses stamped, bit, and kicked, and slowly the tide turned.

"Make a hole!" a female voice shouted over the din of the fighting.

Lord Fergusson glanced back to see Dame Astrid at the head of the next wave of knights. In a flurry of fighting, the cavalry shifted, and an opening formed down the center. Orcs poured into the gap and threatened to outflank the front line.

Dame Astrid spurred her destrier, Wirbelsturm, forward. Men formed behind her in a flying wedge formation and charged. They ran down the orcs, killing them with the flash of a sword and a crunch of hooves.

On either side of the formation, long spears worried at the knights and their steeds. Although their charge devastated the enemy ranks, the humanoids were doing their fair share of damage to the invaders. First one knight, then another was pulled from the saddle. Smaller ballistae, called scorpions, rained stones into their midst from above, hitting knights and orcs alike.

"Stay in formation! Stay in formation!" Lord Fergusson shouted.

Ahead of him, Dame Astrid's wedge hewed through the enemy, killing what orcs they could, and pushed forward.

Spears thrust at them from both sides, smashing against shield and armor in a thundering cacophony that drowned out the sounds of their horses' iron shod hooves.

In the heat of battle, he wasn't aware of the enemy's thinning numbers until he suddenly found himself in the open, staring at the bridge deck.

They were through.

Fergusson caught up to Dame Astrid at the foot of the bridge. For the first time in a quarter century, knights traveled the multicolored deck. He gave the knight on his left a nod of approval and slowed their pace to a trot so those behind could catch up and reform the line.

A loud cheer went up from the ranks.

Lord Fergusson surveyed the expanse of abandoned defenses before him. Now came the hard part: they had to hold the bridge.

Leftenant Gallagher led his infantry at a run behind the cover of the faster cavalry. As they funneled through the gatehouse, the orcs were just starting to flank the stalled cavalry. He paused to collect the front-runners of his unit. The guttural shouts of orc archers preceded a rain of black arrows into the courtyard. Brian spotted the stairs to the battlements and led his troops in that direction.

Horns blared, and Knyaz Dorinkov led his men through the shattered remains of the gatehouse and into the courtyard of the Keep. The Rhodinans reinforced the Iron Tower and hit the orc resistance hard.

As Knyaz Dorinkov's troops surged forward, the orcs resorted to hit-and-run tactics. The battle grew bloodier, both sides refusing to give quarter as they hacked at one another in an orgy of hate and destruction.

CHAPTER 22:
THE CHUCK WAGON

October 29, 4235 K.E.

7:15am

"It won't take them long to get through this trapdoor," Jasper said.

Xandor watched the ladder below catch fire and crumble. "I know, but I don't plan to wait around for them. Chert, can you fix the door so they can't open it?"

"Aye," Chert said, shutting the trapdoor. He stooped over and worked the stone around the edges, pinching it on all four sides and binding the wood.

Meanwhile, Xandor crossed the room to the other ladder. At the top, Sacha canted her head to one side and peeked through the cracked trapdoor. The heavy timber lay propped against the wall beside the ladder.

Somewhere along the way, she'd managed to don the ill-fitting clothes she picked up in Kraagor's harem. *'It's hard to believe she's a Baroness from Pazard'zhik,'* he mused.

"It's similar to the mound we used to enter the caves," she reported. "Only smaller."

"That explains these," he replied, gesturing to a pair of ropes hanging through notches in the doorframe. "Anything up there?"

"Trash. I can't see anything else."

While Sacha climbed down, he quickly checked on the women and children crowded in the cavern, sharing words of encouragement as he went. They were scared, but there was something else. He could read it in their faces — whether they lived or died, they were free.

Sacha laid a hand on his arm. "You ready?"

Xandor turned to her and said, "I'll go first, and you follow. Chert, Jasper, and Grendel, make sure everyone gets out."

When the ranger shoved on the trapdoor, its rusted hinges groaned in protest, but finally gave.

'Outside at last!'

Climbing the rest of the way up, he crawled out and crept to the entrance of the mound. Hidden behind a rank pile of debris and refuse, he watched the orc traffic on the street. Sacha joined him. Behind her, the first of the women and children made room for those below.

"How do we get out of here?" she asked him.

"I was thinking the front door. It's the only one that's open."

Sacha stared at him in surprise but didn't say anything. Instead, she scooped up a toddler intent on making his way outside and hurried over to return him to the other women.

Chert, Grendel, and Jasper crouched beside Xandor. "Everyone's up," Chert said.

"Good, let's finish this," he replied. He returned to the ladder, burned it like the previous one, and had Chert jam the trapdoor shut. Afterward, he asked, "Jasper, can you find that chuck wagon?"

"Maybe. Why?"

"We're going to need it."

Jasper leaned on his staff and concentrated. He turned slowly and finally stopped. He opened his eyes and pointed. "I found it."

"Good. Sacha, can we borrow your necklace?"

"Sure, if you don't mind me keeping your cloak," she answered, handing him the gold chain.

Xandor smiled and placed it around his neck. "Thanks. Can you turn me into an orc like you did Chert?"

Sacha reached up and grabbed the necklace. She whispered a few words, and Xandor changed. His short-cropped blonde hair became thin, black wisps, and his skin turned a mottled green-brown. She kept his height the same even though it was a little tall, but otherwise, he looked like a full-blooded orc.

Turning to Jasper, he asked, "You ready?"

"As ready as I'll ever be," the mage replied. He concentrated and vanished.

After so long in the caves, the early morning light nearly blinded the ranger as Jasper directed him along crowded streets with gentle tugs. Smoke poured from damaged walls and towers. Orcs ran this way and that, and Xandor had no trouble blending in. He took in the devastation in amazement.

Jasper grabbed his sleeve, and they stopped at a small, dilapidated warehouse. Inside, a horse screamed, and Xandor raced through the front door.

Four hungry orcs surrounded a single Percheron. They all turned toward the door when he entered.

"Hwæt syndon gé?" one of them asked.

Xandor shrugged as he approached, giving them a toothy smile. The four crowded around him. In one smooth stroke, he unsheathed his longsword and sliced the first orc across the throat. Reversing direction, he swept his blade across the belly of the next. The third orc was still fumbling with the loop holding his axe when Xandor plunged his sword into the foul beast's heart.

As the last one turned to run, Jasper swung his staff, catching it across the chin. The orc landed on its back and cracked its head on the hard floor. Xandor finished him off with a quick swipe.

After wiping off his blade and sheathing it, Xandor scrutinized the orcs' weapons. He hefted the lone longsword and took a few experimental swings. It was a poor replacement for the one he lost in the cave-in, but it was better than nothing at all.

He made a quick circuit of the warehouse, making sure there was no one else, and ended at the Percheron's side. The draft horse shied away from the ranger's touch, but when Xandor spoke a few words in elven, it began to calm. The other Percheron lay amongst a pile of maggot-riddled straw, its bloodied body missing huge chunks of muscle. Flies buzzed around the corpse, and its stench filled his nostrils. Turning away so he wouldn't gag, he led the Percheron to the waiting chuck wagon.

It looked different without the chuck box. Almost ordinary. Jasper leaned into the wagon bed and turned something over.

Xandor peered over the sidewall. The body of a black cleric lay on its back. There was a gaping hole in his chest where his heart should have been. Flesh and bone had been torn and ripped apart like paper. "I've seen this before," the ranger whispered.

"Really? Where?" asked Jasper.

"In the Haunted Wood. One of Marko's Northmen and an Anak'im ambushed me and Chert. The Northman and I fought a running battle that ended in a ravine. I won, but something took his heart and claimed his soul before he died."

Jasper blinked. "That was Mladen. I wondered what happened to him. What do you think it was?"

"I don't know, but it can't be a coincidence that this Sha'iry suffered the same fate."

"Well, let's get the hell out of here before it comes back," Jasper said. Dark circles underscored his eyes, and he sounded tired.

"How are you holding up?"

Jasper shrugged. "I'll make it. Not far now, right?"

Xandor shook his head in wonder at his overweight companion's fortitude. Just a few days ago, the man seemed to be on the verge of collapse, but here he was, outlasting everyone.

Together, they dragged the body out of the bed and prepared the wagon for travel, cleaning it out as they went.

"Is there room for everyone?" Jasper asked.

"Considering it's all there is, we'll have to make do."

After helping Jasper strip the wagon bare, Xandor checked the Percheron over. He found a few wounds and sores, but nothing serious.

The horse stomped the ground and snorted.

"I know, boy. Me, too," Xandor said, patting the Percheron's neck.

Jasper looked up from the wagon bed and said, "Xerxes will be jealous."

Xandor smiled as he backed the Percheron beside the neck yoke and buckled the girth strap. "Probably."

Jasper opened a box under the seat. He paused, a skillet in hand. After a moment's consideration, he put it back and closed the box.

"We need to lose that extra weight," Xandor reminded him.

"We have to get through the city, and our passengers are going to need weapons," Jasper replied.

Xandor nodded and unhooked the canvas stretched across the bottom, spilling the last of the firewood on the packed dirt floor.

Jasper climbed into the wagon's seat. "It feels odd sitting up here without Dragahn," he said. "I hope the Kral wasn't too hard on him."

"Me, too," Xandor said, and, with a click of his tongue, urged the Percheron forward. The ranger pushed the warehouse doors open and joined Jasper in the wagon.

CHAPTER 23:
THE RAINBOW BRIDGE

October 29, 4235 K.E.

7:30am

The Knight Commander drew his troops to a halt before they reached the apex of the bridge and took a deep breath of fresh river air. Looking at the water far below, he had a sudden desire to go fishing. The bridge was so tall that only the orcs on the far battlements were visible from his position. The gates below remained hidden. Behind him, the sounds of fighting grew increasingly sporadic as Brian and Dorinkov's men mopped up the last of the resistance. So far, their movement had been unopposed by troops on the bridge, and the small war engines mounted on the sides were, blessedly, unmanned. He gave thanks to the Eternal Father that the orcs from the city hadn't organized any faster.

As if in answer, the bridge vibrated with the mad drumming of metal shod feet. Screams and yells erupted from the city gate, increasing in volume as the inhabitants of Chernigov spilled forth.

The surviving members of the cavalry units formed up on either side of the sable-and-argent standard of the Iron Tower. Everyone, warriors and horses alike, caught their breath and awaited the signal for the final charge. Foot soldiers hustled to form into ranks behind them.

Lord Fergusson turned to his second. "Dame Astrid, it has been an honor to have you as my second. Shall we remind these humanoids why they fear the Iron Tower?"

She saluted and replied, "Jawol, meine Kommandant."

Fergusson turned to a second standard-bearer and nodded. The soldier unfurled the commander's personal banner.

The clear, clarion notes of the bugle sounded the charge. The clop of iron shod hooves rang on the stonework, growing in volume as the knights gained speed. With fifty yards between them and the bridge apex, the sound was akin to the pounding of hail on a slate roof. When Lord Fergusson and the rest of the cavalry reached the summit, their hoofbeats had merged into a deafening roll of thunder.

Backed by the sun, the knights crested the bridge with the sable-and-argent banner snapping bravely in the morning breeze. The Knight Commander couldn't tell what made the bigger impact on the approaching wave of humanoids, the charging knights, or the banner. In either case, the orcs' advance slowed, and their front rank faltered.

The charging knights crashed into the mass of orcs. Swords and axes flashed, horses stamped, blood flew, and men and orcs roared, screamed, and died.

Gore flew high into the air as the cavalry plowed through the ranks of the ill-formed orc contingent, leaving bloody furrows behind them.

7:30am

Knyaz Dorinkov stood at the foot of the bridge, where the Keep's flagstones met the bridge deck, and watched the Glaxon Leftenant, Gallagher, lead his infantry up the bridge at a trot. "Vassily, do you know any living person who has set foot on this bridge before today?"

"No, Your Highness," his second replied.

Both men marveled at the fabled stonework before them. The main deck was paved eight across with huge, five-foot square tiles of intricately colored granite. Along either side, five-foot wide pedestrian walkways, also paved in varicolored slabs of granite, abutted short parapets. Despite more than a quarter century of neglect, it was still beautiful. Here and there, the sun sparkled off flecks of quartz. The Rainbow Bridge was aptly named.

The fact that no Rhodinan had set foot on it in nearly two generations energized Knyaz Dorinkov, although he hated what they must do next.

The prince climbed onto his horse and surveyed the Keep. Vassily and the main body of Rhodinan troops would remain within its walls and ferret out any remaining orcs, preventing the vragi on the river from cutting off their retreat. However, the two score men before him had another job. Armed with small shovels, picks, hammers, and chisels, they were carpenters, masons, and engineers. Behind them, donkey carts laden with an assortment of tools, including lumber and generous lengths of rope, formed a line.

Dmitri Rugov and his team of sappers were crucial to the success of this mission. The first part of their job was arguably the most important: fortify the bridge and construct the defenses that would hold the vragi at bay. Approximately a quarter of the men, most barely old enough to shave, wore leather climbing harnesses. These men were reserved for the second part of the team's mission.

A handful of men at the rear of the group wrestled the Keep's heavy gates onto wagons, breaking him out of his reverie. When they finished, the prince raised an arm.

"Comrades, you all know the job we must do today, though you may not know why. The vragi king has found a way to reawaken the plague that claimed so many of our kinsmen in the past. Even now, it does its foul work in villages here, downstream, and to the west in Trakya.

"The Glaxon knights came here, not to help us drive the foul horde from our shores, but to rescue a team of spies they sent among the vragi to find a cure. Although it is madness to even consider, those spies plan to cross the river here, today. A small team is on the river below to aid them. Our battle today is a distraction, but we have driven the enemy from our shore. Now, we must hinder their return.

"It saddens me to undo even a small portion of our ancestor's great work, but this is what we must do. A single span, comrades. Two-hundred feet of stonework and deck, to prevent the vragi from retaking our shore. That is what we must destroy this morning."

Steely-eyed resolve greeted his words. Dorinkov wheeled his horse and signaled Dmitri's team of sappers to advance amid a roar of defiant battle cries.

7:40am

Rugov hustled up the bridge, his wide brimmed helmet adorned with an axe and hammer emblem. He came to a stop at the apex, forcing those close behind to bunch up, and giving the slower wagons a chance to catch them. Taking a moment to survey the situation, the sapper constructed revetments in his mind, figuring placement and supports and overlaying them on the bridge. He also noted that the fighting lower on the bridge descent had stalled.

He hurried forward. "Come, comrades, we haven't much time. We must set the palisade and then start the revetments. Remember: the palisade is temporary."

Sappers hustled forward with the prepared wooden sections, following the infantry down the slope. As they neared the fighting, Rugov stopped at a pair of bridge piers and pointed. Immediately, two sappers wearing climbing harnesses, and a young teenager pushing a handcart disengaged from the group. The rest continued forward.

CHAPTER 24:
TAKING THE COG

October 29, 4235 K.E.

7:30am

"Se gæst faérníða se ceaster!"

"Bregu Kraagor ábrocen se wercynn ciricwág giesterdæg! Se gæst áfréon áfédan!"

Shouts from the wall and the waterfront soon overlapped each other as the number of watching orcs increased. The pair of disguised fishermen only understood a few scattered words, but it was clear the orcs' attention was focused eastward.

"Look, there." Sehraine spoke softly so that only Yevgeny could hear but pointed like many others. However, she pointed a bit closer and higher than the orcs. He squinted, straining to see what had her attention. Finally, Yevgeny thought he saw a dark speck moving in the sky.

A clarion trumpet call reflected off the water, followed immediately by a thundering sound that kept rising until it hit a cacophonous crescendo, a ringing clamor as though a hundred blacksmiths worked in the same room.

All eyes were riveted to the bridge. The sounds rolled off the city walls on the western bluff and echoed from the smooth surface of the river, pounding out its rhythm in the ears and chests of those below the stone deck.

The angry shouts from shore rose higher. Then the anger turned to dismay as a black banner with an argent tower fluttered into view over the apex of the bridge and surged down the western slope, gaining speed as it went.

"Se Írenþréat ancuman!"

"Áfléogan cwealmcuman!"

"Áfléogan!"

"Flæsctáwere béon se éabrycg!"

From the city, a yellow banner sporting a black-mailed fist with blood spraying from something crushed within its grip led the humanoid charge up the bridge. A uniform, braying war cry rose from the unseen ranks around it.

"Hwæt! Týdre hildlatan! Lóclóca hwæt heaðomaére efestan se Írenþréat!" taunted a rough voice from the docks.

The bridge parapet allowed those below to see nothing of the fighting, only the glint of early morning light off steel — swords, spears, lances, and helms. The two groups clashed together. Soldiers — orc and human alike — sailed over the five-foot tall barriers and down to the rushing water of the White River. Drainage outlets set along the bridge bled black and red, streaking the sides of the stone piers.

Some of the orcs on the docks hopped into boats and hurried onto the river to salvage what they could from the floating bodies.

"Psst," Yevgeny hissed a few moments later. Sehraine glanced at him. "There," he pointed with his chin, "is our third cog. What now?"

Sehraine shrugged and stared at the small ship, her face scrunched. He could practically see the gears in her mind turning. It was moored at the end of a long dock north of the bridge, bow pointed upstream. 'A small, cog-like boat' was the description Yana had used. He supposed she was technically correct: it had a mast and was the largest size cargo ship Chernigov had to offer, but the sides and rails were lower than a typical cog, meaning the cargo hold was smaller.

"If the number of Rhodinan soldiers Lord Fergusson gave us is accurate," she finally said, "it's going to be close. We'll have to stuff some of the men below decks; not an ideal place to ride, from what I've seen of the dreyri." She absently picked at the fishing tackle while mulling over the boat's position. "Row us closer to its back end."

"The stern."

"What?"

"The back end is called the stern."

"Whatever. Get us over there, but not too close."

Yevgeny grinned at her. "Soon." From the corner of his eye, he watched Lev in the shadows beneath the docks, surreptitiously daubing eldiálar slime on the boards and painter lines within reach. He tossed their net in a smooth, practiced cast that flared into a perfect circle before hitting the water's surface, but it only brought up a few small fish. As he scooped them up and dumped them back in the water, he glanced at Sehraine, mischief sparkling in his dark eyes. "Can you throw?"

"Hwæt þú efestaþ?" demanded a guttural voice in heavily accented orcnéan.

Sehraine turned, raising her head enough to see the apish face of an orc glaring at them from the end of the closest dock. She kept her face shadowed beneath her heavy hood. "Fisonop," she replied in a growl, and hoped beyond hope she sounded orcish enough. Bending back to her task, she continued to feel his glare for several long moments, but when she glanced back up, he was gone.

"They're getting suspicious," Yevgeny muttered softly.

"Mmhm. Just keep an eye out for Yana," she replied.

Both swept their eyes around. Orcs milled about the shore, their attention fixed on the smoke rising from the Keep and the activity on the bridge.

She watched the two banners amid the invisible lines of warriors. The ringing crashes of steel on steel and the screams of the wounded and dying filled the chill morning air. The two sides pushed one way and then the other, but neither could gain a firm advantage. Sehraine wanted to see what was happening, but try as she might, even her eyes could not pierce the solid stone of the parapet.

"Aiyee! Fýrdraca!" a rough voice screamed nearby. All eyes snapped to the speaker, and then followed the orc's pointing finger down the river.

In the distance, a ship drifted downstream in a blaze of fire. As they watched in horrified fascination, burning figures leapt into the river.

Sehraine strained to make out the details. The fog had lifted, but it was too far away. All she could see was an orange glow as the vessel burned. "I think that's the dreyri cog that almost ran us over," she whispered.

A flitting shadow and a cone of fire leapt down and swept a swath of destruction over several smaller boats in the marina south of the bridge. The fire raced across the old wood and flared when it found the pitch.

Yevgeny stared for all of three seconds, and then threw himself into frenzied action. He whipped open the burlap sack at his feet and took out several ceramic balls. Rubbing off the wax sealing a pair of holes, he dunked it in the water and pitched it into the mass of boats moored downstream. As soon as the first ball was in the air, he dunked another and handed it to Sehraine.

"Throw it."

She aimed for the docks and hurled the ball, holes first. The one Yevgeny threw shattered as it landed. Eerie flames in multiple shades of purple erupted across the nearest slime-daubed craft. Angry shouts followed, along with the pounding of booted feet. A dreyri sailor charged toward the fire but skidded to a halt when the second orb shattered, igniting the boards under his feet in a roiling fireball. He beat at the flames, but they only spread. Bellowing in pain and rage, he plunged into the water and did not resurface.

The fire danced over the sides of the boat and along the ropes tying it to the dock. Soon, others went up, consumed by the unnatural-looking flames. Amidst screams of terror, fishing boats scattered in every direction.

"Keep throwing," Yevgeny ordered as he yanked the anchor up from the riverbed and dropped it to the floor between his feet. Within moments, he had the oars in the locks and pulled them toward the remaining cog.

It took mere moments for Sehraine to exhaust their supply of Yevgeny's clay bombs. A few sailed past their targets to the narrow pier, but the majority landed in the boats or on docks. The violet flames spread, devouring everything in their path.

Sehraine picked out Yana's flyer as it banked out over the river and turned back.

"Hurry! Here she comes!"

More screams of "*Fýrdraca*!" echoed from both the fishermen and the dreyri on the cog.

Yevgeny pulled hard on the oars, and thier boat swept closer to the cog. When they were less than twenty feet away from the stern, a humanoid face appeared at the rail. Feeling the weight of the stare, Yevgeny turned. He braced himself for an attack, then stared, dumbfounded, as a dagger appeared, as if by magic, in the dreyri's neck. The body toppled soundlessly into the water.

At almost the same instant, the soot grey glider swooped overhead, clipped the cog's railing with one wingtip, and cartwheeled into the water just beyond the ship's bow. A banshee shriek of a war cry rose from the deck above. Other voices joined it as they either screamed in pain or roared in anger.

Lev's face appeared above the water's surface near the floating glider and drifted with it toward the rowboat. Yevgeny threw him a line and hauled them to the fishing boat. After tying the glider to the vessel's stern, he helped his brother over the gunwale. No longer wearing his orc clothes, Lev's close-fitting leather glistened with beads of moisture. His gills flared once and merged seamlessly with his skin.

Cat-like, Sehraine sprang up and grasped the edge of the cog's deck, pulling up so she could peer under the aft rail. In the bow, seven dreyri crewmen gathered around a two-on-one battle. The captain and his bosun fought a diminutive shape that furiously spun, blocked, stabbed, and cut anything within her reach.

Sehraine glanced down at the brothers. They already had their rowboat tied to the cog and were pulling on thin gloves that shimmered like fish scales. She eased back down between them. "Yana has the crew distracted at the front of the boat," she whispered. "You two go ahead. I'm going to drag her glider across our boat to dry, and then work my way around to the dock side."

"Port," Yevgeny and Lev muttered in unison before giving her a sharp nod and scrambling aboard the cog.

Seconds later, Sehraine grasped the edge of the ship's deck and hand-walked her way around to the gangplank. From the deck, new shouts of pain and the clash of blades erupted.

The cog's captain held his own against Yana; however, the bosun was not so skilled. He screamed in agony as his guts spilled across his feet and he sank to his knees, desperately trying to put them back where they belonged. A heartbeat later, the first mate kicked the bosun's body aside, leapt forward and, roaring, swung at the tiny figure in the bow.

In his exuberance, the first mate struck wildly. Yana swayed out of range of the dreyri's blade and leapt to his elbow, putting her new foe between herself and the captain. Pivoting on the ball of her foot, she simultaneously beat his returning blade back down with the curved sica in her right hand and slit his throat with the bone-handled karakulak that had once belonged to her father. The heavy hunting knife was almost as long as the blade in her right hand, and often mistaken for a shortsword by those unfamiliar with the Trakyan weapon. A split second later, the first mate stumbled backward, tripped over the former bosun's body, and fell heavily, clutching at his throat as the severed arteries spewed his life over the deck.

Sehraine snuck up the broad gangplank, unnoticed by the combatants, and sized up the situation rapidly. Two of the crew lay in pools of black blood near the cargo hatch; a third lay dead at the bow, but Yana still faced two dreyri. As she watched, one of Yana's opponents went down in a spray of blood from his throat.

The remaining four from the bow battled Yevgeny and Lev with a ferocity bordering on a berserker's rage. The brothers separated, each pushed toward the rails by the humanoids.

Lev was closest, almost directly over their rowboat. He stabbed the dreyri on his left with a mace-like weapon whose tip blossomed into a cluster of six-inch barbed prongs and followed up by punching him in the ribs. When he pulled back for another swing, she saw a six-inch blade protruding between the fingers of his right fist. The second crewman swung low, cutting a deep gash along Lev's leg.

On the far side of the deck, Yevgeny wielded a heavy, saw-toothed blade the length of his forearm. One dreyri rained a flurry of blows on the river elf, and the other circled wide to come at him from the opposite side. Yevgeny caught the first dreyri's blade in his free hand and turned as he sidestepped. Although Sehraine expected to see blood, the scaled glove he wore stopped the blade cold.

He used the captured blade to lever his opponent into the path of the other, gaining a brief reprieve before the crewmen leapt at him again. They traded blows for a moment, then one of the dreyri slipped his cutlass through Yevgeny's defense and sliced the river elf's left arm above his glove. Jaw clenched against the pain, Yevgeny turned enough to bind his opponent's weapon and stabbed his blade into the dreyri's rib cage to the hilt. The dreyri staggered back and collapsed, but his comrade attacked immediately, stepping on and over his crewmate's corpse.

A grunt of pain jerked Sehraine's attention back to Lev and the battle a few steps away. Pressed to the rail, he struggled to avoid his opponents' blades. The two dreyri seemed to sense his growing desperation and their short round muzzles gaped in sharp-toothed grins as they worked through his defenses, gleefully nicking him in multiple places like hounds worrying at a hinde brought to bay.

She crept onto the deck, silent as a shadow, drawing a dagger from her sleeve as she went. Lev blocked a blade aimed at his throat but left himself open to a wicked cut along his shoulder.

Screwing up her courage, Sehraine lunged forward and drove her blade into the nearest dreyri's back, between his shoulder blades. The Bulat steel scraped between bones and sank to the hilt. The dreyri howled in agony.

Lev shoved his knife through the other's throat. Both dreyri collapsed to the deck, spines severed.

The surprised look in Lev's dark eyes came and went in an instant. "Sehraine!" he gasped. Whatever else he might have said was lost in the skittering scrape of steel on the deck boards. Yevgeny's blade slid to a stop near the mast.

Lev and Sehraine raced across the deck. The river elf scooped up his brother's blade as he passed it.

Yevgeny and the remaining dreyri were chest-to-chest, wrestling for control of the hairy monster's sword. Despite the pounding of boots over the boards, the crewman remained intent on killing the river elf. The combatants slammed against the side rail. Yevgeny's eyes met Sehraine's, and he grinned at her before flipping backwards, launching himself and the dreyri into the cold, dark water below.

"Go help your laytenant," Lev shouted, and then he too was airborne over the side.

Sehraine slid to a stop against the thick rail. The river swallowed Lev with barely a ripple. She continued staring at the water, as if she might somehow pierce the gloom and see what happened below.

The sounds of battle, both above on the bridge and off to her right in the bow, reminded Sehraine why she was there.

She saluted the brothers with her blood-stained dagger, then raced away to help Yana.

The captain heard her coming. His blade swept upward, carrying Yana's curved sica with it, and he lashed out with a kick that forced Yana to turn her back to the deck. The big dreyri glanced at Sehraine, seeing only her orc disguise, and expected an ally.

Yana's blade arced out and around during his moment of inattention. The captain's cutlass clattered across the deck, his hand still wrapped around the hilt. She spun past him, as graceful as any dancer ever to set foot on the theater stage. The dreyri's bellow of pain and rage intensified as he went to his knees, his left hamstring cut. He abruptly went silent as his head toppled from his shoulders.

Blood-spattered and covered in nicks and cuts, Yana stalked toward Sehraine. Fear zinged up the elf's spine as she realized her friend did not recognize her. It took everything she had to stand her ground and flip back the hood of her disguise to reveal her flaxen hair and dirt smudged face.

Yana stopped in her tracks. Sehraine wished she could see the wind rider's face rather than the dark blankness of her barbute. Seconds dragged by. Finally, Yana nodded and continued forward, fingers digging in one of the pouches at her belt. She thrust something into Sehraine's hands as she passed, heading for the gangplank. "Raise this on the mast. Where are the Ivanovs?"

"In the river," she replied.

"Here," Yevgeny said, hoisting himself up over the bow near the lines securing the vessel to the dock, followed by Lev. Like his brother, Yevgeny wore slick, dark leather that shed water like sealskin.

Yana nodded to the river elves. "You two clear the hold. I'll take the dock."

The three hurried away, leaving Sehraine at the mast. She unfolded the bright red cloth in her hands, revealing a pennon emblazoned with a black dragon.

CHAPTER 25:
CLOSE CALLS

October 29, 4235 K.E.

7:55am

Yana reached the top of the gangplank just as three orcs reached the bottom. They all stopped for a second, sizing up the opposition. The orcs took in the sight of the small female alone on the upper end of the plank, and their faces broke into wicked grins.

Sounding her keening wail, Yana charged down the plank. Two of the orcs counter charged.

The ramp was wide enough for two to travel abreast, but too narrow for them to fight side by side. The larger orc on her left shoved a half-step ahead of his partner.

At the last second, Yana faked right, juked back to the left, and dropped below the orc's hastily swung blade. She surged up from her crouch, pushing his sword arm farther around with the karakulak in her left hand and into his companion's chest. Simultaneously, she hacked into his groin with her sica, severing his femoral artery. His roar of pain cut off abruptly when Yana's shoulder rammed into his solar plexus, driving the air from his lungs.

The dying orc stumbled back against his companion, and the two pitched over the side of the gangplank into the water below. The third orc remained on the dock, no doubt trying to recover from the shock of his companions' sudden, spectacular deaths.

Yana's lip drew up in a feral snarl, and she continued her charge down the ramp.

The orc sidestepped and swung his broad-bladed shortsword at the spot her back should have been but hit only empty air. Yana came up from a diving roll and faced the orc. He drew a dagger and set his feet solidly. With a leer, he hissed something and waggled his blades at her.

Yana had no idea what he said but could tell it was supposed to be insulting. She held her position: in a slight crouch, left blade high and right blade low. She waited on his move, although he had the advantages of height and a longer reach.

Charging, the orc swung his broadsword down in an overhand attack, forcing the diminutive human to cross-block, and then slashed with his dagger. He opened her armor at her right elbow and drew blood: a minor wound, but first blood in this fight.

The attack drove Yana back a step. He swept his blade out to the right and carried its momentum around in a loop, bringing it back in a horizontal attack, forcing her back another step. He completed the figure eight with another loop on the left and another horizontal cut. The first cut had blocked his own dagger attack, but the second opened up that side, and he swept the smaller blade out again, anticipating that she would focus on the larger blade and the other could slip past her defenses again.

Sensing the ploy, Yana stepped back again, out of range. She spun in a low attack, ducked under the orc's horizontal swing as he blocked his own dagger again, and delivered twin cuts to his lower left leg, slicing high. She pressed forward as the orc staggered backward.

The two circled for a moment, then the orc sliced diagonally from his high left. Putting his weight behind the attack, he struck Yana's blades off center and sent her karakulak spinning from her left hand to the dock.

"Come, little girl, let's do that again!" he taunted in broken Rhodinan.

Suiting words to actions, but coming from the opposite quadrant, he attacked from high right in another diagonal slice. The wind rider was waiting this time. She swayed backward and to her left, letting the blade pass her by and drawing her sica up in a short, vicious cut that opened the orc's sword arm from elbow to shoulder. His arm spasmed and his sword tumbled from his hand into the water.

With a bellow of rage and pain, the orc tackled her, catching her by surprise. Her arms went up and her sword went flying. They hit the dock and rolled over twice before they managed to separate themselves.

Both rose slowly to their feet, bleeding from new wounds and holding daggers. They stood still, each silently daring the other to make the first move.

Yana's banshee shriek split the silence as she attacked in a flurry of hits, kicks, and slices that drove the orc back toward the edge of the dock. She fought like a dervish, always in motion. His armor deflected most of her attacks. Some never hit at all, but enough got through to keep him off balance.

Desperate, the orc lashed out with a wild left-hook that caught her by surprise. She rode the blow, but it killed her momentum and gave the initiative back to him.

He followed up with an ill-timed slice that she took on her left bracer. It stopped his attack cold, and left his arm vulnerable long enough for a jab from her dagger, severing the tendons in his hand and disarming him. She countered with a flurry of cuts in a figure eight motion, her reverse-gripped dagger slicing through his leather jerkin and into his chest as she drove him across the boards.

The orc abruptly pivoted on one foot and spun to land an open palm punch square on Yana's chest. She flew backward and hit the boards in a sliding roll. She skidded to a halt on one knee and surged upward, hurling herself at the orc.

Two long strides away, Yana leapt, coming at him feet first. She connected solidly, kicking hard with both feet, and sending both the orc and herself flying. Sailing across the yard of space separating the dock from the boat, the orc smashed into the hull before dropping into the dark water and disappearing beneath the surface.

Yana tumbled back across the decking and rolled to her feet. She stood still for several seconds, trying to catch her breath. While she took stock of herself, it dawned on her that she was holding only a dagger. She frantically searched for her blades and spotted them where they had fallen. Scooping them up, she ran back up the gangplank.

Sehraine glared at the tangle of ropes attached to the mast, tracing their various twisted paths up past the yards to the black flag at the mast's peak. The ropes and rigging in the theater were never so tangled.

Clashing steel below her feet told the story of at least one humanoid crewman hiding in the hold.

The elf felt her heart racing — this was no theater play. It was real. She had to hurry to keep people she cared about safe. Safer, anyway. Sehraine seized the correct line, brought down the dreyri's black flag and removed it, then attached their red pennant to the rope and ran it up the mast.

The black dragon snapped and danced in the river breeze.

"*Down!*" commanded a voice. Sehraine did not hesitate, hitting the deck as a hail of arrows hissed through the air where she stood a moment before.

Sehraine looked to the gangplank and saw Yana crouched behind the ship's bulwark. The wind rider peeked over the rail, only to receive a handful of additional arrows in response, one of which pinged off her barbute.

Boots pounded on the gangplank, and Yana shot to her feet. Four orcs with longbows slung across their backs appeared at the top. Screaming her unnerving war cry, she buried her shorter blade in the gut of the first and shoved him back against the next in line on the narrow walkway. The second orc took a half step back, grasped his dying leader's shoulders, and shoved him forward as a body shield.

Yana dodged left, and the orc leapt onto the deck, clearing the path for the next in line to attack. The third orc's sword whistled through the air as he brought it down toward her head. The wind rider swept her karakulak in a circle, starting low and moving widdershins. As it rose toward its apex, it connected with the orc's blade just beyond the midpoint, forcing it high and across his body. In the two blades' wake, her sica punched upward through his lower jaw and into his brain. He flipped off the gangplank, taking her sword with him.

Caught up in watching Yana's battle, Sehraine was taken by surprise when a heavy fist closed in her hair. The rancid stench of orc breath assailed her nose.

"Time to die, elf," he growled in heavily accented Rhodinan.

"I don't think so," Sehraine snapped, and drove her dagger deep into his thigh.

Bellowing, the orc spun and flung her against the mast. The petite elf crashed against the mass of wood and ropes, rebounded, and rolled along the deck boards. The orc limped after her, foul sounding orcnéan streaming from his mouth.

He didn't notice the two river elves creeping out of the hold behind him.

The fourth orc barreled into Yana before his companion even hit the water. They crashed to the deck together. Her helmet-clad head impacted with the deck, and the orc's forehead smashed against smokey crystal. The wind rider's world filled with the clang of metal and swirling stars.

The orc pushed up to his knees astraddle the smaller human and snatched the barbute from Yana's head. The ancient metal rang as it bounced across the deck.

Thick, black blood dripped from the orc's forehead to splatter on her face as he wrapped his hand around her throat.

Yana groped for her weapon one-handed while her other hand pried at the orc's thick fingers. A halo of darkness closed in around the orc, and a roaring sound filled her ears. She knew if she didn't break his hold and draw a breath soon, she'd never taste another.

She reached across and gripped the orc's wrist. Simultaneously, Yana dug the fingers of her other hand into the flesh above his elbow in a c-grip and tucked her chin to prevent him from head butting her. On the same side, she hooked her foot under his ankle to trap his leg. Before he knew what was happening, she bucked her hips and rolled at a forty-five-degree angle over her shoulder. As she came up on top, her elbow smashed into his nose, but her second hit was far too slow. His retaliatory strike, a wild and un-aimed slap, connected low and hurled her off him.

Yana came up on her knees, sucking in big gulps of air, her eyes out of focus. Blinking hard to clear her vision, she spied her fallen blade. Uncertain if the pounding she felt was her head or someone running toward her, she scrambled across the boards on her hands and knees.

Yana closed her right fist around her karakulak, snatched a dagger from her boot with her left hand, and pushed up into a low crouch.

Her opponent charged with a wide, curved blade clutched in one hand. Black blood ran freely from his forehead and nose, coating his mouth and chin before dripping onto his leather and chain cuirass.

The orc moved far faster than she expected.

Time slowed.

Yana saw every nick and gouge in the rust spotted sword bringing her death. She brought up her crossed blades, knowing she wouldn't stop the weapon in time.

A streak of silvery steel slid between her upturned face and the descending edge.

Time resumed in a rush of steel screeching over her crossed blades and away without touching her flesh. The orc crashed to the deck, legs twitching, with a dagger protruding from his right eye.

Yana blinked in surprise and turned to find Sehraine only a few steps away. Her platinum blonde hair made a jarring contrast against the greens and browns of her orc make-up in the morning light. Behind Sehraine, the Ivanov brothers were busy tossing bodies over the starboard rail.

The elf dropped a hand on Yana's shoulder as she passed, but said nothing. She wore a grim look as she placed one foot on the dead orc's chest and wrenched her dagger out of his eye. The wind rider saw her shudder when the blade scraped on bone.

Yana picked up the fallen orc's sword and tested its heft. Heavier than her sica, it would have to do until she found something better.

Together, the two women took up positions at the portside bulwark on either side of the gangplank. It gave them the advantage of seeing anyone approach while providing shelter from enemy fire.

Orcs fleeing the burning waterfront south of the bridge shouted and pushed each other in their efforts to get up the bluff road to the city, while a squadron of heavily armed warriors pushed and shoved their way down. Behind the warriors, two Repha'im, giant men more than twice the size of those around them, pulled heavy-looking carts.

They had a breather — for now — but their escape would be a close thing if Dobrynya and his men didn't hurry. Yana glanced at Sehraine. "That thing with the dagger... Thanks."

"You're welcome." Sehraine paused a moment. "Do me a favor and try not to get hit in the head again. Not that there is a whole lot to hurt up there..."

They both chuckled softly as the pain and adrenaline settled.

Lev made his way across the deck, gathering fallen weapons as he came. They were all heavier and longer than Yana preferred.

"Did you see my helmet?" she asked, but the river elf shook his head.

Yevgeny ducked back into the hold and came up with a pair of buckets bristling with arrows. When he placed one on either side of the gangplank, Yana could see each bucket was about half-full of sand. He handed each of them a bow.

"There's plenty of space below decks, Laytenant," he reported.

"Enough room for ten or twenty men down there?" she asked.

"Yes, though no one will be comfortable." Then, with a grin, he produced Yana's helmet and handed it to her.

She nodded her thanks and slapped it in place. "You three didn't happen to recover my glider, did you?"

"It's draped over our rowboat to dry," Sehraine answered.

"Speaking of which," Yevgeny said, "we should bring it aboard and cut loose the little boat."

"Got it," Lev replied as he jumped to action.

Sehraine peeked over the rail to check the progress of the orcs and Repha'im. Turning to her companions she said, "Let me bind those wounds while we wait."

CHAPTER 26:
FLIGHT FROM THE CITY

October 29, 4235 K.E.

7:40am

Shouts and yells from the occasional passerby stabbed into their hiding place, keeping the group of women and children on edge. The waiting seemed to wear at their nerves as time crawled slowly past.

Chert paced across the mound.

"Relax. They have not been gone that long," Grendel said calmly.

Sacha stood nearby with two of the children. Motherless, they clung to her for comfort. It seemed odd to Grendel that the children chose a stranger rather than someone familiar. She ran a gentle hand over the little girl's hair and cast a quick glance at Grendel. There was sadness in her eyes.

Loud banging on the trap door startled everyone. The refugees froze like rabbits under a hawk's shadow.

Sacha was the first to recover. "Hurry! Everyone, hide!"

She and the other women herded the children into the pile of broken timbers and trash. Despite the terror they must have felt, not one of the children made a sound. It occurred to Grendel that these children's lives up to now were not so different from his own childhood. The realization made him more determined to get them out of Chernigov.

Grendel stood slowly and joined Chert. "We can block the door with all this trash."

Chert picked up one of the coils of horsehair rope Xandor placed beside the trapdoor. The other end led to the posts shoring the mound. He touched Grendel on the arm and pointed. "The ropes are meant to collapse the mound from within, but they should work just as well up here."

"Good idea," the half-orc said, "except we will be exposed to the rest of the city."

"Last resort," Chert replied. "You bury the trapdoor. I'll reroute the ropes."

Something pounded on the trapdoor from below. The pile of debris atop the wooden barrier shivered and shifted.

At the front entry, Grendel gripped a thick rope in each hand and waited.

Chert studied the mass of earth forming the mound and smiled in satisfaction. "We might have to step back," he said. "Sacha, make sure everyone's clear."

"You know, if you bring that down, everyone in town will notice us," she replied.

Chert peered out at the traffic of orcs, then turned and pointed at the waste and rubble covering the trapdoor. "You don't think that when they come up, it'll do the same?"

"Not if you keep them pinned down until Xandor and Jasper return."

The trap door bucked again. Wood splintered and the tip of an axe head briefly appeared through a gap in the sliding debris. It struck again, and a chunk fell away. A clawed hand reached through the hole from below and pushed at the barrier. The debris pile shifted farther.

Grendel handed the ropes to Chert and hefted Skyld's two-handed sword over his shoulder. With a fierce thrust, he plunged the sword into the hole. A gurgling scream answered, followed by a loud thud. Lifting with his legs, he wrenched his sword back.

Movement and faint scrabbling sounds came from the orcs beneath the floor. He stepped to the side and thrust his sword back into the hole. Not hitting anything, he quickly pulled it back up before the orcs got any ideas. At least the sounds stopped.

Grendel waited, using the blade as a prop to help support his weight. He was bone weary and could feel his adrenaline levels dropping. A dull ache throbbed in his chest, and he snuck a glance toward Sacha.

The trapdoor creaked ominously, and the pile of debris seemed to shrink. With a resounding crack, the trapdoor caved in. Debris fell into the room below, leaving a huge hole in the floor.

Grendel surged forward as a mass of orcs pushed and shoved their way up a makeshift ladder. He took the head off the first soldier through the opening. The next orc came up blades first and aimed at the half-orc's legs. Grendel jumped back, avoiding the blow, but the effort cost him, and he stumbled.

Chert rushed in and slammed the nearest orc with his shield. He smashed the next orc's head with his hammer and sent him back down the hole.

The orcs proceeded more cautiously, giving Chert time to pull Grendel away from the mound. Out in the street, the women and older children, led by Sacha, heaved on the ropes. Nothing happened. Inside the mound, the orcs, seeing the taut ropes, slashed at them.

"Chert, Grendel, grab a rope!" Sacha yelled. "On three! One... two... three!"

Everyone pulled, and the timbers gave way with a loud groan. The mound collapsed in upon itself, burying the orcs and spewing a cloud of dust.

7:55am

Xandor, with Jasper invisible once again, traveled against the tide of orcs heading to the bridge. The ranger saw the dust cloud near their mound and snapped the reins, urging the Percheron to move faster. They arrived to find Chert, Sacha, and Grendel fending off a half-dozen orcs.

With a shout, Xandor aimed the wagon at the group, and the Percheron gleefully trampled the orcs who were too stubborn to move out of the way. Leaping from his seat, the ranger hit the last orc and rode him all the way to the ground.

Jasper dropped his spell and ushered the women and children into the wagon. He counted at least twenty-three but couldn't be sure because the children kept moving back and forth in the line. He and Sacha piled the smallest into the laps of the remaining women or wedged them between the other children. They crammed together like bundles of cordwood, but no one complained.

Standing up in the seat, Jasper spotted more orcs coming to investigate. He gestured with his staff and yelled, "Vómva fotiá!" Instantly, the orcs' armor and skin ignited, turning them into fiery corpses.

"Jasper!" Xandor yelled while fighting an orc.

"What?!"

"Remember, we're trying *not* to attract attention!"

"Sorry!"

Sacha climbed into the seat next to Jasper and took the Percheron's reins.

"We're getting out of here!"

She snapped the reins and the wagon lurched forward, almost knocking Jasper down. Sacha made a wide U-turn over the charred bodies and yelled, "Xandor, Chert, Grendel! Let's go!"

The wagon slowed and the three warriors dove for the tailgate, leaving a trail of orcs. Grendel, with his long reach, was the first aboard. He stepped on the mothers and the children, but it couldn't be helped. He scooped Chert up while Xandor grabbed the side of the bed and hauled himself aboard.

"Jasper, move aside!"

The mage clambered into the bed, letting Xandor, still in orc guise, take his spot.

"We need an illusion!"

"I'm on it!"

The women and children bore the mage's weight, even though several of the children tried to squirm out from under him. Jasper closed his eyes, reached into his sporran to rest his hand on the black book, and concentrated. Hands reached up to steady him, and he found his magic. Soon, hungry orcs eager for battle filled the wagon — even the Percheron looked different.

They galloped down the street toward the gatehouse and bridge. Orcs, seeing the warriors, raced to join them, but Sacha didn't slow. She snapped the reins, and the lone Percheron tucked its head and surged forward, trampling orcs too slow to clear a path, but no one seemed to care. They were all heading to the battle.

Suddenly, Sacha hauled back on the reins and the Percheron begrudgingly stopped. In front of them was a huge bottleneck: orcs waited to pass through the gatehouse and join the fight on the bridge.

She turned to Xandor and asked, "What now?"

The ranger turned around and said, "Jasper."

"Kind of busy," he replied with his eyes still closed.

"We have a problem."

The mage cracked an eye open and turned so he could see. His face was haggard and grey with fatigue. Xandor feared the mage might collapse at any moment, taking his protective illusion with him.

"Can we go out a different gate?" Jasper asked tiredly.

"Too late now," Sacha answered. She was right — they were surrounded. Orcs stared at them and raised their weapons, encouraged by what they saw on the wagon. They yelled taunts and cheers, working themselves into a frenzy. "Besides," she continued, "this is the only gate that accesses the bridge."

"What do you have left?" Xandor asked the mage.

"What do you want?"

"A path."

"You don't ask for much, do you?"

"Well?"

Jasper muttered a few choice words and rolled up his sleeves. "Trade places."

Xandor moved aside and climbed into the back while Jasper stood beside Sacha to get a better view.

"Hwæt!" one of the larger orcs yelled at the wagon. He pointed and said something else, which Xandor didn't catch.

"That didn't sound good," Jasper said to Sacha.

"Shut up and focus. I owe you for slapping me, and I want you alive to collect."

Her sharp tone drew a surprised glance from Jasper, but the mage quickly turned his attention back to business. He reached into his sporran and closed his eyes, jaw set.

To Xandor, the mage seemed to tap into some hidden reserve of strength. His spine straightened, and his shoulders drew back. The air crackled with power.

With a wave of Jasper's staff, two long walls of orange and yellow flame geysered up. Screams and the smells of burnt flesh filled the air. The walls slowly moved apart, creating a clear lane. The ground was slick with charred gore but seemed passable, if Sacha could get the Percheron moving.

She snapped the reins and the draft horse reared, causing the wagon to back up. The bed of the wagon moved closer to the fire. Shouts erupted all around her when the illusion collapsed.

Xandor scrambled past Sacha and jumped onto the Percheron's back. The shock of the sudden weight surprised the horse, but Xandor's calm words quickly followed, and he urged the horse forward through the gauntlet of fire. The Percheron took a tentative step, and Xandor thumped his heels against the horse's flanks.

Chert jumped from one side of the wagon to the other, hitting orc heads with his hammer.

The fiery lane grew wider. The Percheron lowered its head and charged down it. Their pursuers slipped and slid in the blood and gore, but the surefooted draft horse steadily found his way.

As the wagon moved, so, too, did the walls of flame. The heat scorched the side of the wagon, and the children began crying. Chert moved to the rear, but it wasn't necessary. The wall of flame closed behind them.

Arrows rained down from the archers on the walls above them.

Chert raised his shield to protect the women and children and positioned his body to cover Grendel, but it wasn't enough. Arrows thunked into the wood and into bodies at random.

The wagon lurched and panic threatened to overtake the passengers. Mothers clutched the children in desperate arms. Gripped by fear, a boy jumped out before anyone could catch him. His screams turned from fright to pain when he landed in the fire, but there was no stopping.

An arrow grazed Jasper's shoulder, and he started to fall. Sacha grabbed his belt and hauled him back in.

The wagon entered the gatehouse and, above them in the arched ceiling of the passage, murder holes glared back evilly. Jasper let the flames die and raised his staff, whispering words of magic. Cold air rushed over the wagon, drawing moisture from the river. Thick layers of ice formed around the murder holes, blocking them.

Behind, the horde of orcs rushed after them.

Unwitting guards in the gatehouse poured boiling oil down the murder holes. The ice hissed, steamed, and melted, but not before the chuck wagon had already passed through.

The orcs charged into a rain of scalding hot oil. Flames traveled across the greasy flagstones, and more screams erupted as the oil ignited. The horde balked. Behind them, tohan cracked their whips, but the troops refused to advance while the flames raged. The oil wouldn't burn long, but it gave the wagon a head start.

The Percheron took off at a trot over the level stretch of road between the gate and the foot of the bridge. Surprisingly, there were few humanoids to get in their way, but archers sent a barrage of arrows after them from the gatehouse roof.

With only the smoke from the burning oil for cover, Xandor urged the horse to go faster.

Near the bridge apex, a thick mass of humanoids filled the road and pedestrian walkways. The Iron Tower's black and silver standard flew atop a newly constructed revetment made from the bridge's own pavers. They had to reach that flag.

Two short minutes passed, and the Percheron reached the foot of the bridge rise. The horse continued his run up the slope. Ahead, the sounds of battle grew louder, and the Percheron slowed to an unsteady walk.

They were so close.

Behind the wagon, orcs and dreyri burst from the gatehouse and swarmed after them. The ranger gauged the distances — three hundred yards in either direction, but at their current pace, their pursuers would catch them before they reached the revetment and help. Still in the guise of an orc, Xandor jumped down and slapped the Percheron hard on the rump.

"Go!" he shouted. The draft horse responded with a loud whinny and surged forward, leaving him behind.

CHAPTER 27:
DOBRYNYA SABE

October 29, 4235 K.E.

8:18am

"There!" Lev pointed. "Looks like our men coming this way."

"With der'mo gruz orkov in tow," Yevgeny added. He cast an apologetic glance at Sehraine. "Excuse me, Milady."

Sehraine smiled and put her hand on his shoulder as she looked past him at the approaching soldiers. There were over a score of men, plus four more borne on makeshift litters. She briefly wondered how many Dobrynya had lost. "Let's get ready to welcome them aboard."

Yelling to get the men's attention, Yana and Lev dashed down the gangway to the dock. Sehraine posted herself at the top of the gangplank, and Yevgeny at the tiller.

Yana snagged two walking wounded at the front of the pack and said, "You two, stand here and help Lev keep everyone moving aboard!" After making sure the men followed her instructions, she charged down the dock to the narrow pier connecting it to shore.

As the men crowded past Sehraine, she gave directions, sending those bearing litters to the hold. Those who were able took up positions on deck. Dead on their feet, the Rhodinans didn't question her. Their exhaustion, coupled with her tone, kept them moving.

Eight men fought a slow withdrawal down the pier. They formed two ranks of four each, blocking the orcs' ability to access the dock. Among the four in the second rank was an older soldier using a long gaff as a spear.

Yana slid to a stop at his shoulder. "My Lord, we have to go!" she shouted over the clash of arms. "If the Repha'im reach the waterfront before we get out of range..."

"This lot will cut us to pieces if we turn!" the younger warrior immediately to her left shouted back. He held what looked like an oar but ended in a four-pronged fishgig.

She realized he was right, but they had to get off the pier. Before she could answer, one of the men on the front row staggered back, a broken spear protruding from his left thigh.

The soldier who'd spoken leapt forward into the gap, shoving his gig into the throat of an orc. The man at the end of the row caught his comrade, and the two limped toward the ship.

Yana snatched off her helmet, grabbed the older soldier's elbow, and yelled, "When I give the signal, run for the boat! Leave three men to form on me for rear guard!"

"Who the hell are you?"

"Your rescue party! Now, do it!"

Not waiting for a reply, Yana stepped to the north edge of the pier. She took a quick drink from a metal vial suspended from a cord around her neck and sucked in a couple of deep breaths. Pressure immediately built in her gut. The wind rider bulled her way into the front line next to the last man, hammering at the orcs in front of him. Her sudden appearance allowed the two of them to cut down several of the orcs and throw those around them into confusion.

The space they cleared was enough.

She screamed, "*Now!*" at the top of her lungs, took a half-step forward, sucked air deep into her lungs, and breathed a cone of fire across the width of the pier, sweeping across the orcs facing them.

There was a moment of silence, and then a trumpet sounded. The Rhodinans fell back from the flames, but the six remaining men formed up around her as she slapped her helmet on and retreated backward, facing the conflagration separating them from the remaining orcs.

"Only in Rhodina does this many equal three," she muttered to herself.

The wood burned voraciously where the dragon fire touched it, spreading across the planks as the furnace-like heat dried them. Charred bodies littered the area where the fighting had been feverish but a moment before. Some of the more distant orcs, catching only the fringes of the flaming naphtha, batted at their scorched clothes as they ran screaming in random directions. The lucky ones dove off the walkway and into the water. None willingly remained behind to face the fire breathing Trakyan.

Moments later, the soldiers reached the foot of the gangway and filed onto the ship until only Yana and one other soldier stood guarding the pier.

"Let's go, Milord!" the older soldier called from the rail above.

Yana glanced back at the younger man in surprise. "Vityaz Dobrynya?"

"Dobrynya Sabe, at your service, Trakyan, now let's get out of here," he replied.

As soon as they stepped onto the deck, two soldiers under Sehraine's direction hauled in the gangplank, while another soldier cut the mooring line at the bow. Four of Dobrynya's men used long poles to push the cog away from the dock into the current. Yevgeny held the tiller tight to port, using the rudder to increase the speed of the ship's starboard turn. At his side, a soldier stood ready to cut the stern line the moment the ship was perpendicular to the dock.

Yana stood upon the bow eyeing the keep across the river. If all went well, they'd be well across the river before the bridge span dropped.

Amidships, Lev, Sehraine, and another pair of soldiers had the sail unfurled and worked feverishly to set the lines. Within moments, they were underway.

Yevgeny turned the tiller, sharpening the angle from shore. They crossed the current, putting more distance between them and the giants.

The cog was almost a hundred yards out from the dock when the first attack came. The boulder whistled as it flew through the air from the waterfront. A pair of Repha'im stood near the water's edge, hurling rocks the size of fat pigs.

The stone splashed down eighty feet upstream. Seconds later, another boulder flew toward them. It arced high, well above the bridge deck. The second Repha'im had better aim. Dobrynya watched it pass over and crash into the water thirty feet to their right.

The pilot's twin shouted orders and adjusted the sail to catch more wind.

"No!" Dobrynya shouted. "Make for the bridge! Get us behind the pier!"

Yevgeny ignored him. Dobrynya cast a glance over his shoulder at the waterfront, where orcs prepared to fire a grapnel headed spear from a harpax. One of the Repha'im found a long-poled fishgig and hurled it at the small ship like a spear. The five-pronged head drove through a soldier's shoulder, pinning him to the mast.

"I said make for the bridge!" he ordered.

"We need to stay north of the bridge and reach the Keep," Yana replied. "Lord Fergusson and Knyaz Dorinkov are going to drop a span."

"That's madness!" Dobrynya exclaimed.

Yana shrugged. "So is everything else we're doing today, Milord."

The harpax fired. Its ammunition landed short of the ship's hull, but not by much. The orcs were already drawing it back to shore by the rope attached to the grapnel's shaft. A battery of scorpions fired on them, peppering the hull with bolts.

The second Repha'im hurled another stone. Dobrynya watched the boulder as it reached its apex of flight and started down, seeking to crush the fragile wooden vessel.

"Incoming!" he shouted.

Men scrambled to move out of the stone's flight path. It blasted through the bulwark, snapping the starboard brace and multiple lines. The deck shook violently. The cog heeled over and threw several Rhodinans into the cold waters of the river before it abruptly righted itself, flinging men against the larboard rail.

Ilya, along with several of the men, worked frantically to free the remains of the mooring lines to rescue those in the water before their armor pulled them under. They saved two.

The sail's loose clew flapped uselessly in the river breeze. Despite the helmsman's efforts with the rudder, the current pushed the ship toward the nearest bridge pier and the burning docks beyond.

Sehraine, the petite blonde who appeared to have some orc in her heritage, shinnied up the ratlines to the yardarm, a coil of fresh rope over one shoulder. Dobrynya watched in amazement as she perched herself on the narrow timber, caught the broken line, and replaced it with swift efficiency.

Lev snagged the end of the dropped line and hauled the sail back into position. The heavy fabric caught the breeze and bellied out.

Seconds later, an iron anchor, trailing a section of chain, hurtled toward the damaged cog. The flukes burst through the leading edge of the bow, taking the short bowsprit, a chunk of bulwark, and an unfortunate soldier into the river.

They were just entering the shadow of the bridge when disaster struck. Another anchor scored a direct hit on the yard, shattering it starboard of the mast slings and ripping the sail from top to bottom. Wood, lines, and canvas crashed down, pinning several soldiers to the deck.

The dangling yardarm trailed in the water, dragging against the ship's rudder as it inched across the deck into the river. The Trakyan and her team worked with Dobrynya and his men to cut lines and free their trapped comrades before the wreckage slid into the cold, dark water and carried them away.

A shadow fell over the deck. Dobrynya looked up at the ancient masonry, marveling at the skill and ingenuity of their ancestors. His brow furrowed, and he squinted. High above him, a webbing of thin, pale cords descended from the parapets and turned under the bridge deck. Tracing their paths, he saw the lines connected the arch capstones on either side of the bridge to points along the supporting piers. He hoped the Glaxon knights planned to wait a little longer before dropping the span.

"Yevgeny!" Yana yelled. One of the bridge piers loomed ahead.

"I see it. Keep your pants on," he replied through gritted teeth. The pilot leaned hard against the tiller, and like a drunken elephant, the ship lumbered precariously to one side, trailing broken railings and lines. "Lev, grab the poles!"

The pilot's twin handed out long poles with gaff hooks to the men on the deck not working to clear the mainsail. Together, they pushed against the stone face. The starboard hull scraped the pier and peeled the grime off the wood planking.

"Heave!" the Trakyan shouted. The yard, along with its tangle of lines and sail, slid overboard.

"Now what?" she asked Yevgeny and his brother.

"We go with the current," the pilot replied with a shrug. "It's three miles downstream to the beach we used last night. I can run us aground there."

"Where will that put us in relation to the armiya camp?" Dobrynya asked.

"Practically in it," the other brother replied. "You and your men are almost home, Sir."

CHAPTER 28:
THE FINAL STAND

October 29, 4235 K.E.

8:55am

Xandor ran behind the wagon, a seemingly lone orc in pursuit of the escaping humans. After the stench of Chernigov, the fresh river air filling his lungs was exhilarating.

Orcs rushed from the gate, shouting and waving weapons as they ran. He pushed up the slope, formulating and discarding plans to distract the horde from the wagon.

Two hundred yards to go.

Up ahead, Sacha flicked the reins and shouted at the horse each time it tried to slow. Orcs, ogres, and dreyri attacking the Iron Tower's revetment heard the thunder of hooves and turned to meet the wagon.

One hundred yards.

Xandor skidded to a stop and wheeled around to face the mob at his heels, taking off Sacha's necklace in the process. His orc form melted away as the front runners surged past his position. He unsheathed his blades and shouted, "Aduro!" sending golden flames coursing up the edge of his longsword, while the blade from the warehouse remained cold and lifeless in his left hand. He felt a pang of loss for the magical sword's twin buried under Chernigov, but he shoved it aside. All that mattered now was buying time for Jasper and the others to reach the Iron Tower.

The pall of smoke obscuring the sky split, and a shaft of sunlight illuminated the ranger. He raised his face to the light, thankful to feel its warmth once again.

The orcs around him shied away, arms raised to block the blinding light.

Xandor glanced over his shoulder at the wagon plowing a steady path into the horde. A bugle sounded from behind the stone revetment, and the wooden gate at its center pushed upward. For a moment, it seemed the orcs would pour through, then a pair of knights flanked by infantry pushed out, driving the humanoids back from the gate.

The wind shifted and the cloud of smoke recovered, plunging the ranger into shadow. He turned back to the enemy before him and took up a fighting stance.

Two orcs charged in side-by-side, scimitars held high. Xandor spun to his left, sweeping his left-hand longsword high to beat their blades away. The burning blade in his right hand sliced across the nearest attacker's stomach, and the orc screamed as he went down.

The ranger's action didn't slow. Thrusting his right blade at the second orc, he caught it just above the hip. His sword penetrated its kidney, and the orc collapsed, dropping his scimitar. It reached out with clawed hands, but the ranger had already moved away.

A third orc turned in time to catch the leather-clad ranger's twin attack on his shield, lifted high to protect his head from the taller man's reach. Xandor kicked the orc's left knee, breaking it. The orc fell, shrieking.

Xandor slashed at a pair of orcs who had just turned from watching the retreating wagon. The two didn't have time to react before he passed between them. Both orcs dropped with deep cuts to their abdomens. Black blood bubbled out, painting the deck.

Charging up the slope after the wagon, he roared his Tanjaran war cry and waved his swords, hoping the humanoids' predatory nature would see him as their prey rather than the wagon.

8:55am

Sacha drove like a madwoman.

After Jasper's third attempt to fall off the wagon, she realized he was unconscious and pushed him backward. Hands pulled the mage into the bed, but Sacha had no time to see to his safety. Orcs, dreyri, and ogres charged down the slope to attack the wagon.

Even with the Percheron charging upslope, orcs and dreyri tried to jump aboard. At her back, Sacha's passengers shouted, screamed, and fought their attackers.

An orc leapt from a perch on the running board. Sacha had no idea how he got that far, but now he was leering at her from Jasper's empty seat, a heavy-bladed knife in his hand. He pounced. She screamed her rage at him as she tried to fend him off without losing the reins. The orc pinned her to the seatback and slowly forced her defending arm down. The tip of his knife approached the soft flesh of her throat.

Sacha struggled, putting all her remaining energy into keeping the knife away, but the orc was too big, too heavy, and she was too tired. She was losing the fight.

A cast iron skillet slammed against the orc's head. The creature's weapon fell from nerveless fingers, and his eyes rolled back in his head. Unseen hands pulled the dead weight off Sacha and dragged the body into the wagon bed where, a moment later, Grendel used it as a missile against a pair of orcs who had somehow managed to get hold of the tailgate and were climbing aboard.

Over the din of battle, a bugle rang out. The gate in the stone revetment opened. Humanoids went berserk as they swarmed the opening, but a wave of black and silver liveried warriors fought them back.

Sacha sorted the reins, but the Percheron had the bit between his teeth and charged into the mob. Some of the humanoids tried to get out of the animal's path, others tried to leap for the wagon, but its occupants beat them away.

All around them, soldiers fought the orcs and dreyri back against the parapet wall, creating a lane for the horse and wagon to travel. They were young men with grim expressions, nameless faces she would never forget.

Less than seventy-five yards separated them from the stone revetment and safety.

The Percheron thundered across heavy timber planks spanning a trench dug into the bridge itself. Behind the walls of the revetment, archers fired down into the attackers, and more soldiers filed out of the gate to hold the gap. Sacha hoped they were prepared to leap out of the wagon's path.

Thirty yards to go.

Sacha flicked the reins and screamed, "Hiyah! Hiyah!" She urged the Percheron to greater speed.

A hand axe flashed past her head from behind, narrowly missing the Percheron's skull before embedding itself in the chest of an orc preparing to cut the legs out from beneath their horse.

"Grendel!" she shrieked. "That was too close!"

In response, a second axe flew past, with more clearance, knocking down a second orc.

Over the sounds of combat, a bugle sounded a strange set of notes. A loud *'whumpf!-whumpf!-whumpf!-whumpf!'* answered the bugle's call.

Four explosions ripped through the stone deck behind them, buckling it. The bridge lurched, and the deck beside the trench lifted into the air, flinging soldiers and humanoids to the water far below. Percheron and passengers screamed and yelled as the rear wheels bounced off the pavers.

The concussion from the blast hit the wagon, shoving it and the horse forward.

Whumpf!-whumpf!-whumpf!-whumpf!

Along each side of the bridge, more explosions deafened Sacha. Stone shrapnel flew in random directions, knocking orcs and soldiers to the heaving pavement, and peppering the wagon.

"Aaaaaaaaahhhhhhhh!" Sacha's eyes widened in horror. Cracks raced over the pavement around them. She had a sudden rush of vertigo as the side parapets fell away, revealing the dark, distant river surface.

The weakened deck broke apart into chunks, and the wagon raced over its jagged and shifting surface.

"Faster, Sacha!" Grendel bellowed.

The panicked screams of men and humanoids filled the air. Wild-eyed, the Percheron surged forward, dragging the wagon over the crumbling deck.

Flicking the reins, Sacha grew more and more alarmed. The stone pavement on her right collapsed, disappearing into the abyss.

"Heeeeyaaaaaaaah!" she screamed at the Percheron, whipping the reins in an attempt to coax more speed from the powerful animal.

Beyond panic, the Percheron's eyes rolled madly. Finding a reserve of strength, he strained for more speed. Bloody foam flecked the horse's nostrils even as his mighty leg muscles drove his hooves into the crumbling pavement, and the wagon flew forward. The last of the bridge span tilted alarmingly before it finally gave way.

Bouncing over the corpses of orcs, dreyri, and humans alike, they dashed the last ten yards. Their front axle warped, the wheels wobbled and threatened to fall off at any moment. Following the only path left, the huge draft horse never slowed as it entered the gate. Sacha flinched as the left side of the wagon scraped the stone revetment, and the wheels' iron rims threw sparks with abandon.

The soldiers at the gateway leapt aside and scrambled out of the Percheron's path. Sacha fought for control and tugged on the reins as hard as she could to slow the beast.

Blowing heavily, the draft horse crested the slope, but with each breath, the bit slid farther and farther back in his mouth. Finally, Sacha felt the bit slip completely behind his molars. She hauled back and the Percheron slowed.

The faithful beast covered another fifty yards before Sacha considered herself in control again. She brought him to a walk, and then to a halt. The massive beast's head drooped wearily, and he collapsed to his knees, exhausted.

Sacha turned around to check her passengers. Horrified at the number of dead and wounded women and children, she sought out Grendel, who had already climbed out of the wagon.

Hearing running feet, she looked back to the east. A lone man sprinted up the bridge. His bright eyes took in every detail of the wagon and its passengers, but he neither greeted them nor slowed as he flew past. Sacha turned to follow the man's flight, and noticed Grendel and Chert staring west. Then she saw it — a lone figure on the far side of the chasm, sword flaming, holding back the horde of orcs.

"Xandor!" she breathed in dismay.

In the insanity of crossing the bridge, she had almost forgotten his sacrifice. She didn't like the man — their backgrounds almost forbade such — but she respected him. Other than Grendel, no one had ever willingly sacrificed for her, not even her family.

Sacha sighed sadly. Now there would be no time to find out if she and Xandor might have put their differences aside and actually become friends. Friends — something of which she had a distinct lack.

She studied the half-orc and the dwarf. Grendel and Chert were obviously close friends, and by their expressions, they felt a deep kinship with the ranger.

"Beg pardon, Gospozha," a young voice said. A young man stood at the corner of the wagon. "Will you be traveling to camp with the wounded?"

Soldiers and bearers surrounded the wagon. A burly man coated in rock dust offered the Percheron water and coaxed the exhausted animal back to its feet. A pair of teens wearing climbing harnesses worked loose the girth straps, freeing the horse. After the man led the draught horse away, the teens hooked a pair of mules to the wagon's traces.

"No, not yet," she replied, and climbed down from the driver's seat. She joined Chert and Grendel, and the three walked to the precipice to watch Xandor's last stand.

9:05am

Xandor picked himself up from the bridge deck, his senses still reeling from the explosions and the shaking of the bridge as the span collapsed. Likewise, the orcs around him scrambled to their feet. A tiny part of Xandor's brain mused that he no longer needed to worry about orcs coming at him downslope as he lit his sword again and assumed a guard position.

Without warning, he began to spin, slice, duck, and stab. He flowed from one position to another, leaving a wake of corpses as he passed. Swaying back from a shallow slice, the ranger beat a foe's blade high and thrust below it, running an orc through. Throwing his weight onto his left foot, he dropped low and spun his right leg around, knocking the feet from under two more. Coming back to his feet, he sliced both blades from low left to high right, disemboweling another enemy.

Two orcs attacked him simultaneously, one from each side. He moved into one, cross blocking and spinning such that he wound up beside the attacker, then thrust forward and high, still cross blocking, and caught the second orc's blade as well. The two orcs pulled back, and the three circled one another.

The two orcs charged again with overhead attacks. The ranger swept his blades high from left to right, beating aside both orc blades. He pressed close to the orc on his right and smashed his elbow into the warrior's temple, dropping him. Xandor continued the forward motion, kicked the feet out from under the other orc, and stabbed him in the gut while parrying another incoming attack with his other sword.

The ululating war cry of the Tanjaran clan split the morning air. Though no orc this far north had ever fought an Alashalian clansman, it was impossible to mistake the sound for anything other than what it was — a warning of impending doom.

His newest attacker leapt back. Xandor followed him, his sword trailing fire.

"Beaducwealm dælere!" the orc screamed, scrambling away.

Xandor's blade slipped in under the fleeing orc's shoulder blade, ripping into muscle and sinew. The hapless orc stumbled and fell, black blood gushing from the wound.

The semicircle of orcs grew thicker around the ranger. They kept their distance, navigating around the growing pile of bodies.

The ranger charged those closest to the gap in the bridge and caught the blades of the two opponents closest to the edge. He whipped them both to the right and head butted the second, shattering his nose. As the orc staggered, Xandor threw his weight to the left and body-checked the first orc, hurling him into the abyss. The creature screamed all the way to the river far below.

Dropping to one knee, the ranger narrowly avoided the seeking sword tips of the next wave of orcs. Whipping one blade to the right, Xandor disemboweled an orc while thrusting his left-hand sword into the belly of another. Surging back to his feet, he pivoted to the left, slicing into two more orcs, and forcing them over the edge.

A shadow crossed overhead. The ranger's eyes darted up. A black dragon streaked out of the smoke cloud, jaws agape, eyes glowing in anger. *'Can this day get any worse?'* Xandor thought.

The dragon swept lower, gaining speed as it dove for the crowded bridge, opening its jaws wide. Obsidian scales glistened in the morning light as it descended on its hapless victims.

"*Fýrdraca!*"

The orcs closest to Xandor turned to look.

Sulfurous flames shot from the wyrm's mouth, immolating scores of orcs. The blaze swept the bridge as the beast pulled up to follow the slope of the arching edifice.

Screaming orcs leapt off the bridge.

Xandor saw the flames, felt the heat on his face, and knew that he, too, was helpless in the face of such fury. Bone tired, he sheathed his swords and jumped.

The ranger worried the silver ring on his right hand as he drifted downward. Without the ring, he would plummet to his death in the dark water below, but that might be preferable to the dragon's fire and fangs.

The dragon slammed into Xandor's back and swooped up above the level of the bridge deck, heading northeast. Talons wrapped around his body, and he could see their tips disappearing deep into his chest. The pain had not hit him yet, and he instinctively flailed at the head of the beast. His fist collided with scales hard as iron.

"Hit me in the head again, and I'll drop your sorry arse!" a familiar voice shouted.

Xandor started. "Yana?" He craned his head around, trying to see her. The image of the dragon faltered and disappeared, leaving him looking at her familiar visor. Her legs wrapped around his chest, her feet locked together.

"Can you hold on by yourself? I'd hate to drop you."

Xandor reached up between Yana's hands and hooked his elbows over the control bar. He felt her shake the tension from her legs, one at a time.

"That was insane," she muttered.

They dropped several feet over the next few seconds. "This glider isn't designed for tandem flights!" she shouted over the wind. "We're too heavy!"

"Can you get us to the bridge?" Xandor asked. "Anywhere on the east side will do."

"Are you joking?" Yana demanded.

"No. Hurry."

Yana veered right. The glider streaked through the air toward the foot of the bridge near the Keep, almost one-hundred feet below the bridge apex.

Xandor could tell they were rapidly losing altitude. A combination of the cold air over the river and his extra weight dragged them down far faster than was strictly safe. He watched the rapidly approaching bridge swell in size as they closed.

Ten feet from the bridge parapet Xandor let go, letting the forward momentum throw him above the deck. His ring slowed his descent, but not enough. He rolled with the impact and fetched up against the pedestrian walkway on the south side.

Xandor startled awake to the sound of running feet but was too tired and sore to pick himself up. A shadow fell across his face, and silence followed.

"Next time, warn me before you let go," Yana panted. "And let go with both hands at the same time."

"Sure. Whatever you want," he replied with his eyes still closed.

Another moment of silence passed. "Are you just going to lay there?" she asked.

"Mhm. Until someone makes me move."

Her boots scraped on the stone deck. "Won't be long, then. Here comes Grendel, Chert, and Sacha. That looks like Lord Fergusson and Knyaz Dorinkov behind them." She knelt and placed a hand on his shoulder. "I have to go. I left Vityaz Dobrynya and his men with Sehraine and a pair of river pirates on a crippled cog."

Xandor cracked an eye. "Did you say pirates?"

Yana nodded. "I'll explain later." She started to walk away when Xandor called out to her.

"Hey, Yana!"

She looked back over her shoulder.

"Thanks."

"You're welcome, but let's not do that again."

CHAPTER 29:
DESPARATE MEASURES

October 29, 4235 K.E.

10:20am

"I want that relic!" Knyaz Dorinkov said, slamming his hand on Fergusson's table. The miniature markers denoting troop locations bounced and tumbled to the tent floor.

"Your Highness, Kraagor didn't have it," Xandor replied.

"Are you sure? By your own admission, the place was too large to search everywhere."

"Yes, Your Highness, I'm certain."

"What about that Madasgorski woman you brought with you? Has anyone searched her? And I don't mean just her pockets."

"The Tear of Havel was never in Chernigov," Xandor said.

"Then why the hell did I send my men into battle? Taking the Keep and destroying the bridge doesn't gain us back the White River. Kraagor still controls the west bank."

"This was never about Kraagor or the White River. This was about destroying the poison in those crates. It was about rescuing Xandor and Dobrynya," Fergusson said, his voice calm and measured. "If the relic had been there, it would have been a bonus."

Dorinkov went to the tent flap and watched the soldiers, both Iron Tower and Rhodinan, burying the dead at the edge of camp. Each of the living carried wounds of one sort or another. Some carried their weight on crutches while others bore white bandages like ribbons of honor.

"All this was for nothing," Dorinkov muttered. "Such a waste."

"Your Highness, it wasn't a waste," Fergusson said. "We stopped Kraagor from crossing the river with an army of humanoids."

"And I destroyed the poison," Xandor added. "It's burned to ash and buried under tons of rock."

Turning back, Dorinkov said, "This was pizdets from start to finish. What am I to tell my brother?"

"Tell him the truth."

"Tell him we still don't have the cure? Fergusson, this does not bode well for the relations of our two countries." The Rhodinan prince paced across the tent. "I sent a message to the Korol' asking for a sud'ya to examine the Madasgorksi woman. I want her under constant guard until he arrives. Maybe she knows where this relic can be found, and we can salvage this debacle."

Xandor started to reply, but Fergusson stopped him with a quick shake of his head.

"Yes, Your Highness."

"Remember, gentlemen," Dorinkov said before leaving, "thirty years ago war followed hard on the heels of the plague. The men we lost this morning are the beginning. Without a cure, Kraagor and his minions will march across our borders unchecked." He gave Fergusson a hard look. "I have no wish to be remembered as one of the men who let history repeat itself."

Both men bowed as the prince exited the tent.

From the entrance, Xandor watched the prince stride away, then turned to the Knight Commander. "You can't give Sacha to the prince, Sir."

"Why not? He's perfectly within his right to question her. She *is* a Madasgorski after all. She may even know where the Tear of Havel is located."

"Milord, she doesn't know."

"Are you sure?" Fergusson asked.

"Yes, Sir, I am." Xandor bent down and picked up some of the fallen markers. "Besides, we don't even know if that relic is the cure. Jasper saw it in a vision or some such thing. He thinks it's important, but even he doesn't know if the Tear is the cure, a clue, or completely unrelated."

"Dorinkov doesn't know that," Fergusson replied. "Even if he did, he wouldn't care. He's like the rest of us: a man grasping for hope."

"We still can't give Sacha to him."

Fergusson studied the young ranger, waiting for an answer to his unspoken question.

"The Tear of Havel is at the Sabe Estate. Dobrynya told me as much while we were in the tunnel."

The Knight Commander's eyes widened in surprise at this revelation. "Will he tell Dorinkov?"

Xandor shook his head. "I don't think so. To be honest, I don't think anyone knew Dobrynya was collecting relics across the river, especially the Kral."

"How does your Madasgorski fit into all this?"

"I'm not sure," Xandor said. "She's always been elusive and manipulative, but since her brother left her for dead, she's changed. I can't say if it's a true change of heart or not, but I figure it this way: we keep our friends close and our enemies closer. Once she goes to Dorinkov, she's lost to us, but if I keep her with me, maybe she can lead us to the cause of this whole blasted thing."

"So you want to take her with you to the Sabe Estate?"

"Yes, Sir."

"That's an awfully big gamble."

"Yes, Sir, it is."

The Knight Commander let out a sigh as he studied the pattern of tiny red dots on the map.

Xandor followed his gaze. The majority of the plague markers lay along the river, but tendril-like trails led inland. The latest intelligence reports brought news the disease had spread farther south. The healers were useless. There was no way to stop it. The only thing keeping the world from total chaos was hope.

"Alright," Fergusson said. "Bring her to me, and we'll find a way to get her out of camp without causing a war. You better be right about this or the Highlord will have both our butts in a sling — if we live long enough."

"Thank you, Sir," the ranger said. He aimed for the door, not giving the Knight Commander a chance to change his mind.

"Xandor."

"Sir?" the ranger said, his hand on the tent flap.

"Bring back that relic."

With a nod, the ranger let go of the flap and disappeared into camp.

"Slight change of plans," Xandor said, finding Jasper, Yana, Chert, and Sehraine huddled around a fire amongst the Iron Tower soldiers.

"What? I thought we were leaving," Jasper said, his face haggard and grey from the day's work.

"Not yet. Sehraine, go to the corral and tell Dobrynya I won't be able to leave for another couple of hours."

"Why the delay?" Yana asked as she fiddled with the straps holding her new shortsword and scabbard.

"I can't explain right now," Xandor answered. He searched the nearby faces. "Where's Sacha?"

"Over there with Grendel," she replied nodding toward a tree lined hill.

10:35am

"I'm sorry about Chernigov," Sacha said. She had her hand on Grendel's chest, tracing the dimples in his skin where she stabbed him.

Grendel wrapped his arms around her and pulled her to him. Laying her head on his chest, she felt at home for the first time in her life.

"What do we do now?" he asked.

"I wish I were free to do what I want," she replied.

"But you *can* do what you want. You *are* free. Marko is gone. Come away with me. Let us leave."

"Grendel, I can't. Not while it's out there. Waiting."

They both turned when Xandor coughed.

"I hate to interrupt," Xandor said. "But Dorinkov knows you're a Madasgorski."

A wild look crept into her eyes, and she pushed away from Grendel. "Is he going to arrest me?"

"More or less."

"He cannot have her," Grendel said. "We will fight."

"Hopefully, it won't come to that," Xandor said. "Dobrynya and I will be leaving soon. I need you to talk with Fergusson. He's going to keep Dorinkov busy so you two can escape."

"Why can we not leave with you?" Grendel asked.

"It's complicated."

10:45am

Passing the outer ring of guards, Lev, Yevgeny, and Sergei led Sehraine into the Rhodinan camp. Zack ran ahead of them, weaving his way in and out of the crowd.

"I swear that boy would explode if he were forced to stay still," Lev said.

"Were we any different?" Yevgeny asked. "What about you Sehraine? What were you like growing up?"

Sehraine glanced surreptitiously over her shoulder at the guards as she pulled her hat even lower over her ears. A shiver of fear raced up her spine, sending her heart pounding. Even in broad daylight, harsh faces loomed at the edge of her vision, and she drew closer to Yevgeny without realizing it.

The riverman wrapped an arm around her slim shoulders.

The bard gave Sehraine a worried look. "Dama, you are safe with us," he said.

"Sehraine, do you want to go a different way?" Lev asked.

"Yes. No," she replied. "Let's just hurry."

10:50am

At the corral, Dobrynya's men gathered around three horse-drawn wagons. Poruchik Tirinko helped them load the wounded into the bed. Healers in brown robes administered poultices and prayers, and worked to make the wounded comfortable for the trip.

Ilya, along with the rest of his men who were able, snapped to attention when the young Vityaz arrived with Knyaz Dorinkov.

"Your Highness," Ilya said with a bow.

"At ease, men," Dorinkov said. "Looks like you're about ready."

"Yes, Your Highness."

Vassily gave a kind word to the last of the wounded, hopped off the wagon, and said, "Vityaz Dobrynya, I hate to see your men go. They're good fighters."

"No, Vassily," Dorinkov said, patting Dobrynya on the back. "Gertsog Sabe expects his son to come home, and I can't say that I blame him. Besides, these men have seen enough action for the time being."

The prince spotted Sergei and the Ivanovs and said, "And here are the heroes of the day."

"Nay, Your Highness. We were but one act in this play, and a bit part at that," Sergei said.

"I doubt Dobrynya thinks your service was insignificant."

Dobrynya smiled. "Yes, Your Highness, you are correct. My men and I owe them our lives."

The prince looked around and asked, "Where are the ranger and the wind rider? Aren't they going with you?"

"Yes, Your Highness," Sehraine answered, "but Xandor asked me to let Dobrynya know it will be a bit later, after he's released from duty."

"Alright," Dobrynya replied. "Ilya and the wounded can go ahead now, and we'll catch up with them."

12:30pm

"Why do we have to walk?" Jasper groused as he leaned heavily on his staff.

"You could move faster if you didn't complain," Yana said.

"Seriously? I have the most weight to carry," he said.

"Do you expect one of us to carry you?" the Trakyan countered.

"The exercise will do you good," Xandor added.

"Really? After all we've been through, you're going to throw that in my face?" Jasper huffed.

"Come on, we're almost there," Xandor said.

"You're just in a hurry to see Xerxes again. You and that horse."

"You see! It's not just me," Chert said. "You should have been with him when we were following Dragahn's caravan. Downright scandalous."

"At least I didn't talk about dirt the whole time," Xandor parried.

Dressed in fur-lined riding leathers, Dobrynya stood next to a pale stallion in blue and gold barding. A soldier in a silver and black surcoat brought out the Percheron Xandor rescued from the mudpots and tied it to a hitching post. With a loud whinny, Xerxes trotted up to the gate as soon as he saw the ranger. Two dun-colored ponies with moist eyes joined him.

"It's good to see you, boy," Xandor said, laying a hand on the black Andalusian's neck. The horse shifted closer and rested his cheek and jaw on the man's shoulder.

"By the Eternal Father," Chert said, "what is it about rangers and their horses?"

"Xandor, that's a fine horse," Dobrynya said.

"Don't encourage him," quipped Jasper.

The young lord laughed. "Master Mage, you look winded."

"Tell me about it," Jasper replied.

"Where's Grendel?" Dobrynya asked.

"He'll meet us later," Xandor said. "You're sure your father won't mind visitors?"

"Definitely. Knyaz Dorinkov sent a courier to let him know I'm on my way home. If I know my father, he'll send someone to meet us."

Off to one side, Sehraine took Yevgeny's hand and gave it a squeeze. In return, he wrapped her in a hug.

"Goodbye, kotenka," he said. "Be careful and keep your claws sharp."

Zack grabbed her waist, sandwiching her against Yevgeny. Sehraine twisted around and gave the boy a kiss on the forehead. "I proclaim you King of the Camp," she said.

Beaming, he hugged her tighter.

"Come, we must go," Lev said, mussing the boy's hair.

Yevgeny helped her up onto the Percheron behind Yana and slipped one of his daggers into her hand. "So you'll remember us," he said.

Laced with intricate scrollwork that resembled lapping waves, the slim dagger fit perfectly in her wrist brace. "It's beautiful. Thank you."

12:30pm

Lord Fergusson chewed his cigar. Brian stood between Grendel and the door while Sacha paced back and forth.

"Make up your mind. Dorinkov's runner will arrive at any moment," Fergusson said.

"You're not giving me much of a choice."

"No, I'm not."

When Sacha didn't respond, Fergusson said, "Don't you understand? I'm letting you go. I just want your cooperation."

"Letting me go," Sacha scoffed. "You're recruiting me."

"Call it what you will. It's either this or I hand you over to Dorinkov."

"And if Grendel and I choose to run from you both?"

"Go ahead. Every bounty hunter in the Confederated Nations and Michurinsk will be after you by nightfall. Is that what you want?"

"Damn you. I helped your ranger. We saved your precious Rhodinan. What more do you want from me?"

"I want the cure to this plague you caused."

Sacha stared at the maps and realized there wasn't anywhere they could go. They were trapped. "What, exactly, do you want me to do?"

"What you've been doing. Help Xandor. He's on his way to the Sabe Estate as we speak."

"I don't understand why we couldn't have joined him earlier. I have ways of blending into a crowd."

"You're forgetting Dobrynya. He is duty bound to turn you over to Dorinkov and this sud'ya. There's no way you could have made it out of here without causing a scene. As it is, I am putting a lot at risk just by talking to you."

"Do you expect me to thank you?"

Grendel laid a hand on her shoulder. "We accept."

She spun around to argue, saw the look on his face, and her mouth closed with a snap.

Brian held out his hand and Sacha gave him her necklace. The leftenant looked at his commander and asked, "You want Anders?"

Fergusson grinned despite himself. "No, we need our fastest runner."

"Yes, sir." Gallagher said.

"What about us?" Sacha asked.

"I'm afraid you get to ride with the sutlers."

12:40pm

Sacha streaked through camp, hurdling over saddlebags and weaving past the tents. Behind her, Rhodinan and Iron Tower soldiers gave chase. Anders sat with his head back, a bloodied rag pressed to his nose. Sir Brian shouted orders to release the dogs.

"Fergusson! You let her escape," Dorinkov accused. He sat astride his Lundellan Charger, Vassily at his side. "I hold you personally responsible."

"My apologies, Your Highness, but I don't see how it's the Tower's fault. She struck my squire and slipped past the escort you sent."

"We'll see," he said as he spurred his mount.

12:45pm

Wrapped in a dirty cloak, the real Sacha flicked the reins to her troika and rode in the opposite direction from the crowd. Grendel lay in the back under a pile of potatoes. Other sutlers, their wares packed away in boxes and bags, fell in line behind her.

7:00pm

Xandor, Dobrynya, and the other riders caught up to the slow-moving wagons an hour outside of camp. Although Xandor chafed at the slow pace, he did not argue Dobrynya's decision to ride alongside his men. They stopped outside a modest village and circled around a campfire. After a quick supper, Xandor slipped out into the darkness. Minutes later, the sound of receding hoof-beats drifted down the road.

Hours passed, and everyone settled in to sleep, except the men on guard duty and Dobrynya. The young nobleman had a bad feeling in his gut that trouble was headed their way.

Midnight came and went.

The moon had long since sunk below the horizon when Dobrynya heard the sound of a wagon coming. He and Ilya were standing in the center of the road when Xandor and Xerxes topped the hill, followed by two figures in a sutler's troika. Although he couldn't make out their faces, there was no mistaking the form of the big half-orc.

Dobrynya waited, arms crossed, for the ranger to dismount and the wagon to draw to a stop before he spoke. "Xandor, what are they doing here? She's supposed to be with Knyaz Dorinkov."

"I know, Dobrynya. Please forgive this bit of skullduggery, but I need them."

Dobrynya heaved a sigh. "Xandor, what do you expect me to do?"

"Milord, I expect you to trust me," Xandor replied.

Emotions warred on his face. "She's a Madasgorski. Duty demands I turn her over to the crown." He pinched the bridge of his nose, eyes closed. "If I didn't owe you my life, I'd clap all of you in irons right now."

Xandor laid a hand on the young lord's arm and said, "I know this is asking a lot, maybe more than you're able to give, but I need you to listen." Stepping closer, Xandor said, "She knows more than she's letting on, and if she fell into the prince's hands, we would lose her, one way or the other. With us, she may let slip the origins of this plague or lead us to the cure."

Dobrynya stared at Sacha, weighing her.

"She is our only chance."

"Xandor, nothing good can come of allying yourself with a Madasgorski, but I will trust you. Just be aware that it's not only my honor at risk, but that of my entire family."

CHAPTER 30:
THE SABE ESTATE

October 30, 4235 K.E.

7:00am

The next morning, everyone woke to a layer of frost on the ground, trees, roofs, and wagons. It gave the village a sparkle in the sunlight.

"I told you," Dobrynya said.

"What's that?" Xandor asked.

Dobrynya pointed at a pair of opulent carriages bearing the Sabe crest. "I told you my father would have someone meet us."

The carriages pulled to a stop beside the three wagons bearing Sabe's men. The drivers clambered down and helped the soldiers prepare for the morning ride.

Xandor gave the carriages a dubious look. "How long until we reach your father's estate?" he asked.

"About four hours on horseback, but with the wagons, as well as a stop of lunch, probably closer to eight or nine."

2:00pm

Sehraine leaned back into the plush seat of the carriage, tucking her feet under her as best she could. She savored the heat and scent of the warm cocoa before taking a luxurious sip. She enjoyed it for a moment, listening to the rhythmic tread of the horses, before turning back to the man sitting across from her. Yana slept in the corner with her head propped on a tiny pillow. Sacha sat opposite, looking out the window, lost in her own thoughts. Outside, trees slid past as they traveled north to the Sabe Estate.

"This is a wonderful treat you are sharing with me."

Sergei dipped his head and gave her a gallant smile. "A drink worth sharing with a lovely lady."

"And you want to hear all the details of our little adventure on the river," she laughed.

"That was part of our agreement," he noted.

"Too true." She paused for another sip. "Once we shoved off, we headed across the river, arriving at the western shore south of the city. We worked our way north through the fog..."

Sometime later, she wrapped up her story with the battered rescue boat reaching the eastern shore with Vityaz Dobrynya's people aboard. Then she turned her attention back to the present.

"Thank you again for helping me with supplies. We couldn't have pulled off that rescue without you."

"I played a trivial part, but what a grand story I received in return — one that I will enjoy telling in the coming years. My first will be tomorrow night. I promised Vityaz Dobrynya to buy his men a round of ale for their actions. I think a song about their exploits is also in order. I would be honored if you would join us."

"If I can, I certainly will. However, I suspect we will be moving on shortly." Her expression darkened. Sergei waited for an explanation, but none was forthcoming.

He visibly perked as a thought struck him. "A young man recovered this from the cog. Your laytenant might appreciate it." He handed her a carefully folded textile.

She partially unfolded it, revealing the pennant she hoisted on the rescue boat the previous morning. "Master Bard, this may be a trivial item to most, but it holds great meaning for my cousin. In all the excitement yesterday, neither she nor I thought to retrieve it. In truth, I thought it lost. Thank you again for your thoughtfulness."

Sergei simply smiled.

"Tell me," she continued, "were you responsible for the dragon? I can think of no one else, save Jasper, who might have done that, and I heard he was unconscious at the time."

"Yes, Milady. Another miniscule part I played to make the story stronger, and to help in my own way. Many of us gathered to watch the ranger's last stand. I saw her take to the air and head for the west bank, and it didn't take any genius on my part to guess what Yana was about to do when she streaked toward him. I cast the illusion, hoping to slow the orcs from firing arrows at her, as well as to make the tale more spectacular." He smiled brightly at her.

She laughed delightedly. "Rest assured you did more than that. More than half of Dobrynya's men are convinced she's a dragon in disguise!"

His eyes danced merrily at the thought of what that could add to his tale, and he laughed aloud.

"Tell me, though, why did you cast the illusion as an obsidian dragon? I thought fire to be inappropriate."

"Maybe a red dragon would have been more appropriate for the fiery breath, but I've heard it said that obsidian dragons live in volcanoes and spit lava. Besides, at such great range with a moving target, I struggled with the visuals. Truth be told, I put little into the sounds other than amplifying the ambient noises from the wind on her glider." He shrugged. "As I said, a bit part."

"A bit part, indeed! She and Xandor would both have wound up pincushions but for your 'bit part.' They have much to thank you for."

He smiled. "A chance to hear their stories firsthand would be more than ample thanks..."

A narrow pass-through at the head of the carriage opened, and one of the drivers interrupted the bard. "Ladies and gentleman, we'll be stopping in the village of Zdorov'ye for lunch in a few minutes. You won't have time for a bath, but the inn has set aside a room for everyone to freshen up."

4:00pm

The light from the fading sun painted the western sky in swaths of gold and red by the time the convoy carrying Vityaz Dobrynya's men arrived at the two pearlescent towers guarding the gates to the Sabe Estate.

Soldiers in bright plate and chain armor rushed out of the towers to greet the drivers and their passengers. Dobrynya nudged Xandor's boot, waking him. The ranger looked around through bleary eyes and asked, "Are we there?"

His question woke the others, all except Jasper, and they shifted in the cramped space. Xandor nudged the mage with his elbow and Jasper leaned over, resting his head on the ranger's shoulder.

"Hey, wake up," Xandor said as he pushed the mage upright.

Jasper straightened and looked out the window, wiping the sleep from his eyes.

"How are you feeling?" Xandor asked. "You look a little flushed."

"I feel fine," Jasper replied tersely. "Just tired."

Once the guards were certain all was as it should be, they opened the ornate iron gates set into the whitewashed walls, revealing a red brick lane. Huge oaks stood like sentinels on either side of the drive.

The carriage horses advanced at a walk, followed by the wagons bearing Ilya and the soldiers, and the tether-line of horses bringing up the rear. A dozen yards beyond the gate, the wagons turned down an unpaved lane to the barracks and stables, leaving the carriages to continue alone in the fading light.

The trees lining the drive suddenly ended, revealing an expansive lawn and a massive, two-story stone mansion with multiple wings and tall chimneys. Dozens of leaded glass windows surrounded by carved trim work graced the home's face, each glowing with candlelight.

Jasper's mouth formed an *O* as he gawked at the estate. "You live here?" he asked.

"What kind of question is that? Of course he lives here," Xandor responded before Dobrynya could say anything.

The vityaz laughed at the pair. "I'd forgotten how good it feels to laugh," he said. "It has been a long time."

The two carriages slowed to a stop at the foot of an hourglass-curved marble stairway lined with glowing lanterns. Servants swathed in blue and gold livery stood ready. One placed a low stepping stool beside the carriage while another opened the door.

Xandor looked at Vityaz Dobrynya and said, "After you."

The young lord declined and motioned for everyone else to exit first.

With a groaning of springs, the carriage tipped precariously as Grendel exited, and righted itself when the half-orc's weight touched the ground. Sounds of protest bombarded him from within the carriage.

Chert, followed by Jasper and Xandor, climbed out to stand beside his friend and ran his hand through his curly hair, trying to comb it. The four men waited shoulder-to-shoulder. A marble colonnade graced the top of the stone steps, where a throng of people waited for them. By the looks of it, every soul in the manor had come out to greet them. No one made a move.

Dobrynya stepped down from the carriage and took in the apprehensive looks on the four men's faces. "What's wrong?" he murmured.

"Nothing," Xandor answered quickly. He cast a furtive glance toward the distant stables hidden among trees on the far side of the lawn.

Sehraine appeared beside Jasper, smelling faintly of lilac and roses. She wore a blue gown that sparkled in the evening lights. Her thick, pale tresses were twisted into a complicated up-do that hid the tips of her ears with amazing artistry. Tiny pearl and sapphire strands woven amid the curls and braids sparkled to match the dress.

"Where did you get that?"

"Sergei."

The mage stared intently at the bard, who was currently helping Yana and Sacha exit the carriage. Sergei had also managed to change into something more formal, even if it was outdated.

"Jealous?" she asked.

"No," Jasper lied.

She laughed and linked her arm in his, guiding him toward the line of people waiting at the top of the steps. "You know you're the only mage for me," she whispered.

Following Jasper and Sehraine's lead, Xandor took Yana's arm, and Sergei took Sacha's before she reached Grendel's side. She glanced at the bard in surprise and flinched before casting an apologetic glance over her shoulder to Grendel.

Scowling at the strange bard who'd attached himself to their group, Grendel took a place beside Chert and Dobrynya Sabe.

Dobrynya's father, Gertsog Leonid Sabe, stood at the top of the stair. A broad-shouldered, fit man like his sons, he wore his black hair in a long, stylish braid and his beard and mustache neatly trimmed. His dark clothes fit snugly and contrasted with a heavy golden ring adorning his left hand.

A step behind him, his wife studied the warriors with a hint of amusement. Her milky-white skin seemed to glow against the contrast of her dark blue lace and satin gown. The other members of the household, also dressed in their formal garb, formed two lines that started four steps behind the gertsog and ended just outside the foyer door: the proverbial greeting gauntlet.

As they traveled up the marble steps, Sehraine whispered excitedly in Jasper's ear, "Gertsog Sabe is the equivalent to one of your dukes. He reigns over a tiny, quasi-sovereign principality adjacent to Knyaz Dorinkov's."

"So you're saying I should be nice," Jasper said sarcastically.

Ignoring him, she continued, "He's probably descended from the first Korol' Melikhov."

"Doesn't that make him a prince like Dorinkov?"

"No. But he's probably a cousin to the throne, so you need to address him as 'Your Serenity' and his wife as 'Milady.'"

Before they reached Gertsog Sabe, a mousy man with a white wig approached them and asked their names and titles.

As they passed, he announced them: "Your Serenity, may I introduce to you Master Jasper Thredd of Tydway and Dama Sehraine Marchenkova of Trakya."

When they approached Gertsog Sabe, Sehraine curtsied and Jasper, using his staff for support, bowed as well as his stomach allowed. "Your Serenity," he said.

The gertsog spoke in a baritone voice and said, "I am Leonid Sabe, and you are all welcome in my home. Be at peace here." He turned and gestured to the lady standing beside him. "This is my lovely wife, Yelizaveta."

A servant ushered them between the two lines of greeters. Behind him, Jasper heard the other team members being introduced, including Gospozha Sacha Aleksandrova, teamster driver of Pazard'zhik.

Everyone seemed eager to meet the warriors who had saved the gertsog's son. Sehraine floated between the two lines like a butterfly, eliciting open smiles and warm comments. Jasper followed in her wake, giving the bare minimum of greetings, and forgetting both names and faces as soon as they were given to him. However, when they reached the end of the line, he stopped dead in his tracks. He scrutinized a serious looking little boy who appeared to be only a few years old. The boy held the hand of a beautiful young lady with sad eyes.

The servant announced, "May I introduce to you the Lady Mariya Sabe and her son, Alyosha."

Jasper cast a quick glance at the elder Sabe, but Sehraine elbowed him discretely and whispered, "That's Dobrynya's wife."

The mage peered down at the young boy as he gave Sehraine a deep, courtly bow. When she curtsied in return, the child took her hand and kissed the back of her fingers. Maybe he was feverish, but all he could see was a younger version of August. Noticing the attention her son was getting, the mother curtsied and said, "Thank you, Sir, for saving my husband."

Jasper bowed, his thoughts a jumble, and said, "You're welcome. He's a good man."

Lady Mariya nodded, her eyes on her husband, who was talking with his father. Her face was a mask as she watched the two travel the line.

Sehraine tugged on Jasper, pulling him toward the door.

Inside, a sparkling glass chandelier, suspended from the ceiling by a silver chain, illuminated the two-story foyer. A tile mosaic of the Sabe crest, a seven-pointed star of gold on an azure field, decorated the floor. On the opposite side of the room, two ornate double-curved stairs with dark wooden treads gently rose, mirrors of each other, to the balustrade lined second floor.

Servants separated Jasper and Sehraine and led them up opposite stairs to their rooms.

Jasper's servant led him down the lofty hall and opened the door to his room where another servant waited. Behind the manservant, warm flames crackled in the fireplace, and a large four-poster bed, covered in thick, wool blankets, added to the cozy feel of the room.

"May I ..."

"No," the mage snapped. "Get out."

"Yes, Sir," the servant replied with a bow, his face neutral.

Jasper followed the servant to the door and shut it behind him, exhaling deeply. Alone at last.

He stood in the middle of the room and slowly peeled off his shirt and pants. He grimaced in pain. An expansive mirror atop the dresser gave him a clear view of the angry red blisters and scab crusted wounds covering his body, punctuated by deep bruises. Fingers exploring the swollen wound at his shoulder, he turned to get a look at it in the mirror. Angry, red lines of infection spread out in a starburst. His body reminded him of the dark-robed mages he encountered at the White Circle in Pazard'zhik.

In the mirror, he could see his sporran with the *Veritas autem Sutekh* waiting for him to take it up and claim all of its power. It lent him the strength to survive Chernigov, but at what cost? He dared not depend on its help again. The warning he received from the ghost of Guildmaster Kolev whispered from the recesses of his mind.

Beads of sweat trickled down his face and body. Jasper retreated into the bathroom where a steaming tub of water waited. Ignoring it, he lay naked on the cold tile floor. He closed his eyes but didn't fall asleep. His mind was too busy for that luxury.

A knock on the bathroom door broke him out of his reverie.

"Jasper?"

It was Xandor's voice.

"Yes," Jasper answered weakly.

"Are you ready? They want us downstairs."

"Just a second."

"You have fresh clothes out here."

"Thanks," Jasper said as he sat up, looking longingly at the bath cold water. Maybe later.

Whispering, "Katharizōn," he stood up.

Although he had a day's rest, Jasper's magic responded slowly, oozing through him like thick sludge. When he looked in the shaving mirror, he looked refreshed, but he didn't *feel* clean. He walked stiffly into the bedroom and found red robes laid out on the bed. His freshly polished boots sat beside the door.

Downstairs, everyone had gathered in the foyer, waiting for the call to dinner. Jasper stood on the bottom step, leaning against the rail. He could smell the food, but instead of being ravenously hungry, he felt nauseated. The corruption inside him twisted in his guts like a slimy worm. Maybe his connection to magic made him more aware, maybe not. In either case, he made up his mind to skip dinner, despite not having eaten all day.

He saw Sehraine kneeling to talk with little Alyosha. The child smiled and handed her a white rose tipped in blue to match her dress. She carefully tucked the bud into her hair, leaned forward, and placed a kiss on the child's cheek. The boy's eyes grew wide, and he placed his fingertips on the spot her lips touched.

Again, the image of August filled Jasper's fevered brain. Another wave of nausea swept through him, and he headed toward Sehraine to ask her help in making his excuses. Before he reached her, Mariya appeared before him.

"May I speak with you?"

"Perhaps in the morning?" Jasper asked, still looking at Sehraine.

"Oh. I... I suppose so."

The sadness in her voice drew Jasper's undivided attention. He could see the glisten of unshed tears, and he sighed inwardly. "My apologies, Milady. Of course I'll speak with you."

With a slight nod of thanks, she guided him to an adjacent sitting room. "Your name is Jasper, yes?" she asked.

"Yes. You're Dobrynya's wife?"

Her features clouded when she nodded. She sat on an uncomfortable looking bench opposite the window and gripped Jasper's hands fervently. "How is he?"

Jasper looked around, oblivious to the emotion welling in Mariya's eyes.

"How's who?"

"August."

She said the name in a hushed whisper, but the pain and longing in her voice were clear. Jasper stared down at her and saw the same deep sadness in her eyes he noticed earlier. He settled on an adjacent chair and said, "He was fine when we parted ways."

"Where is he?"

"I don't know." His answer didn't satisfy her, so he continued, "He's traveling with some very good friends of ours."

"Do you count him as your friend?"

"Yes."

She closed her eyes, and a tear slowly worked its way down her cheek. "It's been almost three years since I've heard any news of him."

Jasper found a handkerchief in his new clothes and dabbed her tear. Before he could say more, Dobrynya stepped into the room and announced, "Dinner's ready."

The young knight stopped cold when he saw them together. His face turned beet red, and he stalked out without another word.

Mariya stared after him, her hands in her lap.

"It's my fault he runs away," she said. "He'll be gone again before the week is out."

"He's more serious than his brother, that's for sure," Jasper remarked.

Mariya smiled at the mage's understatement, but it was short-lived. Her face lost all humor. "Dobrynya challenged August to a duel to the death when he found out about us. August couldn't bear the thought of killing his brother, so he fled."

"That's why Dobrynya hates August," Jasper murmured.

She placed a hand on Jasper's arm and said, "Please don't tell anyone. Only Dobrynya and his parents know. No one else suspects."

"In just the few minutes I've been around him, I can see both August and Dobrynya in Alyosha. Which one is his father?" Jasper asked softly.

"I do not know, and there lies the problem," Mariya answered.

Jasper sat beside Sehraine at the long dinner table, across from Yana and Xandor. The servants marched in with decanters of wine, followed by others with covered trays of silver and gold. They placed the dishes on the table and, in a flourish of perfectly timed choreography, lifted the lids away to reveal the feast.

He saw platters of burned flesh, rotten vegetables, and side dishes filled with glistening pools of grease. Jasper closed his eyes and reopened them. His mind registered what the dishes were, but his senses revolted. Even the bread sticking out of a delicate wicker basket appeared to be covered with thick layers of green and black mold. Jasper's stomach lurched.

Leonid Sabe stood up, silhouetted by a large, stone fireplace, and lightly rang the edge of his wine glass with his fork, calling for a toast. Everyone stood with a glass in hand.

Gertsog Sabe faced Xandor. "Thank you for saving my son and bringing him home. You and your team have the undying gratitude of a gertsog and a father."

Half listening, Jasper watched one of the servants cut into the carcass of a charred bird using a rust-pitted knife. Black blood seeped from the wound. A tiny screech echoed in his head. He mopped his forehead with his dinner napkin, but the cloth came away dry. Sehraine looked at him strangely, and that was when he saw it. Near her neckline, powdery makeup hid a patch of grey skin.

Jasper's mind reeled. Guilt overwhelmed him and he took a step back, knocking over his chair. Everyone turned at the noise. The mage muttered an apology to Gertsog Sabe and rushed from the room.

He stumbled up the stairs with only the handrail to prevent him from falling, and staggered to his room, unmindful of the furnishings he knocked askew. The fire of guilt warred with the fever wracking his body. Jasper locked the bedroom door behind him. His sporran lay on the bed where he left it.

The *Veritas autem Sutekh* waited inside, eager to do his bidding.

Clutching the book, he sat cross-legged on the floor and prepared his mind. He had to find the answers. He had to save Sehraine from the dwolma inside her. He had to make a deal.

Hands shaking, Jasper opened his mind and felt the book stirring in his lap. He gripped the cover and prepared to open it.

The pain from a hard slap across his cheek broke the spell. In front of him, Sacha stood with her hands on her hips, glaring down at him. Xandor and Dobrynya stood a step back on either side of her.

"What are you doing?" she asked.

"I have to find the cure. This book is the only way."

"No, it's not," Sacha said. She held out her hand.

Jasper gripped the book defensively, unable to let it go.

Sacha's glare softened as she knelt in front of him. "It's a book of lies," she said, the pain and sadness in her heart laid bare in her voice. "That's all Sutekh does."

"He knows how to cure Sehraine; he told me."

Everyone looked at one another. Sehraine pushed through the crowd to stand in front of Grendel in the shattered doorway.

"Jasper, you have a choice," Sacha said gently. "I didn't. If you open this book, there is no turning back. He'll show you what you want to see, tell you what you want to hear. In the end, it's nothing but lies with just enough of the truth to keep you hooked."

Jasper glanced down at the book and back up to Sacha. Voices whispered in his head as he struggled.

Sehraine crossed the floor and knelt next to him. "Please, Jasper. We'll find another way."

Her voice carried a certainty that he didn't feel.

"What if there's not another way?" he said in desperation. "We don't even have the Tear of Havel."

Dobrynya cleared his throat, drawing everyone's attention. "Master Thredd, put away the book and let me show you something."

Before Jasper could reach for his sporran, Sehraine snatched the book out of his hand and darted to the fireplace. Jasper cried out and lunged after her, but he could not gain his feet before she tossed the book into the blazing orange coals.

A wave of power exploded from the fireplace, tossing Sehraine across the room like a ragdoll. Black flames roared up the chimney. The temperature in the room plummeted, and frost formed on the edges of the mantel and stone hearth. Everyone backed away, their breaths forming vaporous clouds.

Within the black flames, a shape began to form. A reptilian shadow crept out of the fireplace and slid along the walls, growing as it went. Lines and cracks appeared on its body as it moved, each one resembling a river of lava. A pair of cherry red eyes fixed them with a baleful glare.

Bat-like wings flared out, covering the ceiling. Rooted in place by fear, no one dared move. Silent as a grave, the shadow shot up the chimney.

The *Veritas autem Sutekh* was gone.

Xandor snatched out his longsword, and bright flames coursed up its blade. He searched the room, but no signs of the dragon remained. A greasy, black stain marred the fireplace, wall, and ceiling. "What was that?" he asked once he found his voice.

Dobrynya glared at Jasper. "Mage, you brought evil into my family's home."

"It's my fault," said Sehraine. "I took it from the vault in the Guild Master's office in Pazard'zhik."

Jasper hugged himself, and dark stains appeared on the sleeves of his red robes.

"Where do you think it went?" Grendel asked as he helped Sehraine to her feet.

"Who cares, as long as it doesn't come back," Sacha said.

After extinguishing his sword, Xandor turned to the mage and repeated, "Jasper, what was that?"

"I don't know," Jasper replied. His eyes remained focused on the fireplace.

"It was the Tugarin," Sacha supplied, "a manifestation of the Dark One."

Chert shoved his way into the room and grabbed Jasper by the arm. The mage cried out at the dwarf's touch, as though it stung him.

"This Tear of Havel," Chert said, as he inspected the ulcers along the mage's arms. "Do you think it will cure you and Sehraine? Do you think it will put a stop to this evil?"

Jasper blinked. "I... I don't know."

"Who told you about the Tear of Havel?" Dobrynya asked.

Jasper's gaze darted back to the fireplace.

"Great! Just great!" Yana stalked across the room, her fists clenched. "You think that book told you the truth? My people, my *brother* needs a cure, and all you've done is lead us on a wild goose chase!" Sehraine threw Yana a reprimanding look, but she was too furious to notice. She reached for her karakulak, but Xandor grabbed her wrist before she could draw the weapon.

"Take a walk and cool off, Yana," he commanded. The room's tension grew taught as the pair engaged in a battle of wills.

The wind rider snatched her wrist out of the ranger's grip, turned on her heel, and strode away, muttering under her breath.

"Dobrynya, what do you know about this Tear of Havel?" Xandor asked.

"Follow me." He led them into the hallway where his father stood waiting at the head of the stairs, the rest of the household and guests ranged below him.

"Son?"

"We have to show them."

With a nod, Gertsog Sabe let them pass. He turned his attention to the audience that had gathered and asked them to follow him back to the dining room. Sergei and Mariya deftly stepped out of the crowd and joined the smaller group.

Dobrynya walked past the stairs and foyer, heading toward the opposite wing. He entered an anteroom and started down a spiral stair.

"Normally, only the servants use this, but it's the fastest way to the chapel," he said over his shoulder as he descended.

The group wound down the stairs to the first floor and found themselves standing in a hallway outside a pair of double doors made of oak fitted with narrow, rectangular stained-glass windows. They each bore a golden Korsun cross on a field of white.

"We go to church in town but have the chapel here for special occasions." He gave Mariya a pointed look.

Dobrynya produced a skeleton key and inserted it into the lock, which released with an audible click. The knight pushed the door open, revealing a dark chamber filled with four rows of pews. At the far end, they could barely make out the altar and pulpit in the gloom. Light from the hallway shimmered over a silver cabinet sitting on a small table at one end of the rostrum.

A wave of deep sadness washed over them as they stepped inside, and Jasper recalled the same sadness emanating from the monastery outside Chernigov.

Dobrynya took a lantern from the wall and lit it with flint and steel. The warm light illuminated the chapel, but the flame flickered back and forth, causing the shadows to jump about like gremlins. Before he continued, he turned to the group and said, "I must warn you: the Tear of Havel is dangerous. It is sadness incarnate."

The young knight walked to the altar and knelt, saying a brief prayer. When finished, he approached the reliquary and unlocked the door with an ornate key. Inside, a long, dagger-shaped gem sparkled with a bluish-purple fire.

Grief and sorrow poured out of the relic in waves. It rolled across the room and crashed against the chapel walls. Memories swirled about the room like ghosts, reminding everyone of their mistakes, their sacrifices, and friends they had lost along the way.

Jasper turned back to the door and the escape it offered from the Tear's effects, only to be confronted by the haunted looks in his companions' eyes.

On either side of Grendel, Sacha and Sehraine fell to their knees, their faces filled with agony as they wept.

A choked gasp from the doorway drew Jasper's attention to Mariya. The young woman's eyes were wide, and trembling hands covered her mouth. He followed her gaze to Dobrynya, who stood by the reliquary, his head hung in shame. Jasper turned back to the door, but Mariya was gone. Instead, Sergei had taken her place. He made no attempt to enter the chapel, yet his expression remained impassive.

Grendel crouched between Sacha and Sehraine, and wrapped an arm around each of their shoulders, drawing them to him. His dark green eyes held shadows of their own.

Xandor faced away from the group, his shoulders stiff and his fists clenched, and the mage wondered what ghosts haunted the ranger.

The Tear's power seemed to have the opposite effect on Yana, though. To Jasper, it seemed the Trakyan grew angrier, a feat he hadn't thought possible after her display upstairs.

Another wave of sadness crashed across the chapel. Jasper fought against the gem's power as he fought against the sickness and despair that writhed inside him. Using his years of training, he compartmentalized his emotions and used them to fuel the magic inside him, creating a shield. Chert stood beside him, his face like stone. The two approached the rostrum and stopped.

"Is that the cure?" the dwarf asked, forcing out the words.

"I don't know," Jasper whispered. "I wish I knew."

"What are we supposed to do with it?"

Jasper simply stared, unable to speak.

"Where did it come from?" Chert asked, trying to use his voice to break the spell of sadness.

Before Jasper could answer, Sehraine said, "My village."

Everyone turned. She had moved to one of the benches and sat with her arms clenched tight across her torso, as if she feared she might fly apart.

"The same village where the Blood of Cayn was spilt?" Jasper asked.

Sehraine nodded and cradled her forehead into her palm.

"Where's your village?" Xandor asked.

"Less than a day's ride north of here."

Dobrynya looked at her, his eyes wide in surprise, and said, "How can that be? I thought all those elves died during the Plague War after sealing off their village."

"Why did I run away?" she said, her voice filled with grief.

"Gregori must have known of your village," Sacha said in hushed tones. Her eyes darted around the room, as if expecting the dark mage to leap from the shadows and attack them. "That's probably where he got the Blood of Cayn."

"How did he get through the barrier?" Dobrynya asked.

Sacha shrugged. "Gregori must have found a way."

"Why?" Dobrynya asked. "What kind of depraved man purposely spreads a plague?

It was a question with no answer.

"Sacha, what does the Madasgorski family know of the Tear of Havel?" Xandor asked carefully.

"I don't know. Maybe everything, maybe nothing. Either way, it was information to which I wasn't privy."

"It seems too coincidental for a village with an item such as this to be the target of a random attack," Jasper said. "I think someone intentionally sent them a barrel full of the Blood of Cayn thirty years ago with the intent of getting their hands on the Tear of Havel, but the elves escaped, taking it with them."

Sacha stared at the relic inside the cabinet.

"The Tear must be the reason Gregori created and released this horror," Jasper said, staring at his blackened fingers. "Based on what Lord Fergusson said, it's already out of control."

"What are we going to do?" Sehraine asked.

"Jasper, can you destroy the Blood of Cayn like you did in the city?" Xandor asked.

"I had to use dark matter to destroy what little there was in the soap. Assuming I could find more, I don't know what would happen if I used it against more than a handful."

Xandor shook his head and said, "There's only one way to find out."

"What about the Tear of Havel?" Dobrynya asked.

Jasper studied the intricately carved gem and asked the young knight, "How did you get it here?"

"No one was able to touch it, so we carried it in the reliquary."

"Have you tried taking it out of the cabinet?" Xandor asked.

"We've tried everything," Dobrynya answered. "We even tried breaking the reliquary."

"May I?" Jasper asked.

"Sure," Dobrynya said as he stepped aside.

Jasper took his place at the reliquary. Elven sigils decorated the gilded edges of the framed opening. Around the back and sides, a battle between two giants played out in detail. Inside, the Tear of Havel glowed with an inner light that, through the sadness, made the churning in his gut subside. He felt a surge of hope akin to what he felt when he used the *Veritas autem Sutekh* to search out the dagger-shaped gem. At least that part wasn't a lie.

It took both a physical and a magical effort to pass through the reliquary opening. He used his magic to unlock each of the elven sigils, and the opening shimmered with a golden glow. Pushing his hand through the barrier, Jasper felt a tingling sensation and watched, fascinated, as his corrupted hand reverted to its original skin tone. Whatever was inside him didn't like the magic and retreated up his arm. He would have been excited if not for the maelstrom of emotions emanating from the Tear.

Jasper threw caution to the wind and grasped the hilt-like portion of the gem.

The world vanished, and Jasper felt himself sliding down the skin of a giant's cheek. He saw Gaia's surface far below him. He tried to stop, but gravity held him firm. The giant's head whipped around violently as if struck, flinging him high into the air. He couldn't tell how far he flew — the landscape was all a blur.

Gravity took over again, and Jasper plummeted with his heart in his throat. At first, it was a slow arc, but as he gained speed, the ground rushed toward him faster and faster. He kicked his feet and waved his arms, trying to slow himself. Jasper tried to remember the words of magic that would slow his descent, but none came.

A presence brushed against his mind, soft as a feather, and he suddenly felt as though he was in two places at once. He could still see the ground rushing toward him, but he could also see his hand within the reliquary. He managed to pry his fingers loose from the dagger and stepped back, almost falling off the rostrum in the process. The others turned to him in alarm, but Jasper waved them back.

"What happened?" Xandor asked.

"I fell," Jasper replied absently. He stared at his hand and saw the grey creep back into his fingers. *'Well, it's a start,'* he thought. The Tear of Havel's inner light teased him with the solution to his riddle: how do you cure the corruption caused by the Blood of Cayn?

"You don't," someone answered behind him.

"Huh?" Jasper said, forcing himself back into the moment.

"You can't cure an orc or an ogre. They're not a disease — they're alive like you and me," Chert said. "You heard the old elf."

Jasper turned to Grendel, who looked uncomfortable under the mage's scrutiny. He pushed to his feet, drawing Sacha up with him. Hand in hand, they took a step away from the mage.

"Do you remember the witch doctor?" Jasper pressed.

Grendel's eyes grew wide at the question, darting around like those of a trapped animal. A grimace of pain flashed across his face, and he gripped Sacha's hand harder.

"Do you remember the stuff in his bowl?"

Sacha grew angry and said, "Let it go, Jasper. Can't you see what you're doing?"

Grendel licked his lips and swallowed. The half-orc's sudden fear vied with the Tear's sadness for dominance in the room.

Jasper ignored Sacha's question and plunged ahead. "I've seen the Blood of Cayn twice now. It's black and oily, not grey and muddy like the stuff the witchdoctor used.

Perhaps his was a derivative." He focused on Sacha and asked, "What was that stuff supposed to do?"

She glanced quickly at Grendel before answering. "Kraagor said the ritual brought out the primal spirit of the orc inside half-breeds."

"Why would it do that?" Jasper muttered. "Damn it. I feel like we have all the pieces, but I can't see how they go together." Turning back to Grendel, he asked, "Grendel, during the fight with Gregori, you purged the stuff the witch doctor gave you. How did you do that?"

"I do not know."

"Think. It's important," Jasper urged.

Sacha let go of his hand and wrapped her arm around his waist.

Grendel's brow furrowed in concentration. Silent seconds ticked by, stretching into minutes before he spoke. "I do not know how I did it. I remember wanting to cause that human pain. I remember you telling me not to kill him; otherwise, I would have torn him apart," the half-orc said, staring down at his clawed hands. "Something deep inside me fought against the effects of the witch doctor's magic. All I could feel was hate and rage. I wanted to destroy the world."

Sacha hugged him tighter.

"But you won," said Jasper.

"I think so, but I still remember how it felt. Part of me still craves that violence. To do it all over again."

Xandor asked, "Are you saying that the orcs at Chernigov were already using the Blood of Cayn? It's somehow part of them?"

"Maybe. It makes sense, especially if it's supposed to awaken their primal nature. If what Kraagor said is true, it takes them back to the beginning, when they were first created."

"Is that what happened to Grendel?" Sacha asked.

"Yes —" Jasper started to answer.

"But we all have a primal nature," Chert interrupted. "A devil inside us, if you will, but we also have a spark of divinity."

"Sehraine and I are infected with the Blood of Cayn," Jasper mused. "I'm certain that elves didn't start life as these dwolmas. Whatever it is, it's not affecting us like it did Grendel."

"No, it's not," Chert agreed. "Which means you're right about the witch doctor's slurry being different."

"It's almost as if the Blood of Cayn is sentient," Jasper said. "Something was controlling everyone at the guild in Pazard'zhik. I felt its presence there and at the clearing before we entered Gregori's lab.

"What about all those formulas he had written down?" asked Xandor.

"I don't know. He rewrote most of what was on that board in his cabin. However, the presence I felt could have been controlling him, as well." Jasper reached into his sporran and pulled out the sheaf of folded papers containing his copy of Gregori's formulas. Sitting on the rostrum, he leafed through them. "The more I look at these, the more I think Gregori was trying to contain it. I bet he didn't know what he was dealing with, and it got away from him.

"Let's move forward with the assumption that the witchdoctor used a watered-down version. Something different than what's inside the soap," Xandor said. "How does that bring us closer to the cure?"

Jasper and Chert stared at one another.

"In the vision the book showed me, the elves turned into dwolma the moment they touched the Blood of Cayn," Jasper answered. "It means that the Blood of Cayn, by itself, doesn't cause the plague. We have to fight the intelligence that's controlling it."

"It also means the orcs are working with this thing — Cayn or Ka'Sehkuur — whatever they to call it," Chert added. "Otherwise, we would have either sick orcs or uncontrollable savages running around."

"Does that mean Grendel is immune to the soap?" Xandor asked.

"The soap, yes. The slurry the witchdoctor used — as we have already seen — no," Jasper answered, "but all this is speculation."

Xandor looked at him with a shrug and said, "Speculation is all we have to go on."

"If the Tear of Havel is the cure, why didn't the elders use it to save the village?" Sehraine asked in a small, hopeless voice.

The mage and the dwarf both glanced at her, their brows furrowed in thought.

Jasper stood, leaving the papers on the altar. He walked to Sehraine and held out a hand.

Arching her eyebrow, she asked, "What?"

"Let's try something," Jasper said casually, but his voice didn't match the look in his eyes.

She slowly gave him her hand, and he led her to the reliquary, where she gazed deeply into the Tear of Havel's purplish fire.

"Feel anything?" Jasper asked.

Everyone watched, unsure what Jasper had in mind.

"Nothing," Sehraine answered, giving him a quick glance.

He took her hand and brought it closer to the Tear until he stopped just outside the gilded box.

"I want you to place your hand inside the reliquary, but don't touch the dagger. At least, not yet. I want to do this one step at a time."

Jasper pushed back Sehraine's sleeve, exposing her arm, while she slipped her hand past the shimmering golden light. Instantly, a grey ring appeared on the surface of her skin at the light's edge.

"It hurts," she said through gritted teeth, her eyes squeezed tight. The portly mage grabbed her arm and held it in place when she tried to pull her hand from the light.

"Jasper, stop it," Yana said. "You're hurting her."

"Not yet," Jasper said, keeping his attention focused on the grey ring. "Sehraine, you're going to reach farther, but do not touch the dagger."

As he pushed her hand deeper into the reliquary, the ring of grey retreated up her arm and grew darker. Sucker-like mouths pressed against the inside of Sehraine's skin, each voicing a silent scream.

"Owww! Jasper!" Sehraine screamed as she jerked her hand out of the reliquary. She pushed past him and retreated to the far corner of the room, where she huddled against the wall on the last pew.

Yana placed herself between Sehraine and the mage, giving Jasper a threatening glare.

The mage ignored them both and turned to Xandor and Chert. "The Tear of Havel works!" he said excitedly.

"How did it work?" Yana demanded. "All you did was hurt her. Meanwhile, Marcus is *dying*." She didn't have to state the obvious fact that it might already be too late for Marcus and Pazard'zhik.

Xandor studied the reliquary and said, "You think if the dagger were removed, it would drive the dwolma out of her?"

"Yes," Jasper answered.

"How are you going to get it out if you don't want anyone to touch it?"

Jasper's face fell as he realized the flaw in finding a cure. Then, just as quickly, his face lit up and he asked for a dagger. The group watched Jasper prod the magical barrier with the blade's tip. Try as he might, he couldn't get it to cross the threshold of sigils. He tried lacing the blade with magic, tried different combinations, but nothing worked. The dagger wouldn't budge, yet he could reach inside the reliquary with no problem.

"It won't work," Jasper said in frustration. "I can't get the dagger to pass through the door."

"Would a different dagger do it?" Xandor said, offering his own.

"No, I don't think so."

Xandor turned to Sehraine and asked, "Sehraine, did your people ever use the Tear of Havel?"

Sehraine shrank back, fear and sadness warring across her delicate features. Finally, she nodded. "Once a year, during the winter solstice, one of the Elders would open the reliquary, and the dagger would rise in the air. They used it to mark the beginning of the New Year and to celebrate our creation."

Jasper perked up when she mentioned the dagger rising and asked, "How did they do it?"

"I don't know. It was a long time ago. I haven't thought about home, family, or my people since I chose Pazard'zhik and a life among humans." She shook her head slowly and massaged her temples. "It might have been something the Elders did, or it could have been the time of year."

"We can't wait that long," Jasper said softly.

"Dobrynya, have you ever seen it do anything?" Xandor asked.

"No."

"We could take it to Sehraine's village and see what happens," Jasper suggested.

Silence settled over the chapel.

Jasper looked at everyone's faces. "What else can we do?" he demanded.

Xandor considered the plan and asked, "Dobrynya, how dangerous is it to take this thing outside?"

The young knight shrugged and said, "We didn't have any trouble bringing it here. Other than that, I can't say. However, before we go any farther, we need to ask my father's permission."

"Let's show him," Jasper said. "After he sees what it can do, he won't have a choice but to grant us his permission."

"I still don't see how it's going to help us. There's no way people like Marcus will be able to make a pilgrimage to Sehraine's village, and that's if it works," Xandor said doubtfully.

"Maybe Gertsog Sabe will have a suggestion," Jasper responded hopefully.

"It is worth a try," Grendel said.

"If the Tear of Havel is the cure, we'll find a way to either get Marcus to that dagger or get that dagger to my brother," Yana stated.

"You're all forgetting something," Chert said dourly.

Everyone turned to the dwarf, waiting for him to continue.

"Dobrynya said the elves sealed off the village."

"If Gregori found a way in, we can too," Jasper said.

"We're not even sure he's been there," Yana said.

"What would you have us do? Sit here and wait for Sehraine to turn into a dwolma?" Jasper snapped. He regretted saying it the moment the words left his mouth, but the damage was done. Sehraine burst into huge wracking sobs and buried her face in her hands.

Grendel glared at the mage, rose, and made his way to the back of the chapel. He sat beside Sehraine and wrapped an arm around her shoulders, pulling her against his chest. Beside him, she looked like a child.

"All I'm saying," Chert said calmly, "is this has the feel of a fool's errand. We should tread carefully."

Grendel's hulking form shifted, and he said, "I say we try."

Jasper smiled, thinking he'd found an ally, but Grendel wasn't looking at him. He was looking at Sehraine.

Xandor turned to the young knight and said, "Vityaz Dobrynya, it is your decision to make."

"No, it's my father's."

9:30pm

Gertsog Sabe walked with his son to the Chapel, listening to him summarize the events of the past few days. Dobrynya left nothing out, including Xandor and Jasper mistaking him for August. Rumor had already reached the estate, but sharing that part of the tale reopened old wounds.

The two stared into the chapel, watching the mage and the dwarf study the reliquary. In the background, little conversations helped fend off the effects of the Tear of Havel.

Stepping into the chapel, Dobrynya's father asked, "Can you open it?"

Everyone turned and bowed at his approach.

Jasper straightened and answered, "Maybe, Your Serenity, but it will take us time to decipher all the symbols."

Weighing each word carefully, Gertsog Sabe said, "My son has explained your plan. Is this the cure?"

His only answer was silence.

"That dagger is not going anywhere unless you give me a clear answer."

Running his hand through his short blond hair, Xandor said, "Your Serenity, we don't know. The dagger seems to have the power to drive away the disease, but until we get it out of the box, we won't know for sure." He gestured to Jasper. "Show him."

The mage pulled up his sleeve, exposing the weeping sores and grey streaks running down his arm. Wiggling his fingers, he inserted his hand into the reliquary. Like the previous times, the dark grey in his fingers retreated up his arm, forming a black ring at the edge of the shimmering glow. Jasper pulled his hand back out and wiggled his fingers again. They were back to normal, but it didn't last long. The grey slowly returned.

"It works, but it's not permanent," Jasper explained.

"And you think that if you can remove the dagger, it will be permanent. It will drive out the contagion."

"Yes, Your Serenity."

Gertsog Sabe turned and scrutinized Sehraine. "An elf, here in my own home, after all these years," he murmured. "Have you seen the dagger taken out of the reliquary before?"

Sehraine hiccupped and sat up, giving Grendel a grateful half-smile. She rubbed her eyes with her hands and answered, "Yes, Your Serenity. It was during the winter solstice, many years ago, but I don't know how it was done."

Leonid Sabe raked his gaze over the people gathered in his family's chapel. His jaw clenched, and his eyes turned hard.

After telling his father the full story of how he came to bring these people home with him, Dobrynya understood why his father would be suspicious. After all, they claimed friendship with his traitorous brother. Despite what they'd done to save him and his men, Dobrynya wondered if his trust was misplaced.

"Your Serenity, please allow us to continue studying the reliquary and see if there is a way to open it," Xandor said. "If we don't make any progress, the dagger stays. If we do, please allow us the opportunity to use it."

Gertsog Sabe considered the ranger's words, quietly studying each person in the room. His gaze finally rested on his son. "Dobrynya, what do you think?"

"So long as they stay here, I say we give them a chance. The last thing we need is for the disease to spread and Kraagor to move across the river. We gave him a black eye yesterday, but he is massing troops at Chernigov. I think this new plague is a harbinger of war. This may be our chance to stop it, here and now."

Leonid mulled over his son's words and replied, "This poses a risk not only to my lands, but to all of Michurinsk. I received a message from the Korol', informing me that he is sending his men here. You have until morning. After that, the Korol's men will take over."

Questions bombarded Gertsog Sabe, and he held up his hands for silence. He turned to Sacha and said, "Lady Aleksandra Madasgorski, your presence here has put me at conflict with the Korol'. His men are coming here to take you to the capital. Your family's crimes against the people of Michurinsk are numerous, and when the Kral hears of your capture, I expect he will issue a formal request for your extradition back to Pazard'zhik."

Everyone stood, and the air became brittle with tension.

"I am disobeying a direct command by warning you, but you helped save my son's life."

Sacha bowed slightly in thanks, but her eyes remained cold and calculating.

"Of course, the Korol's men will be interested in hearing about the dagger, and its potential to stop the disease. They may choose to take it with them."

"Father, you can't let them take it," Dobrynya urged. "It's our responsibility."

"What would you have me do, son? Fight the Korol'? It is out of my control."

Dobrynya opened his mouth to argue, but nothing came out. Whatever he was going to say was lost when he saw his father's expression.

Gertsog Sabe turned and said, "I have guests to attend. Let me know if you have any success." He walked out of the chapel, leaving everyone staring at his back.

"We can't let them have Sacha or the Tear of Havel," Jasper exclaimed once Gertsog Sabe was out of sight. "We need to flee. Tonight."

Dobrynya's eyes grew wide.

Xandor rounded on the mage. "We will do no such thing! Jasper, get a hold of yourself. You're on edge, you're sick, and you can barely stand without your staff." His voice softened. "We all want to find the cure."

"They will bury this dagger, and we'll never see it again. Besides, I don't think Grendel will let the Korol' take Sacha without a fight. Neither will I," Jasper said, surprising even himself.

Xandor looked around, shaking his head, and said, "No. Gertsog Sabe is right. We can't fight the Korol'. If we run, it will only make matters worse for us and for Sacha. We need to find a way to open that reliquary, and when the Korol's men get here tomorrow morning, we tell them how to use it."

"We need to take it to the village," Jasper explained, tiredly. "It's the only way."

"You don't know if taking it to the village will help."

"We're wasting time arguing," Chert said. "The Korol's men are coming."

CHAPTER 31:
THE RELIQUARY

October 31, 4235 K.E.

12:01am

Jasper and Chert pulled the reliquary away from the wall, studying every side of the box. Sehraine hovered beside the altar, her brow wrinkled in thought.

Xandor paced down the aisle between the pews, glancing frequently into his journal for a reply from Lord Fergusson. Grendel and Sacha sat in the back, talking in heated whispers. Servants had come and gone with refreshments. Cups and half-eaten plates of food lay scattered. No one had left the chapel.

Dobrynya lounged in the front pew with his long legs stretched out in front of him, his attention divided between the ranger and the men studying the box.

Yana sat down beside him.

"You holding up?" he asked.

"Yes. You?"

He nodded with a quick smile, but worry lines etched his face.

Sehraine knelt beside the reliquary and traced her finger over the embossed silver metal. She inhaled sharply when she realized it was a thin sheet of mithril, beaten and shaped to form images in low relief. She ran her finger down the length of a tall man holding a sword. He was fighting another man. Tiny figures huddled at their feet.

Chert squatted beside her and said, "It's an amazing work of art. See how they joined the corners over the wood: seamless."

Looking over his shoulder, Jasper said, "The two figures represent Havel and Cayn fighting in a field. Down here are the newly formed elves created from his tears." The mage moved over and motioned to another location. "Here is where, I guess, Cayn strikes Havel." "And see this," he continued, pointing to a small dimple, his hand shaking, "this is the Tear of Havel."

Sehraine's eyes grew wide as she traced its course across the back of the reliquary to the other side. Below, more tiny figures watched its progress.

On the other side, Jasper pointed to the terrain. "The Tear of Havel never fell and created an elf. It flew across the world and landed somewhere up north. See these ridges: ice and snow."

She looked where Jasper pointed and saw the Tear resting on a smooth patch of mithril.

"It froze," Chert added, "and never had the chance to create something."

Sehraine looked around toward the front, dazzled by the brilliance of the Tear of Havel. Its inner light illuminated her face and reflected in her eyes.

"If we take it out, will it melt?"

"I don't think so," Jasper and Chert said together.

Jasper moved around back and studied it carefully.

"Chert, take a look at this."

The dwarf shuffled over and watched Jasper trace his finger over several more dimples.

"Are these more tears or stars?"

The dwarf backed away and said, "It's a constellation."

"Really?"

Jasper backed up as well and looked again. "You're right. I don't know why I didn't see it before. It's Cetus or Tiamat, and it's looking over Cayn's shoulder."

"What does that mean?" Sehraine asked, joining them.

"It's hard to say," Chert said. "It could be that the elves blame that constellation, or what it represents, for Cayn's actions."

"What's down here?" she asked, pointing toward the bottom edge of the reliquary.

"Some kind of symbol," Jasper said. "Xandor and Dobrynya, can you lift this up so we can get a better look at the bottom?"

Dobrynya stood and stretched while Xandor checked his journal one more time before putting it away. They stepped onto the rostrum, and Dobrynya closed the reliquary door. They took up positions on opposite sides of the cabinet, grasped the mithril handles, and lifted the reliquary from its resting place.

Underneath were more elven symbols.

Xandor asked Jasper, "Can you use them to open it?"

The mage shook violently, and Sehraine wrapped her arms about him. His flesh burned with fever, and she caught a putrid whiff of decay.

Jasper closed his eyes until the shivers passed. When he reopened them, he grabbed Sehraine's arm, and whispered words she didn't understand.

The faint etchings glowed, and memory flooded her mind. A gasp escaped her lips, and her eyes filled with tears. It was the lullaby sung by the Eternal Father to the elves the first night of their creation. The song that soothed their fears against the sons of Cayn. All elven parents sang it to their children.

Memories of her grandmother and father singing this lullaby filled her head, and she began to sing with them. At first, the sounds came out jumbled and hushed, but as she continued, the music became bolder and elven magic wove into the song.

Closing his eyes, Jasper grasped Sehraine's hand and when the verse repeated, he joined her.

Good evening, good night,
With roses, bedight,
With cloves adorned,
Let your fears be in vain.
Tomorrow morn,
You will wake once again.
Tomorrow morn,
You will wake once again.

Good evening, good night,
My elves, faeries, and sprites,
Calm the racing of your heart's beat,
And lay you down by the cool stream,
Sleep now blissfully and sweet,
See paradise in your dreams.
Sleep now blissfully and sweet,
See paradise in your dreams.

Grendel and Sacha left the back of the chapel and came forward. Light from the Tear of Havel shone brighter, and its purple hue faded. Xandor and Dobrynya quickly set the cabinet down and backed away, looks of awe on their faces. Blinding lines appeared at the edges of the box as it slowly opened, and the Tear of Havel rose above their heads. The light changed to a brilliant silver, and the gem resonated in the air, answering the call of the elven music.

Basking in its glow, Sehraine and Jasper continued singing. The Tear of Havel grew brighter still, and an inaudible wave of sound seeped into their skin and bone, forcing out the corruption caused by the Blood of Cayn.

Formless shadows appeared around them, held at bay by the pure silver light. Sehraine and Jasper continued to sing. The darkness behind Sehraine coalesced into a single shape, and the mouths of the dwolma filled the chapel with pain-filled shrieks. With a loud crescendo, the shadow exploded into black dust motes that ignited and burned away, one by one.

They collapsed onto the rostrum, and the singing stopped.

Sehraine pushed herself upright on shaky arms and rubbed at her makeup. The grey blotches were gone. No trace of the disease or the dwolma remained. She reached over to feel Jasper's forehead. He slept soundly, the fever broken.

Standing in the hall outside the chapel with several of the servants, Sergei hummed the tune, a twisted smirk on his otherwise handsome face.

CHAPTER 32:
JUDGE AND JURY

October 31, 4235 K.E.

7:00am

Two rows of horsemen cantered down the brick lane. The morning frost crunched under their hooves and steam wrapped around the horses' muzzles, giving them the appearance of breathing smoke. The leader carried a swallow-tailed pennon emblazoned with a purpure-and-argent checker-pattern, the heraldic badge of the Korol'.

A team of stark white horses pulled a gilded carriage past the main gate. After the carriage, another ten horsemen followed, guarding an empty jail wagon.

Gertsog Leonid Sabe waited on the top step with his son. Behind them, a grim-looking Sacha stood beside Grendel, who was adjusting the straps on his leather armor. The hilt of Skyld's sword rose above his shoulder, within easy reach. Xandor and the rest of his team stood back amongst the colonnade, trying unsuccessfully to look relaxed. Jasper had a tight grip on his staff, his clear eyes focused on the approaching parade.

The horsemen broke formation, splitting apart and allowing the carriage to pull around and stop at the bottom of the marble steps. The waiting servants placed a footstool beside the carriage and opened the door.

A gloved hand reached out and gripped the dark door handle for support. Out stepped a short, elderly man who wore official court robes. On his right hand was a gold signet ring similar to Gertsog Sabe's. After him, came a tall, powerfully built man wearing black judge's robes, but the expression on his face was one of an executioner. In his hand, he carried a wooden rod tipped with a steel ball.

At the front of the line, the captain barked an order. The horsemen dismounted and formed ranks beside the horses. He eyed the men in the recessed entry, but his face remained impassive.

"Velikiy-Gertsog Vsevolod, how good it is to see you again. Be at peace here," Gertsog Sabe said, bowing his head as the two new arrivals walked up the steps.

"Gertsog Sabe, thank you for seeing me this early. May I introduce to you Sud'ya Oleg Belousov," the elderly man said. "You may have heard of him."

"Only by reputation," Gertsog Sabe said, turning to the judge.

The judge, however, swept his gaze across the group behind his host. A cold chill raced down Xandor's spine when he met the other man's eyes. Something about the judge didn't feel right.

The elder Sabe continued with the customary greeting, "Welcome, Sud'ya Oleg Belousov. Be at peace here."

"Thank you, Gertsog Sabe," the judge said, bowing.

"The Korol' was most pleased to find you captured a Madasgorski alive," Vsevolod said. "Where is she?" He made a show of looking around.

"I'm here, Your Eminence," Sacha said, stepping out from Grendel's protective shadow.

Vsevolod's eyes grew wide at her sudden appearance. "What is the meaning of this, Leonid?" he demanded. "Why is this criminal not bound in irons?"

Before the Gertsog could answer, Sacha replied with a bow, "I voluntarily surrender myself to your authority, Velikiy-Gertsog Vsevolod."

The nobleman's head drew back, and his eyes narrowed with suspicion. "Who are you, young lady?"

"If I may?" Oleg asked politely. Vsevolod nodded and the judge gave Sacha a short bow. "Baroness Aleksandra Madasgorski Krakova, cousin to Imperatritsa Malraisa of Zhitomir, I have heard so much about you," he said. "This is indeed a fine catch, Gertsog Sabe."

The judge's voice was smooth, but his eyes lingered on Sacha's body longer than they should have. Xandor watched the judge, and his hand involuntarily moved toward the hilt of his sword. Yana, who stood next to him, noticed his intent, and touched her shoulder to his arm. He glanced down at her with eyes that had gone cold and hard. Yana gave the barest shake of her head in the negative. On Xandor's other side, Chert's beard bristled at the judge's attitude, and his fingers rubbed over his palm as if his hand itched for the hammer nestled in its belt loop.

Sacha's eyebrows rose slightly as she studied the man in front of her like a piece of meat. The barest hint of a smile curled her lips. She held up her hand, palm down, and said, "It's been a long time since anyone has addressed me formally."

The judge took it and brushed her fingers with his lips.

Straightening, he said with a smile, "Had I known it was you, I would have chosen better accommodations."

Sacha glanced at the jail wagon before waving her hand airily and said, "No, you chose well."

The judge's his smile froze. If he couldn't tell whether she offered insult or compliment, her next statement left no doubt.

Awarding the judge with one of her best smiles, she said sweetly, "Given the present company that surrounds me, I much prefer the solitude of the kibitka."

Oleg's smile vanished and his eyes flashed dangerously. "Baroness, it will do you no good to insult me."

Sacha took a half-step toward the judge. There was no outward difference in her appearance and, except to those who knew her, it might have gone unnoticed, but the judge couldn't keep his eyes off her, trapped by his own desires. She was in her element.

Gertsog Sabe grabbed her arm and motioned to his son. "Please escort the baroness to the kibitka. See to it that she is made comfortable."

"Yes, Father."

"Are your men ready?"

"Yes, Sir."

Dobrynya nodded to Ilya, who had taken a position near the bottom step. His second signaled to the dozen men standing near the line of trees. Leading their horses, they formed up behind the jail wagon.

The young knight offered Sacha his arm with a kind smile. She took it graciously, letting Vityaz Dobrynya escort her past the lecherous judge.

The Korol's men openly stared at Grendel following Sacha and shifted uneasily. Hands gripped weapons up and down the line.

The grand duke's wrinkled face went livid. "Leonid, what is the meaning of this?"

"I'm sorry, Your Eminence, but since I could not go with you, my son offered to escort the baroness to face the Korol'." Gertsog Sabe stared at Oleg meaningfully as he continued, "We would hate for something to happen to her along the way."

Oleg eyed the gertsog with a brief flash of undisguised hatred but wisely kept his mouth shut. He turned and followed Dobrynya and the baroness to the jail wagon.

Watching the group approach the wagon, Vsevolod said thoughtfully, "Leonid, you and I have seen many campaigns. Why do you do this?"

Gertsog Sabe watched his son open the jail door and said, "She saved his life, Bazyl. I owed her that much. Besides, she has freely surrendered herself to you. I believe she deserves to be treated better than some animal locked in a cage."

"She's a Madasgorski, Leonid. One of the enemy. Are you certain she has not beguiled your son?"

Without hesitation, Gertsog Sabe answered, "I am certain, Your Eminence."

The unquestionable confidence in Sabe's voice made the elderly man pause. "Then I will do what I can for her," Vsevolod promised. "Now, what is this about you finding a cure for the plague?"

"Your Eminence, please, follow me." Gertsog Sabe gestured toward the door to the foyer. "Master Thredd and Xandor, if you would follow us."

A half-dozen of the Korol's men stood in the chapel dressed in their purpure-and-argent surcoats over chainmail shirts. They had just witnessed the Tear of Havel rise up from its reliquary and glow with astounding brilliance. Having heard its song, every man there wore the beatific expression of one who witnessed an unexpected miracle.

"Master Thredd, you said that this gem does what again?" Vsevolod said after finding his voice.

"Your Eminence, it forces the corruption of the Blood of Cayn out of the body."

"Gertsog Sabe, we will need to take this to the Korol'."

"Of course."

At a gesture from the old man, two soldiers cautiously approached the reliquary.

Xandor and Jasper stood back, giving them room. Their faces were masks, but deep down, Jasper felt like they were losing the battle. He knew Xandor felt the same, even though this was the right thing to do. Gertsog Sabe had already told them to be ready to travel with the Tear of Havel. Without asking, he had made them its unofficial guardians.

The two watched the soldiers walk the box down the aisle toward the exit while the others marched out in front to clear the way. Velikiy-Gertsog Vsevolod and Gertsog Sabe walked behind the reliquary, deep in conversation about the Tear of Havel, and whether the Korol' should expect the Elven Nation to lay claim to it. They hoped their leader could broker a deal with Trakya and the Confederation of Nations that would avoid war and be mutually beneficial.

The moment the two noblemen crossed the threshold, a blanket of darkness enveloped the hallway. In the seconds it took Xandor to register the danger and reach for his weapons, soldiers shouted for help and were brutally silenced in mid-cry. Wet noises echoed off the stone as something spattered the walls. Jasper reached for his magic. Rough hands threw Gertsog Sabe back into the chapel, knocking them both down.

Before the mage and ranger could disentangle themselves, the darkness in the hallway fled and light from the lanterns returned. Jasper wished it hadn't. Six soldiers lay at odd angles like torn and discarded rag dolls. The walls ran red with their blood.

Velikiy-Gertsog Vsevolod's upper torso lay at the threshold, his body ripped in half. Xandor and Jasper searched the hallway, but the reliquary was gone.

Shouts echoed from the foyer. Gertsog Sabe looked up from the bloody mess as one of his servants rushed toward him.

"Your Serenity! Come quickly! Trouble in the courtyard!"

Xandor and Jasper immediately stood, ready for action, but Gertsog Sabe said, "Stay here. Figure out what happened. I'll handle what's going on outside."

"Yes, Your Serenity," Xandor and Jasper replied and reluctantly turned their attention to the spatter patterns on the wall.

8:35am

Outside, the jail wagon was empty. Sud'ya Belousov turned to Dobrynya, who stood staring at the empty space inside the bars.

"Vityaz Dobrynya, you have acted disgracefully! I blame you for the baroness' escape!"

"Sud'ya Belousov, I had nothing to do with her escape," he said calmly, a rock amidst the sea of the judge's fury.

With a sly look on his face, Oleg whispered, "What happened between you two? Was the sex good?"

Dobrynya ignored the question. The clenching of the muscles in his jaw was the only evidence he had heard the judge's comment.

Digging further, Oleg continued, "Now if you had been your brother..."

Dobrynya lashed out and the judge's head snapped back. Closing in, the young knight followed up with several jabs to the man's lower ribs.

Lowering his head, the judge tucked his elbows and raised his forearms to defend against the blows.

Hurried footsteps crunched on the frost-covered ground.

Ilya grabbed Dobrynya's arm as he reached back to throw a right cross. He forcefully dragged the knight toward his men, who immediately formed a protective ring around them.

On the other side of the jail wagon, the Korol's men surrounded Sud'ya Oleg Belousov with their weapons drawn, and yet they hesitated.

Between the small knot of battle-hardened veterans and the Korol's men, Grendel brandished a huge sword. He glared at the empty wagon. His nostrils flared and he drew in a great lungful of the frozen air.

The two groups eyed each other, waiting for the order to charge.

"Vityaz Dobrynya Sabe! You are under arrest for striking a member of the court and helping a member of the Madasgorski family escape!" Oleg yelled, gesturing with his metal-tipped rod to emphasize every word.

Gertsog Sabe rushed down the marble steps and yelled, "What is going on out here?"

Oleg turned to Gertsog Sabe, revealing a swollen left eye that was already beginning to darken.

Father glared at son, who only gave him a slight, apologetic shrug.

"I demand to know what happened!" Gertsog Sabe said, staring at his men.

"Gertsog Sabe, I demand justice. Your son helped the baroness escape and struck me in the process."

"I had nothing to do with it!" Dobrynya said vehemently and tried to slip out of Ilya's grasp, but the grizzled soldier tightened his grip. Realizing his struggles were getting him nowhere, Dobrynya drew himself up to his full height and said, "She simply vanished!"

"You were standing beside her! I saw you!" the judge accused, pointing toward the empty jail wagon like it was all the proof he needed.

Dobrynya's father held up his hands, gesturing for both men to calm down.

"Drop your swords! Rhodinans will not fight Rhodinans today!" he shouted, walking straight to his men, his face set in grim determination. His soldiers were slow to respond, so Gertsog Sabe grabbed the first soldier he came to and made him drop his weapon. It fell to the frozen ground with a metallic ring. He walked to the next one and the next, and slowly, his men dropped their weapons. Gertsog Sabe didn't stop. He continued around the group, making sure every one of his men followed his order. Until he came to Grendel.

The half-orc stared at the cage, confusion and frustration waging a war across his face. Gertsog Sabe grabbed his wrist while everyone watched.

Grendel jerked, as if seeing the Gertsog for the first time. The two made eye contact. Neither spoke, but something passed between them. With a sigh, Grendel sheathed the long, two-handed weapon.

Ilya let Dobrynya go. The soldiers around him made ready to grab him, just in case.

Gertsog Sabe turned, ignoring his son, and inspected the jail wagon. Oleg joined him. Neither saw any signs of forced entry or obvious means of escape.

"Count yourself fortunate, Gertsog Sabe, that you were able to stop your men when you did," Oleg said smugly.

"Velikiy-Gertsog Vsevolod is dead," Gertsog Sabe said abruptly, wiping the smug look from the judge's face, only to have it replaced by one of righteous fury.

A collective gasp escaped the soldiers.

Stepping back as if he might become a suspect through sheer proximity to the elder Sabe, he spat, "Gertsog Sabe! You were responsible for his safety! What happened?"

"Come see for yourself," he offered.

Oleg eyed the gertsog suspiciously and said, "And put myself in your care? Do you think me stupid?"

With the mask of a diplomat, Gertsog Sabe responded, "You asked what happened. It would be best if I show you."

Glancing around, Oleg motioned to the captain of the guard. The soldier ran up, keeping a wary eye on Sabe's men. "Sud'ya Belousov."

In a voice loud enough for everyone to hear, Oleg ordered, "Send a message to the Korol'. Tell him that Velikiy-Gertsog Vsevolod is dead and Baroness Aleksandra Madasgorski Krakova has escaped. Tell him that Gertsog Sabe is responsible."

With a short bow, the captain of the guard rushed off.

Turning on Gertsog Sabe, he said, "I will personally see to it that you are stripped of your lands and title for this debacle."

"Before you jump to conclusions, Sud'ya, perhaps you should see the evidence first," the gertsog requested. "You have my word of honor that nothing will happen to you."

Oleg weighed the elder Sabe's words, then whipped around and yelled, "Captain of the Guard!"

The soldier stopped and turned.

Oleg studied the gertsog's face as he said, "I agree, on one condition. I want your son as my hostage until the baroness is found. And if anything goes wrong..."

"Nothing will go wrong, Sud'ya," Gertsog Sabe said quickly, and then yelled, "Dobrynya!"

The younger Sabe turned to his father.

"Surrender yourself to the Korol's men. Now."

"But, father..."

"Do it!"

With his head hung low, Dobrynya crossed the clearing toward the awaiting soldiers. He could feel Ilya and the other men watching him, and a feeling of helplessness washing over him.

An evil smile twisted the judge's face, and he said, "Captain, delay that order. If I'm not back in fifteen minutes, then send it and Vityaz Dobrynya as well."

"Yes, Sir."

"Gertsog Sabe, you have bought yourself some time," Oleg said graciously. "Please lead the way."

The elder Sabe nodded and gave his son one last look before heading into the mansion.

Chert followed the guards inside. His compact stature allowed him to escape most of the attention as he pushed his way through the crowded hallway. When they approached the chapel, the air turned coppery and smelled of death, but there was another smell as well: brimstone.

Jasper leaned over one of the dead soldiers and checked the man's vitals one more time. Deep red gashes crisscrossed his chest. He picked out a bloodied chain mail link embedded in one of the wounds. The damage looked to be from some type of bladed weapon, but Chert wasn't sure. Whatever it was that attacked these soldiers was both inhumanly strong and fast.

Suddenly, the soldier opened his eyes wide and screamed. Oleg, who stood observing the body of Velikiy-Gertsog Vsevolod, turned around and watched as Chert rushed to the wounded man's side and placed his hands on the soldier's chest.

"You there! Get away from him!" the judge ordered.

"I can save him!" Chert replied.

Not waiting for a response, the dwarf prayed to the Eternal Father for healing. Blue light spread from the dwarf's hands, seeping into the wounds.

"Jasper, keep picking out the links. I can't heal him with those inside him."

With Oleg standing over his shoulder, Jasper carefully dug into the wounds, pulling out piece after piece of metal. Fresh blood seeped from the wounds, and the warrior flinched each time one came out.

As Jasper cleaned, Chert slowly knitted the flesh back together, mending the wounds inside. The soldier's eyes became sharper as the pain receded. They darted around until they focused on Sud'ya Belousov.

The judge knelt beside him, placed a hand on his head, and asked, "Who did this?"

The soldier's face clouded as he remembered the attack. His body trembled with fear, and he stared wide-eyed at the judge. Grabbing Oleg's arm with a bloodied hand, he gasped, "It was the Madasgorski woman."

Standing, Sud'ya Belousov slipped out of the warrior's weakened grip and said, "Gertsog Sabe, I have seen enough!" He turned and addressed his guards. "No one leaves this house. Is that clear?"

The sud'ya faced Gertsog Sabe and announced, "You are all my witnesses of the court. You will be confined to this house until a proper trial can be arranged."

"Sud'ya Belousov, you can't be serious," Gertsog Sabe said.

"As you said, Your Serenity. You wanted me to see the evidence first, now I have witnesses. The Baroness is guilty, and so is your son."

Xandor glared at the judge, then turned to Gertsog Sabe for an explanation. The gertsog motioned him to silence. Sud'ya Belousov smiled and walked away, leaving one of the guards behind to protect the evidence.

As soon as he was out of earshot, Xandor asked, "What was that all about?"

"My hot-headed son hit Sud'ya Belousov."

"Why?"

"Does it matter? It happened," the gertsog said sadly. He turned to Xandor. "Against my better judgement, I trusted you. Worse, I trusted her."

"I am sorry, Your Serenity. We all trusted her," Xandor replied.

Chert looked up from his healing and asked, "You can't seriously think that she did all this?"

The look on Xandor's face said it all.

Gertsog Sabe saw it, and his shoulders slumped in defeat. He bowed his head as if to pray, but his eyes locked on the bloody footprints near Xandor.

Xandor followed the direction of the gertsog's gaze to several smaller booted prints. Despite their smeared and streaked state, it was obvious that none of the men made them.

"They're Sacha's," the ranger said with certainty.

"You can't know that for sure. They could be from any of the women in this household," Chert said.

Xandor studied the tracks, wishing they would change. "You're right. I can't know for sure, but they match her weight, size, and the way she carried herself."

Chert stopped and spread his arms. "Can't you smell it?"

Xandor and Jasper's heads snapped up. They both looked pointedly at the guard stationed in the hallway.

Chert glanced from them to the guard and back again.

"It would only muddy the situation," Xandor said. "We're stuck here."

Gertsog Sabe looked at the men through narrowed eyes, clearly not understanding what they left unsaid.

Chert finished closing the deeper wounds on the young soldier's chest and put him into a deep, healing sleep. Jasper leaned on his staff and gave the bloody mess another good look. He was no expert like Xandor, so the spatter patterns and footprints were a mystery to him, but to the ranger, they were an open book. If he said Sacha was here, then she was here. He cast a furtive glance at the ranger and then at Chert. Jasper felt confident they were all thinking the same thing: it was her demon.

But did she send it so she could escape? What was really going on here?

Jasper and Xandor shared a look. After a moment, the ranger nodded toward Gertsog Sabe. Jasper closed his eyes and concentrated.

'Gertsog Sabe.'

The elder Sabe looked around suddenly — the voice was in his head.

'I apologize for this intrusion, but we felt you needed an alternate explanation to these events.'

'Master Thredd?'

'Yes, Your Serenity.'

'What's going on here? Why can't you talk openly?'

'The judge's guard, Your Serenity. He's listening to everything we say and will report it to Sud'ya Belousov. There are some things that need to be left unsaid for the time being.'

'Like what?'

'We have reason to believe a demon did this.'

'A demon?'

Gertsog Sabe swept the gory hallway and the untouched chapel beyond the threshold with new eyes.

'Unfortunately, Your Serenity, the baroness had a demon bodyguard. Grendel definitely saw it, and Xandor said he thought he felt its presence, once. She may have sent the demon for the explicit purpose of collecting the Tear of Havel.'

'Why are you telling me this?'

'We thought you needed to know. We don't think the judge is aware of the possible connection, but if he finds out, it may only strengthen his case.'

'Is that the only explanation?'

'Maybe not. It is Winter's Night, after all.'

'You mean Vetrnætr?'

'Yes, Your Serenity.'

Gertsog Sabe looked thoughtfully at the guard before turning back to Jasper, Xandor, and Chert. The mage could see the man's struggle to give them his trust. On the one hand, they helped save Dobrynya's life. On the other hand, they may have ruined his position with the Korol'.

'Can you find her?'

'I can't by myself, but with Grendel's help, I can.'

'I need her to get my son back.'

Out loud, Gertsog Sabe asked, "What do you know of my other son, August?"

The question caught Jasper by surprise.

"Your Serenity?" Xandor asked.

"Do you really know him?"

The ranger nodded. "We do."

Gertsog Sabe searched their faces.

Reaching a decision, he said, "Master Joalheiro, see to it that this soldier is stabilized and meet us in the foyer. Xandor and Master Thredd, please come with me."

CHAPTER 33:
STAMPEDE!

October 31, 4235 K.E.

11:00am

Gertsog Sabe led Xandor and Jasper past the servants' stair and glanced down the hallway. A pair of the Korol's men moved from room to room, collecting those within and directing them to the dining room. The gertsog paused briefly as they marched past, and then continued toward the entry foyer.

Sud'ya Belousov was outside, talking to the captain of the guard. Ilya and his men knelt on the frozen earth with their hands behind their heads. Soldiers collected weapons and deposited them in a pile. Several of the Korol's men surrounded Grendel, who still wore Skyld's sword and refused to give it up. Dobrynya had taken Sacha's place in the jail wagon.

Mariya ran up to Gertsog Sabe, on the verge of hysteria.

"Not now, woman," he snapped.

Lady Yelizaveta, Yana, and Sehraine watched the events transpiring on the lawn. They turned when Gertsog Sabe and the other two men approached.

"Leonid, what's happened? They've taken Dobrynya."

"Sud'ya Belousov accused him of helping the baroness murder Velikiy-Gertsog Vsevolod, and your son struck him. Not the most diplomatic of gestures."

Sehraine raised a hand to her mouth in surprise.

Yana looked at Xandor and Jasper and asked, "Did she do it?"

"The evidence suggests that she did," replied Xandor.

"I don't believe it," Sehraine said.

"Your Serenity, can't we beat some sense into Sud'ya Belousov?" Jasper asked.

"No, I'm afraid not. He has apparently made it his personal mission to bring down this family, and if I resist him, the Korol' will only see it as a sign of guilt. We must take the higher road."

"It seems the Madasgorski reputation does far more damage than the actual individual," Xandor mused.

"Perhaps, but none of this would have happened had I not accepted her into my house."

"I disagree," Jasper said. "I believe that whoever is behind this was after the Tear of Havel and used us to get it."

Everyone stared at the mage.

"How? The only people who knew what we were after and where to find it were Dobrynya and Lord Fergusson. Surely you aren't accusing them?" Xandor asked.

"What about Knyaz Dorinkov? He knew Sacha's identity and that we sought the cure."

"Knyaz Dorinkov didn't know the Tear was here," Xandor said. "Only Lord Fergusson received that information."

"Still," Jasper pressed, "the prince knew we were coming here. He has the power and resources to have us followed. How else do you think the Korol's judge arrived here so quickly? And what about us? We all knew."

"Are you suggesting we have a traitor amongst us?"

"I'm just saying that the list of suspects is longer than you think."

"Where's Sergei?"

"I'm here," the bard said from a position near the windows.

"If it's not one of us, then that only leaves Sacha," Jasper said, watching Grendel.

"And her demon," Chert muttered.

"If we can bring her back alive, then, maybe, we can save Dobrynya and the Sabe reputation."

Xandor said quietly, "You know that Sud'ya Belousov won't let us go without a fight. We're his *witnesses*."

Gertsog Sabe looked pointedly at each of Xandor's team and said, "I cannot help you in this matter, but remember you are not bound by Rhodinan law. You represent the Iron Tower, Trakya, the Elf Nation, and the Dwarf Nation. As such, you can request certain rights, but remember, your actions reflect not only upon you as an individual, but upon your countrymen as well."

His piercing eyes focused on Xandor. "Without the Tear of Havel, there is nothing to stop the plague."

"What will happen to you and your family?" Xandor asked, feeling the weight of the world on his shoulders.

Gertsog Sabe smiled sadly and said, "I will seek an audience with Melikhov and plead our case."

11:20am

Xerxes stomped the ground impatiently. He snorted, and his breath came out in twin jets of steam. Xandor huddled close to him, the hood of his mottled cloak pulled up, helping to conceal him from watchful eyes.

Yana stood on the other side of Xerxes, wearing a borrowed cloak. It billowed loosely about her slight frame, but she managed to cross the yard between the estate house and the stables unobserved.

The Korol's men patrolled the grounds, waiting for reinforcements. Once they arrived, there would be no escape, so she and Xandor had snuck into the stables to prepare the horses. Xerxes was still bitter about Xandor riding in the carriage, but after a few sweet treats, the Andalusian began to forgive the ranger. In addition to Xerxes, they had two mares, the Percheron Xandor rescued from the mudpots, and the two mud-colored horses Jasper created from earthworms. She shook her head. The two horses didn't act right and probably never would, but they were all they had. The other horses were trained warhorses, and unlikely to carry a new rider unchallenged.

They both ducked when a guard walked past the stalls, checking the barn. Fortunately, the stalls were full height with tall doors that concealed their preparations.

She watched Xandor finish cinching Xerxes' saddle and recalled his plan with a dangerous smile. It was elegantly simple and lacked the complications inherent in Sacha's plan at Chernigov. When asked, he had simply said, "Let's make a run for it." So here they were.

They had horses for everyone, including Sergei, who had requested to "tag along and write their story." At the very least, the thought was that he could provide a third-party account and maybe sway the Korol' to their side. Who could say?

Grendel remained outside, watched by a handful of the Korol's guards. Across the way, the judge and the captain of the guard spoke in low murmurs and occasionally gestured in his direction.

Truth was, Grendel felt adrift. He had heard the accusations and watched as Sacha had simply vanished from the jail wagon. His heart sank to his feet when he thought about it, an anchor that weighed him down more than any chains.

"Yah! Yah!" The shout burst from the nearby stables, followed by the sudden pounding of hooves. The frozen ground shook as a dozen horses galloped out behind Xerxes.

Everyone in the yard turned.

Spread out like the head of a spear, the line of horses galloped past the edge of the house and angled toward the jail wagon. In the lead, Xandor clung to the side of his horse, trying to make himself as difficult a target as possible.

Not believing what they were seeing, the Korol's men formed loose ranks with weapons ready.

Instead of going around, Xandor guided Xerxes directly toward them. "Move! Move!" he shouted.

Gesturing wildly, the captain's eyes went wide when he realized they weren't going to turn. The thundering hooves drowned out his orders and his men flung themselves to the side.

Xandor aimed Xerxes directly at Sud'ya Belousov, forcing the judge to dive out of the way and hide behind one of the ancient trees lining the lane. At the last second, Xerxes veered toward Grendel.

The half-orc watched the horses stampede toward him and saw the massive Percheron near one side. They turned, and suddenly the Percheron raced along the edge of the herd.

With speed unlike any the soldiers had ever seen before, he slammed an elbow into the mouth of the nearest guard and spun to one side. The guards fell back from the oncoming horses as Grendel raced across the field.

Xerxes, still in the lead, slowed enough for Grendel to catch up and grab the Percheron's saddle.

Yana emerged from the opposite side of the house, riding at the head of a second group of horses. Sehraine and Chert rode tandem on the horse immediately behind her, with Jasper and Sergei bringing up the rear.

Her eyes swept across the tableau. Sud'ya Belousov had his back to the bole of a huge oak, his face twisted with rage. Gertsog Sabe held his wife on the broad marble steps, eyes wide with shock. Clustered around the jail wagon, the Korol's guards seemed frozen.

"They're stealing my horses!" Gertsog Sabe shouted.

The nobleman's voice set the captain of the guard and his men into motion. The leader and half his men leapt into their saddles and spurred their horses to a gallop behind the fugitives.

Xandor glanced over his shoulder and made eye contact with Yana. His eyes narrowed when he caught sight of the soldiers closing in on them. He crouched lower in Xerxes' saddle and urged more speed out of his mount.

CHAPTER 34:
THE ELF RING

October 31, 4235 K.E.

11:40am

Kicking up chunks of frozen ground, Xandor and his team's horses raced out of the main gate at a dead run with their tails flowing behind them like streamers in the morning light. The forested landscape flew by, and the ranger occasionally glimpsed blurry patches of snow in his peripheral vision. The cold air nipped at his fingers as his adrenaline wore down.

He felt bad about stealing the gertsog's mounts, but there had been little choice. Now, the herd mentality had taken over. The ranger glanced over his shoulder. The warhorses from the stables followed Xerxes, easily keeping pace. Two horses back and to the left, he saw Grendel's tall form, his face unreadable. The others clung to their horse's backs.

A shrill whistle grabbed his attention, and he saw Yana signaling. He gradually pulled up on Xerxes' reins and slowed to a quick trot.

Yana urged her horse closer. "We need to stop!"

Xandor tugged on the reins a little harder, and Xerxes came to a walk. As Xerxes slowed, the excitement of the chase evaporated, and the herd broke up behind him. They milled about along the side of the road and searched for bits of grass.

The thunderous pounding of the Korol's horses drew closer.

With a gesture, Xandor had everyone slip from their saddles and walk their horses into the woods, using the gertsog's warhorses for cover. Yana led the others deeper into the trees and underbrush while Xandor obscured their tracks.

"Halt, in the name of the Korol'!" a voice shouted.

Thinking the soldier spotted him, Xandor stopped moving and watched the horses for signs of trouble. The warhorses looked up from their browsing, but they quickly lost interest in the arriving soldiers.

Xandor didn't make the mistake of making any sudden moves that might give him away and counted the seconds. On the count of eight, he realized that the voice had come from the opposite side of the herd.

"Sir, there's no one here."

Xandor raised his hood and crouched silently in the underbrush beside a tall hardwood.

"Check the herd!" the captain shouted as he wove his way through the horses. Once on the other side, he stopped and jumped down to inspect the woods.

One of the horsemen came within a few feet of the brush concealing Xandor. He searched the forest floor intently, but there was no sign of anyone leaving the road, just the creaking of the trees in a light wind.

A soldier made a sign to ward off evil. "Witchcraft," he whispered.

"Elf magic," another suggested, and a few glanced about nervously.

The captain ignored them and ordered, "Circle back around and find them. They're here somewhere."

Peering through the leaves, Xandor counted seven soldiers on his side of the road as they fanned out. He waited by the tree and watched them efficiently divide the areas adjacent to the road into a grid. After a few long minutes, most were ready to give up, but the captain made them expand their search farther and farther away from the road.

Xandor remained silent and still, watching the soldiers for any indication they'd spotted him or his companions.

The sun rose higher, and it became apparent the soldiers would find no one. Moving back to the road, the captain collected his men and the gertsog's warhorses and headed back to the Sabe estate.

Xandor emerged from the shelter of a tall oak with low hanging boughs. In the distance, the air shimmered as Jasper lowered his staff, canceling his mirage.

"That was close," Yana said when Xandor joined them.

The ranger nodded.

"They may come back," Sergei said. "We should have killed them, or at least tied them up."

Xandor glowered at him and shook his head. "No. They are good soldiers, just doing their duty," he replied. "Letting them go was best."

"Maybe, unless they're corrupt like the sud'ya."

"Sud'ya Belousov might be corrupt, but I believe there is honor amongst the ranks of men," the ranger replied.

"Some men," Yana corrected.

"True," Xandor admitted. Looking to the sky to get an idea of the time, he motioned everyone deeper into the forest. He led them along a game trail and around a bramble thicket into a thick copse of trees with a canopy of frost-covered branches.

The trees gave way to a secluded dell, well hidden from the road. Xandor nodded with satisfaction and brought the group to a halt. "Jasper, where to now?" he asked.

The mage turned to face the half-orc and said, "Grendel, I need your help finding Sacha."

"How should I know where she is?"

"You don't, but your memories and your connection to her can provide me a way to locate her."

"She is innocent!" Grendel exclaimed as he read the expression on everyone's faces.

"Grendel, we don't know if she's innocent or not," Xandor said. Before Grendel could interrupt, he held up a hand and continued, "The evidence seems to be against her, but we also know she's bound to a demon that cannot be trusted. It wasn't until I saw the devastation in the hallway outside the chapel that I truly understood. We must find the Tear of Havel — that is our mission — and to find the Tear, we must find Sacha, regardless of her guilt or innocence."

Grendel stared at Xandor, letting his words sink in. "What can I do?"

"Jasper?"

The mage moved in front of Grendel and motioned for him to kneel in the loam. "I know you haven't trusted me in the past, but I need your trust. I need to reach inside your memories and find Sacha."

"Will it hurt?"

Jasper shrugged. "Only as much as remembering a painful memory."

Xandor quirked an eyebrow. "You can find her with a memory?"

"It depends on Grendel. Sacha may have severed their connection when she tried to kill him, or it may have made it stronger. I won't know until I look inside."

Standing beside Grendel with his arms crossed, Chert asked, "Can this affect his mind?"

"Only if he resists, which is why I need him to relax and trust me."

Grendel looked calm, but the vein throbbing near his temple revealed his inner turmoil.

Jasper placed his hands on each side of Grendel's face, with the tips of his middle fingers on the half-orc's temples. "You have a big head, did you know that? Maybe I won't get lost."

Hoping it was only a jest, Grendel kept quiet and listened as Jasper explained what he was doing.

"Emotions are the key. They can become a link between one person and another. These links are tenuous at best, but are stronger between two people who love each other, like the bond between a mother and her child. Strong links can actually exhibit physical traits, such as pain if the other person is hurt. Sometimes, it may even prevent a person who died from moving on."

Jasper's words became hypnotic, and Grendel found himself relaxing.

"Only strong emotions provide links, but what constitutes a strong emotion is subjective. I prefer emotional events to feelings. They tend to be more stable. For example, links often form between people who share a near-death experience, and they may not even know it. The shared memory exists even though there may be slight differences due to perception, and it can be used to help locate one another."

"Is it magic?" Grendel asked. He couldn't tell if he spoke aloud or only inside his head.

"Good question. I have heard both sides of the argument and still don't have a good answer. I guess to answer that you must ask, 'what is magic,' which is also hard to define. For me, I have the ability to reach inside myself and draw upon a power to manipulate the elements or create something, even if it's just an illusion. Is that magic? I think most people would say so. But then couldn't we also say that childbirth is magic? Or feats of great strength that come only in times of need? Or faith, which fuels Chert's ability to manipulate the earth and to heal others?"

Jasper moved deeper into Grendel's head. Memories long forgotten came to the surface. The half-orc saw the faces of people flash in his mind: friends old and new, foes on the battlefield, strangers he met in passing. They all swam together.

"Grendel, this is where it gets tough. Are you ready?"

The half-orc nodded.

"I need you to focus on Sacha."

An image of Grendel kissing her in the tunnel outside Chernigov floated in his mind.

"Good. Now focus on the memories of when she tried to kill you."

Grendel jerked like a fish on a hook and tried to break Jasper's grip but couldn't. Jasper was inside his head.

"Calm down. You have to remember."

Slowly, Kraagor's torture chamber came to the surface. Pain clung to the memory like a scratchy wool cloak, but it wasn't physical. It was emotional. He saw Sacha chained to the wall and rushed to her side. The dagger suddenly appeared in her hand, and Jasper felt the memory of the blade plunging into Grendel's chest. He saw the moment when Sacha realized what she had done, and then he was inside her head. Sacha was unconscious, but there was an evil presence watching over her.

The demon.

Jasper jumped out of Grendel's head and tumbled backward.

"Well?" Xandor asked, holding out his hand.

"I found her. She's unconscious," Jasper replied, grabbing Xandor's hand to haul himself up off the ground.

Grendel opened his eyes and stood up, looking but not really seeing. "I feel her," he murmured in an awe-filled voice. "She's alive."

"I opened the door a little too wide, so to speak. Don't worry, it will wear off after a while."

Xandor glanced at both of them and said, "Does it work both ways?"

"Yes."

"Jasper," Xandor said, his voice growing angry, "she'll know we're coming."

"Well then, I guess we'll know if she's innocent or guilty. Besides, it couldn't be helped."

Sehraine laid a hand on Grendel's arm and asked softly, "Can you find her?"

"Yes, she is that way," he said, pointing due north.

Sehraine's gaze followed where he pointed. She grew pale.

"What is it?" Sergei asked.

"I don't know if she's there, but that's the same direction as my village."

6:28pm

The sun had already set behind a blanket of clouds by the time Xandor called for a stop. They had traveled most of the day cross-country through fields and wooded glens, with Grendel leading them farther and farther northward into the environs of winter. The ranger studied the ground and guessed that this area had seen its first snow several days ago. Patches of white stuck to the frozen ground and nestled in the crooks of tree branches. All around him, glistening snowflakes drifted down and landed gently on the needles of the evergreens, giving them a frosted look.

Xandor's boots crunched in the fresh snow as he jumped down from Xerxes' saddle. He wrapped his cloak tighter about him and collected some wood for a small fire while the others dismounted and prepared for the last leg of the trip: Sehraine's village — Välavtårar.

Sehraine stretched the kinks out of her muscles and looked nervously at the wall of trees marking the ancient boundaries of her people, expecting at any moment to see ghosts. Jasper joined her, his staff making tiny holes in the snow.

"You alright?" he asked.

"Yes. You?"

"Much better, thank you."

Her low-light vision made the dark forest as bright as day, but she still saw shadows at the limits of her vision.

A warm orange glow appeared behind them as Xandor risked a fire. Everyone huddled close and rubbed their hands together, trying to get the blood flowing again.

Sergei began humming the elven lullaby. Instead of comforting Sehraine, the bard's slow, deep-toned rendition sounded sinister and sent a shiver down her spine.

Xandor looked across the fire at Sehraine and asked, "Which way to your village from here?"

After getting her bearings, she pointed to an overgrown hollow in the wall of trees a hundred yards from their camp.

"That's the main road over there. We can follow it all the way to Välavtårar."

"How close are we?"

"Maybe an hour if we walk."

"Well, let's soak up as much heat as we can, then get this over with."

The road, as Sehraine called it, was a leaf-covered path bordered by ancient hardwood trees, barely wide enough for a single wagon. Following a step behind Xandor, Jasper used his staff to light the way. Small animals scampered out of their path. A snowy owl followed their progress and hooted before flying away to chase a tasty morsel.

Xandor stopped and raised a closed fist. While the others waited, he moved forward with caution and investigated something lying across the road.

Jasper couldn't see an immediate threat. He crunched through the snow and joined the ranger. In front of them, a solitary line of snow-covered toadstools over a foot high barred their path. Tilting his staff to direct the light, Jasper contemplated the puzzling scene. No snow lay beyond the toadstools. Alongside the oversized myconids rested a row of gleaming white stones that sparkled in his light. Filling the space between the toadstools and stones was a narrow line of white crystals — salt.

Jasper peered deep into the forest to the left and right. The intricate pattern traveled beyond the reach of his light. Even more bizarre, no trees grew within a dozen or more yards on either side of the toad stools, and no tree limbs crossed them overhead. He stroked his beard and turned over the conundrum in his mind.

"You might want to step back some," he told Xandor.

"What are you going to do?"

"Test a theory," the mage replied.

The ranger didn't ask for an explanation. He slipped back down the path to where Yana and the others waited.

Jasper wove a thin trace of magic over the tip of his staff and extended the charred wood across the toadstools.

Despite his efforts, he could not force the staff-tip beyond the line of salt. However, when Jasper released the magic, a surface shimmered into view and reflected the staff's light like a mirror. In its surface, he could see distorted images of his companions and the forest behind them.

"Wow," he breathed. Without warning, he doused his light, provoking protests from Xandor and Yana. Silence fell over the forest, lit by a dim green glow emanating from the barrier.

On its surface, fiery symbols swirled. Some appeared to be words written in runic script while others were complicated, geometric shapes. They danced about as if alive, each with the same dim, green glow.

Soaring over the trees, the mirror-like surface formed a dome of incredible proportions. With no easy way to judge its size, Jasper could only guess the magical barrier covered the entirety of Sehraine's village.

"What is it?" Xandor asked in amazement.

The mage used the tip of his staff to prod one of the fiery symbols. Shimmering ripples spread out in a circular pattern along the surface like water, but otherwise, it felt solid. "That, my friend, is the biggest containment circle I have ever seen." Re-illuminating his staff, the mage turned right and struck off into the woods.

"Uh, Jasper?" Xandor queried.

The mage, studying the circle, did not respond or even realize that no one followed him. His light bobbed up and down as he shined it at the surface of the barrier. Every once in a while, Jasper prodded the barrier with the end of his staff, and the shadows of the trees careened wildly to one side or the other.

The group waited but sounds of the mage's passing continued to recede. Xandor shrugged and looked at everyone else. "I guess we follow."

Yana asked, "What about the horses?"

"This is as far as they go," he replied, watching their small herd shift and stamp each time the light from the dome flared.

The ranger patted Xerxes on the neck. The horse somehow managed to look embarrassed. "It's alright, boy," Xandor said, slipping the bit and bridle from the horse's head and tucking it in a saddlebag. "Look after the others and keep them together. If we don't return by noon tomorrow, go to Gertsog Sabe. He'll take care of you."

The horse nickered affectionately and nodded.

"Good boy," Xandor said and then turned to the others. Everyone had followed his example and tended their own horses. He took care of Jasper's steed, then waited until the last saddlebag was buckled before speaking again. "Alright, let's follow the mage before he gets hurt."

Most everyone smiled at his attempt at humor, but Grendel and Sehraine shared haunted looks as they glanced around one last time.

Before Sergei took a step, Xandor put a hand on his chest and said, "You don't have to come. It'll be safer with the horses."

"Of course I'm coming. I wouldn't miss this for anything," the bard replied without hesitation.

Xandor slapped Sergei on the shoulder lightly before jogging into the woods to catch up with Jasper.

8:00pm

In the glow of his mage light, the floating symbols written on the surface of the barrier disappeared, so Jasper doused its glow and followed the dim green line along the ground. Taken in short segments, the bottom of the containment circle seemed almost a straight line. Looking back, however, he could not see Xandor and the others, proof he traveled in a wide arc. Jasper considered going back, then caught a glimpse of movement through the trees, and saw the others hurrying to catch up. He turned his attention back to the dome, his face illuminated by the green glow.

There was no denying that the magic used to create the barrier was impressive. Jasper had a bad feeling that whatever was inside must be just as impressive, and dangerous to match.

"How do we get through?" Xandor asked when he reached the mage.

"We have to break the circle," Jasper answered.

"Jasper, I don't think that's such a good idea," Yana volunteered from the back of the line.

"I would bet the demon or Gregori has already broken it."

"Then why is it still here?"

"A strong barrier like this probably cannot be dispelled by simply passing through it, but I think it could be weakened. That is what I meant by breaking the circle. In order to keep the circle intact, a door must be cut — normally on the east side — which is where I am heading."

"Can the door be closed?" Sergei asked.

"Yes. You simply reconnect the lines."

Xandor smiled to himself. Jasper's explanations always sounded so easy, but he had a way of seriously understating what really needed to happen. He recalled seeing Jasper writing in one of his ever-present *cookbooks*. The ink smelled awful, and a series of complicated equations took up an entire page. He remembered pointing to a line and asking Jasper what it meant. The mage had told him he was working on an incantation to heat his teakettle to perfection.

An owl hooted and brought Xandor back to the present. Apparently, the local animals were used to the barrier. He couldn't tell if that was a good sign or a bad one. He wasn't usually one for omens or portents, but at this point, he was willing to try just about anything.

Jasper finally stopped at a portion of the circle that looked just like everywhere else. The mage stared, oblivious to those around him.

In the dull glow, Xandor noticed a crushed patch of wiry grass. He knelt for a better look, but the dome's light wasn't bright enough. The ranger pulled his journal and stylus from his belt pouch and used its light to study his find. "One person waited here, while another walked to where you are now, Jasper. It looks like the one who stood here was weighted down, based on the deep impression their boots made." Xandor spent another long minute shifting the blades of grass with his hand and studying the ground. "Sacha stood here, holding something."

"Are you sure?" Sehraine asked.

Xandor stared at her a moment, stony eyed, before turning back to Jasper.

"So, Jasper, is this where they opened the door?"

"I expect so."

Chert walked around a tree and asked, "So if Sacha stood there, who opened the door?"

"My guess: Gregori," answered Jasper, stroking his beard.

Chert fidgeted with his hammer and said, "So we either have Gregori and Sacha working together, which I still say is unlikely, or we have Gregori and her demon working together. Is that even possible?"

"I don't know if it's possible, but it would certainly explain a lot," Sehraine said.

"What was she carrying?" Yana asked. "And where did she go?"

Grendel pointed toward the circle and answered, "In there."

"Jasper, can you open it?" Sergei asked.

The mage examined the green dome. He followed the movements of the different symbols, tracing them with his finger. Eventually, he saw a pattern form — not really a pattern, more an irregularity in the surface of the circle. Some of the symbols moved erratically when they touched an imperfection in the magic. Tracing it, he found a vertical crease in the surface of the barrier.

Jasper illuminated the head of his staff, and the symbols disappeared, making the crease impossible to find.

"Sorry, just wanted to double check."

"What did you find?"

"I found the door. Now all I have to do is open it."

"Can you do that?" Sergei repeated.

"Maybe," Jasper answered, dousing his light again. He stepped up to the barrier and traced the crease with his finger. Green ripples propagated from his touch. He closed his eyes and called up the magic inside him. With the corruption purged, it was like tasting the cool mountain waters of Ozera. He opened his magical sight. The containment circle glowed brightly, all except for a dark line marring its surface.

Jasper studied the door. It puckered along the edges where it had worn thin from repeated use. Only a few more times, and this door would be permanent. This was where the elves charged with protecting the Tear of Havel must have escaped, with the Elders sealing it from the inside. This was where they had closed the circle thirty years ago. He also saw the magic Gregori used, recognizing it from the cabin near the edge of the Haunted Wood in Trakya. It was a similar spell.

Stepping forward, he repeated the word he used on Gregori's cabin, "Patefaciam."

CHAPTER 35:
VÄLAVTÅRAR

October 31, 4235 K.E.

9:40pm

The crease opened like a raw wound not allowed to heal. The smell of rot and decay wafted out. Jasper stepped through the doorway, followed by the others. The mage turned and waved his staff, and the doorway closed behind them, sealing them in.

Tall, majestic trees marched into the distance bearing long, winding branches, some of which ran along the ground for tens of yards. Spanning over the tops of the trees, the green dome provided just enough light to silhouette the soaring canopy.

Jasper lit his staff and wished he hadn't. It was like being inside a gargantuan mausoleum. Covered with moldy growths that clung tenaciously to the bark, the dead trees appeared skeletal in the light. Black and barren, the ground grew no underbrush to hide the broken limbs that lay strewn about, their jagged edges blackened from rot. There were no animal sounds, just the eerie quiet of a graveyard.

Sergei let slip a giggle, which he squelched when everyone stared at him. The bard bit his lips together, but Jasper saw them twitch.

Sehraine buried her face in her hands. Grendel laid a hand on her shoulder, offering what comfort he could. The others drew in around them.

This was the village of Välavtårar, and Jasper could only imagine what it looked like during its prime. There was no denying that there was something seriously wrong about this place.

"Alright, people, let's get moving," Xandor whispered after a moment.

Sehraine collected herself and wiped her eyes with her hands, clearing them. Xandor looked at her expectantly. She nodded.

Xandor drew his longsword and said, "Aduro." Golden flames ran along the edges of the blade, driving away some of the gloom. Behind him, the others drew weapons and prepared for the worst.

Grendel and Sehraine led the way through the dead trees and detritus. Next came Jasper, holding his staff high and trying his best to illuminate the area. Behind him came Sergei and Yana, with Xandor guarding the rear.

Jasper couldn't shake the feeling they were being watched, and he could tell Grendel and Sehraine felt the same. Both of them seemed to be trying to watch every shadow, darting their heads from side to side. Somewhere out there was a malignant, evil presence. Whether it was the demon or something else, he didn't know.

They crept deeper into the village. Ancient trees that once held the homes of Sehraine's family and neighbors within their embrace now stood barren and lifeless. Dark yawning holes opened where doors once hung, flanked by black hollows in place of windows, like warped faces stretched in eternal silent screams. Sharp, twisting pain ripped through Sehraine's heart with each new sight.

Underfoot, the dry ground crunched and cracked. Not even Xandor or Yana managed their usual quiet tread. With each passing step, the color seemed to bleach from the world until all that remained were black trunks and the sick green glow from the distant dome. A limb broke and crashed to the ground somewhere off to the right. Sehraine and her companions dropped into crouches, expecting an attack. Instead, the putrid scent of rot and death assailed their nostrils.

Lichen-shrouded holes in the trees became more frequent, glaring at Sehraine in accusation. She edged closer to Grendel as they followed the path toward the village center. Fear and dread of what they would find grew steadily in her mind.

With an audible hiss, the flame along Xandor's blade extinguished as if swallowed by the night. A moment later, Jasper's light winked out, leaving only the dome's eerie green glow overhead. It seemed more the symptom of some evil disease than her ancestors' magic. Shadows danced all around them, far more than one light source could produce.

Sehraine gripped her daggers in white-knuckled fists. At her side, Grendel turned in a slow circle, a growl rumbling deep in his chest. The flicker of movement came faster and faster. Whatever was out there surrounded them.

CHAPTER 36:
THE WAGON AND THE DWOLMA

October 31, 4235 K.E.

10:45pm

Grendel raced ahead. Sehraine darted after him and heard the pounding of footsteps in her wake. Past a row of trees, they skidded to a stop in the center of town.

Multiple lanes came together like the spokes of a wheel. Light from Jasper's staff flashed of its own volition, throwing off glimpses of the town in an odd strobe effect. The on-again, off-again lighting messed with her vision, but it was better than not being able to see at all — or so she thought. One brilliant burst revealed an old, dilapidated trader wagon sitting ominously at the end of one of the lanes.

Sehraine cried out, breaking the silence. Tears of anguish streamed down her face as her worst nightmare came true: it was her father's wagon. The one she had run away from so long ago. Daggers fell from her nerveless fingers, and she stumbled forward. Yana followed, but Sehraine pushed her away.

"Get away from me!" she screamed. The shadows seemed drawn to her voice and closed as the radius of light slowly shrank.

With her hands pressed to the sides of her head, Sehraine sank to her knees, oblivious to the shadows, staring at the bed of the wagon. Everyone caught up with her in a rush.

In the wagon's bed, two barrels sat upright, still lashed to the deck. A third barrel lay on its side. Like a cracked eggshell, its lower half rested on the tailgate. Some type of unnaturally preserved grease lined the inside of the barrel. However, the wood of the tailgate had deformed and sagged as though melted. On the ground, the remains of the upper half of the barrel lay partially submerged in an irrationally large pool of glossy, black liquid: the Blood of Cayn.

Even after more than thirty years, the Blood of Cayn pooled on the sagging tailgate still dripped to the ground.

Grendel cocked his head to one side, confused, until he noticed a drop of the Blood of Cayn rise back up to the wagon, maintaining a constant volume.

The air constricted like a vise and held him tight. Maniacal laughter drifted in the still air. Grendel noticed a fresh set of footprints in the Blood of Cayn. He followed them with his eyes to where Gregori stepped out from behind a tree. The spiked iron collar of the orcnéan mancatcher no longer circled his throat.

"It's good to see you again, Jasper. And you brought friends! So nice to have an audience."

The portly mage closed his eyes and seemed to try to turn his head, but the air prevented it.

Gregori swiped his hand in front of him, and a mad gleam appeared in his eye. "Bow before your master!"

Grendel struggled against the invisible bonds, but he, too, was helpless against Gregori's power. In his peripheral vision, he could see the others slowly forced to their knees. However, instead of bowing to Gregori, the magic forced the group to look in the opposite direction.

On the other side of the town center, Sacha stepped into the flashing light of Jasper's staff, holding something in her hand — a human heart that somehow still beat.

Grendel pushed harder against the air, but to no avail. He watched her cross the lane toward them. The heart in her hand dripped red blood between her fingers. He wanted to scream and shout.

The clothes Sacha wore accentuated her lithe form, but when she drew closer, Grendel recoiled from the streaks of dried blood across her face, hair, and skin, leftovers from the morning's events.

'*How could she*?' he thought to himself. He closed his eyes, trying to block the images that ran rampant in his head, but he couldn't stop them. Remembrances of their short time together on the wagon train and the kiss in the tunnel came back to him. That's when it hit him: whoever this was, she was not Sacha. He felt her nearby, struggling against the unseen bonds just as much as he was. Relief flooded him, but so did frustration. He was so close.

Opening his eyes, he saw the Sacha lookalike standing in the middle of the Blood of Cayn. She held the beating heart up into the air like an offering. "Welcome to Winter's Night," she said. "A time when old bonds are broken."

Her attention focused on the dark mage, and she ordered, "Gregori!"

Gregori stepped forward, carrying the reliquary. Shadows hovered about him like moths to a flame. The evil mage stopped at the edge of the black pool and knelt, placing the cabinet inside the Blood of Cayn.

Sacha hummed the elven lullaby, repeating Sergei's lower, more sinister rendition from earlier. Gregori leapt back as brilliant purple light broke through the seams. The mithril sheets peeled away like old paint, and the reliquary burst open, revealing the Tear of Havel.

The Tear hovered above the Blood of Cayn and burned with an inner light untouched by the black liquid. Sacha's double dipped her free hand into the black pool, dribbled some of it on the heart, and gestured toward the gem. Its dagger-like shape looked more pronounced as it drifted to the woman's waiting hand.

When she grasped the hilt, the fire within the Tear of Havel burst forth and seared her flesh, but she didn't let go. Pain etched Sacha's features as she fought for control of the dagger and stabbed its tip into the beating heart, killing it.

Green light flashed, tracing its way along the dome, and something heavy crashed against the protective barrier.

"With this death, I sever my ties to the Dark Lord! My promise to him is broken, and I am free to remain in this world!"

Sacha dropped the dead heart into the Blood of Cayn, where it dissolved. Closing her eyes, she licked the blade of the dagger clean. Steam wafted up from her mouth as it scorched her tongue. She shuddered in excitement and leaned her head back, giving voice to a deep sonorous laugh at odds with the shape of her throat. When her eyes opened, they filled with an unholy ecstasy.

She glanced toward Gregori, who knelt at the edge of the pool, and nodded.

"It is almost time."

Gregori waved his hand, and the real Sacha appeared beside him. Gagged by a red scarf, she struggled against the thin cords that bound her hands and feet. She rose and floated over the Blood of Cayn, toward the other Sacha.

Grendel saw her and pushed harder, but the air remained solid, with no signs of weakening.

Again, green light flashed. Something huge pounded on the dome. A monstrous roar of frustration resounded above them, shaking the ground, but the creature remained outside, unable to break through.

"Lady Aleksandra Madasgorski, I am disappointed in you," the other Sacha said, ripping off the gag.

Sacha spit in the other girl's face, but it only evoked more laughter.

"Razrushitel! I command you to let me go! I command you!"

"You are no longer in a position to give me orders! You know the rules. It is Winter's Night."

Sacha looked confused. The demon grabbed her by the throat and screamed, "Did you think I wanted to be your slave?"

Loosening his grip, Razrushitel continued, "I have done the bidding of generations of your ancestors. Now, that time is past. At midnight, the height of Winter's Night, I will sacrifice you to Ka'Sehkuur, the sleeping god, and break my ties to the Madasgorski family forever."

"Sutekh will stop you! Even now, his Tugarin is breaking through the dome."

"It's too late. He cannot stop me now. I will kill you and take your place. Gregori's plague will spread to every living human and elf, and Kraagor, with his orc horde, will rise up to dominate Parlatheas. All thanks to you," Razrushitel said and turned slowly toward Sehraine, "and this elf."

"It is time, Milord," Gregori said.

Looking about, Razrushitel said, "So it is."

The demon, still in Sacha's form, bent and scooped up a handful of the black liquid in his palm. Bringing it to his mouth, he gulped it down. Gulp after gulp, he drank the Blood of Cayn. Grendel watched in horrified fascination until he noticed that the Tear of Havel stopped burning the demon's skin, and it began to heal. Even his tongue no longer seemed damaged.

Sehraine felt one of the shadows watching her. It recognized her. Perhaps the demon drinking the Blood of Cayn lessened its influence on her village, but the shadows seemed different.   One in particular darted away from the others.

Gregori watched Razrushitel raise the Tear of Havel over Sacha's heart, oblivious to the approaching dwolma.

"What do you plan to do with my friends?" Sacha asked.

The dagger-like gem remained poised over her, "If by your friends, you mean Grendel, he will share the fate of the others."   Razrushitel looked up at the dome, where long cracks scored the surface. "Gregori and I will be gone, and your friends will be the only things left alive when the dome collapses," the demon said, looking down at her with an evil grin. "I am sure Sutekh will take out his frustration on them as only he can."

"You bastard!" Sacha yelled, struggling against her bonds.

"Relax. You won't feel a thing," he smirked.

The dwolma launched itself out of the shadows, catching Gregori unawares. With a loud, wet splat, the dark mage fell to the ground. The creature's tentacles wound around his lower torso and legs like a pulsating cocoon. He cried out under its weight and fought desperately as the thing slowly ate him. Gregori reached out a supplicating hand toward the demon.

Razrushitel ignored him.

The light of Jasper's staff flashed, and Grendel appeared at the edge of the pool as if by magic, with Skyld's sword in his hand. Arrayed behind him, Xandor and the others stood ready for battle.

CHAPTER 37:
THE FINAL SHOWDOWN

November 1, 4235 K.E.

12:00am

With a defiant yell, Razrushitel plunged the Tear of Havel toward Sacha's heart. He put all the weight of his years behind that fatal thrust.

Sacha cried out.

The blade never struck.

The magic holding her up failed, and Sacha fell into the pool of oily blood.

Grendel let loose a guttural growl and leapt at the demon, slashing with his blade.

Making Grendel's attack look slow and clumsy, Razrushitel ducked under it and stepped on Sacha's body, pushing her deep into the Blood of Cayn. It seeped into her ears and crept up her face like some living thing. She screamed and fought the weight of the demon, but only managed to mire herself further.

Holding the Tear of Havel like a weapon, Razrushitel said, "You can't win this fight, half-orc. I cannot die unless she dies."

The demon lunged, and Grendel beat the dagger aside with a sweep. The Tear of Havel flashed with a brilliant purple light as the two weapons met.

Behind the demon, Xandor made to step into the black blood.

"No!" Grendel shouted. "The demon is mine!"

Pushing off Sacha's body with his left foot, Razrushitel slashed with his empty left hand and the curved blade of a falchion cut toward Grendel's face.

Grendel leaned left and took a long step backward to avoid it.

Razrushitel followed up with a thrust from the Tear of Havel toward Grendel's abdomen.

Off balance, Grendel backpedaled to regain his footing. As he did, he lifted his blade straight up, sliding his left hand high to grip the ricasso. With a jerk, Grendel brought his sword pommel straight down, smashing the hand holding the dagger. The Tear of Havel fell with a plop and slipped beneath the oily surface.

Following up instantly, Grendel thrust with the shorter-gripped sword, seeking Razrushitel's belly. The demon hopped backward. Grendel resumed a standard grip and whipped the sword in a high circle, forcing the demon back another step.

Advancing, the former gladiator stepped over Sacha.

Dark shapes crawled out of the trees. Chert shouted, "The dwolma! They're coming!"

Xandor and Yana moved to meet the creatures. Jasper and Chert flanked them, forming a defensive arc.

The gelatinous dwolma slithered forward on roiling, flailing tentacles far faster than Chert felt they aught. The creatures launched themselves into the air. Xandor swept his flaming longsword and his scavenged blade up and across the first dwolma. Flesh singed with a putrid stench as tentacles went flying. Yana's attack mirrored Xandor's and left another dwolma short a few tentacles. Both wounded creatures retreated, but others crowded forward, intent on a fresh meal.

Chanting, Chert focused on the two dwolma stalking Sehraine, and a nimbus of light grew around them. They writhed and shrieked under the bright light, but the very nature of the village struggled against the priest's magic, as though the entire area strove to maintain its darkness, and the light dimmed. The dwolma resumed their oozy, slurping march toward the despairing elf.

Jasper pointed with the ring finger on his left hand and yelled, "Ilíos!" White energy lanced across the clearing and ripped into the side of a beast trying to flank the wind rider.

Black ichor sprayed from the deep gash, and Yana flinched as small drops of its digestive juices burned her. Keeping her eyes on the approaching danger, she called out through gritted teeth, "Jasper! Watch where you're aiming that thing!"

Grendel thrust with his blade again, stamping forward.

The enraged demon slid to Grendel's left, out of line with the thrust, and stepped inside the two-handed weapon's optimum range. Razrushitel stabbed toward Grendel's head with the falchion. The abyssal blade hissed as it cut the air. Out of position, Grendel shifted to a crouch and lunged forward, jabbing at the demon's chest.

With hellish speed, the demon spun widdershins and struck the half-orc a mighty blow with his fist. Grendel's head popped back, and he flew through the air, landing in the black blood with a splash.

Razrushitel, still using Sacha's image, now held two falchions, the right blade full length while the left was shorter. He swiped them back and forth and asked, "Son of Cayn, how is it you survived my gift?"

Light flashed around them. Grendel stood, the Blood of Cayn clinging to him. Holding Skyld's sword in a guard position again, he stared at the demon and answered, "Demon, my father may have been a son of Cayn, but my mother was a daughter of Havel."

Razrushitel closed, and the demon's blades became a blur. His first real attack shot toward the half-orc's shoulder. Stepping back on his left foot, Grendel half-turned and let the weapon slide on his. Razrushitel twisted sharply and cut at Grendel's exposed hip with his other blade. This time, Grendel passed back on his right foot, and the shorter falchion swept in front of him.

Letting go with one hand, Grendel dropped the tip of his blade behind both falchions, temporarily binding them. Stepping in and forward quickly with his left foot, he aimed his elbow at the demon's chin.

That close, he caught a whiff of Sacha's scent, and it saturated his senses. Memories hammered at his concentration, clamoring for attention. His attack faltered as he pulled the punch at the last second. It was a foolish mistake. The blow landed, but with only a portion of the half-orc's strength.

With a sinister smile, the demon in Sacha's lithe form spun to the right and lashed out with a sharp sidekick to Grendel's gut. The air went out of this lungs with a whoosh as he doubled over in breathless agony.

The demon brought both his falchions to bear, hacking at Grendel's neck. Dropping to one knee to brace himself, Grendel brought his sword up horizontally, gripped with one hand on the hilt and one on the blade, catching both falchions just above the quillions.

Feeling as if he had just stopped an avalanche, Grendel struggled to keep the keen edges from his skin. They inched closer and closer as the demon brought its true strength to bear.

Sehraine screamed as a glistening tentacle latched onto her leg. The attacking dwolma dragged her toward itself. The elf reached for her daggers, but the sheaths were empty — she had dropped them on the other side of the clearing. She rolled onto her belly and scrabbled for purchase on the dirt track.

Chert pivoted to his left when he heard Sehraine's scream. The dwolma raised its body up, tentacles waving, preparing to smother the elf.

The dwarf hurled his hammer with a shouted prayer. It struck the creature squarely as the beast dropped toward its victim. Thunder clapped and the blunt head burst through the unnatural thing, but its tentacles remained fixed around Sehraine's leg.

The force of the blow threw the creature into the air, dragging the slim elf with it in a trailing stream of black mucus. Elf and dwolma landed in a heap several yards away.

Chert hurried to Sehraine's side, catching his hammer as it returned to his hand.

Two dwolma leapt at Xandor. He ducked past them and spun his blades, each at a separate target. Thousands of sucker mouths shrieked as the burning blade clove through rubbery skin. The creatures landed behind the ranger, writhing and spitting mucus as the screams continued. Xandor speared each of them, and the screams died amid the viscous dissolution of the two unnatural creatures' bodies.

Nearby, Yana focused both blades on her single opponent, who was missing a few tentacles. Lacking Xandor's flames, her blades bit deeply into the body of the beast but did not cauterize the wounds. Black ichor splashed and pitted her blades.

The dwolma screamed from its myriad mouths and spat at her.

Dodging the acidic spit, Yana didn't see the tentacle snaking toward her until it snapped around her ankle and yanked her foot out from under her. She fell heavily to one side, barely keeping her weapons.

The tentacle drew her toward the dwolma's mouths. Squirming around, she hacked at the offending tentacle, cutting it in half.

She rolled back over one shoulder to escape another grasping tentacle, the first still wrapped around the ankle of her boot. Before she could regain her feet, a burning blade impaled the pursuing creature. The screaming tapered off and the dark grey mass collapsed in on itself.

Xandor offered her a hand up, and they readied themselves for the next wave.

Not-Sacha's eyes gleamed as Grendel struggled. A feral smile splitting the beautiful face, the demon pushed harder, forcing the kneeling half-orc backward.

Sliding in the blood, Grendel fought against falling. Summoning the reserves of his strength, he pushed against the demon, muscles bulging. A metallic crack resounded as Skyld's sword snapped in two.

The sudden release of pressure threw both fighters off balance. Not-Sacha regained its balance after only a couple of steps while the half-orc, still grasping the hilt of the broken sword in one hand and the blade in the other, fell flat on his back into the black pool with a splash. Grendel rolled and pushed himself up with one hand while flinging the blade toward the demon's head with the other.

The demon sneered as he batted it aside. "Did you really think you could defeat me, warrior?"

Sacha's form melted away, replaced by a cadaverous, burnt-sienna-colored body with feral, ochre eyes. Broad, bat-like wings spread out behind him as he grew taller. In his hands, two abyssal blades of pure flame took the place of the falchions.

Razrushitel glared at the half-orc and said, "I fought and won battles long before the pernicious lives of man were first conceived. How dare you think that you could defeat me?"

Grendel crabbed back through the Blood of Cayn.

Without seeming to move, the demon appeared in front of Grendel and grabbed him, one handed, around the neck.

Grendel cut and slashed with the jagged edge of his broken weapon, but the blade simply bounced off the demon's hide without a scratch.

An evil laugh escaped Razrushitel's throat as he flung Grendel into Xandor, Yana, and Jasper, who were charging toward him. All four bowled over in a tangle of limbs. Jasper's light blinked out, plunging the village into darkness.

Razrushitel stood over Sacha, searching for the Tear of Havel. The half-orc charged toward him, Skyld's broken sword in his hand. With a powerful backhand, Razrushitel crushed Grendel's nose and sent him back into the air.

"Give up, son of Havel," the demon's voice boomed mockingly.

Grendel shook his head to clear it as he stood, red blood streaming down his chin.

Rolling off Xandor, Jasper found his staff, aimed it at the demon, and yelled, "Astrapí!"

Lightning arced from the mage's staff but diverted toward the green dome. It hit the barrier in a shower of sparks that rained down like flaming glitter and briefly illuminated the center of the village.

Jasper looked around in the fading light and spotted Sergei, one palm extended toward Jasper as if to signal him to stop.

With a flourish of his staff, the portly mage brought his shield up a split-second before a jet of yellow and red fire engulfed them. Waves of heat from the blast shook the trees, and dead limbs rained down, most catching fire as they fell.

Sergei flicked his fingers, and balls of lightning lit the town center with their ever-searching fingers of electricity.

Swords in hand, Xandor crouched behind Jasper's shield. Beside him crouched Yana, her face hidden by her ever-present barbute.

The alternating flashes of fire and electricity illuminated a line of dwolma waiting beyond the fire's reach, but it was spreading fast. Once the trees caught, there would be no escape.

"You two go. Get out of here," Jasper said through gritted teeth.

With a nod, both leapt through the small gap in the fire and charged toward the dwolma.

Grendel spat blood. Each breath came wet and ragged. Several of his ribs felt broken, but he wasn't giving up on Sacha. The half-orc trudged through the pool, formed one giant fist with his hands, and brought it down on the demon's back. He hit stone.

Razrushitel rose from his search in a spin, grabbed Grendel's right wrist, and yanked him off balance. Still in motion, the demon's left fist crashed against the side of the half-orc's head, snapping it to the side.

Light flashed behind Grendel's eyes. His legs buckled and he could not coordinate his arms to break his fall when the demon slung him to the ground.

Grinning, Razrushitel dropped to his knees, straddling the half-breed. Like a cat playing with a mouse, the demon battered his foe, raining blow after blow into Grendel's unresisting body. Loud cracks echoed off the dead trees as the demon broke bones, one by one. Even after the last bone shattered, the demon did not stop. His punches landed with sickening, fleshy thuds that sank deep into battered flesh.

Chert and Sehraine watched helplessly from the edge of the pool, grimacing each time they heard something break. Time slowed. The demon struck Grendel one last time, and then resumed his search for the Tear.

The half-orc lay in a shapeless heap. Red blood mixed with that of the black pool. Grendel's chest shuddered and hitched.

Leaving Sehraine to find her daggers, Chert dashed to his friend's side, wincing in sympathy as he recognized the wheezing sound of punctured lungs. "Grendel, I'm here," he said as he laid his hands on his friend and prayed. The big man did not respond — there was too much damage, too much pain. Blue light formed around Chert's hands and spread into the gladiator's body. It kept Grendel alive, but that was all it could do.

"Pyros!" Jasper shouted, with one hand extended. A jet of fire shot forth, coming to a splashing halt just short of his target as the bard countered with fire of his own. The mages locked eyes through the waves of heat.

"Gregori," Jasper breathed softly, his tone a mix of wonder, anger, and self-castigation.

Sergei/Gregori smiled evilly and gestured with both hands, pushing hard. His flame grew stronger, forcing Jasper to hide behind his shield once more. The fire scorched the air around him and slowly melted holes in the shield.

Yana threw herself to one side in a vain attempt to avoid a dwolma's low leap. Two of its tentacles whipped around her thigh in a vice-like grip. She hit the ground and pivoted, driving both blades into the creature's wet body. The dwolma convulsed and dissolved into the earth.

Taking a quick glance around, she scrambled to her feet and charged across the clearing toward the black pool. "This is really, really stupid, Yana," she muttered to herself.

Watching the ball of lightning wander toward Chert, a snapping twig brought Sehraine's heart into her throat. Daggers clutched in her fists, she turned to find a dwolma watching her. Although she could not see any eyes, the thing followed her swaying movements in a macabre dance.

Sehraine's scalp prickled, and it felt as though her hair attempted to crawl from her head. Without looking, she knew a ball of lightning loomed right behind her. Shouting at the dwolma, she waved her arms. The creature leapt. Sehraine threw herself sideways, rolling out of the way. The dwolma flew through the space she vacated into the ball of lightning.

The ball exploded and hurled black rubbery pieces of flesh into the air, onto Sehraine and the trees. The ball of lightning slowly moved off in the opposite direction.

Tentacles lashed out at Chert. The dwarf turned in time to hide behind his shield and protect his friend. He felt the tentacles smash against the shield, followed by a slimy scraping sound as they dragged at it before sliding off its face. The dwarf swung his hammer, striking the dwolma, and sent it sprawling.

The thing hissed and spat black mucus at him from a score of mouths. Chert retreated behind his shield and heard the bubbling hiss of the acid eating at its surface. Grimacing, he peeked around the edge just as the creature leapt at him. The priest planted his right foot behind him to brace against the impact.

"Eternal Father, please help me," he prayed as the creature flattened out, spreading wider to envelop him.

A startling pain jolted through the dwarf, starting at his back. The pain was so intense his vision went black. A loud "pop" deafened those nearby. The concussive blast threw Chert and the dwolma into the trees, both partially obscured by an ozone haze.

Waves of heat searing his face, Jasper gripped his staff with both hands and shouted, "Anemostróvilos!"

The still air in the clearing shifted, becoming a ripple of current that grew steadily. The wind picked up speed, swirling about the clearing. Concentrating, Jasper compacted the area, holding it tight about Gregori's position. Dirt, sticks, and pebbles sucked up into the forming funnel. The wind gained enough velocity to first bend and then capture Gregori's fire, turning it back and suspending it in the twisting vortex. Flames licked out as the whirlwind grew taller and taller, almost touching the green dome.

The other mage shouted, his words muffled by the wind. Jasper grinned, but he knew it was only a matter of time.

Suddenly, the wind stopped spinning. Dirt and stone shot out in every direction. Jasper's grin melted, and he frantically reinforced his shield. Stones pummeled the solid wall of air, clicking together like castanets in a mad, Espian dance.

Kneeling, Razrushitel continued his search for the crystal dagger. He shifted left, trailing his hands through the Blood of Cayn. His head came up when a pair of boots appeared at the edge of the pool.

"No wonder you like parading around looking like Sacha. You are butt-ugly!" Yana exclaimed before stabbing him in the face.

The demon jerked his head to the side as her blade scraped over his stony cheek.

He rose with an annoyed sounding bellow and beat his wings, generating a gusty wind that built with each forward thrust and spattered his diminutive foe with the Blood of Cayn.

Yana leaned into the wind to remain standing, and the demon grinned, revealing multiple rows of curved teeth. Unable to move forward and unwilling to go to her knees, Yana shifted her stance. She pushed her shoulders back and held her blades low, leaning forward into the wind.

Leering at her, the demon brought his left hand back, and his fiery blade reappeared. He paused, as if to be certain she saw it coming, and then thrust at her chest, never letting up on the beating of his wings.

Yana raised herself to a more vertical position, spread her arms, and went up on her toes, allowing the wind to snatch her up and toss her backwards before the flaming blade reached her.

The demon snorted as the little human tumbled away and turned back to his search through the black blood.

Still lying in the Blood of Cayn, Grendel felt a measure of strength return and opened one bleary eye. Fifteen feet away, Sacha's face barely broke the surface of the black pool. He thought it odd because the pool wasn't that deep; nonetheless, she looked to be on the verge of going under.

'*Arise,*' a voice said inside Grendel's head.

His eye roved about and found something lying next to him, emitting a faint white light.

'*Arise, Vanin Grendel's son. This fight is not over.*'

The half-orc struggled, but every part of his body protested. He stretched his fingers toward the white light. It dimmed to nothing, leaving a long hafted, double-bladed battle-axe in its place.

Surprised, Grendel sought the one who left it.

"I failed you, Eternal Father. You lent me this axe, and I lost it," Grendel said.

The voice answered, '*The most important things you have — your life, your friends, your strength — are, in their own way, borrowed. Why do you focus on just an axe?*'

Grendel couldn't answer. He thought of Sacha lying in the Blood of Cayn and used the dregs of his strength to move his arm a few inches.

'Remember that I am always with you, and your strength will never fail.'

'Remember that I am always with you, and your strength will never fail.'

CHAPTER 39:
THE TEAR OF HAVEL

November 1, 4235 K.E.

12:20am

Razrushitel's hand closed around the hilt of the Tear of Havel. "At last!" he cried out in orgasmic joy. The Blood of Cayn trailed down his arm as he brought it out. He dragged Sacha out of the pool by the leg and dumped her on the wagon within easy reach. "Your time is up, Lady Aleksandra. No more delays."

She looked up at the demon's face, all fight gone. She had witnessed what happened to Grendel and knew the demon killed him.

"What? No smart remark? No last-minute plea for mercy? You disappoint me."

"Get it over with, demon," she said in a hoarse whisper.

"Oh, I will," Razrushitel said smugly. He raised the dagger above her heart and gripped its hilt with both hands.

Something struck his left wing with a fury. The demon ducked reflexively and roared his frustration as a blade slapped against his impenetrable hide, interrupting him once again. Raging, he spun toward the source of the attack. His glowing eyes reflected in the black depths of Yana's barbute.

She launched another attack at him. The demon lashed out at Yana with a backhand, slapping her right blade from her grip even as her left blade bounced off his abdomen.

Slashing horizontally with the Tear, Razrushitel hammered into the wind rider's two-handed block. Yana splashed into the black pool on her back. The demon pivoted on his right foot and stomped down on her chest with his left. Her helmet slipped off as her head sank beneath the surface of the Blood of Cayn.

Teeth bared, the demon ground his foot into her chest, cracking ribs. Sputtering black blood, Yana stabbed her remaining blade against his calf. He reached down and snatched her up by the neck of her leather cuirass. His fist closed around her blade, wrenching it from her grasp, and threw it across the clearing. "You cannot beat me!" he roared.

Yana glared back at him and gasped, "Who said... anything... about... beating you?"

His eyes narrowed. Snarling, he flung the impudent woman after her blade.

The rush of wind was the demon's only warning. Grendel tackled Razrushitel from behind and, spinning to his left as they fell, hurled him away from Sacha.

Infuriated, Razrushitel rounded on his attacker, surprised to find Grendel in his way. In his hands, a double-bladed battle-axe shone brightly.

A flicker of fear crossed the demon's face, and he asked, "Who are you?"

"I am Vanin." Grendel crossed his forearms in front of his heart and dipped his head without breaking eye contact. "Alea iacta est." *The die is cast.*

Razrushitel threw the Tear of Havel into the wagon bed, and blades of flame sprang from his hands. The stench of brimstone filled the air as his bat-like wings beat an infernal wind. In a blur of motion, the demon slashed with the blade in his right hand.

Matching the demon's speed, Grendel instantly shifted his grip and brought up the haft of the axe, blocking the attack above head level. Grendel pivoted and twisted the axe blade down. Using the demon's own strength, he forced the blade into the other, fouling them.

With the edges of Razrushitel's swords still in contact with the haft, Grendel stepped closer and, lowering his fighting crouch only marginally, slammed his left foot into the demon's lead knee.

Razrushitel roared and staggered as the joint gave with a loud crack. Thrown off balance, the demon tried to disengage. Grendel followed up by jabbing the knob of his axe toward the demon's face. The demon dodged backward and only the use of his wings kept him vertical.

Pressing forward, Grendel slid his right hand down the haft as he brought the axe up again. The blade suddenly righted and, backed by the might of Grendel's shoulders, came crashing down toward Razrushitel's skull in a two-handed vertical cut.

Razrushitel leapt back, his wings churning the air to avoid the descending attack, and followed up by sweeping both his blades in a dual horizontal arc to knock the axe aside. He reversed his attack and cut back toward Grendel, forcing the half-orc to scramble.

The demon landed and the two circled warily, each looking for a gap in the other's defenses.

"I broke you. How do you still stand?" the demon said, his tone warring between curiosity and outrage.

"I am Vanin," the half-orc repeated grimly. "Son of Cayn and Son of Havel." Mortal eyes met demonic, glare for glare. If Grendel had any inkling his abyssal foe outmatched him, he gave no indication of it.

Crisscrossed with lacerations after the whirlwind, Gregori-in-Sergei's-body closed on the portly mage.

Still standing behind his shield, Jasper shouted, "Fýllo tou págou!" This time Jasper did not target his foe. Instead, he focused on the ground beneath Gregori's feet until a shimmering sheet of ice appeared. As the faux bard took the next step, his feet slipped from underneath him, and he fell.

Jasper rushed forward, his shield of air still encircling him. It flashed and sparkled as he moved, reflecting the balls of lightning and the green dome above. Staff gripped tight in both hands, Jasper swung it at the prone man's head.

Gregori quickly gave up on standing. He slashed with his hand and yelled, "Iter!"

An unseen force slammed against Jasper's legs, bowling him over.

Jasper rolled as he landed and brought up his staff. Several crackling balls of energy sped toward him. They struck his shield, shrouding it in a cloud of ozone.

Concentrating on his right-hand ring, Jasper yelled, "Pyros!" Yellow fire leapt out and struck Gregori's shield.

"Your attacks are weak," Gregori said with a scowl, standing. With a wave of his hand, liquid fire lashed out toward Jasper.

A literal moat of molten lava surrounded his little shield, and Jasper had flashbacks to Kraagor's throne room. *'Probably one reason Gregori keeps using the blasted stuff,'* he thought to himself.

Xandor slipped in behind the traitor, Sergei, and raised his longsword to strike him with the pommel. He didn't know why the bard turned against them, but suspected it had something to do with Gregori. A full yard before reaching the bard, the ranger encountered an invisible wall — an arcane shield. Feeling around, he detected no edge. Giving up on getting around it, he raised his blades and hammered against it. Magic and flames arced, casting sparks into the night as the blades slammed against solid air.

Sergei turned toward Xandor and gestured with his hand. A wall of flame sprang up at the ranger's feet. Throwing himself down, the ranger rolled away, slapping at his armor to extinguish where the leather had caught fire.

With another gesture from Gregori, a randomly floating ball of lightning suddenly had direction. Xandor sprang to his feet and jumped to avoid the approaching orb. He was surprised when it followed him rather than continuing on its previous path as it had done earlier. He moved to the left. Again, it followed.

'*This isn't good*,' he thought. Glancing around, he saw an orb tracking toward Sehraine as she moved away from a dwolma; likewise, another drifted toward Yana.

Dodging again, he called, "Yana! Sehraine! Chert! The orbs aren't random anymore!"

Razrushitel lashed out with his left-hand sword, slicing from high right to low left. Grendel shifted back and left, letting the sword slide through empty space before slicing in horizontally at the exposed ribs. The demon blocked the counterattack with his right blade, and sparks flew from the clashing weapons.

Attacking from his left again, Razrushitel circled the sword low to maintain momentum and, with a snap, brought it up from below. Grendel jumped back to avoid disembowelment, but the infernal blade scored a shallow cut along his stomach. Flames blackened the skin on either side of the wound.

Without acknowledging the hit, Grendel stepped in and swung his axe, two-handed. The demon hammered his blades against the softly glowing axe, rebounding it. Whipping the double-bladed axe down and around, Grendel dropped the blade below the hilt of the demon's sword and then back up in a rush. It was Razrushitel's turn to hop back too slowly. The tip of the axe sliced open his chin, creating a new cleft.

As they circled again, Razrushitel rubbed the blue-black blood off his chin with the back of one hand, the wound already closing. Moving almost faster than the eye could see, the demon lashed out with a double attack aimed at Grendel's head.

Thrusting upward with his axe, Grendel grunted as he caught the demon's weapons between the tips of his axe blades.

The demon pivoted on his right foot and drove a roundhouse kick into the half-orc's chest, hurling him to the ground.

His reflexes honed by years of fighting in the arena, Grendel hit the ground rolling.

Stomp!

Roll.

Stomp!

Roll.

Stomp! This time, the demon connected and drove the remaining air from Grendel's lungs as he pinned him in place.

Kicking away the half-orc's axe, Razrushitel smirked at his opponent. "Don't worry, Grendel. I won't kill you yet. First, you will watch your dear Sacha die and after that, your friends. Then, I promise, I will make certain that you die slowly and painfully."

Grendel pushed futilely at the foot pinning him to the ground, but he had no leverage. As the demon spun his blade, slowly moving the tip down toward his pinned opponent, Grendel's squirming grew more frantic.

Smiling in anticipation of the coming pain he was about to inflict, Razrushitel was unprepared for Yana's sudden attack. Her blades, while ineffective against the stone-like skin, distracted the demon for a fraction of a second as he faced the new threat.

It was all Grendel needed. The half-orc heaved and twisted the demon's ankle. Razrushitel toppled heavily to one side. Clinging to his foot, Grendel twisted and snapped it hard. The demon kicked at the half-orc while Yana let loose another barrage.

Razrushitel disappeared, only to reappear a few feet away, this time standing. Yana shifted and charged while Grendel scrambled to his feet and retrieved his axe.

The liquid fire ceased. At first, Jasper didn't notice as the naphtha-like magic blazed and ran down the sides of his shield to collect at the perimeter. In the same moment he realized it had stopped, he spotted a flash of light. Reacting instantly, he thrust his staff out and shouted, "Astrapí!" A bolt of lightning burst forth.

The two bolts impacted, combined, and streaked up to crash against the dome, emitting a boom of thunder that echoed throughout the enclosed village.

"Págos!" Jasper yelled, congealing the cold, damp air around Gregori, freezing it in place, and locking him inside. Sweating profusely, Jasper let out a breath. The irony of a huge ice cube sitting not twenty feet from a moat of lava was not lost on him. He took a deep breath. There was no doubt in his mind that Gregori was the more powerful mage. He could only hope that his friends worked things out on the other end quickly and came to help.

The block of ice exploded, sending shards flying in all directions. Chips hissed and melted against Jasper's shield, still superheated from the liquid fire. Even as Jasper noted the reaction, fingers of earth crept up and encircled his legs. He looked down with a yelp and tried to pull free, but the ground held him tight.

Gregori slowly approached Jasper with a cold smile on his face. He was coming in for the kill.

Dodging another orb, Xandor thought about the lightning arcing toward Chert's armor, even with a gap between them, and remembered a conversation with Jasper about Trakyan architecture and lightning storms. An idea blossomed.

He thrust the longsword he scavenged in Chernigov into the soil. Moving back slowly, Xandor kept the sword between himself and the ball lightning. The crackling orb followed the ranger as he backed away — until it connected with the sword hilt.

Whumpf!

A blinding flash of light followed by a crash of thunder staggered the ranger. The stench of ozone hung in the air, tingling his nose. Xandor looked at his sword. The bronze pommel was slagged, the leather and wood of the hilt burned away, and the steel blade blackened. There was no sign of the orb.

Xandor turned toward Sehraine. She was already heading his way, having seen, and heard, his solution. Next, he looked for Yana. He found her with Grendel, facing the demon.

Whumpf! Sehraine's orb disappeared as it connected with his planted sword, leaving the blade further warped.

Xandor and Sehraine glanced around, noting the locations of the three remaining orbs. Then he looked up, and his face paled. "Get ready to run."

Stamping forward, Razrushitel thrust with his left blade. Grendel parried it to the outside, and then retreated a step as he brought up his axe to block the follow-up, a hacking attack from on high. Sparks flew every time the weapons met.

Seizing the initiative, the demon thrust again from the left while sweeping up with his right blade. Forced on the defensive, Grendel dodged and blocked.

Twice more, the warriors repeated the intricate flash of blades and dance steps. Each time Grendel gave up a single step.

A shark-like smile split Razrushitel's face. Thrusting yet again, the demon's expression morphed from smug satisfaction to surprise when Grendel parried to the inside instead of out. Already, slicing in with his other blade, the two weapons fouled one another.

The half-orc spun in next to the demon's exposed flank and jabbed, thrusting the tips of the axe blades like a spear into Razrushitel's side. The attack failed to penetrate the abyssal hide, but it cracked ribs, evoking a cry of pain from the demon.

Snapping his elbow down and back, Razrushitel caught Grendel in the chest, forcing him back a step. With a flick of his wings, he held Grendel with the pinions and hurled him away. Appearing beside the fallen half-orc, the demon swung both blades down from his shoulders, trying to catch Grendel on the ground.

Grendel rolled over his left shoulder and back onto his feet in a low crouch, one hand in the pool as a brace. Avoiding the incoming attack, he leapt to the right just as Yana, who stood at the edge of the pool, hurled a dagger at the demon's eye.

The wind rider's blade flew straight and true. Against any other target, it would have sunk to the hilt. The demon flinched back from the stinging blow, his pursuit of the half-orc temporarily forgotten.

Grendel stepped close and brought his axe down on the demon's left forearm, severing it above the wrist. "That is for Sacha!"

Razrushitel shrieked in pain and lashed out with the elbow of the wounded arm, slinging blue-black blood and landing a glancing blow of his own. Thinking to hurl the half-orc away, he crouched and flicked his wings.

Grendel was ready for the attack and hacked at the flailing pinion with his glowing blade. "That is for me!"

The demon screamed again and leapt away.

Grendel followed. Razrushitel's wounds were already closing, his hand regenerating.

With a roar, the demon charged with his single weapon, and it took all of Grendel's skills to stay alive. Recalling all his fights, all his training, Grendel knew he had met his match. The demon responded stroke for stroke, block for block.

Stripped of everything else, all Grendel had left was faith. Gripping the axe tightly, Grendel lashed out with a feint.

The demon took a long step back and raised his sword as the half-orc switched and cut at him from the inside. The axe blade struck and slid down the fiery blade.

Grendel pressed his advantage, stepped inside, and thrust forward with the haft. Slipping past the demon's blade, he jabbed forward with the axe ferrule, landing a blow against the demon's chest and forcing him back a half step. Grendel grabbed Razrushitel's sword wrist. Raising his axe with his right hand, he brought the blade down on the demon's exposed chest with all his might.

Razrushitel buffeted his wings and flew backward, lifting Grendel a few feet off the ground when the half-orc refused to relinquish his grip on the axe lodged in the demon's hide. Overbalanced, flight was not possible. The pair landed a short distance behind, near the edge of the pool of black blood.

Grendel wrenched at the battle-axe, pulling it free.

The demon took a single step back, then he seemed to freeze. His back arched, and his face twisted in agony. Although his lips peeled back from his jagged teeth, no sound escaped his gaping maw. Behind him, Sacha held the Tear of Havel, the demon's blue-black blood dripping from its glittering tip.

Razrushitel spun toward her.

The fire inside the dagger flared blindingly white. Unable to tear his eyes away, Razrushitel raised his arm to block out the light. He thrashed his wings, trying to get away, but Grendel rushed forward and held him down.

As they struggled, a cold wind blew past Grendel, and the smell of fresh air replaced the fetid stench of death and brimstone. Feeling something alight on his face and melt, Grendel chanced a brief look around.

Snow.

Something stung Jasper's cheek, and he wondered what new torment Gregori unleashed. Another stinging pinprick struck his forehead, and he realized it was cold. Only then did the portly mage realize his opponent's advance had stopped.

Snow drifted down, and Gregori seemed terrified of the sight. The body-thieving mage muttered words of magic and vanished.

In his place, Jasper caught sight of Yana, Sehraine, Xandor, and Chert staring up with open mouths. He followed their frightened gazes.

Above them, an enormous pitch-black dragon perched on the jagged edge of a hole ripped into the green dome. Its cherry red eyes reflected the images dancing in the barrier and scanned the ground, watching the unfolding drama. Sutekh's Tugarin had come.

Grendel released Razrushitel's arm as he shoved the demon away from Sacha. The combatants separated.

Oozing blue-black blood from his nose and mouth, Razrushitel glared at the half-orc. So intent was the demon on Grendel that he failed to feel the falling snowflakes or the drop in temperature.

Grendel planted his feet, carefully placing himself between Sacha and Razrushitel in a position where he could protect her and see the dragon behind the demon. He lifted his axe in a two-handed grip, readying it near his right shoulder.

Razrushitel blinked and shook his head as though he had something in his eyes and approached his opponent warily. He whipped his sword around in a short horizontal arc aimed at Grendel's neck. When the glowing axe matched it, the demon's blade rebounded off the crescent shape.

Whipping his fiery blade up and over, the demon aimed for Grendel's opposite shoulder. Again, the axe blade beat the sword aside. Yanking his arm back, the demon drove it forward, thrusting the flaming war brand at the half-orc's guts. The glowing axe again interposed, parrying the sword to the side so that it slid past.

Not once did the gladiator move his feet. Not once did he attack.

Grinning, Razrushitel said, "You cannot defeat me, mortal!"

Seeing the dragon launch itself from its perch, Grendel replied, "I already have." He whipped his axe up and back over his head, then hurled it at the demon.

The draconic Tugarin dove at the embattled pair as the demon easily dodged the heavy missile.

Motion attracted Razrushitel, and he looked up, only then noticing what was coming for him. His eyes found those of the dragon, and he screamed, *"No!"*

As soon as he released the haft of his axe, Grendel turned and tackled Sacha, wrapping her in his arms. He took her to the ground and rolled to the tree line.

The dragon roared and spat a torrent of superheated lava at the demon. Razrushitel crossed his arms in front of his face in defense, but it did no good. His wings drooped and melted, leaving charred stumps, and his skin boiled, exposing blackened muscle and bone underneath.

Still, lava spewed from the dragon's mouth.

Xandor and his companions shielded their eyes as the center of town glowed brighter and brighter. The demon's dark shadow transformed into a figure of pure fire within the dragon's breath. A piercing shriek split the air and the demon exploded, throwing blazing chunks high into the air.

With a fury born straight out of hell, the dragon whipped his head all around the clearing. Xandor, Jasper, and the others fled to the shelter of the trees. Billowing waves of heat engulfed the center of town, focusing on the wagon and the pool of black liquid, and still lava spewed from the dragon's mouth.

The Blood of Cayn hissed and popped as it boiled before bursting into flame. The wood of the wagon instantly disintegrated.

Fingers of fire trailed across the ground, seeking out the last vestiges of the Blood of Cayn. Anyone who had even a trace of the dark liquid on them cried out as it burned away. They fell to the ground in pain, feeling just an echo of the dragon's breath.

Small flashes appeared on the trees all around them as the Blood of Cayn burned. The dwolma writhed on the ground, their rubbery skin melting and dissolving into the earth. Their amorphous carcasses sloughed off, revealing the pale ghosts of the elven elders.

When the dragon finally stopped, it left nothing but a charred stony crust where the pool had once been. Hovering over the town center, the dragon's flapping wings stirred up a cloud of ash. Its glowing eyes seemed to rove over every inch of the domed forest before it landed.

Xandor felt the Tugarin's burning gaze on him. He held his ground and gripped his weapon tighter.

The elves bowed to the dragon, seemingly more out of courtesy than reverence, and turned toward the Tear of Havel, now floating in the center of town. Their voices rose in an eerie song of sadness and grief. The Tear glowed with an inner light that seemed to answer their call.

A voice whispered in Xandor's head, *'Thanks to you and these others, my brother still sleeps.'*

Xandor felt disturbingly unclean. Questions formed in his mind, but he was afraid to ask them, remembering Sacha's comment back at the Sabe estate. Following the elves' lead, he bowed his head out of courtesy and tried to temper the rage building inside him against this minion of the Dark One. He gripped the Korsun cross on its leather thong around his neck until its arm-tips bit into his palm and said, "We tried to destroy a wagonload of it a couple days ago. It's buried in Chernigov." The dragon stared at him a moment longer then turned his attention away.

After looking around the clearing once more, the dragon spread its wings, and launched itself into the night sky.

Xandor was the first to emerge from the trees. He brushed off the ash and looked up. Snow drifted down through the breach in the green dome, reflecting the tiny fires that remained. On the other side of a massive trunk, Jasper and Sehraine helped each other over the roots. Beyond them, Chert and Yana approached the smooth, ropy surface of the hardened lava. They all had singed patches on their clothes, skin, and hair where the Blood of Cayn had burned off, but it could have been much worse.

In the center of the town, the Tear of Havel hung in the air, giving off a pale white light. The sadness remained, hidden beneath the surface. Ghostly figures stood around the light without moving. They continued their singing, and something akin to music emanated from the Tear. It blended with that of the Elders, filling the town with a melody unheard since before the Plague Wars.

As if the trees were old men standing up after a long sleep, the wood gave off a tremendous creaking and popping. The trees seemed to come alive, straightening and standing tall. The pall of the Blood of Cayn was gone. No signs of the demon, the dwolma, or Gregori remained.

On the opposite side of the clearing, at the edge of the light, Grendel and Sacha lay huddled in each other's arms. Seeming to sense everyone's eyes upon him, Grendel helped Sacha to her feet. She swayed and stumbled until Grendel wrapped an arm around her waist. In one hand, she clutched the black cords the demon used to bind her, still blooded from where they had gouged her wrists.

Xandor watched Grendel lead Sacha past the ring of ghosts and across the lane. Something about how she walked struck him as odd. It took him a moment to realize she was blind.

Xandor heaved a sigh. "I'm glad to see we all survived," he said.

"Is the Blood of Cayn gone?" Yana asked.

Chert looked everyone over, ending with himself. "I think so."

"All of it?" Xandor questioned.

"Doubt it," Jasper answered, looking up at the snow-filled sky through the crack in the dome.

They stood quietly, digesting what they had witnessed.

"We need to get that to Pazard'zhik," Yana said, breaking the silence and nodding toward the Tear of Havel.

"What about the elves?" Chert inquired. "Will they want to keep it?"

"And what about Sacha?" asked Grendel.

"We can't all go to Pazard'zhik. Some of us will have to stay," Xandor said pensively. His eyes held a distant look as he struggled with the plethora of things that needed doing. He knew they had to tread carefully, or they might inadvertently start a war over the Tear.

"I'm going to Pazard'zhik," Yana stated in a tone that allowed no room for argument.

"Marcus isn't the only person who needs help," Xandor replied.

Sehraine stepped between Yana and Xandor. "It doesn't matter what either of you thinks or wants, if the Elders don't agree," she said. She gestured toward the Tear of Havel and the ring of elven ghosts. Their song finished, they watched the small group of mortals.

"Can you get it away from them?" Xandor asked.

"I don't know," she replied. Taking a deep breath, Sehraine approached the ring of ghosts.

"We have long awaited your return, Sehraine," one said, his voice echoing hollowly.

She bowed her head. "Please forgive me."

"It is not our forgiveness you need, child, it is your own," the ghost replied. "Had you returned here with your father on that long ago day, there would be none to take up the burden of the Tear of Havel now." The ghost waited for her to look up. "Many need Havel's Mercy, child. Will you be its bearer?"

Sehraine stared up at the Tear of Havel, contemplating the daunting task before her. Finally, she nodded.

The ghost bowed to her and stepped aside. "Then take the Tear of Havel. It is yours by birthright."

Sehraine entered their circle and stood beneath the floating Tear. She raised her hands above her head, palms flat to receive the blade, and sang the elven lullaby once more. Her soprano filled the clearing in a rising aria of peace echoed by the crystalline tear. It settled in her waiting hands, its light pulsing softly in time with her heartbeat.

Another elder stepped forward, bearing a shining mithril box in her transparent hands. "When your task is done, take the Tear to our cousins in the mountains to the east," she said. "They will keep it safe until it is needed again."

Sehraine bowed deeply. When she straightened, the elves were gone. All, except two: a male elf in plain riding leathers, and an older female in a homespun gown of green and silver.

Sehraine faced them. "Amma, Isä, I'm so sorry I ran away. Please forgive me." Tears glistened in her eyes and rolled unheeded down her cheeks.

The pale hand of her father caressed her hair gently and he said, "We love you, Sehraine. We always will." He stared deeply into her eyes, and she smiled, but her voice was lost.

Her grandmother said, "All is as it needs to be. Remember that your father and I will always be with you."

Sehraine reached out one trembling hand, and her father's fingertips brushed hers. Then they, too, were gone. She wiped the tears from her cheeks and drew in a steadying breath. Then, she turned and faced her friends. Even inside its new home, she could feel the Tear of Havel's presence.

Yana and Xandor stood on opposite sides of the group, watching her. The tension between them had a physical presence.

Sehraine approached Jasper. "Can you get us to Pazard'zhik, like you did when we escaped from the theater?"

"I can only send two people," Jasper answered cautiously. He had everyone's attention.

"Well, I guess that would be Sehraine and me," Yana said.

"We need it to save Dobrynya," Xandor said. "Lord Fergusson and the Iron Tower expect me to bring it to them, as well."

Yana stepped in front of Xandor and said, "You know my brother is in Pazard'zhik, fighting for his life. You can't expect me to just let it go."

"I know," Xandor said.

Sehraine could see the conflict between his sense of duty and his personal feelings reflected in his mismatched eyes. She joined Yana and added, "The Tear of Havel can't be in two places at once. You heard the elders. This is my birthright, my task to complete. The Tear goes to Pazard'zhik first."

Raising his hands in defeat, he said, "Fine, you win. But remember, it can't stay. There are a lot of people who need its help."

Sehraine smiled and hugged Xandor tightly, catching him off-guard. He gingerly returned the hug, as if he feared he might break her. She stepped back and approached Jasper. Lifting a cord from inside her shirt, she revealed his signet ring. "One day, you'll have to tell me the story behind that ring," she said.

"One day soon," he promised, and slipped the ring onto his right hand. He looked from Sehraine to Yana. "I need the two of you to do me a favor."

"Oh? What would that be?" Yana asked suspiciously.

"Tell Ms. Violeta Galabova that I would like to fix her a nice dinner." He grinned at Yana's confused expression.

Sehraine gave Jasper a sly smile and said, "This better not be like last time."

Jasper rewarded her with a shocked look and replied, "I sure hope not." He became more serious and said, "Good luck."

"You too," Sehraine said, hugging him.

After the elf let go, Yana walked up to the mage, punched him in the shoulder, and said, "Get this right, mage, or I'll hunt you down." She gave him a mock glare as she spoke.

"What was that for?" Jasper asked, rubbing his shoulder with an exaggerated expression of pain on his face.

Yana wrapped the mage in a tight hug and then turned away. The two women quickly said their goodbyes to everyone else and stood together as the mage finished his preparations.

Jasper looked at each one, getting a quick smile from each. He nodded and raised his staff, speaking words they couldn't hear, and released his magic. Their images slowly faded, and the last thing the group saw was their hands waving goodbye.

"What about us?" Chert asked.

"We need to take Sacha to the Korol'," Xandor said.

"What!" Grendel barked. "There is no way I am handing her over! Not now."

Not backing down, Xandor stared the half-orc in the eyes and said, "I have no intention of letting Dobrynya take the fall for something he didn't do!"

The two men studied each other warily, neither backing off.

Following their voices, Sacha stepped between the two of them. She pushed gently on Grendel's chest and said, "Xandor's right. I must take responsibility for what my demon has done."

She turned toward the ranger's voice. "I will go back with you."

Grendel stared at his feet and said, reluctantly, "We will go together."

Turning back, a sad look came over Sacha, and she said, "Where I go, you cannot follow. It is my task, and mine alone."

"But I am trying to save you."

Sacha placed a hand on Grendel's cheek and said, "You already have."

CHAPTER 40:
MARCUS

November 1, 4235 K.E.

1:40am

Everything went dark. Yana felt Jasper's magic surround and move through her. Suddenly the bottom fell out, and she felt like they were falling. The quick rush of adrenaline ended when she and Sehraine landed in a small room filled with cloth and dress designs. Embers in the fireplace lit the room with a warm glow. Yana hadn't realized just how cold she was until she felt the fire's warmth.

Working late, Violeta Galabova was sketching a new dress on a thin sheet of paper pinned to a cutting board. She didn't notice the two people in her shop — at least at first. Screaming, she dropped her charcoal pencil and leapt toward her crossbow.

Yana slowly held her hands up in front of her and tried not to look threatening, but the blood and grime covering her masked her intent. Violeta snatched up her crossbow and pointed it at the two females, her hands shaking.

"Who are you, and how did you get into my shop?"

Sehraine pointed toward the rough circle in the floor with her toe and said, "Jasper sent us."

"Jasper. Jasper Thredd?" the seamstress asked with an odd mixture of exasperation and curiosity.

"Yes," Yana answered with a snort. "Round mage. Has a habit of getting into trouble and dragging other people down with him."

The point of the bolt in the crossbow dipped as Violeta studied the two women. Her eyes went wide, and she gasped, "You're an elf!"

Sehraine nodded while Yana said, "Sorry about intruding, but we must get to the Kral."

"Have you found the cure?"

"We think so."

"He said he was looking for a cure," Violeta said to herself. "Is he well? Jasper, I mean."

"Yes, he's fine. Actually, he wanted us to tell you that he would like to fix you dinner when he returns."

Violeta smiled, laid the crossbow on the table, and said, "Please do not let me keep you any longer."

Yana and Sehraine thanked the seamstress and walked past her to the front door. Violeta reached to open it and asked, "Do you need anything? You look a mess."

A blast of winter air hit the three ladies, and snow drifted across the threshold. Sehraine laid a hand on Violeta's arm and shook her head. "No, I'm afraid we must be off." Before stepping outside, Sehraine added, "Thank you for believing Jasper."

Violeta chewed on her lip for a moment and then said, "Tell Jasper anytime, but make sure he uses the front door."

"I will," Sehraine answered.

Tugging what was left of their winter cloaks tighter, the two raced up the empty street. A light dusting of snow covered the cobblestones. Along the edges, piles of snow had turned to grey slush and refrozen during the night. They continued up the hill and stopped at the main gate to the royal estates.

"Who goes there?"

A guard dressed in the livery of the Kral peered through the bars of the gate.

Yana stepped forward and announced, "I am Laytenant Yana Marchenkova, Black Dragon Squadron, Trakyan Wind Riders, and this is Lady Sehraine Marchenkova. You will let us pass."

"I'm sorry Milady, but I have strict orders. No one is allowed inside."

"What?! Why?"

"The plague, Milady. The Kral's estates are off limits."

Sehraine pulled out the Tear of Havel. It glowed dimly.

"Soldier, stand aside. We have the cure."

Lit by the Tear of Havel, the look on Yana's face made the guard swallow his next response. He stared at the two ladies as doubt riddled his face.

"I have my orders."

Thinking quickly, Yana pulled Marcus' signet ring from beneath her cuirass and held it up for him to see. "Do you recognize this?" she inquired harshly.

The guard held out his hand, and she gave it to him. His eyes widened as he realized what he held, and he nodded.

"Open the gate," she ordered.

They heard the lock snap open, and the gate swung back. The man held out his hand to return Marcus' ring.

Two more guards approached from behind him, their pikes ready. "Nikolai, what the hell are you doing?" one demanded.

"They carry the signet of Lord Marchenkov, sub-head of the Ochi i Uchi."

"I don't care if they're angels from on high, they are not getting past..."

Pain exploded on the man's face, followed by more pain in his solar plexus. The guard found himself on the ground, his nose bloodied, and unable to draw a breath.

"If your captain asks you what happened, tell him you were hit by a girl."

Yana and Sehraine casually stepped over the prostrate guard. The other two backed away, but they didn't yell out, either. Yana took it as a good sign.

"Come with us," she told the first guard. "Lock the gate, and man the post," she ordered the other.

They immediately headed for the chapel infirmary with the guard hurrying to keep up. As they approached, Sehraine began humming the notes to awaken the Tear of Havel. Its glow spread out before them, chasing away the shadows.

"Here we go."

Ahead, red crosses painted on the doors glowed eerily in the Tear's light. A padlock bound the chain wrapped through the handles.

Yana turned to the guard and asked, "Do you want to help these people or not?"

Gripping his pike tighter, he nodded and struck the wood around the handles until one broke free. When the door opened, the stench of death, sickness, and fear hit them like a solid barrier. They waded through it. There was no light or warmth. No one remained to light the candles or stoke the central hearth. Half-frozen people lying in their own filth covered the chapel infirmary floor and filled the pews.

Sehraine sang, and the Tear of Havel floated above her raised hand, casting its brilliant silver light to the far corners of the room. Elven words blended with the music from the Tear, forcing out the Blood of Cayn. People awoke as if from a nightmare and stared into the light, a beacon of hope to guide their way home. Sehraine worked her way through the nave, making sure the light touched everyone. When she and Yana reached the chancel, they stopped, bowed their heads, and said a silent prayer to the Eternal Father.

Dropping his pike, the guard raced outside and yelled for help.

Darkness clung to the walls of the hallway leading out of the north transept. The two walked slowly toward it, afraid of what they might find. These were the first arrivals, the ones who had suffered the most. Death leered hungrily from behind thick curtains drawn across small alcoves.

The music of the Tear of Havel soaked into the stone and found every recess. The ancient battle between Cayn and Havel raged again, but this time, it was in the hearts and minds of men, not on a battlefield.

Sehraine found some were already lost, their blankets pulled up to hide their faces. Others, weak from lack of food and water, burst into tears as the light of Havel's Mercy washed over them.

Voices echoed from the chapel infirmary, followed by cries of praise and thanksgiving.

Sehraine followed her friend past bed after bed. Finally, Yana found Marcus. Their aunt still sat by his bedside, holding his hand.

He looked deathly pale, and when Yana placed a hand on his chest, agony filled her face. Still singing, Sehraine eased past the wind rider and placed the Tear of Havel over Marcus' heart. The light grew brighter as her words flowed with emotion.

Lady Marchenkova woke and blinked away her sleep. "Yana? Sehraine?"

"We're here," Yana replied.

"I'm thirsty."

Yana stepped out into the hall and yelled, "Water! Someone, fetch us water!"

Sehraine placed a hand on Marcus's brow. She felt the struggle waging inside him. She felt Cayn's grip on his soul. What had Gregori and the demon done?

Like a drowning man plucked from the sea, Marcus gasped for air. His eyes flew open, and he stared at the Tear of Havel on his chest. A strange look came over him. He gripped Sehraine's wrist, making her wince, and said in a voice that was not his own, "Caino dorme, ma risorgerà." *Cayn sleeps, but he will rise again.* For a moment, his eyes burned fever bright before rolling back in his head. His hand fell slack onto the bed.

"Marcus!" Sehraine exclaimed.

Marcus' eyes slid open. Confusion clouded his features, followed by relief as he recognized Sehraine, his aunt, and his sister beside him.

"You made it," he whispered, his voice his own once again. He reached a hand to Yana, and she gripped it in hers.

"Of course I did."

CHAPTER 41:
REDEMPTION

November 8, 4235 K.E.

11:00am

"Gertsog Sabe, your son is responsible for the death of Velikiy-Gertsog Vsevolod. Whether or not he had a personal hand in it does not matter, he's responsible for letting the person who did escape. It's as if he had held the knife himself," Sud'ya Oleg Belousov said with a theatrical flair. Strutting across the bowl-shaped audience chamber, he waved his steel-ball-tipped black rod in the air and cast his gaze upon the nobles who watched from the tiered benches. Surrounding him, evenly spaced marble columns streaked with blue and white veins lined the walls, supporting both the gallery and the lofty, domed roof. Directly above them, a round stained-glass skylight let in the morning light.

On the topmost step along the north edge of the chamber, Korol' Melikhov VI of Michurinsk sat on a majestic throne made of white marble. He was a middle-aged man whose dark hair showed faint streaks of silver. Today, lines of worry creased his careworn face. Wearing robes of judgment, he presided over the testimony presented by Sud'ya Belousov and Gertsog Sabe. On the right arm of the throne rested a mahogany gavel, and on the left was a golden scepter encrusted with purple and white diamonds. Normally, the office of the sud'ya handled such affairs, but since this involved the death of one of his closest advisors, the king had a personal stake in the matter.

Two steps below and to his right, the master of ceremonies held his staff of office, while the captain of the royal guard was two steps below and to his left. In the first seat of the gallery on the Korol's right sat his brother, Knyaz Dorinkov.

Dobrynya Sabe, wearing his soldier's livery, remained beside his father. They both stood at the bottom of the chamber, railed off from the current speaker. He glared at the judge but wisely kept his mouth shut as the sud'ya explained in lurid detail the events of eight days ago.

His family had followed the jail wagon to the capital, where his father requested an immediate audience with the Korol'. Sud'ya Belousov must have smelled blood, because he demanded there be a public trial. Once word spread of the graphic nature of the death and who was involved, the Korol' had no choice and sent word to the other gertsog. The nobles put aside all other business and flocked to Michurinsk.

The young knight listened to the sud'ya explain how the Sabe family conspired with a ranger of the Iron Tower and allowed him and his men to escape. Exaggerating a limp, the sud'ya continued by recounting how he personally tried to arrest the ranger and was nearly trampled. From the corner of his eye, Dobrynya saw his father clench the rail, otherwise the elder Sabe kept his face expressionless as he listened. The events described by the sud'ya were slightly different from what Dobrynya remembered — the horses were much closer, and the man seemed in constant peril throughout his retelling. The judge sported his fading black eye like a badge of courage.

"Dobrynya is a young man, easily swayed by the wiles of a succubus." The sud'ya looked the younger Sabe in the eyes and added, "In this case the Lady Aleksandra Madasgorski Krakova, a vile and reprehensible creature from Zhitomir. He fraternized with this woman and welcomed her into the Sabe estate. This alone is proof of his duplicity."

With a wide sweep of his arm, Sud'ya Belousov concluded by saying, "The Sabe family's loyalties to the crown are in question. On that fateful day under the leadership of Gertsog Sabe, they acted more like agents of the Confederation of Nations than loyal subjects of Michurinsk. They have no honor! I humbly suggest that their lands and titles be stripped away."

Gasps of disbelief echoed in the hall. Many came to their feet and shouted in protest. The master of ceremonies slammed his staff against the floor, demanding order.

Silence crept into the hall like an unwanted guest, and all eyes turned to the Korol' when he said, "Gertsog Sabe. What have you to say in your defense?"

Leonid looked around the audience, meeting the heated glares of his peers. He took a deep breath before proceeding. "Sire, I cannot deny the events that took place at my estate; however, I argue the specifics of the honorable Sud'ya Belousov's interpretation of those events. The fact remains that Velikiy-Gertsog Vsevolod, a friend to both my father and myself, died under my roof. I do not know how he died, and to claim that Lady Aleksandra Madasgorski Krakova had anything to do with it is premature."

Sud'ya Belousov spun toward the Korol' and shouted, "Your Majesty, I object! Lady Aleksandra's luring of Velikiy-Gertsog Vsevolod to the Sabe estate is on record."

Gertsog Sabe rounded on the judge and countered, "She voluntarily gave herself to the justice of the Korol'. You and Velikiy-Gertsog Vsevolod being the ones to claim her was pure chance based upon your proximity, not a plot."

"I disagree. I suspect she knew all along who among the aristocracy would be available."

"How could she know that? She had just come from Chernigov after playing a significant role in the rescue of my son."

"Now we come to it," Sud'ya Belousov said, his eyes focusing on Dobrynya. "What were you doing in Chernigov?"

All eyes turned to the youth. Dobrynya turned to his father, who gave him the barest hint of a nod. Addressing the Korol', the young lord said, "Sire, my men and I were trapped in the monastery by Kraagor's humanoids."

"I repeat the question. What were you doing in Chernigov?"

"We were salvaging relics from the old towns abandoned by the Trakyans."

"Was this activity sanctioned by the court?"

Gertsog Sabe looked up at the Korol', pleading with his eyes. The Korol' sighed before addressing the crowd. "I was aware of this activity, but it was not public knowledge, for obvious reasons."

A collective gasp went up from the assembled noblemen. Sud'ya Belousov turned to Dobrynya, a cold and calculating expression on his face.

"Did anything of interest come from this?" the judge asked.

"You know it did," Dobrynya interjected. "It brought us the Tear of Havel."

"The relic stolen when Velikiy-Gertsog Vsevolod was murdered."

"Correction," Gertsog Sabe interjected. "A relic which was stolen after it was removed from my family chapel."

Sud'ya Belousov smiled and said generously, "Gertsog Sabe, I stand corrected. A relic stolen after it was removed from your personal chapel, where a succubus could get her hands on it after she was welcomed into your home."

Dobrynya frowned. The sud'ya was twisting everything they were saying.

The Korol' looked down at Dobrynya and asked, "How did Lady Aleksandra escape from the jail wagon?"

"Your Majesty, I do not know. She simply vanished."

"Could she have been a succubus?" the Korol' asked.

The doubt in Dobrynya's eyes was obvious, and Oleg's face split in a victorious grin.

"I don't know, Majesty. We were so busy trying to escape that I didn't spend any time with Lady Aleksandra. All I know is that we would not have escaped without the help of the Iron Tower and their ranger, and he trusted her enough to walk with her into the bowels of Chernigov."

"This ranger is not the one on trial. You are."

A sudden commotion rose in the hall outside, and the grand double doors swung open. The crowd of noblemen parted along the south end of the chamber, revealing three newcomers.

Xandor, wearing his mottled cloak, strode down the steps. Sacha, wearing a conservative grey dress, and Grendel, who still wore his bloodstained leather, followed. The half-orc's low-pitched instructions to the woman at his side carried over the crowd. Her left hand rested on his right wrist, and she tilted her head as she listened. Her white, sightless eyes stared straight ahead, unblinking. Behind them, light flared at the entrance and the ring of steel on steel echoed loudly.

The Korol' stood and shouted, "Who dares to bring arms into my hall?"

He motioned with his scepter. The captain of the royal guard signaled for his men to intercept the three intruders.

Guards carrying crossbows appeared amongst the noblemen and on the balcony.

Ignoring them, Xandor kept moving toward the center of the chamber, a sword strapped across his back. Jasper and Chert blocked the doorway, stemming the tide of guards who rushed to protect their king.

"Your Majesty, please hear us out!" Xandor shouted over the din of the crowd.

The captain of the guard interposed himself between Xandor and the Korol'. The ranger stopped, keeping his hands open before him as a sign of non-violence. The Korol' sat and eyed the ranger speculatively.

Banging the butt of his staff on the floor, the master of ceremonies yelled, "Ladies and Gentlemen! Ladies and Gentlemen!"

Sud'ya Belousov was livid. He turned to the Korol' and shouted, "Sire, these people are criminals! I demand their removal from this court! This one in particular tried to run me down with his horse!"

The Korol' leaned forward and studied the trio. He picked up the gavel and struck the arm of his throne. From either magic or the acoustics of the domed roof, the sound cut through the yelling and the clash of arms, causing everyone to pause.

After a quick bow of his head, Xandor said, "Your Majesty, my name is Xandor ap Kynan of Clan Tanjara, a ranger in the service of the Iron Tower. May I speak? I bring one who has information pertinent to this trial."

Sud'ya Belousov yelled, "I protest!"

The Korol' silenced the judge with a stern glance and said, "Ranger, you have my attention. Speak."

"Your Majesty, Ladies and Gentlemen of the court, may I present to you Lady Aleksandra Madasgorski Krakova."

The hall became deathly silent when Sacha stepped forward. She gazed around the room with milk-white eyes. Grendel helped Sacha face the throne, and she bowed to the Korol' of Michurinsk. "Your Majesty, I have come to proclaim the innocence of the Sabe family, in particular Dobrynya Sabe. They are not responsible for the death of Velikiy-Gertsog Vsevolod. I am."

Making a face, Grendel turned toward Sacha, but Xandor put up a hand and shook his head at the half-orc. The two stared at each other, their unspoken argument plain in their expressions, and the Korol' quirked an eyebrow at the byplay.

His jaw clenched tight, the judge went pale as he faced the audience surrounding them. With a subtle cutting motion, he wiped his mouth with the back of his hand.

One of the Korol's guards burst through the crowd of noblemen. Eyes filled with fervent determination through the visor of his helm, he raised his crossbow and trained it on the small crowd in the center of the hall and fired before anyone could stop him. With a sharp whistle, the bolt shot across the chamber.

Grendel twisted, pushing Lady Aleksandra into Xandor. The ranger staggered under the impact but kept his feet under him. He held her close while searching for the one who had shot at them. Behind him, Grendel roared, and shocked murmurs ran through the crowd when they saw the fletching of the bolt sticking out of his back. With a lurch, the half-orc dropped to his knees.

Guards erupted from the crowd of noblemen and tackled the rogue soldier, forcing him to the ground.

"Bring him!" the Korol' ordered. Two of the Korol's men held up the assassin and dragged him to the chamber floor for all to see.

Chert fought his way through the crowd, Jasper right behind him. With a final shove, they broke through the last line of noblemen and reached Grendel's side. Tearing away from Xandor's grip, Sacha knelt beside the half-orc, resting her hand on his arm.

Guards disarmed the assassin and threw him down. The captain held his sword to the man's throat and asked, "Who hired you?"

At first, the assassin didn't respond. He simply looked at the Korol' with his mouth forming words that no one could hear. Sud'ya Belousov leapt forward and struck the assassin with his rod. The steel ball crushed the man's skull like a grapefruit.

Dobrynya could hardly believe the speed with which the judge had moved and the explosiveness of his action.

The captain of the guard jumped back and leveled his sword at the judge.

"He was trying to curse the Korol'," the judge explained.

The captain turned to the Korol' for direction, and the monarch gave him a curt nod. Sheathing his weapon, he motioned for two of his men to remove the body.

"It seems that someone doesn't want me talking to Lady Aleksandra," the Korol' mused softly. "Ladies and Gentlemen, in light of what has happened, we will recess for lunch. In the meantime, I would like for Sud'ya Belousov, Lady Aleksandra, Gertsog Sabe, and Xandor to join me in my private chambers."

Everyone stood while he exited into a small side passage behind the throne.

Grendel held Sacha's hand while Chert dressed the wound in his back. "I am fine. Go before someone else tries to shoot you."

She squeezed his hand a little tighter before reluctantly allowing Xandor to lead her away.

Xandor guided Sacha as they followed the captain of the guard down the lush hallway. Behind them walked two more soldiers. Couldn't be too careful, he guessed.

They didn't say anything, but the ranger thought it odd that just a little over a week ago, he had been ready to kill the woman in his care. He thought about the look that had passed between her and Grendel and wondered if the two would ever see each other again.

Standing outside a dark, wooden door, the captain held up his hand and the two joined Gertsog Sabe in the hallway. Worry creased Xandor's brow — the sud'ya was already inside with the Korol'. After a few minutes, the door opened, and the captain motioned them inside.

The office was a lavish affair that spoke of wealth and pageantry. Glass cabinets, filled with delicate items that sparkled, lined one whole wall. On another, leather-bound tomes rested on shelves, well used but maintained. At the far end, the Korol' sat in a comfortable leather chair behind an ornately engraved wooden desk with lion's claws for feet. A lamp glowed warmly in the corner, and it seemed to Xandor that the king of Michurinsk spent much of his time here.

Xandor turned his attention to the judge standing in front of the desk. The man smirked, and Xandor glared in return. Something about the judge grated on his nerves.

"Leonid, I don't see you enough. You should come to the capital more often."

Gertsog Sabe took encouragement from the Korol's relaxed manner and replied, "The duties of our offices seem to conspire against us, Your Majesty."

The Korol' nodded and turned to Sud'ya Belousov, "You have claimed grievances against the Sabe family. You have questioned their honor. What say you now?"

"Sire, as you know, my only wish is for justice to prevail. Lady Aleksandra has publicly confessed to the murder of Velikiy-Gertsog Vsevolod. She is a succubus and should be put to death before she can claim any more victims."

Xandor rankled at the man's words, wanting to shove them down his throat, but Sacha put a hand on his chest, stopping him.

"A succubus, you say," the Korol' said, studying Sacha's face. "Karl, please find Otets Jovid and ask him to join us. In the meantime, find a servant and have someone send up refreshments." The captain of the guard nodded and sent a runner to find the archbishop and another to find food.

It only took a few minutes before the butler arrived to offer the Korol' and his guest glasses of wine. One of the kitchen staff followed on his heels with small meats and cheeses. Sacha heard the soft chime of the silver tray as the girl placed it on a side table. Although Xandor offered to bring her something, Sacha found she had no appetite.

Talking from the hall attracted her attention. Two men deep in conversation arrived at the office door. Sacha had heard of Otets Jovid. The priest had been with the Korol' many years. He had come to Michurinsk with the Iron Tower after the Plague War and fell in love with the country and its people. When given the opportunity, he stayed. One thing led to another, and Korol' Melikhov V came to rely on the priest's advice. Now, the ex-army chaplain was the archbishop of the royal chapel, teaching the Korol's children of the Eternal Father. Gossip said his years were leading to senility, but those closest to the archbishop staunchly defended him. Of course, that might have had to do with the fact that he didn't get involved with court intrigue, and those who tried to use him found themselves flustered by his open candor. There were a number of noblemen who blatantly avoided the archbishop — except on Sundays.

She imagined the priest's apolitical stance was a refreshing change of pace for the Korol' and found herself wondering if the priest's neutrality would extend to her as well.

"Your Majesty, it's good to see you again," one of the men said. His voice was strong despite his age. "A shame about that killing in your hall."

The Korol' walked around his desk and led the elderly man inside. "Otets Jovid, please let me introduce to you Sud'ya Belousov, Gertsog Sabe, Xandor — a ranger of the Iron Tower — and Lady Aleksandra Madasgorski Krakova."

After a slight hesitation, a pair of wrinkled hands clasped hers in a firm but gentle grip. "The peace of the Eternal Father be upon you," the man said.

She bowed her head. "Thank you, Otets."

"Otets, can you tell me if Lady Aleksandra is a succubus?" the Korol' asked.

The man continued holding Sacha's hand in his but moved the other to her forehead. The archbishop whispered a short prayer, and silence settled over the room.

Fabric rustled as the sud'ya fidgeted with his court robes.

Despite her inability to see, Sacha felt Otets Jovid's vision penetrating into her soul. Sadness welled up in her heart. Although she herself was no demon, her sins were too great. She knew this holy man would see the stain on her soul and condemn her.

The old man's hand brushed across her forehead and cupped her cheek. She heard the smile in his voice when he spoke. "You are fine, my dear. Not a succubus — and not possessed. You are a child of the Eternal Father."

Sacha let out the breath she had been holding, and a tear slipped from her eye. "Thank you, Your Grace."

The younger priest found a chair and offered it to Jovid.

"Well, Sud'ya Belousov, satisfied?" the Korol' asked after the archbishop was settled.

"Not hardly, Sire. She is still a Madasgorski and not to be trusted."

Taking back his seat, the Korol' asked, "Lady Krakova, what happened at the Sabe estate?"

Looking down at feet she couldn't see, Sacha recounted the events of the morning before Velikiy-Gertsog Vsevolod's death. She tried not to leave out any detail, but in the end, she realized there wasn't much that she actually knew. She turned toward the direction of the Korol's voice and concluded, "The last thing I remember was being in the jail wagon. I awoke in the clutches of the demon bound to my family's service. He had the Tear of Havel and wanted to use it to sacrifice me to Cayn."

The Korol' cast a questioning look at Otets Jovid, who sat listening with his eyes closed — or maybe he was asleep; it was hard to tell.

Sud'ya Belousov said a little too loudly, "Majesty, there is no proof. It's a story she made up to conceal the truth."

Trying very hard to control his anger, Xandor turned to the judge and said, "I know for a fact that her story is not made up. I saw both the demon and the Tear of Havel. The demon killed Velikiy-Gertsog Vsevolod — not Lady Aleksandra or Vityaz Dobrynya. You saw the damage done to the bodies!" He pointed at Sacha, "Can you honestly stand there and tell me she has the physical strength to rend bodies like that? I don't think even Grendel could do that kind of damage, especially in the seconds in which the killing happened."

"Where is the Tear of Havel now?" Sud'ya Belousov prodded. "Don't tell me you let this so-called demon keep it."

"The Kral has it in Pazard'zhik." Everyone turned. It was the younger priest who answered.

Otets Jovid broke the silence. "Your Majesty, I apologize. I did not introduce my friend, Otets Georgiev, from Pazard'zhik. We checked the pigeons this morning and found two came in during the night. You were busy with the trial this morning, so I haven't been able to give this to you until now."

The priest handed the small message to the Korol'. It bore the royal seal of the Kral in miniature.

"Your Highness, the Kral wishes me to express his gratitude to you for helping save his people. As you can see, he would have come personally, but is currently hosting negotiations between the Emissary of the Elven Nation and the Confederation Council on where the Tear of Havel should travel next. He requests you send him a message if you also need the Tear."

Otets Jovid leaned back in his chair and said to Sud'ya Belousov, "It seems that, despite your efforts, these people have managed to avert the plague and another possible war. Instead of executing them, I recommend they be heralded as heroes."

Oleg's mouth opened and closed as he floundered, trying to find something to say.

The Korol' hid a smile by stroking his beard, but Xandor could see the relief in the king's eyes. "Otets Jovid has a point," the monarch said. "I see no reason to punish the Sabe family for what they have done. In fact, it seems that their actions were warranted."

"Your Majesty, you are justifying their actions based upon the end result, not the means. No one is above your law. I need not remind you that your people died. Their families seek restitution."

"Are you suggesting a monetary solution?" the Korol' asked, his eyes narrowing.

"No, Sire, they want the one responsible. If you want to spare the Sabe family, give them the Madasgorski woman."

Xandor looked between the judge and the Korol' and said, "You can't seriously be considering this? Sacha did not kill anyone. The demon did."

Sud'ya Belousov grinned maliciously and said, "She publicly took responsibility for the death of Velikiy-Gertsog Vsevolod. He would be alive today if she hadn't sought shelter at the Sabe estate."

"You don't know that," Xandor argued.

Laying a hand on Xandor's shoulder to calm him, Sacha said, "I have many crimes to atone for. I am sure that once the Kral hears of my presence here, he will want to have a say in what happens to me." She turned toward where she thought Otets Jovid was sitting and continued, "I seek to do the right thing, and a part of that is not hiding from what I've done."

"That could mean a death sentence. I will not stand here and let that happen, and neither will Grendel," Xandor said, surprising himself with his vehemence.

The Korol' stood and said, "Otets Georgiev, you are dismissed. I will speak with you later. Gertsog Sabe and Sud'ya Belousov, please wait for me in the audience chamber. Tell the master of ceremonies that I will resume the trial in fifteen minutes."

As soon as the door closed behind them, the Korol' said, "We have one other thing to consider."

Everyone in the office turned to him, and he motioned to Sacha, "Someone tried to kill you in my audience chamber today, Lady Krakova. I don't think it was a Vsevolod family member seeking revenge — that leaves us with the Madasgorski family. I imagine they are concerned you will divulge family secrets."

Sacha's brow furrowed as she thought over the new angle.

"If I'm right, they won't stop until you and everyone you care for is dead."

1:20pm

A guard ran into the hall and shouted, "The witch attacked the Korol'!"

Voices drowned each other out as everyone sought news. Grendel bounded up the steps to the throne and raced toward the hallway with Chert and Jasper behind him. Guards moved to intercept him. Behind them, a grim-faced Xandor emerged.

"What happened?" Grendel asked, peering past the ranger. He tried to step around Xandor, but the ranger blocked him.

"Grendel," the ranger said.

The half-orc wasn't listening. He pushed against the ranger. Xandor gritted his teeth and pushed back. "Grendel! Stop!"

"What are you doing? She needs me!"

Jasper glanced questioningly at Xandor. Something wasn't right.

Behind the ranger, the Korol's guards carried Lady Aleksandra into the hall. Her body hung limp. A dark bruise marred her neck.

Grendel saw Sacha and bellowed. He shoved Xandor aside, intent on reaching her. His friends tried to hold him back, but he was impossible to stop. It took six guards, Xandor, and Chert to wrestle him to the floor.

Escorted by more guards, Otets Jovid helped the Korol' to the throne. Blood spatters covered both men's robes.

Sud'ya Belousov stood a safe distance away from the raging half-orc. "Your Majesty, what happened?" he asked. Although his voice sounded concerned, Jasper thought he saw a hint of self-righteous glee in the man's eyes.

"Lady Aleksandra attacked me. You were right. I should have listened to you," the Korol' replied.

The guardsmen laid her at the foot of the throne. The sud'ya scurried forward to examine her. Unable to conceal his surprise, he announced, "She's dead."

Grendel heard the judge's proclamation, and the fight went out of him. Xandor moved everyone off him and knelt beside his grief-stricken friend.

Chert strode across the room and placed his fingertips on the vein below her jaw. He closed his eyes and waited. One minute passed, then two, before he stepped away from Sacha's lifeless form. He looked at Grendel and shook his head slightly. The half-orc closed his eyes and trembled.

The Korol' stood and announced in a weak voice, "Justice is done. The murderer of Velikiy-Gertsog Vsevolod and those in his service has revealed her true form. Dobrynya Sabe, you are free to go."

The crowd of noblemen was shocked to silence and could only watch as the Korol' retired from the audience chamber.

Otets Jovid knelt beside the grieving half-orc and placed a comforting hand on his shoulder. The old man gripped the half-orc's hand and slipped a small note into his palm and whispered, "Read it later, when you are alone." In a louder voice he said, "You are welcome in the chapel, should you choose to come for prayer. May the Eternal Father's peace comfort you in this time of sadness." The archbishop directed the guards to bring the body to the church for funeral preparations and led them from the room.

Sud'ya Belousov watched the procession briefly and stomped away.

CHAPTER 42:
ALEA IACTA EST

November 10, 4235 K.E.

3:00pm

At the front of the chapel, the citizens of Michurinsk pressed close together, trying to catch a glimpse of a Madasgorski. Sud'ya Belousov mingled with the crowd, smiling, and sometimes pointing — the triumphant hunter displaying his kill. Otets Jovid held up his hands for quiet. With a nod from the elderly priest, carpenters stepped forward carrying a pine lid. The staccato sounds of hammers hitting nails cut through the murmuring.

Grendel sat in the last pew with Chert on one side and Jasper on the other. He flinched at each ringing blow. In his fist he held a blank piece of crumpled paper, but the words that had been there burned in his mind.

G

I have so much to say but so little time. The Madasgorski's will do anything, torture and kill anyone, to keep what they deem is their own. They are a ruthless people and would use you against Aleksandra. That is something that she could not bear. No one — not the Korol', the Kral, nor the Highlord could protect you or her. She knew there was only one way to keep you safe.

Aleksandra Madasgorski Krakova is dead.

Do not linger here, mourning the past. Be content to carry her love in your heart, always.

S

Xandor leaned over the back of the pew and said, "They're taking her outside."

Six soldiers wearing white gloves lifted the plain pine box by its huckles. Led by Otets Jovid, the procession filed into the graveyard between the press of spectators. Rather than the air of solemnity a funeral deserved, the crowd buzzed with festival excitement.

4:00pm

Glistening snowflakes floated down from the pale sky, adding to the inches already covering the grounds. They dotted the dirt surrounding the unmarked grave that held the plain pine box. Gravediggers advanced with shovels in their hands. Outside the graveyard gate, Otets Jovid said a kind word to each person as they left — even Sud'ya Belousov.

Witness to the death and funeral of a Zhitomiran princess, Grendel stood silently with Chert, Xandor, and Jasper at his side. He watched the gravediggers dump shovelful after shovelful of dirt on top of the coffin until only a small hump marked where Lady Aleksandra Madasgorski Krakova lay buried. His thoughts traveled back to their campfire conversations. She was right. Her arena didn't have boundaries. He had been able to walk away from his arena, but not her — not her.

Stepping away from her grave, Grendel crossed his forearms in front of his heart and dipped his head. He lifted his eyes and grumbled, "Alea iacta est."

THE END

THANK YOU FOR READING!

We hope you've enjoyed <u>Blood of Cayn</u> as much as we enjoyed bringing it to you! No author would be where they are without readers, so please accept a HUGE thank you for taking a chance on our endeavor. Whether you loved it, hated it, or landed somewhere in between, it would be of immense help to us, as well as other readers, if you would take a moment to leave a review on Amazon and/or Goodreads. Even a single sentence will mean a lot.

We love to hear from readers! Feel free to drop us a line at mcdonald.isom@gmail.com Let us know what you loved (or what you hated). If you have questions about the story, we'll do our best to answer them. For more information about cultures, countries, creatures, and races of Gaia, visit the glossary on our website, www.mcdonald-isom.com. You can also find us on Facebook, @McDonald.Isom.author.

There are more adventures yet to come!

ABOUT THE AUTHORS

Jason McDonald

An engineer by day and a world builder by night, Jason is an advocate for using both sides of the brain. Unfortunately, it seems his best (and worst) ideas come to him while driving — much to the chagrin of his family and coworkers.

With his stepfather as a guide, Jason traveled the worlds of Edgar Rice Burroughs, Robert E Howard, and JRR Tolkien at an early age. As he grew older, he discovered Dungeons and Dragons and the joys of creating his own campaigns. Combined with the creative genius of his co-writers, whom he met in college, these adventures grew more complex, and an entire world sprang to life.

During all this, Jason graduated from Clemson University, embarked on a career in engineering, and became a partner in a successful engineering firm. Still a practicing engineer, he continues to design a wide range of projects. His attention to detail and vivid imagination helps shape the various scenes and adventures that challenge his characters.

Alan Isom

Alan began his adventure with science fiction and fantasy literature as it should begin: with JRR Tolkien's The Hobbit, read to him as a child by his father. Since that auspicious beginning, he has fostered a love of reading a variety of fantasy and science fiction types and that led him to RPGs, most notably Dungeons & Dragons, where world building became a fascination.

Growing up in northeast Alabama, Alan moved north to South Carolina for college. He fell in love with the Upstate of South Carolina and forgot to go home afterwards. While initially majoring in Physics at Furman University (Go Paladins!) and then moving on to Clemson University for additional studies in Civil Engineering (after deciding that his options for a Physics career were decidedly thin), he became a licensed engineer and now works for an international

Engineering-Procurement-Construction company.   During all of this he served a number of years as a soldier with the Army National Guard.   Each of these careers, as well as a multitude of hobbies, helps bring depth and creativity to the characters and worlds he brings to life.

Stormy McDonald

Born in the midst of a thunderstorm in the darkest hours of a solstice morning, Stormy has been told she has a personality to match: full of sound and fury, and highly unpredictable.   She comes from a family of traditional, oral storytellers, so it's little wonder that she's driven to weave words as well.   She can't remember a time when she didn't love books — from the feel and smell of the pages, to the information they hold, to the tales that they tell.   However, storytelling is a labor of love, which doesn't always pay the bills.   Over the years, she's worked a ridiculous variety of side jobs to support her writing habit, including waitress, security guard, library minion, engineering drafter, and small business owner.